F122503   EW

GREENE'S SUMMER

PART III
OF
COPENHAGEN QUARTET

Thomas E. Kennedy, an American expatriate in Europe since the mid-1970s, is the author of nine books of fiction, including most recently *The Copenhagen Quartet* (*Kerrigan's Copenhagen, A Love Story*, 2002; *Bluett's Bluet Hours*, 2003; *Greene's Summer*, 2004; and *Breathwaite's Fall, in progress for 2005*) – four independent novels about the loves and seasons of the Danish capital. Kennedy's fiction has won numerous awards including the *O Henry, Pushcart, Gulf Coast,* and *European* prizes, the *Charles Angoff Award*, and the *Frank Expatriate Writers Award*. He has also worked as a translator for Copenhagen's Rehabilitation Center for Torture Victims, serves as Advisory Editor of *The Literary Review* and International Editor of *StoryQuarterly* and has published a book of essays on the craft of fiction, *Realism & Other Illusions* (2002). He is a member of the International Reading Faculty of Fairleigh Dickinson University's Master of Fine Arts in Writing program.

Portions of Greene's Summer were originally published in altered form in *The Literary Review* (Vol 47, No 3), *New Letters* (Vol 60, No 3), *The Gettysburg Review* (Vol 5, No 4), *Americas Review* (No 6) and *Mediphors* (No 11) and received honorable mention in the *Pushcart Prize* anthologies.

Photo Credit: Alice Guldbrandsen

Novels

Crossing Borders (1990)
A Weather of the Eye (1996)
The Book of Angels (1997)
Kerrigan's Copenhagen – A Love Story (2002)
Bluett's Blue Hours (2003)

Short Story Collections

Unreal City (1996)
Drive, Dive Dance & Flight (1997)

Essay Collections

Realism and Other Illusions:
Essays on the Craft of Fiction (2002)

Literary Criticism

Andre Dubus: A Study of the Short Fiction (1988)
The American Short Story Today (ed.) (1991)
Robert Coover: A Study of the Short Fiction (1992)
An Index to American Award Stories (1993)

Anthologies

New Danish Fiction (1995)
Small Gifts of Knowing: Contemporary Irish Writing (1997)
Stories and Sources (1998)
Poetry and Sources (2000)
The Secret Lives of Writers (co-ed.) (2002)

GREENE'S SUMMER

THOMAS E. KENNEDY

Wynkin deWorde

2004

Published in 2004
by

Wynkin deWorde

Wynkin deWorde Ltd.,
PO Box 257, Galway, Ireland.
info@deworde.com

A CIP catalogue record for this book is available from the British Library

ISBN: 1-904893-02-3

Typeset by Patricia Hope, Skerries, Co. Dublin, Ireland
Cover Design: Roger Derham
(Adaption of a Thomas Kennedy photograph)
Cover Design Coordination: Design Direct, Galway, Ireland
Printed by Betaprint, Dublin, Ireland

GREENE'S SUMMER

PART I

The Woman with Eyes of Blue Light

'I look for a green gate
in the black depth . . .'

– RAFAEL ALBERTI

translated from the Spanish by
Christopher Sawyer-Laucanno

PART I

The woman with eyes of blue light

*'Silence and screams
are the end of my song.'*

Victor Jara
September 1973

1

A car door slams

The first time Nardo saw the woman with eyes of blue light he woke from a dream in which the angels had forsaken him. He bolted from beneath the covers and huddled in the corner of his bedroom. It was dark. He did not know he was in a new land.

Through the window he could see stars trembling in the clear black night. It might have been the sky over Valparaiso. He listened for the sound of a car door slamming shut, footsteps on the wooden staircase . . . But there was nothing. Just tires sizzling past on the roadway and two or three young men talking loudly on the lake bank, staggering home from a Saturday night serving house. No angels. No woman with eyes of light. But he had seen her. Her gaze was cut into his mind.

Slowly he became aware of the sweat that soaked into the underwear he'd slept in, that wet his scalp, his temples. And the pain, of course. In all the usual places: teeth, joints, head. Within.

But no one was coming up the staircase. For here he was now. Far away. Delivered. And that, anyhow, was something. The angels had kept their word.

He remained crouching there for a long while.

Even if you live to go out and tell this, Nardo, no one will believe you. Do you think they will? No one will. No one outside of this room will ever believe the things that happen here, and the more you try to tell of what happened, the less they will believe. To make them believe, you will have to edit, to distill, to tell only the tiniest little portion of it, and when you tell only the tiniest little portion, why then they will be inclined to think, after all, perhaps there was a reason for this, perhaps the police sometimes need to employ certain means and measures.

This was the frog-eyed one speaking, the worst of them perhaps, one of the worst. He spoke quietly, meditatively, pausing to puff on a cigar while Nardo hung by one foot and one hand, and Frog-eyes pushed him, like a swing, holding an imaginary conversation in which he pretended first to be Nardo – 'Let me tell you,' he said to the imaginary person Nardo was supposed to be informing about this, 'Let me tell you what these animales did to me, listen!' – and then he would reply, playing the role of the person Nardo was to have been telling, 'Oh come now, you can't mean this, surely you exaggerate. What do you take me for? This is too bizarre really . . .'

Then he interrupted himself. No, my swinging friend, he said and gave another push. Nardo could hear the cartilage that held arm to shoulder creak and pop. No, it will be worse than that. They will not even say anything. They will seem to listen to you with the face of great sympathy and say nothing, but in their little heads . . . He circled his forefinger at the side of his own skull. In their little heads they will be thinking, This man is full of the shit. He is nuts. That is what they will think of your tales, my swinging friend. No one likes the little boy who tells tales out of class. And he removed the cigar from his lips and smiled, and Nardo began to scream even before the glowing tip pressed against his nipple.

2

The Place of Screaming

We had come so far. Yet any further step began to seem hopeless. He sat across from me, perfectly still, body aligned with the sharp angles of the chair, so immobile his face might have been cut from a brown paper bag: two eye slits, a rectangular mouth that said nothing. Watching him, I became aware of the chair he sat in, how rigidly he conformed to its severe lines. I thought of a chair I had seen the weekend before while browsing with my wife in a department store; the one with gently curving arms and a molded seat; light and comfortable to sit in, springy – an Arne Jacobsen chair of deep lacquered green.

Alfonso Laurencic, who designed torture cells for the Spanish Republicans – the so-called 'cells of color', had claimed that red was stimulating, blue relaxing, while green evoked melancholy and sadness. I did not agree. The green of that chair was full of peace, of quiet hope. It was expensive, too. The center's finance department could never approve its purchase. I decided I would pay for it myself. Perhaps it would help him to release the sorrow in his body, to set free the poisoned emotion coiled within him.

My gaze moved around the office, alert to other possible

subtle obstructions, but the colors were soft and cheerful, the green of the potted palm calming to the eye, the bookshelf lined with multicolored spines of books, the dreamy Chagall prints on the walls.

The silence continued. I watched him. He was dressing with more care now I had noticed. No longer the dark, colorless garments, not black or grey or brown, an indistinct mix, like spillage, shades and styles that seemed to suggest a desire to be invisible, clothing that seemed to say, *I am no one. No reason to look at me. No reason to see me.* Now he was neat, elegant even. A shirt of deep clear blue, squarely knotted brown wool necktie, dark green Irish tweed jacket with hand-stitched lapels. And his arm, unfrozen now from its bent immobility, hysterical paralysis. That has been our triumph. It seemed to me he must have been fully aware of the progress we had made together, but still he sat there and stared at nothing, motionless.

What question could I pose to break the ice of his posture? *Why did you scream?* It was in the grip of that screaming, that terrible screaming those weeks ago, that he began to flail his arms, clawing at the air with both hands, reclaiming the movement of his paralyzed arm. A dramatic change! I had been trained to consider dramatic change suspect, but this was a genuine, and seeming permanent, dramatic change.

I still did not know what he had seen, what memories had induced his screaming. He told me so little, just bits of it, glimpses, some few details, the man he called Frog-eyes, who closed the door on his hand. He had had to invent names for them all because it was not permitted for detainees to know the names of their keepers. Frog-eyes. Tweedsuit. Flatnose. Moustache. Frog-eyes was the one Nardo had had most contact with, and slowly I began to feel I knew that nameless man. I felt in myself a desire *not* to know him, *not* to witness. The thought occurred to me that were I to look into Frog-eyes' face, so to speak, were I to come to *know* him, the knowledge would sear me like acid.

I thought again about something one of the other survivors once told me in response to a question I posed about what had been done to him. *You do not want to know the answer, my friend*, he said to me. *Just to know the answer to this will damage your soul. Maybe forever. Better change jobs. Become a fireman. Save people from burning rooms; it is safer.*

But I had to return to that place with Nardo, the place of the screaming, had to help him relive those memories. I was afraid, too, but I had to go there with him.

'How is the arm?' I asked. A circuitous approach.

Without turning his eyes from the nowhere on which they were focused, he lifted the once-dead arm, extended one finger, flicked it against his cheek, as if shooing a mosquito, lowered it to the wooden arm of the chair again.

I waited. He waited.

'Tell me where you are, Nardo. What are you thinking?'
His eyes contracted visibly. He saw something. I could see that he saw something far away from us but alive still, inside him.

'Tell me, Nardo.'

But he said nothing.

3

Source of the fertile God

Fresh air scented with the sap of newly clipped grass drifted in the window. Through the gentle angle of the blinds, I could see mid-morning sunlight on green leaves, and across the road, the great looming beast of the State Hospital. Fronds in the potted palm beside my bookcase drifted in the breeze.

Last time Nardo announced that he would not return. I could not know if he meant it or not so I have reviewed my notes, preparing for his visit as usual. I have replaced the straightback chair with the more comfortable Arne Jacobsen model, which suggested nothing of a state facility. Nardo's experiences with state facilities have, to say the least, not been conducive to trust. The new chair's green is cheerful. I defy Alfonso Laurencic and his sick research. The chair was very expensive. *For your clinic?* my wife asked. It must have been difficult for her to understand, especially when I suggested we wait until the end of the summer to buy the children's new shoes, but she was patient with me.

I had to make Nardo understand the difference between interrogation and anamnesis, and this was not an interrogation chair. Together we had to dredge through the memories, the

9

emotions behind the memories. He seemed to remember most of what had happened, but I had to help him fill in the blanks and especially to remember what he had been feeling in order to free him of it. To begin to free him back to whom he was before, a man who read, taught, who held convictions he valued more than his own safety.

An idealist? Naïve? Self-destructive? Tempting his own ill fate? Perhaps he had to be helped to see himself more clearly to avoid those traits, which led him into that hell – but this was a fine line to tread; on the other side of it lay the game of blaming the victim, punishing the wronged instead of the wrong-doer.

I remembered what Nardo had told me the other day in an uguarded moment about the things he was accused of teaching. *I just taught them,* he said. *They existed and they were beautiful and true and so I taught these things to the children so that they would know they existed, too. I did not think about it. I did not think. Now I think. So they have won.*

But I thought it was not so simple. I knew that his father had died in the stadium with Victor Jara when Nardo was only a teenager. What our fathers do, the fates they choose and that choose them, drive us as surely as Oedipus toward our own fate, whether we run from it or not. That is what a man must understand.

I could not contain my smile when Nardo appeared at the door of my consultation room, right on time, for his appointment. I rose, beaming. To hell with professional objectivity! I was glad he had come! He nodded formally, looked at the new chair. He touched the smooth green line of its back. 'A beautiful object,' he said and sat.

I could see something new. I waited. Then, 'How was your week?'

'Weak.'

It took a moment for me to catch the pun. 'The weak week of a strong man.'

His face registered nothing. He reached to the name plaque on my desk, held it before his eyes and said, 'Dr T Kristensen. Son of Christian.'

'You are welcome to use my first name if you prefer. Thorkild. Source of Thor.'

'Source of the fertile God.'

'My parents played both sides.' I regretted the words as soon as they left my mouth. Anything said can break the spell of objectivity, blur the necessary border between us. Now he had an opening, might ask which side I was on, and we would be back into the pointless ideological fencing on which we had wasted so much time earlier – even as I myself had to confront the daunting question of which side I would have been on if I had been born there where Nardo came from: the dangerous side that sought democracy or the easy side that protected privilege?

But Nardo let it be. He put the plaque back onto my desk and said, 'I think I will just to call you doctor.'

'Fine. Tell me about your week.'

'I met a woman.'

'Ah!'

'A Danish woman.'

'*Ah!*'

'See, the blackheads come and steal your womans.'

'Is that what you feel people think?'

'Some do.'

'What *you* think is what matters.'

'Well, anyway, I lied. I did not meet a woman. I *saw* a woman. And she smiled at me. A beautiful smile.'

'Next time you can say hello.'

'Hello,' he said. "Hell. O.'

His gaze was nowhere again, in some pit of hopelessness perhaps where even the faintest glimmer of hope served to remind him there was no hope, only an abyss. I watched him, waited to catch his eyes, but he was better at waiting.

I took a breath. It would be so much easier just to chat, but that was not what we had to do. 'We have to go back,' I said.

He remained silent. Then, 'Back to the future.'

'No. Back to the place of screaming.'

4

Because I do not know the names of things

El Domingo. Sunday, Nardo finished his work early and went out to walk through the streets of this new city, this new land, in search of his hunger. He fancied he was looking for her, a woman whose name he did not even know, but whose eyes had met his one afternoon in the café across the lake. Eyes like blue fire; warm, full of life. He had seen her three times, and once she smiled at him. If only he could remember what one said to a woman, he thought surely he would speak to her. He wished he could learn about her, know her name, so that he could think about her more clearly, prepare himself in case there was to be some meaning in this.

He gazed into the sadness of closed shop windows, dress-mannequins alone in their shadows. Obliquely he gazed into the faces of the Danes he passed on the sidewalk, at the strange long words on street signs that he had to read letter by letter to construct what he could rarely be certain was their correct pronunciation or meaning. His lips formed words of his own: *Por no saber paner los nombres, no las expresos.* Because I do not know the names of things, I do not express them. Worse, without

13

the names, without words, he was not certain he could see at all. What does a tree look like whose name you do not know? A flower without a name might be invisible.

A man without a name is a stranger.

At home, the summer night was alive with sound whose names were so familiar he needn't even think them: birds crying out, the movement of leaves, tall ferns, the dark filled with sounds of insects and frogs. But he was not home. There was no home.

He walked boulevards, allés, narrow winding streets whose cobblestones sounded sharply beneath the heels of his boots, along the curving facades of buildings that had stood since the last great fire in 1795, before his own *flaco* stringbean of a country had finished driving the Indians south, then freed itself to redefine liberty as the freedom to acquire, always punishing not the wrong-doer but the wronged.

He sat to take a coffee at an outdoor café on Coal Square where Søren Kierkegaard once lived, preparing words that would define the consciousness of Nardo's father's generation: to decide one's own essential nature with action.

Words. Like the ones that ended him here alone in the chill summer air of this northern capital that had been shelled nearly two centuries before by the British, his great-grandmother Norton's people, who would marry an Irishman, give birth to a mother who would mother the girl who married Nardo's father. The family of man and its betrayals.

Beautiful women crossed the square, and he watched carefully, but none had the eyes of blue light. Couples pushing prams, vital young men with blue eyes and good teeth. A man ran past pushing a jogger baby carriage that glided along before him – ingenious! A very old couple, arm-in-arm, supported one another across the square. Surely, he thought, they had seen the last great war here, perhaps remembered grey-green German uniforms on these streets, remembered their own flag, a white cross on red, supplanted by the jagged black fascist wheel on that same red field. The red of my own flag, too, he thought, is for the blood of patriots. All flags are red with blood. *Sangre perdido.* History exonerates no people. We have all betrayed each other. Only the animals live in innocence, eating grass, eating flesh, but only to stay alive.

His stomach growled. He was hungry now at last and could stop thinking. To be hungry was a blessing. To be hungry and have food. Hunger was optimism. His small booted feet led him through the upside-down season of this country back to his own quarters by the lake. He should be glad. At home now, there would be the winter rain, endless and cold.

But there was no home.

Light sparkled on the lake as he ate. Watching the street and banks below his window, he cautiously registered the fact that his restless eye was not guided by dread.

Perhaps at last peace had begun to open her heart to him. He cautioned himself not to prepare a welcome place for such thoughts. Instead he chewed – shallowly where his remaining teeth registered pain – and let the juices of the fried meat nourish his senses, his thin body, his trembling hands.

The sound of children screaming in the street stirred uneasiness. Emotion? The only emotion he felt was a half-slumbering memory of terror that sometimes woke abruptly in sweat, roused by the sound of a car door smacking shut, rapid footsteps on a staircase, interminable moment before the pounding on the door began, and in his ears the screaming the doctor so enjoyed taking him back to.

Serfa bello ir por las calles con un cuchillo verde y dando gritos hasta morir de frio. Beautiful it would be to run through the streets with a green knife screaming until I died of cold.

Let Neruda speak for me and leave me in peace, doctor. It is Sunday. It happens that I am tired of being a man. Of being a person. I am tired. That is all I feel now.

The other emotions were buried with the dead ones he once loved, who unlike him had not survived. Survivors they were

15

called now, those who had lived through this plague. *The Plague of the Twentieth Century* they called it at the rehabilitation center. The word *victim* was avoided now, with its reek of reverse blame, blaming the victims. To be called a survivor was to be congratulated, acknowledged as triumphant. A victim was a marked person; a survivor was an individual of resource, strong.

One question, Dr Kristensen: How much of a survivor, in fact, survives? How much must remain of a survivor for him also to be called a man? Some of us who are still present and accounted for perhaps are *desparacedo* nonetheless, invisible pieces missing from the whole. You tell me to remember. All over again. *To remember*. Perhaps there is nothing left there, doctor. Perhaps it is all gone. Perhaps all that is left is the screaming. Empty screaming to fill empty ears.

He dipped his hooked broken nose into the bell of the glass and inhaled the earth smell of the grapes, then flooded his tongue with wine, and uneasy questions disappeared.

I am free now, he thought. The others are gone, but I have found my center. Alone.

And even as that thought found him, she turned the corner below, stood on the street beneath his window, waiting for a truck to pass so she could cross to the lake bank. He felt yearning and happiness, an invasion of his solitude that he welcomed and dreaded. He felt her beauty as delicate tendrils of root that clutched the earth of his consciousness.

She grew smaller as she took the path along the narrow edge of the lake across *Fredens Bro*, the Peace Bridge, and he guessed she might be headed to the café on the other side where he had seen her before.

She had met his eyes so warmly, smiled, scared up a smile onto his own lips. Without meaning, of course, a passing glance, the Danish smile they were all so proud of. Part of the Gross National Product. Blue eyes and Danish smile. They marketed it, a commodity each of them possessed. Could it ever be trusted?

She was, of course, too young for him. No doubt. And how did one do it again? Say something, anything. Tell her 'hello,' Dr

Kristensen said. Let one word lead to another until some manner of contact was made, some . . . what? Never mind. Perhaps you will speak to her one day. Perhaps you will not. But whether you do or whether you do not, you will not daydream like some stupid boy, will not allow hopes to build that can only fail.

He wondered what her name might be. If only he knew her name, he would feel better.

The light of sunset slanted through his windows, reddening his eggshell walls, the paintings he had collected in his time here, an Italian artist named Giancarlo Savino whose paintings had no names and depicted, it seemed to Nardo, souls disconnected from their bodies, angels of some sort, large dark eyes peering out from a place that is matterless to a place of matter.

These pictures were important to him; he had denied himself necessities to purchase them, slowly. He was interested in angels. He had read that angels are interested in human beings, and he knew this to be true. He dreamed recently of an angel that sat on his head like a hen on an egg. It was a passionate, sexual dream, and he emitted seed in its thrall – the first time in longer than he could remember. He had music about angels, too, and literature. He collected these things in tribute to a memory that was perhaps the only remaining substance at the core of his being. He could tell a story about angels, but he wished not to. Marquez had said that to tell a story, you must be a hypnotist. You must make the listener forget everything but the story you are telling him. Nardo had no story he wished to tell.

His Irish mother had taught him a love of reading. He carried her name now, Greene, for the distance its English syllable gave him from the past, from his father's name. He was Bernardo Greene now. Bernardo for Bernardo O'Higgins, the Irish-born viceroy of Chile, then a leader of the Chilean revolt, then first president of the Republic in the early 1800s. Named for a revolutionary: thank you, father.

Nardo had read that there was a current fashion among the young people of Denmark, and perhaps elsewhere as well – he no longer knew what was original here in this little country, what was assimilated from without – to change their names, to consult numerologists and mystic counsellors who helped them select new names for themselves, dropping those their parents had given them at birth or baptism, dropping the names of their fathers or their mothers, selecting names whose numerical composition of letters, whose sound, might deliver them to a new reality. And if those changes did not help them, then they chose another. A grappling with surfaces it seemed to him.

Nardo's father had been 'pure' Chilean with a touch of Indian that Nardo carried in his own face. Nardo had dropped his name for practical reasons; best not to carry it beyond the life he had escaped. So even if his English was weak, he wore his mother's Irish name, like a mask over his Indian face. His father's name was a mask, too – a mask of ideas Nardo had shed as soon as he realized how deadly serious it was taken. His father had taught him about ideas, about dying for an idea. Taught by example. A choice he once thought noble. Now his choice was escape, although he was not certain that was a good choice either. Perhaps in evading the danger of ideas one evaded a truer life than that of survival. Perhaps it was better to die, as so many others had. But they had not chosen their death. Death had chosen them. No. Men serving simple policies of greed had chosen them to die. Hands that signed papers chose them without ever knowing their names or faces or personal histories; unimpeachable as the sentiment of grass, of trees. Did the trees bear witness beneath the crust of their bark, within the heart of their sap? Did they cry out beneath the blades of axe and saw, in the agony of flames that warmed the bodies of men? Did grass rejoice beneath the dance of joyous feet? Or did it snap and bleed?

These thoughts made his head ache so he refilled his glass of Merlot and lifted it to his lips, gazing out at the lake, though he saw not the lake but his mother.

His mother's name had been Angela. A teacher and a poet; she did not live to know her only surviving son's fate, but he remembered well the poem she wrote about the child who died before he spoke, before he had a name, Nardo's younger brother.

She would go out on the cliff at night, over the crashing waves of the Pacific, calling, but he died without a name, and all she could hear in response was the answer of silence and of the blue-dark night, and he thought it was good that she had died before she could know all the things that were to happen. He wondered if she did know anyway, wondered if she were a spirit in the ache of the wind sometimes, even here, when the air wrapped about the walls of his building with a moaning force that lifted the waters of this little lake as though it were a sea.

His leg had stiffened after sitting too long. He limped from the window, empty glass in hand. The ache was echoed in his lower back, his kidney which still sometimes passed blood, the elbow and wrist and hand of his no longer dead arm, the arm they suspended him from and slammed the door on, the arm that the Danish doctor, Thorkild Kristensen, had coaxed life back into. But even now it ached as he lifted the wine bottle and discovered in his mind a thought: I do not even know her name, the girl who smiled at me.

Could she know how I think of her? Could she feel my yearning, like a force trying to find her? Could her life be waiting, as mine does? He felt the danger of desire rise in him again, and the anticipation of the next glass of wine was already sour on his tongue, so he jammed the cork back into the bottle.

He tied a brown woollen necktie at the throat of his dark shirt, shrugged on his jacket, donned his grey beret. From the kitchen he gathered the ends of bread that had gone stale, packed them in a plastic bag, then let himself out, double-bolting the door behind him with two keys.

All but a sliver of red sun had disappeared behind the low blue buildings across the lake, but the vault of the sky was still yellow, as if the day would never end.

He crossed the road, walking slowly along the narrow end of the lake. He paused to dig into his plastic bag. As if on command, swans and ducks and divers came paddling from all corners of the lake toward him. Seagulls gathered screaming and circling above his head. Pigeons strutted on the bank around his feet,

19

eager for the spillage. He chuckled at how cheap it was to gather an audience here. For nothing more than crumbs of old bread. He broke off bits of the crusty ends and distributed them, favoring the slower, weaker, smaller birds, ignoring the aggressive seagulls in their diving squawking frenzy. They got more than their share anyway.

Then he deposited the plastic bag in a refuse can, dusted his palms and continued across the lake, away from the language class he should be attending, through the chill, light, northern summer night, toward the café on the other side of the lake where he had seen her before, the woman whose name he did not know.

5

A little time the leaves are green

Michela was early again. She crossed the bridge through late afternoon sunlight, wondering why she always put herself into this position. Always the first one there, waiting for him, or whomever, to show up. Why couldn't she be late just once, let Voss sit and wait for her? It was like some kind of disease with her, a psychological warp. Hurry hurry hurry, wait. Too many years of Little Miss Nice School. Used to drive her ex-husband to fits. How many times had she nagged him to be ready for a dinner or a party only to arrive so early they had to circle the block a few times not to ring their hosts' doorbell while they were still frantic, snapping at one another, in the kitchen?

Midway across the bridge, she paused to gaze down the sloping grass bank at the lake, rippling in the sunny breeze. Tatters of cloud shadow skimmed its surface, and she thought it must have been her teachers who did this to her. That dread of being late to class, everyone looking as her eyes made a panicked search for an empty chair, the dry acid of Frøken Jespersen's or Herr Carlsen's commentary placing her at the center of all attention until she was finally seated: *How nice of you to honor us with your presence today, Michela Ibsen. I do hope we're not interfering with your other activities, Frøken Ibsen.* The boys smirking, eyeing her breasts while she searched for a place to sit. She hated her breasts.

The chestnut flowers along the bank stood like off-white candles amidst the summer-green leaves of the trees. A green Michela now filled her eyes with. So short a time, this green, and changing every day, deepening with summer, yellowing to autumn.

What was the poem?

> *A little time the leaves are green*
> *Then yellow, falling to the earth,*
> *And turn to dust.*

It was a very old poem she remembered from her gymnasium literature-class. She had written it carefully on a strip of paper she carried in her wallet for years. The paper too had yellowed and torn and was now who-knew-where? And no one knew who wrote those lines that had lodged in her heart as a teenager, a quarter century ago, 1,200 years or more after it had been written by someone, whose name no one remembered.

Children in T-shirts ran screaming on the lake bank outside the Café Noir, and a tall grey building loomed up above the café roof. How she dreaded that place, its tall grey walls. And behind tall grey windows her mother and father had their rooms now; his two floors below hers. Mother would be sitting up in her bed, or in the little armchair by the vanity table, staring out the window or into the mirror, it didn't matter which, having conversations with dead faces only she could see, including her dead husband who was, in fact, alive, two floors beneath.

She paused outside the glass door of the café, twenty minutes early for her meeting with Voss who would anyway be twenty minutes late.

Instead of entering the café, she strode further down the embankment to the tall grey building and went in through the concrete gateway. A woman behind the information window looked up from her newspaper, saw Michela and nodded. In the little gift shop, Michela bought a bunch of tulips for her mother and rode up in the elevator with a ruddy-faced old man wearing a dusty, striped bathrobe. She smiled at him, and his thin purple lips moved against each other. He clicked his tongue. 'Oh!' he exclaimed. 'Isn't it . . .?' but could find no name because they had never even seen one another before.

She nodded, smiled, stepped off at eight, the top floor, but he remained inside, his face still puzzled and expectant.

The door to her mother's room was open. Mustering cheer, Michela called out, 'Hello, mother!' startled again, as always, by the wild white hair, the shrunken face, lips stitched with wrinkles.

'No,' her mother said, her voice vague, and looked at Michela, her eyes swimming like blue fish behind the heavy lenses of her spectacles. 'Your mother looked in yesterday,' she said, 'but went out for a walk with Aunt Ida. I've been waiting here ever since. I just don't know what to make of that.'

Aunt Ida had been Michela's mother's baby sister, a countess by her last marriage to a bankrupt nobleman. Ida had been Michela's favorite aunt, full of fun and play. Michela used to visit her and they would dress up together in costumes when Michela was a girl. Her aunt would read the funny papers to her, laughing and laughing as she did all the different voices. The year before she turned 40 she opened the gas and went to sleep, and it occurred to Michela suddenly that she now had been on the earth a year longer than the dear sweet aunt who had been dead for over 30 years. Michela's mother used to tell her how she resembled Ida, fear in her eyes as she told her.

In the small white bathroom, Michela filled a metal vase with tap water and arranged the tulips. 'See, mother! Pink tulips! Your favorites!' She placed the vase on the window ledge in a sphere of sunlight.

'Your uncle brought those,' her mother said.

Michela hummed. 'Nice of him.' Then she asked, 'Shall we go out for a visit, mother?'

The old lady's face went still. 'Yes,' she whispered, and

Michela heard in her tone fear that this little promise might be broken, and she felt guilt because it had been many days since, and it was getting harder and harder for her to come here, to render these little pleasures to an old woman and an old man she only knew were her mother and father by repeating the fact to herself. In the sorrow of her mother's eyes, she found resolve: Voss would just have to wait, for a change.

Then her mother's lips pursed slyly. 'Where?'

'Down to six.'

'To see *him*? The fraud?'

'Let me brush your hair and do your face, and you can wear your good pearls.'

'And the brooch?'

'Of course. What a good idea!'

As Michela brushed and pinned the thin white hair and rouged her cheeks and lips, held each brittle finger, painting on mauve polish, nail by nail, her mother hummed the song that seemed always in her mind now, from her days as an *au pair* in Paris nearly 70 years before. '*Grand Amour*,' she hummed, then paused to speak into the mirror to someone about a Bornholm vase that she said had disappeared although she suspected it had been stolen or *accidentally* broken.

'No doubt by the dark girl who comes to clean. If you could call that cleaning. I'll bet she sold it,' she whispered. 'I'm not saying she is a negro, but she is very dark.'

'*Mother!*' Michela chided. Expressions of bigotry had always evoked a sharp word in her home, but her mother was already back to the subject of the vase that was not there.

'It was given me by mother's mother after her holiday. That was long before the Russians came. They raped a girl, you know,' she whispered, talking again directly to Michela. 'And she had to *keep* the baby.'

Abruptly her expression changed and she said matter of factly, 'Your brother is a horse now, you know.'

'I have no brother, mother.'

'Well that's because you ate him. You always were a greedy child.'

24

In the mirror the reflection of the blonde duty nurse passed outside the open door to the room, and Michela's mother cried out, 'Oh look! It's Michela! Why didn't she stop to say hello?'

Michela kissed her mother's neck. 'She's right here, mother.' And her mother's thin rouged lips went slack. 'She is?'

The old bathrobed man was still in the elevator when Michela rolled in her mother's wheelchair.

'Good afternoon, Fru Lise!' he said with hearty warmth, his ruddy face brightening. 'How nice to see you again! How lovely you look today!'

Michela's mother pursed her mouth with irony and rolled her eyes. When the old man looked away again, she tapped her temple quickly, furtively, and glanced into Michela's eyes.

'Are you still hanging around, Herr Kragh?'

'I like to watch the reflections,' he explained, gesturing at the unpolished brass of the sliding doors where their three images shimmered dimly. 'See how elegant you look there, Fru Lise!'

Michela's mother sniffed. 'Flatterer!' she said, but a smile played on her lips. The old man's face was tender as a child's.

On the sixth floor, Michela tapped at her father's door and peeked in. He lay there as always, half propped up against the headboard, his right hand clutching the little trapeze above his bed, strings of sinew taut in his scrawny arm. The room stank of cancer. He looked up from a slim paperback book in his left hand, held open by his thumb, and his one good eye crackled in his wasted face.

Michela rolled her mother's wheelchair briskly through the doorway, announcing, 'Look who's come to visit with you, Father!'

His eye lightened. 'Don't you look lovely, Lisa!' he said, his words thick in his toothless mouth. 'Michela, doesn't your mother look lovely?'

Her mother sniffed. 'It smells in here.'

Michela's father said nothing, only glared from among the

25

turned tables of his consciousness, clinging to the trapeze with his right arm, amidst the reek of his dying. He jiggled the book in his free hand as though he might fling it.

'Who is *he*?' the mother asked, tipping back her head to look up at Michela behind the wheelchair. 'Is he the fraud?'

'Oh, that's good,' her father's gravelly voice muttered. 'You really have the power now, don't you? And you use it.'

'Yes,' said the mother mildly so that Michela wondered for a moment if it was all an act, a way to justify her rejection of him, a screen of confusion to hide behind. She tried to signal him to be easy, but her mother whispered loudly, 'He needs a bath. He looks like a sack of rags. Do we have to stay here?'

'No!' said her husband in a phlegmy bark. 'Feel free to go!' The exertion left him gulping for air, his frail chest heaving, bald now Michela saw through his pajama lapels; gone the curly red hair she had always thought so beautiful and that her mother had made faces about. The skin was now puckered, bald-white blotched with purple.

'Dad!' Michela pleaded, hoping to make him recognize that his wife's mind was gone, for his was strong enough to see that, but he cut her off, snapping, 'Weak! Weak and simple. As always. A woman's love is weakness.' And, 'Look!' he added. 'She's even smiling. This is how it is in Denmark now by God! Smile and smile and cast the bullets!' Holding the book up alongside his face, as though to witness, he smiled poisonously and hissed, 'Pernicious woman! Frailty!'

Now his wife was looking elsewhere. Her smiling face was aimed toward the window, the yellowing sky. 'My view is better than this.'

Michela punished her father with silence, let it extend until she could no longer bear it, then asked, 'Do you need anything, Dad?'

'Yeah!' he snapped. 'About 30 meters of intestine and a new asshole!'

She chuckled despite herself and was surprised and relieved to see in the turn of his lips that he appreciated her appreciation of

26

his irony. She admired that he could muster even that much of a smile, even that much irony. His strength was not depleted. Yet perhaps that was not good either, she thought, observing how desperately he clung to the trapeze suspended above his bed. She moved closer and sat on the edge. Her fingers touched the taut strings of muscle in his right arm. She stroked the papery, veiny skin on back of his hand, clenched around the bar of the trapeze. This close the smell was very bad. 'Don't you get tired holding on like that?' she asked softly. 'Why don't you let go? You'd sleep better. You've earned it.'

'What rubbish!'

'Are you afraid?'

'Afraid of *what* for the sake of the devil and Christ in heaven!'

'I'll be here for you.'

'Rubbish,' he muttered, but more softly now. 'Pure and simple rubbish.'

But she knew him too well. She could see the cracks in the facade. The tremor of a dessicated eyelid, his thin collapsed lip. 'You've always been so strong, Dad. You don't have to anymore. You can relax now. Your arm will get all cramped if you don't let go of that. Let yourself relax.'

Staring straight ahead, he slowly, laboriously, began to clear his throat, and she knew it meant he wanted to speak, to ask something, and she knew she had to wait. Her mother silently studied her own hands now, turning them over and over before her eyes in a snapping movement, as though she expected the side not visible to change character while it was out of sight, as though she might catch it in the act of transformation.

Finally, the long slow process of throat-clearing was completed. He had smoked nonfilter cigarettes, Cecils, 20 or 30 a day, for nearly 70 years, but the cancer was not in his lungs, and he still smoked she could see from the heaped ashtray on his bed stand, the half-empty green pack of cigarettes.

'Will you give me an honest answer to a serious question?' he asked.

'Yes.'

'Do you believe in . . . in ghosts?'

'*Ghosts!* Have you seen a ghost?'

'I asked for an answer, not a question! Do you believe there's another life after this one?'

'That's your question? Well the answer is, yes.'

'Simple as that?'

'Yes.'

'Jesus and all the rest of it?'

'Yes.'

He lumped up his mouth and grumbled, 'Heaven, too, and all the rest of it?'

'Yes. Does that answer your question? Yes.'

'That wasn't the question.'

'Well, what is the question, then?'

He jerked his forehead upward. 'Do you think I have any chance of going . . . up there? Or will I go *down*? Below?'

'Nay,' she said with purposeful gruffness. 'You probably deserve a quick trip down, but even Satan must draw the line somewhere as to who he'll let in.'

The watery red eye turned to her. What a beautiful brown his eyes had been. She held her mouth in the only kind of ironic smile he would be able to believe and the grumble in his throat she recognized as laughter. 'I said it was a serious question.'

'And I said the devil won't have you so Christ will have to take pity.'

'You,' he growled breathlessly. 'You're just like me. Stubborn!'

'Only when I'm with you. You taught me everything I know.' And she bowed forward into the stench and touched her lips to his forehead. She glanced at the title of his book. *Hamlet*. Of course. *Hamlet and the trapeze.* 'Still reading that play, Dad?'

'*Yes!*'

'It's so short, how long could it take you to read it?'

He glared at her. 'Until I know which part I played.'

'Dad, why don't you start writing again? Why don't you let me bring you some other books? Why waste all your time comparing your life to some play?'

'Some play,' he mocked. 'It is the *only* play. This play is about my life. You'd know that if you ever picked up a decent piece of literature yourself!' And she saw in his eyes that he could see in hers he had gone too far. Gruffly he tried to tip his harshness back toward affection. 'You've got a good head on your shoulders. Make some use of it!'

'I think I'll make use of my feet just now, Dad. Have a good day.'

6

One fair daughter and no more

As the door swung shut behind them, he grumbled, 'Pernicious woman,' though not loud enough for Michela to hear. He shifted his legs beneath the sheet and carefully placed the book in a little hollow between his thighs, reached for his cigarettes and lighter, inhaling carefully not to evoke a coughing fit that might pop his catheter. The smoke calmed the anguish of his regret at having been too harsh with Michela.

'One fair daughter,' he recited softly, 'And no more, the which he loved passing well.'

All his adult life he had worked to focus a vision of his world with words; no matter the assignment – pieces on municipal politics, prisons, the library system, Copenhagen cafés, the fishing industry, unions, hospitals, the doctors unions – always plumbing for the story that was true to himself (*This above all, always to thine own self be true* . . . words of an old fool), always careful, measured. On his desk he'd kept a sign: *Big Words Not Spoken Here.* Now it occurred to him he had no big words, no big topics, no big ideas, nothing. He had always taken it for granted that he had something great in him. He had felt it there within, incubating.

Must have been simple dyspepsia. For it never emerged. The sum total of everything he had written in all the decades was a lifetime's collection of small serviceable pieces. Something between fillers and features, a three-quarter column on page 2, page 4, an obituary, portrait of the day . . . Still, the words had been his. Now it was easier for him to find himself in the words of others, written in someone else's book.

One fair daughter, and no more, the which he loved passing well. That communicated now the real total of his life. What else of substance did his life amount to? Yet the line spoke not only of Michela but also of Ria, his sweet little girl's sweet little girl. End of the line! Just like Ophelia. The end even Hamlet didn't dare to take. The parallels to his life seemed increasingly uncanny. Even the name 'Ophelia' he had read somewhere meant 'opening', and what opening remained for him now, if not the opening young Ria had chosen?

He meditated Michela's answers to his questions. Facile answers. Glib. Was such simple faith really possible? Tenable? *Yes*, she answered. *Yes*. And, *Yes*. Christ and Satan. Heaven and hell. And if the water comes to a man and drowns him, there is no fault. But if the man comes to the water . . . Ria was buried in hallowed ground. No one questioned that anymore, but that was not the question anyway. The question was . . .

The door of his room popped open again, and a long bony face peered in beneath a mess of white hair. Focusing his left eye, Mikhail saw it was Kragh, whose brain was wispy as his wig. Mad as birds. Old lech.

The bony face grinned. 'Ib!'

'My name is not Ib!'

Kragh's face went stupid. 'It's not?' He stepped into the room, his dusty striped bathrobe flapping, unbelted, around his long rangy frame.

What's worse? Mikhail wondered. *Sound mind in unsound body or the reverse? Happy fool. Oblivious as a cockroach. Imagine if a cockroach was doomed to consciousness.*

'Here's a riddle for you, Kragh.'

32

The spacey-toothed smile returned. 'Riddle?'

'Yeah, riddle. *Riddle!* Why is a king like a fish like a worm?'

'I give up.'

'You can't just juice-sizzle-me give up! You got to think about it first.'

The slack mouth. 'Think about it?'

'Oh what's the use?'

Kragh blinked, staring at the wall. 'The use?'

Mikhail sighed. 'What do you have on your heart, Kragh?'

'My heart?'

'What do you want? What are you doing here?'

'Doing?'

'Why have you come to visit me?'

'Visit?'

'Would you please just get out,' Mikhail shouted. 'And leave me in peace!'

Kragh began to cry. He wiped his nose with the striped sleeve of his bathrobe and stared at Mikhail with the face of a stricken child.

'For *Satan*,' Mikhail muttered, 'Sit down, then, have a chair.'

Kragh drew in a tremulous breath and sat, elbows on his lolling knees, pajama flies agape so Mikhail could see something he had no wish to see. 'Will you please button up, Kragh? Tuck in that damned oversized eel, and button up?'

'On my heart!' Kragh exclaimed then, eyes bright in his wasted face. 'She *likes* me. She told me so. Not in so many words, but I could see it in her smile. And tomorrow she said she likes them tall and long. That's what she said to me, "I like men tall and long."'

'Said that tomorrow, did she?'

Kragh nodded emphatically.

'Congratulations, then,' Mikhail said. 'Have you set a date yet? How about last year?'

'Date?'

'Well if you're in love I presume you will do the right thing and marry the girl.'

Kragh's lower lip thrust out. 'She's already married.' Then he brightened. 'But her husband's dead. She's a widow. I still call her *Fru*, but he's dead all right, she's available. And she is a beautiful woman!'

An ugly vapor rose slowly from Mikhail's belly and filled his mouth, his nose. He narrowed his good eye to sharpen its focus and saw Kragh's long, stupid face in a frame of tear. 'Who is she?' he whispered gruffly. 'What's her name?'

'I always want to call her Alexandria, but I think her name is Fru Lise. She has the *bluest* eyes!'

'Get out!' Mikhail barked. 'Get the hell out! You false Danish dog!'

Kragh leapt up in a crouch, face cracked in terror, and fled, the tails of his bathrobe streaming behind him.

In one brilliant instant comprehension flooded Mikhail's consciousness. He felt himself on the edge of knowing the ugly core of all secrets of his existence . . . Then he groaned from the base of his chest, and the flaming metal was at his arse again, moving slowly upward, twisting, twisting, as he tightened every flaccid stringy muscle against the attack. He felt his mouth pop open, his eyeballs bulge, and pain beyond anything he had ever imagined.

'Help!' he gasped. 'Help!' Grabbing for the call button pinned beside his pillow, pressing, pressing, until the fat ugly nurse was there with his pills, and he saw there again a revelation – all power of existence focused in that lackluster face. She cradled his head, placed the tablets under his tongue, held the water glass to his lips.

The fire! he thought, holding the word inside the pit of his consciousness. To know the word was action: an act in and of itself. *The fire below! Up my arse, you arse-fucking Satan! The fire!* But the word was already blurring behind his eyelids, fading from his ears as he floated downward. And far away he heard the tinkle of a razzamatazzy piano, a voice singing words. He knew that voice, those words. Leo Mathisen. Poor doomed crazy Leo, during the war, singing English in the smokey bar, a cigar clamped between his manic smiling teeth:

> To be
> Or not to be
> That's the question
> But not to me.
> Cause you know I'll always be
> In love with you . . .

Somewhere outside the thickening dark, he felt fingers prying gently at the fingers of his own right hand, but he held tight, sinking, still a question somewhere to answer . . .

7

Gone where?

Upstairs, as Michela helped her mother out of the wheelchair into her bed, the old woman surprised her with a lucid question. 'That man who was here with you last time, the one who waited outside, why didn't he come in with you? Is he afraid of me?'

'There was something he had to do, Mother,' she said rather than go into it. In fact, Michela had asked him to wait outside; that time and every other time. She didn't want to have to see Voss seeing this. He was too young and she didn't want to have to see the way he would see it. He didn't argue the point with her either.

'Is he your cavalier? Your beau?'

'He's a friend, mother?'

'Where is Mads, then?'

'He left me, mother. You know that very well.'

'And where is my little grand-daughter? Did Mads get custody of her? Where is little Ria?'

'You know very well, Mother. She's gone. *Gone!*'

The old woman's eyes were bewildered. 'Gone?' she repeated. 'Gone where?' she asked, sliding back into her mist. Michela hadn't the heart to try to explain it again, couldn't bear to put it into words once more, not for her mother's sake and not for her own. Any thought of her daughter now was pain for her, unhappy years and happy years both. She could not bear to think of her, in some ways especially not the sweet young face of her childhood. She let the silence be her answer, waited while it filled the space between them and receded.

'That other man,' her mother asked then, timid obstinacy in the set of her lips over her false teeth, 'The one who waited outside. You don't . . . do anything with him, do you?'

Yes, I fuck him, Michela wanted to say, but instead she said, 'I just have to use your toilet, Mother,' and let herself into the cubicle. She rolled off some sheets of paper, blotted her eyes and blew her nose. Then she looked at her face in the mirror over the cold white hospital sink, and she could see the lines and pouches, the sag beneath her chin, incipient wattles, that had not been there five years before.

Waiting for the elevator, she had to keep clearing her throat and wondered why. She thought of her father's question, hoping her response was good enough. But the thought of his... his arrogance nagged at her still. *If I would read a decent piece of literature once in a while!* As if he hadn't been the one who blocked her from college, tricked her into taking a job as a secretary, promising her the boss was his friend and had assured him it would lead to greater things. A lie he later denied. *I never went to university; it's not necessary.* She wondered if she would suddenly start weeping here.

The elevator doors slid open, and Torben, her family doctor, stepped off into the corridor. She got in, but held the door from closing so she could have a quick word with him.

'Hi, sweet Torben,' she said. 'Are you looking in on them?' He was also Michela's parents' doctor. 'Have you been down to my father?'

'He's sleeping the sleep of the just, which is hardly just.'

The comment stung – he was still her father! – but she only said, 'He's still holding on.'

Torben laughed. 'When he goes out they'll have to pry that bar from his hand.' Then, seeing Michela's face, quickly added, 'Sorry, listen, you mustn't be so hard on yourself. This is the natural course of it all. I hope you don't spend too much time here.' His tone was mild, his smile kind, camouflaging the toughness of his message. 'There's nothing more you can do. Limit your time with them or you'll get depressed again, and we don't want that. They'll eat you alive. You've been through enough.'

'What about Dad? He's taking it so bad, I think.'

'He's taken everything bad his whole life. Except for his pleasure.'

'But . . .?'

'Look, honey, it could be a day. Could be a month. Or six months! There's no use coming here all the time. Once in a while is more than enough. Think of yourself now. Now you have to decide whether you want to live your life or do something stupid like get cancer yourself. It can be contagious, you know, if you give it the chance. What are you doing for dinner tonight?'

She'd had lunch with him a couple of times, but never dinner. Dinner seemed an escalation to intimacy somehow. She looked at him, skinny as toothpicks with the dark of overwork under his eyes, the excess of caring that was consuming him, the sweetest man you could imagine. With a warm smile, she said, 'Let's keep it to lunch, Torben,' and let the elevator door slide shut.

8

Who are you?

Mikhail's eyes opened. Had he fainted? Slept? Again? It seemed hours ago he woke and lit a Cecil. Brain clear for the challenge of what he had learned. But the cigarette had burned out, a bowed pillar of ash just above the yellow skin of the fingers that held it. It hadn't even burnt his skin. Miracle it hadn't set fire to the bedclothes, burnt down the whole home. No, not a miracle, he thought, merely a simple phenomenon. The cigarette was pointed upward between his fingers. Cigarettes go out when they're pointed upward. There are no Goddamned miracles!

He reached to drop the spent butt into his ashtray, exhausted, the pillow wet at his back. There was a thought he had lost and wanted to find again, a question . . .

The question was in the locked metal box in the drawer of his bed table, its key on a string around his neck: the key to the opening, his little treasury of ketogan. The nurse delivered two pills three times a day, and he saved one of them whenever he could, whenever he could manage on just one. Saved two sometimes, too. There was the question. In the box. By thus opposing end them.

41

One more piece of the play coming true. False bitch. With Kragh, of all arse-fucked people! *Kragh!* He hated the name. It sounded like the cackling laughter of a rook. Mad as birds. Lech. A crown of mockery on him. Horns!

He smiled bitterly, fueled by rage that swept across him in a wave, then passed, leaving him spent and slack. All save his right arm. His one good eye turned to the arm. An arm against a sea of troubles. It was the only tool he had left: his writing arm, holding him up.

Take the pills, he thought. *Take them.*

And what then?

A question little Ria could answer for him. He had prayed to her to answer. What happens, dear? You were braver than I, you just went right ahead. But maybe in your case there were mitigating circumstances? Perhaps you would not be taken to task for it, young and innocent as you were. You were so hurt, perhaps your mind was hurt; perhaps you could not be held responsible.

But there is nothing wrong with my mind. Or is there?

As a boy in religion class he had been taught that despair was the only sin that was unforgiveable, and he remembered thinking, *They would have to say that. They would have to.* All those truisms. Life is a gift that must not be thrown back in God's face! All that rot. Rubbish!

Where was his certainty now? Where had it leaked away to? Perhaps it had never before been a real possibility for him. Perhaps before it had only been a consolation, the pillow of despair that could comfort the self-pitying spirit for a time, then be put aside again when things were going well once more.

And now?

Japs did it. The Romans, too. Fall on the sword. Death before dishonor. Life without honor is not a life. Decisive action. But it seemed to him a man who chose to take his life would necessarily know what that life had been, who he had been and thus who he no longer was. He thought he knew, had taken it as a given all his years: I am Mikhail Viggo Ibsen. And that was enough.

Who are you?

I am Mikhail Viggo Ibsen. Full stop. The next question never came. Until now.

And who, precisely, is Mikhail Viggo Ibsen?

Well, now at least you've got one answer. A cuckold. Wear your horns. Or take revenge. Reason to go on. *Hurt* them back. You, dear Lise, are no faithful Penelope! You are a stupid, unfaithful, pernicious Gertrude!

And I am a stranger to myself. How can you end the life of a stranger? And at what price? Even the Buddhists, he had read, believe in immediate punishment for self-slaughter: Instant recycling as a lower form. Death as a man, rebirth as a cockroach. Or something of the sort. And then you have to work your way back up through the whole infernal system again, living in garbage, in drain pipes, in sewers. Mating with female cockroaches. Right up the ovipositor! Eat shit, eat the dead! Maybe meet Kragh there. Miserable lecherous cockroach! After my little bug of a wife.

Read about this in Herodotus, too. Report on the Egyptian belief that when a man died, his immortal soul began a series of further lives until it had experienced life as every living species on earth and was embodied as a man again. This process Herodotus estimated to take 3,000 years.

Ludicrous.

Or is it?

What is worse: To return as a cockroach or to burn in eternal hell-fire?

Rubbish.

There is no hell.

Or is there?

He turned his head and his good eye fell on the blue paper cover of the book in his lap. The slender volume seemed a lifetime to him. If only he could know which part had been his. For years he thought of himself, without really thinking at all, as a prince, a king. Then later as a broken king. Then, more recently, as a prince broken from birth. Broken by circumstance. What circumstance? The false pernicious cheating wife! My most seeming virtuous queen! Horrible, horrible, most horrible! Smiling damned villain!

He felt the preserving venom of fury rousing his blood, but in the instant of recognizing it, he slumped again, saw himself trying to play the role of king. Who are you? Never the king. Never the prince. Not for a moment. Not even the covetous treacherous uncle, bold sinner, no. My sins were bold, but puny. Who are you now, then, right now? The old fool Polonius with all his words and blind certainties? No, not even Polonius. Less. Some more or less indifferent functionary? Marcellus announcing the rot in Denmark? Horatio putting aside felicity to send the prince with angels to his sleep and tell the tale? *Felicity!* No, not him either. Just a common fool? Yorick maybe, with a hunchbacked soul. Am I Yorick? Or maybe the gravedigger, the one who had a way with words, yes: We fatten pigs to fatten ourselves and fatten ourselves for maggots, for cockroaches. Who builds the strongest mansion? The man who builds a grave, for it lasts until Doomsday.

The Day of Judgement.

There it was again. The cowardice of conscience. Can't even build your own grave. To act or not to act. Inaction is a worse form of death. Not to act a kind of slow bleeding of the self until the water finds the man. To carry him where? To cockroachdom? And what is better? To live here like this or to crawl through miasma for a new lifetime?

Think of Kragh. Think of his stupid face. Think of the false Lise. Think! he thought and tasted the bitterness of his smile.

9

A thirsty girl

Torben's invitation cheered her, to be desired. Her step was light along the lake bank beneath the green trees.

At the café door, she scanned the scatter of customers seated, standing, and she tried not to think about the fact that she had crammed her parents into her schedule like that, a stray 30 minutes. She looked for Voss's face, hunching a bit to hide her breasts.

He was not there yet, even though she was a quarter hour late. She glanced at the big glass case of sandwiches and deserts, thought of chocolate mousse, tiramisu, lemon tart, and in the pleasure of the moment's yearning remembered how she would feel afterwards. Full but not satisfied. A few moments' sweetness on her tongue before vanishing. She remembered Voss last time they were together in bed, pinching a lump of fat up over her hip and smiling at her without a word.

'Does it bother you?'

'Juicy,' he said in a drawling whisper, as though he were admiring it, but she remembered once as they strolled in the King's Garden how he had looked at a younger woman sunning herself on a blanket and muttered, 'Slim as an eel.'

'So go and fuck her if that's what you want.'

'Let's both fuck her,' he said, and she slapped him happily on the arm.

She chose a table beside the plate-glass window, far enough back from the door so she could see everything – lake, chestnut trees, the room, and anyone coming in the door as well. Music played over the sound system, a smooth reedy saxophone she recognized. Stan Getz. Brazilian. *Desafinado*.

At the table beside her was a young woman wearing tiny glasses. Skinny and dry, Michela could not help but think. No party lights in those eyes. She looked like she was ready to take her goodnight shit, as old Uncle Viggo used to say: I'm about ready for the long goodnight shit, but pour me a little dram of snaps first, will you? The woman with tiny glasses was reading *Information*. Michela felt vaguely guilty. Her interest in the world beyond Denmark, never great, was vanishing. She subscribed to *Politiken*, but hardly glanced at it over her morning coffee anymore. She looked at the first page headlines, the first page or two of the cultural section, the two intelligent comic strips – Nicoline Werdeline and Strid – and the TV page. It was enough for her to watch the seasons. Wasn't that enough? The doings of the world seemed so relentless and unstoppable: terror, slaughter, carnage, suicide bombings. Hatred of people for their race; their religion; their nationality; their wealth; their poverty. She could not bear to read about it all, to see it on television. World events were repellent and the local news was increasingly disturbing, too – stabbings, rapes, race conflict.

Voss could talk circles around her even if he was nearly ten years younger, but she knew what he wanted and loved to watch his face dissolve in the pleasure of the phantoms they evoked in whispers as they made love.

Outside, sunlight shone through the trees, casting its final sparkles across the water, as a swan paddled past, followed by two grey chicks and another larger swan, the male. Monagamous, they say, a perfect little family. Sometimes Michela packed stale bread in a plastic bag and carried it to the lake to feed them from her hand, felt the tickle of their beaks on her palm gobbling the dry crusts. Should do that more often, she thought. She hated throwing away bread. Seemed a sin. On the grassy bank a full-throated bull pigeon ducked its head and strutted after a delicate little she, who scurried off. No monogamy there. More like human males.

Three tables away a girl of twenty or so sat with a book and a bottle of *Jolly Cola* with a glass of ice cubes. Michela studied her face, her posture, the book she held open in one hand. The girl poured cola so it sizzled over the ice, swirled the glass without looking up from the book and raised it to her full lips. Michela squinted to read the title on the dove-blue spine of the book, but could not make it out. Looked like a university text book. Student. About Ria's age, The age Ria would have been, but she would not think about Ria today, and she would not have dinner or even lunch with Torben who would turn 60 this summer, a widower with a daughter who was a drug addict.

Involuntarily an image appeared in her mind, Ria at five, face beaming with joy, chin thrust out, eyes squinted. But the image dissolved at once into the pale, drained face Michela had discovered that spring morning four years before. So still. She had tried giving the kiss of life, even though the cold lips – her little girl's cold lips – told her it was futile.

Michela closed her eyes now with a shudder, remembering.

Not even a note. Just gone. And Michela remembered then the scarf she kept tucked away in a chest of drawers; Ria had given it to her the Christmas before she died, and it was so ugly Ria had feared it was some kind of sarcastic joke, an insult even, Ria had been so strange during those months. No words came to her mouth, no thanks, nothing. She tried to be discreet by not mentioning it, hoping Ria would think it had just been forgotten amidst the shuffle of gifts when in truth it was the only gift Ria had given her and Michela could not find a single kind word to say about it, it was so garrish. She regretted that. The scarf was still packed in its clear plastic packaging in her drawer, buried there, though she never looked at it. She could not bear to, could not bear to think of the hug and the thank-you she had not given in return for the gift.

If she herself ever should take her own life it would be with that scarf in her arms, an embodiment it seemed to her of all her failures as a mother, as a person who could not manage to assume the best and hug her little girl fondly and say, 'Thank you, honey.'

She tried now to picture Ria's sweet face in the innocence of childhood, smiling down on her from heaven, forgiving her, giving *her* the hug *she* had not given and saying, 'It's ok, Mom. It doesn't matter. I knew you loved me. It wasn't your fault, Mom. I just . . .'

She had to be in heaven. Michela could not believe in a God who would punish a little girl for the sorrow that had overwhelmed her. If there was a sin, let the sin be her own, hers and Mads's. It was not natural for a person so young to want to die, to do that. The sorrow could only have been stronger than her will, and it was a mother's responsibility to nourish strength against such sorrow, to protect her child from it. Michela would take that discussion with God when the time came. She was already discussing it.

Purposefully she moved her gaze to an elderly man seated near the door, looking out the plate window. Early 60s maybe. White-haired and firm-jawed, wearing a striped tweed jacket and mustard-colored necktie. Nice-looking man. She wondered if he was alone in life, pictured him coming home to a stale lonely apartment; pictured herself at that age alone. Not so far off really, 20 years or so, only half again the time she'd lived so far.

Look at all the lonely people, she thought and lifted her hand to the waiter. He was tall and slender, long-legged, slim-hipped in black jeans, dark, his skull shaven to a peppery stubble. She asked for a cappuccino, wondering why she did so when what she really wanted was white wine, and watched his back as he walked from her, black apron around his slender hips, a younger man than Voss, himself nearly a decade younger than she.

She felt uncertain about the age difference. In one sense flattered, in another foolish. She wondered if people would think she had not grown sufficiently in experience or maturity to attract a man her own age. Was nine years such a difference? (nine-and-a-half really.) There were some traits in him she saw that made him seem immature: his pouting, his sometimes transparent manipulations, naked selfishness – grabbing the last cake, the last slice, the last chop, the last glass of wine. Made her feel awkward in her own greater maturity. But weren't most men like that really? And other times his cleverness dazzled her, his insight. Wouldn't it always be that way between a man and woman? A melding of strengths and weaknesses?

How did that explain Mads, his walking out after Ria?

I want to quit the job. I want to try my music now.

Ok. I'll give it a try with you.

That, uh, wasn't really my plan. I never thought we would be together, you know, forever, he said.

Oh? What was it you said yes to in the church, then?

You know. It was just the ritual. People don't stay together forever anymore.

16 years. A dead daughter. And that was it.

She found herself wondering then when Voss would walk out, and with the same thought came the realization she had no claim on him. Or he on her for that matter. They'd hardly been together a year. If roots couldn't grip fast after 16 years, how long *did* it take? Maybe Mads had been right. People don't stay together forever anymore. Just keep each other company for a while until they can't take it any more. Until the kids are grown. Or dead. And they can't take it any more. Then go try their own music.

She glanced up at the bar, saw the tall North-Indian manager there, Sudeep. He smiled, heavy-faced, pouches under his eyes, and she nodded. Sudeep had come to Denmark as a refugee from Kashmir, she knew, though she was not certain why. She heard someone ask him once if he favored India or Pakistan in the Kashmiri dispute, and Sudeep said coldly, 'I favor Kashmir.'

Michela continued to berate herself for not having ordered a glass of wine instead, but the waiter was already coming with her cappuccino. He put it down too hard so the coffee slopped into the saucer. She wanted to order the wine, too, but instead she asked for a napkin, her pointed red fingernail tapping the table as she did so – a gesture she recognized as impatience with herself even as the waiter gave her a look.

'*Og et glas hvid vin, tak*,' she blurted then. And a glass of white wine.

'You don't want the cappuccino?' He looked confused, which she liked. 'I want both,' she said with a smile. 'I'm a thirsty girl,' pleased at the relief her words brought her.

He laughed, perhaps accommodatingly, and said, 'Well that's the best kind,' and she felt like an old babe badgering flattery from a young dude. It occurred to her she had no right to expect a damn thing from Voss which put it all at a distance for a moment and made her happy at the thought of his company, made her wonder if perhaps what she felt might even be the first stirrings of love. All things were possible. She was open to whatever.

The café door opened, and her eyes moved gladly toward it, but it was not Voss. It was that fellow she had seen in the café a couple of times before, a dark-haired, grey-eyed man of indeterminate age, wearing a grey beret that matched his eyes, slender legs in black jeans, a tweed jacket and necktie. Vaguely Indian, but fine-featured face, though his nose had been badly broken – a boxer? –; mournful eyes that brightened as their gazes met. She smiled. He nodded and took a seat two tables away.

10

How pretty is your scraf

Nardo doffed his beret and sat, near enough to exchange a word. What word? Seeing her there alone, he felt fear drop like a lead weight inside his stomach. The fear he knew as an adolescent seeing a beautiful girl he knew would not be his. That she was perhaps accessible made everything somehow worse. For now he could try to approach her, and then she could rebuff him, and he would have lost even the distance to dream of her. Or, if she said yes, he may join her at the table, then he would have the opportunity of witnessing how inadequate he was to fulfill even the most common movement toward another human being.

You are not a man. You are not even a man. If you understand nothing else from this, then understand that one thing: You will never again be a man to a woman. That I shall see to, Mr Poet-taster! You want to say a poem for me now, ey, Greeenbag?

At the table beside him a young man opened his laptop computer. The sound of electronic symphonic fanfare crescendoed in the air. Nardo lifted his eyes to her. She smiled and looked away, and in that moment he remembered once, years before, when he was teaching in Temuco, in the south, its dried mud, unpaved

51

roads, its poor beleaguered illiterate Araucanian Indians, its endless winter rain; and the little man who had come all the way from New Delhi to teach English to the Indians was sitting by himself in a restaurant when Nardo came in and looked for a table. The man blurted out, 'Greene! Come and sit with me! I am all alone here!' His voice near panic. A beautiful naked confession, unabashed dread of being cut off. To be alone. A loner. The lone wolf driven from the pack. Easy prey. Nardo had never imagined he could prefer this fate. He had smiled inwardly at the man's terror, recognizing it in himself, although it was a terror he didn't have the courage or desperation to express himself. He feared simply to say something to this woman.

Then he noticed that on the table before her were both a wine and a coffee. So! She was not alone. But she tasted the wine, then shook powdered chocolate on the coffee, and sipped it, too.

'No!' she exclaimed softly in Danish to no one in particular. '*Nej!*' she said with an apologetic smile. 'It tastes so good.' And it seemed to him for a moment a key to the Danish mentality: When they are excited and pleased about something, they exclaim, *No!* But he could find no way forward with the insight, it left him there no wiser. Yet she had addressed him.

His eyes lit on her scarf; brilliant silken rectangles of yellow, blue, red. He was close enough to speak, and he opened his mouth and said, 'How pretty is your scraf,' amending quickly, '*scarf*, I mean.'

'*Tak!*' The word left her pretty mouth with surprised gratitude, smile so light, eyes so blue, pain in his throat.

'It is from *Suomi*?' he asked. "From Finland?'

'Yes, how did you guess?'

And words came, meaningless meaningful sounds, the opening of mouths, sounds to inscribe a common circle around them.

'You are Finnish?' he asked.

'No, but I admire their style. Their sense of color.'

'You have been to there?'

'Once. To Helsinski, we ate blinis with champagne every time.'

We, thought Nardo.

'My ex-husband had business there,' she explained, 'and invited me once to go with him. It was years ago.'

The waiter was approaching, and Nardo thought he might request to join her. May I join you? May I sit with you? Are you alone here today? Is that chair occupied? Waiter, serve my drink at the lady's table, if you please. What does one say? *Lady's*, or woman's? May I . . .?

But the waiter walked right past him and he felt foolish, insulted. The door opened, and her face turned to it and smiled at a tall young man whose slouching posture and too long steps Nardo did not like. His glance, however, was intelligent and not unsympathetic, as he clearly surmised Nardo had been speaking with her. Civilized. He nodded rather formally, though with a broad smile. Nardo was uncertain what the smile might mean, returned only a formal nod of his own and looked away, watching from the corner of his eye as she gave her mouth to the young man, thinking this was a demonstration to tell him she was taken.

'Well *joyeuse fumée*,' said the young man. 'Sorry I'm late.'

'I can understand that,' she said.

'Are you sour?'

She smiled at him. 'I only said I can understand you're sorry you're late because you are late. But that's nothing new.' She spoke mildly, with a smile that said she was only telling facts, not pushing for a fight. He shrugged, matching her smile, and sat.

The rippling surface of the lake soothed Nardo's gaze as he separated himself from their banter, tiny spires of water rolling eastward in the wind, snakes beneath a blanket, dapples of color – green, brown, black, silver, blue. A swan with wind-ruffled feathers floated past. Nardo cursed himself for not having a book in his pocket with which to busy himself as the woman and the man rose to leave, her arm in his. But it was he who looked again at Nardo, to nod once more, and only then did she offer a parting smile and say softly, in the Danish manner, '*Hej hej*,' which in English sounded like *hi hi*; a double greeting that meant farewell.

53

They glanced back once from outside the closed glass door. Why? Did he appear a funny little man to them? A funny little foreigner, ignored by waiters? The ones some Danes called *Perkers*, a blanket slur combining Turk and Pakistani and Persian and Palistinean and Philippino and all other foreign *black-heads*. *Fejl-farvet*, miscolored, some said, or *spaghettis*. Just as in Nardo's country some called the Cubans *sardinos*. Always someone at the bottom of the heap and those just above could care less who you were, whether you had a profession, a culture, a history.

Nardo could feel the set of his face harden into the unreadable mask he had learned to don, felt his eyes blacken and glaze, and the waiter still had not approached him. He found himself staring at a poster on the wall announcing Tango Day at the Café Bopa, over on Bopa Square, with a profiled picture of a man and woman in Argentinian cowboy clothes, bodies wound round one another in dramatic shadow. Nardo laughed bitterly.

He reasoned with himself. Perhaps the waiter did not see him because he had made himself invisible by his silence, by his own averted gaze, as Dr Kristensen in the rehabilitation center had suggested. Perhaps he was employing the tricks his body had learned to avoid being seen, to avoid engagement. Nonetheless, abruptly he rose and knew he was foolish, saw by the round white-faced clock on the wall that it still was possible for him to attend his language class, saw in the periphery of his vision the waiter turn toward him in confusion reading now the offense his posture projected, and it was too late to reverse this exchange. Instead, Nardo softened the set of his shoulders before he left.

As he crossed *Fredens Bro* toward the Centrum, the wind along the lake played in his hair, and he remembered a story told by Neruda about a man, a Chilean painter, arrested by the Nazis in Paris and sent to a camp. He survived and returned, a walking skeleton, to Santiago where 'Death completed its work.' That phrase. Why, you fool? Because a woman you fancied already has a man whose posture offends you? Because a waiter does not see you, having correctly read the signals you had sent him? Fool.

11

Flying lessons

Nardo had given me glimpses of his experiences, sometimes intricately detailed glimpses, yet still no indication of the emotion. Only the screaming, but the screaming and the description were two distinct parts of his memory, two compartments sealed off from each other.

I felt a terror sometimes of what might seethe beneath that absence of emotion. Something I sensed in the grimly playful names they gave to procedures too ugly for contemplation – 'flying lessons', 'the submarine', 'roast chicken', the *picana*. I had seen pictures, sketches, heard descriptions that defied distance. We had regulations in the center limiting our sessions with patients like Nardo. The problems they presented were dangerous. They had been so close to evil. At times they seemed like mirrors reflecting distant images brought suddenly too close. Nardo reminded me of the limits of the objectivity we learned to don in medical school. Of the stink of the pathology lab; the electric, even sexual power radiating from the scalpel in your palm as it sliced into an abdomen. These were slight compared to what Nardo brought into the room with him.

I had to coax him from his hiding place, but cautiously. Too much might lose him, perhaps forever.

At home at night, I was exhausted. I avoided my wife and children, sat behind the closed door of my study. Sometimes I sat there and wondered where I was. What was my aim? What mattered most really? In truth, I had to ask myself how seriously I cared about this little brown-faced man who had suffered so horribly. *Why do you want to do this, doctor?* he asked me. *What is in it for you? Do you enjoy hearing these things?*

It is my profession, Nardo.

Ah, your profession, you and the priest perhaps, who never repeats secrets outside the box? Well, let me tell you, doctor. Priests are not always so good at keeping secrets. No, not always so good.

It was necessary to be faithful to routine. I sat at home in my study over my notes, uncapped the fountain pen. The formality of a fountain pen forced me to write more slowly, contemplatively. I sat over the bound journal in which I recorded impressions of Nardo and closed my eyes and waited for words or images to assist me.

To care or not to care, I wrote, *is not your profession. To help him become who he was is the objective. What you feel or do not feel at any given moment is not at issue here. You are to remain faithful to a commitment greater than the passing mood.*

Me, I think. *More about me.*

You know nothing, doctor, he said to me, *nothing about the human race.*

The secret is in Frog-eyes, I thought. I have to look for it there. At once, a door slid shut in my mind.

From the living room came the sounds of the television, the recorded laughter behind some American comedy series that my children so enjoyed watching before dinner. A program about a happy family and all the little problems they solve by their humor and love and commitment to one another. Unreal, but probably harmless. I pictured myself on the sofa between them, an arm over each of their slight dear shoulders, a martini cocktail on the table before me, the sentimental simplisms, half-truths, dusting over my heart as the gin gently numbed my thought.

I must face this. Why did he smile? What did I say to him that caused him to smile? I said, Nothing you say to me will be repeated outside this room, and he said, Where will you tell it, then, doctor? Here, behind your desk?

In an A4 basket at the corner of my desk, dust gathered on the clear plastic jacket containing my book in progress: *Psychiatric Sequelae of Torture,* a book that grew slowly from a series of papers. I had not worked on it for nearly four months. The structure I so laboriously developed and carried in my consciousness for months was no longer with me, no longer a part of me. I would have to reread my own half-finished book to recall what the intended structure of the work was. It would be like reconstructing another man's study, a dead man, as though I were serving as my own literary executor.

I considered these thoughts, heard the self-pity, the melodrama in them. But also the fear at the core, something far worse, a chaos of formlessness where an identity can fall asunder.

Had it been for the book that I turned from private practice? A ground-breaking study that might establish me soundly in the community? Had it been for that I chose this field? Or did this field choose me? Had it been to help or to seek my own comfort, to help myself? To escape the endless series of grey lonely people, the marriages broken, breaking, children of affluence suffering pains of excess, the incessant self-love, self-focus, solipsistic narcissistic masturbation. Moral weakness. There had been a time I would reject that phrase in an instant, turn from it as from a bad smell, yet now it sprang into my mouth, my thoughts, constantly. Spiritual cripples, moral flab. And now I was free of them, now I faced real, concrete problems.

For a time it had seemed to be of use. There were people I helped, truly helped. I saw it in their eyes; the occasional note; a Christmas letter confirming that they were well, strong again. Antonio from Uruguay who returned to his village, reclaimed his land. The Bergi family from Lebanon and their 12-year-old son.

We helped him. His story . . . their stories were all in the book, inside the clear plastic jacket in the red plastic A4 basket at the corner of my desk which I had not touched in four months and which might be dead by now, aborted.

In the quiet of my study then I felt a presence breathing near me. Smelt foul breath. Who? What? Wheezing laughter. No, I was tired. I ran my palm across my eyes. My brow was damp. I heard the television laughter outside, my children's laughter. I thought of their shoulders in the palms of my hands, their warm bodies touching mine, their innocence protecting me from evil.

I rose, closed my journal, recapped my fountain pen, left the room.

12

Spy Eye

In the classroom on the second floor of a building on Peter Hvidfeldts Street, above a grocery shop, half a score of students sat awaiting the teacher. Nardo took a seat in the back and listened to the antics of a young Palestinian man named Muhammed Ali who was showing a small Philippino man in the seat beside him an advertisement he had cut from a comic book.

'See this thing,' Muhammed said. 'It is called Spy Eye. With this I will to be able seeing through walls, through doors.' He lowered his voice. 'It is even to suggest with this one can see through a garment.' He chuckled happily. The little Philippino clearly saw through it all, but only smiled and nodded while an Israeli, who sat sidewise on his chair by the window, guffawed. 'Muhammed,' he said. 'You would believe anything.'

Instantly Muhammed was indignant. '*You*,' he hissed. 'You know nothing. *Nothing!*'

'I know that you have wasted 79 crowns plus postage on a worthless object that must be fitted in a hole you first shall drill into the door. Anyone can look through a drilled hole. It is no wonder your people make no progress.'

'And you are stupid as you are ugly,' said Muhammed.

The Israeli cackled, his laughter high in his throat but slightly subdued as if to avoid too dangerous a provocation.

'You are so stupid and *evil*,' Muhammed continued, 'that your people murdered Jesus Christ!'

The Israeli sat forward showing the gap between his front teeth, dark eyes glittering merrily. 'You think that? You do not even know that Jesus Christ was a Jew himself?'

'This is lie!' Muhammed said through parted teeth.

'No. I am true.'

'Jesus was not Jew. He was great prophet. Bernardo,' he said, turning back toward Nardo who for some reason he seemed to believe the only trustworthy source of information in the room. 'This is true? Jesus was Jew?'

Nardo wished that he could refrain from replying, that he could lie, that he could feast instead his eyes on the auburn-haired Canadian girl sitting two rows ahead in her tight beige jeans, but reluctantly he admitted, 'Yes. It is true.'

'You see! Even Bernardo confirms this!' The Israeli laughed with his gap-toothed smile. 'You see!'

And Muhammed buried his face into his palms and cried out in anguish just as the teacher, Merete Sørensen, entered the room; a plump young woman with extraordinarly large breasts and a lisp. Merete had a master's degree in Danish literature and tried to teach them Danish by reading poetry to them – Pia Tafdrup, Bo Green Jensen, Marianne Larsen, Inge Christensen, Henrik Nordbrandt, Michael Strunge, Dan Turrell, Thorkild Bjørnvig – which touched Nardo so he prayed she would not discover how hopelessly disinterested most of the students were. Several of them had no language at all really. Muhammed, the Israeli, even the Philippino spoke a little bit of several languages, but had no mother tongue, were master of not even one language.

It was the most terrifying situation Nardo could imagine: to have no language, only bits and pieces of the languages of others; to have to say only what you could, never what you wished to say, might have said, never what you felt straining within you to

60

be expressed. It was difficult enough when you were master of a tongue. Without the words to mix with thought and feeling, one might as well bark, shriek, gabble.

He knew that neither Muhammed nor the Israeli had ever had a full language. They had lived in camps, in settlements, parentless, bits of English, Arabic, German, Yiddish, East European languages, but no mother tongue, no father tongue. The Danish they would learn could scarcely serve as more than a merchant's patter.

Abandanado. Perdido. Por no saber paner los nombres no las expresos. Because I do not know the names of things I do not express them.

There was a great uneasiness amongst his Danish hosts that the refugees to whom they offered shelter were not embracing the Danish tongue. This language had survived a thousand years or more but had trouble holding ground in the European Community. Nardo wanted to tell them that as long as there were Danish poets, this language would thrive. Yet, although he did not wish to insult his Danish hosts, their tongue was not a tongue of the world. It was the language of a small, enclosed place. A few million people spoke it, and he doubted he himself could ever learn it so well that it would become the pulse in his veins. And even if he did, what then? What then would happen to the language he shared with hundreds of millions of people? The language of Cervantes and Unanumo, Garcia Ortego and Alberti and Neruda and Lorca and Marques and Borges. Would he lose it? Already now, after only a few years, wrong prepositions sometimes found his mouth, wrong ordering of words, wrong phrases, translations of Danish modes that would be recognized in an instant as counterfeit by those who spoke his father tongue.

What choice had he? To live with the other Latins in a little circle of expatriates? And who were they? From which side had they fled? In the rehabilitation center where his body had been healed here, where movement had been given back to the arm he had thought forever dead, where he had been helped to free from his heart some of the images that were crippling him, even there he had seen them. More than once. Faces that he knew from the wrong side of the door. *El Pacto del Silencio*. To live among his own people was too dangerous. Even to live among the Danes was uncertain. Who was Thorkild Kristensen really? To whom did he report? Madness perhaps. And perhaps not. The only safety now was in solitude, away from the river of blood in which all who do violence to others are boiling, to the place Rilke defined when he said, *It is important to be lonely and attentive when one is sorrowful.*

Yet even as his ears listened to the sweet lisping words of Merete Sørensen as she recited for them lines from Pia Tafdrup concerning a butchered hare bleeding onto the pages of a newspaper, his eyes moved to the softness of her extraordinarily large breasts – breasts which seemed to define her as a woman fated to spend her life in an attempt to give succor – to the graceful lines of the back of the Canadian girl, the whirl of the red-brown hair pinned to the nape of her slender neck, and he knew that he was forever a slave to the sensual beauty of women and could not live alone for very much longer without withering inside.

13

Why did you laugh?

I knew that I had to press him, to dig into that place to which he did not wish to return. I did not wish to either, but it was necessary. Yet as I sat preparing the question that might nudge him toward it, he suddenly asked, 'May I leave, doctor?'

'Leave? Why yes, of course, if you wish, but I hope you will stay and tell me more about what you experienced?'

'And when I rise?'

'I do not understand. Please, Nardo, tell me what you are thinking, what you are feeling?'

'You say that I may leave, but when I rise to go, what then?'

I studied his face, immobile, eyes averted in their paper bag slits, and I recalled something he had told me about the first time he was arrested. They left him alone in an interrogation room. Then another policeman stumbled in, smiling, to tell him he was free to go whenever he pleased, that he was guilty of nothing illegal. He had only been doing his job as a teacher and that is, of course, to teach. The policeman left, closing the door behind him, and when Nardo rose and moved to open it, Frog-eyes and Moustache were waiting just outside. The moment he opened the door, their fists began to fly at him.

'And when I rise, doctor?'

'No one will try to stop you, Nardo. You are a free man.'

He laughed, a single bitter note. 'Free,' he whispered.

'You are free,' I repeated. 'You only have to remove the remaining bonds. The bonds of memory,' I said, to be certain there was no misunderstanding of my meaning, no secret calculations furiously elaborating behind the paper bag of his face.

'Please, Nardo, trust me. Please take your time and try to put into words what you are feeling, your thoughts. Please trust me. My silence is the silence of a priest, and I take that silence seriously. I do not breach it at any time, for anyone.'

'And if you were moving on? If someone else was to take over for you? You would share your notes?'

'I am not moving on.'

'Stuck in a rut, doctor?'

'I have chosen to be here.'

The glimmer of a smile crossed his lips and was gone. Words leapt to my tongue. *Why did you smile?* But fortunately I stopped them before they left my mouth. I did not dare ask that. I remembered Pinto, the Brazilian, who told me about a torturer who would demand to know why he had laughed when he had not laughed. When he had only been squatting in the corridor, waiting to see if it would be his 'turn' again that day.

The smile was gone now anyway. I had no proof it had ever been there in the first place beyond my own faith in the accuracy of my observations. Something I said made him smile briefly, bitterly. What? Finally, choosing my words as steps across a minefield, I said, 'My words seem to have touched you in some way that I did not intend them to. What is it, Nardo? Did I say something stupid?'

His face tilted, his eyebrows lifted. '*You*, doctor? Something *estupid?*'

I tried to outmaneuver by taking his sarcasm for its literal value. 'Yes, I too can choose my words poorly, say something stupid. Anyone can.'

'Hard to believe, doctor.'

His sarcasm was complete, a closed circle of dry understatement. It locked me out. 'True nonetheless,' I said.

I waited. He waited. His face, as I watched it, seeking the eye contact he would not give, began to assume an eerie quality. He was a mix of races, but his father had been part Indian, and I felt suddenly that I was studying some Inca mask on a wall. So foreign. I cautioned myself to turn from this line of thought, even though I knew that such intuitions often led the way to discovery. I had to focus on the humanity of the face, had to seek the glow of life behind the affectless features. I had to see the man there.

He was not much older than I, educated; he had a degree in philosophy, had written poems. He was not so unlike myself really. The differences were more of form than sort, even the religious differences. The only thing, the main thing that separated us was what he experienced in the prison, those many months, nearly two years. A difference of geography differentiated our fates. That question rose up inside me again: had I been born there, which side would I have been on?

'So,' he said at last. 'You are a priest.'

'No, I only compare my silence, my ethical obligation, to the vow of the priest in confession. I know you told me not all priests honored their vows, but I want you to know that I honor my obligation. Here in the center, we must or everything is lost. You told me you were Catholic.'

'Was,' he said. 'Until they cracked the face of the Catholic god for me. And you are an atheist. No, don't object. I know what you are, doctor. You are an atheist. When I tell you about God, when I tell you about the angels who spoke to me, you interpret these things as the ravings of a primitive, as some manner of compensation, sublimation, the mechanisms of an inferior mind. You glorify yourself, the power of your own mind because it recognizes no power beyond itself. You believe, literally, in nothing. And you congratulate yourself for that. Pitiful.'

'I notice how good your language is when you argue, Nardo.'

'You avoid the question of your belief, doctor.'

'My belief, or uncertainty, is not at issue here, Nardo. I know you are an educated man. I respect your beliefs, whatever they may be. I am in awe of a belief that could make a man so strong to stand up as you have done.'

'You can only respect the belief of an educated man then?'

'I didn't say that. I respect both your intelligence and your belief. And your strength.'

'So you would like to take instruction perhaps?'

'I would like to help you stop being so strong. Your strength is now locked against you.'

I saw a brief glimmer of something cross his face, uncertainty. At least my words had touched him.

'But *where* will you tell it then!' he shouted. '*Where*? Am I an imbecile? Do I not understand your twisted riddles!'

'What riddles, Nardo?'

'And when I rise?'

'Rise? I don't . . .'

'And when I rise, what then?'

'Please tell me what you mean, Nardo. Please take your time and try to put into words what you are feeling, your thoughts. Please explain to me so I can try to understand what you are feeling and thinking. Please trust me. Nothing you say to me will ever be repeated outside this room.'

I could see in his eyes, in the tremor of his mask that he was sliding back into that place again, and it was like watching him fall in terror into a dark pit from which I must not try to hold him back.

Outside in the street beneath his window, Nardo heard a car door slam. Footsteps sounded on the sidewalk, in the lobby, on the stairs. They came to his door in civilian clothes. This time they were polite, almost apologetic. No uniforms. No rifles. 'There has been a complaint,' the one said. He looked like a senior clerk, a man of responsibility, concern. His eyes were not hard, his gaze did not probe. He wiped his face with a clean square of handkerchief, a nervous man. 'We must ask you some questions. Will you come to Headquarters with us? We do not have a warrant. We cannot force you, but if you will come voluntarily, it will simplify things tremendously.'

'Very well, then,' Nardo said, and for some reason he recalled having read that a demon may not enter your home unless you invite it. He did not yet know why he thought that, and he brushed the thought aside.

In the station, the other one, who had not spoken before, the one with the flat nose and flat brown eyes and pencil moustache, leaned too close. His breath smelt of cigars and coffee and spiced sausage. He spoke very softly, as though cautious not to be overheard. 'I know what you have done. It would be wise of you to make a clean breast of it now. Before we have to try to get it out of you, which we easily can do anyway. You have broken the law, the spirit of the law. You know it. I know it. Confess now, and it will be infinitely easier for you. Resist and, well, see for yourself. I will leave you now to think things over in peace.'

The room was small, dim, without windows, the chair hard wood, the table green metal with sharp corners. Nardo would not want that table in a house with children; they could fall and strike their heads on those sharp corners. The walls were bare, chipped, stained, no identifiable color, the floor raw wood, dusty. The door was shut, perhaps locked. He thought about leaving, slipping out the door, passing unnoticed through the confusion in the front of the station, out onto the street, take a bus to the *countryside*, walk to the border, up in the mountains where there was no sentry. Leave his wife and child behind.

From the ceiling a dim light bulb hung, shadeless. Were there observation holes in the walls? Was he being watched?

They had taken his wristwatch when he arrived. Watch, belt, shoelaces. He had no idea how much time had passed. He thought about his 'crime', searched in his mind hoping to discover what they might think him guilty of. Could it have been the complaints of the parents? What the principal called him in for? Impossible!

The lingering odor of the flat-nosed one's breath hung in the air of the room, mingled with the smell of his own body, sweat, gas. He looked at his fingers. They were trembling. His legs and back were stiff from sitting too long in the wooden chair which was the only place to sit in the room. He decided to rise, stretch his legs, but just at that moment, as his knees locked, the door opened abruptly. A man in a yellow tweed suit, three-piece, wearing a yellow necktie, stumbled into the room, stopped, surprised.

'Excuse me,' he said. 'I did not realize this room was in use.'

'Please,' Nardo said. 'How long must I wait here?'

'Have you been waiting? How long?'

'I don't know.'

The man raised his eyebrows. 'You don't know how long you have been waiting? You have been waiting, and you do not know how long?'

'They took my watch.'

He punched the palm of one hand sharply with his own fist. It startled Nardo. 'Those bastards!' he said. 'Thieving bastards!' He looked at Nardo again. 'Perhaps there has been some error. Why are you here?'

'I was told I was suspected of something, but I don't know what. I have broken no law.'

The man laughed. 'Everyone has broken some law. It is not possible to draw breath without breaking some kind of law. Still, perhaps there has been some mistake,' the man in the yellow tweed suit and tie said. 'You do not look like a criminal to me. And I should know. You would be amazed to see the scum I must deal with every day. Scum. It makes me feel unclean when I go home in the evening to my beautiful wife and my children.'

'My wife and child are waiting at home, too,' Nardo said and his eyes met the policeman's for just an instant, dropped to his jacket, yellow tweed with leather-lined buttonholes, an elegant jacket, nicer than any Nardo himself ever owned. He was a high-ranking officer perhaps, whose bribes were received on the highest level, beyond the extortion line.

'Tell me the name of your wife and child,' the man said. 'I will see they are taken care of.' He pulled a piece of paper from his pocket, took from his shirt pocket a pen that was clipped there. 'Here, write them down. Quickly. Before the others return. Come on! Hurry up! Don't you want me to help them?'

Desperately Nardo tried to think of an excuse for not writing down their names. Surely the police knew their names already.

They had been to his house to collect him. They had seen his wife's frightened eyes, his little boy clinging to her leg, his large dark gaze.

'You are a queer egg,' the man in yellow said. 'I offer to help you and you ignore me. Peculiar behavior. Well, never mind. Let me go make some enquiries. I will let you know your status. One way or the other,' he added and left Nardo wondering what he meant by that phrase. But he returned almost at once, smiling, at the door. 'Just as I suspected,' he said. 'It is a big mistake. All you did was teach, right?'

'Yes.'

'There is certainly no law against a teacher teaching, is there? A noble profession. You taught young teenagers, junior high school? They are wonderful at that age, aren't they? So pliable.'

Nardo said nothing.

'You taught them the poems of Domingo Gómez Rojas?' He had the paper and the pen out again. 'Here, would you write down the name of that poet and some of his best poems for me. I would like to read them myself.'

Nardo leaned on the metal desk and watched his hand print the poet's name. The ink in the pen was purple. He watched the block letters forming in purple ink on the page, and the man leaned over Nardo's shoulder and watched, too. 'Now sign your name, too, won't you? I will cherish this piece of paper signed by the man who introduced me to the poetry of Domingo Gómez Rojas. That is José Domingo Gómez Rojas, no?' Nardo did not sign his name. He only scribbled something illegible, which was not his signature, and the man took it from him and shook his hand.

'A pleasure,' he said. 'You are free to go. And please accept my apologies on behalf of the others. Sometimes they are . . .' He shrugged. 'Overzealous.' Now Nardo dared to meet his eyes. They were kind. His face was angular, but gentle, his haircut impeccable. His teeth were good. Nardo recalled thinking only an affluent man could have such good teeth.

'May I leave then?'

'Yes, yes, whenever you please,' the policeman said, although suddenly Nardo thought he heard some tone of impatience in the

man's voice, as though in the tick of the last second, Nardo had done something wrong, had offended him in some way. He shut the door behind him and was gone.

Nardo rose from the wooden chair, crossed the room. The doorknob was smooth against his palm. He opened the door to see a face close behind it: the flat-nosed policeman with the pencil moustache. He was holding a piece of paper, the paper on which Nardo had written the name of the poet. He folded it and tucked it into his inner jacket pocket. His mouth smiled, dark lines between his teeth, but his eyes were hard as glass.

'Good news,' he said. 'They are going to help you.'

'In what way to help?' Nardo asked.

'To help you become a human being.' Abruptly his fist flew into Nardo's face. This blow changed everything forever. It put a crack in the face of God.

Nardo staggered back. Another man crowded into the room behind him. Frog-eyes. Their fists struck from left and right, again, again, Nardo had never been hit so hard, so repeatedly. His head bounced back and forth from blow to blow. He sank to the floor, saw stars. He thought, I am seeing stars! Just like in the comic books! He opened his mouth to laugh, but heard another sound, wondered if it could really be himself making such a strange, high-pitched sound, but could no longer distinguish anything now, only the little piece of wall molding fading in front of his eyes as their shoes collided with his ribs, back, groin. He felt hands grasping his ankles to part his legs. A foot kicked between them, missed the target. He turned slightly to see what kind of shoe, it seemed of interest to know what kind of shoe. A scuffed black toe of perforated leather leapt toward his face. He jerked away and it struck the side of his nose. Pain glided like an electric current along the bridge of his nose, through the eyeball, into the brain where it burst into a bouquet of glittering sparks where a room was filled with screaming, and then that was all of his existence, all that he was, a raw red scream from his bleeding throat, through his bleeding mouth.

14

Only a secretary

She was just the right height. Her shoulder came up beneath Voss's armpit so he could hang his arm across her as they walked, his hand dangling over her chest, holding the fingers of her opposite hand. They strolled in the evening light across Coal Square, down Butcher Street, toward the Centrum, and he felt easy and proud beside her. He felt other men's eyes on her, and he was proud she was with him, the first truly adult woman of his life. That she would be with him seemed to him to confirm that he was a man now, a man among men.

He leaned to kiss her neck, and her eyes turned up to him with a happy smile. Her arm circled his waist, her hip warm and round against his, the sky above them lighter than the street, and he whispered in her ear.

Her mouth formed that droll smile he so cherished, heating him even more.

'Do you think of nothing else?' she asked.

'It's hard.'

A moment passed before she heard it and smirked affectionately at him. She touched the small of his back. 'I have to find a dress for your company dinner,' she said. 'I want you to be proud of me.'

'Already am.'

'Aren't you embarrased to be seen with an old lady?'

'I'm proud. That an adult woman cares for me.'

'You're sweet,' she said, 'but do not exaggerate please,' and steered him toward a shop window with a row of mannequins wearing summer formals.

Exaggeration is a sin in Denmark, but the way he felt at just that moment, he wanted to say to her that he was not exaggerating, in fact he was understating. If he gave full expression to his admiration for her, he feared she would think him weak. In fact, he adored her. He adored everything about her. He adored the small wrinkles at the corners of her eyes and the smile lines bracketing her full mouth. He worshipped the slightly used look of her hearty, capable hands – he wanted to seize them in his own two hands and cover them with kisses in honor of the duty they had seen – the cooking of meals, ironing of clothes, scrubbing of kitchen and bathroom fixtures. He pictured her in yellow rubber gloves to the elbows, a curl of hair askew on her forehead, pictured her at the stove, the sink, or he himself serving her breakfast in bed while she watched him happily with a sleepy smile on her face. He adored her feet, even the incipient bunions at the outer base of her big toes which seemed to him like badges of experience; the tiny wavy lines that had begun to mark her rather large earlobes; the faint wrinkling on her chest, just where her breasts separated. He loved that when she opened her mouth to laugh he could see some silver there; that there was the silvery iridescent remnant of a pregnancy stretchmark on one side of her belly; that she had been a mother; that, though he would never have told her so, she had weathered the death of a child for he believed it had enhanced the slightly distant, sorrowful, wise, dreamy look to her eye. He loved the strong lovely lines of her back and the frightening thrill he felt when it was turned to him. There was no part of her body he would not kiss with relish. He even secretly coveted the towels she dried herself with, the warmth her body left behind on the sheets when she rose from bed, the scent of the clothing she threw over the chairback in her bedroom at night, and it filled him with joy that she was wiser though less intelligent than he. These were the secrets he would not reveal to her lest her knowing might dissolve their powerful aphrodisiac effect upon him.

'How about that one?' she asked.

'Too frumpy. *Joyeuse fumée*, what about *that* one?' He pointed at a slinky red number, low off both shoulders with plunging neckline and back.

'Isn't that too sexy for a business function? Wouldn't it make me look cheap?'

'With your shoulders and back and chest? You'd look like half a million!' Not to mention, he did not say, how tantalizingly beautiful her breasts would be in it, breasts that were his alone to fondle.

'What would your Chairman of the Board say?'

'He wouldn't say a thing. He'd just think it and eat his fat heart out. Come on. They're just about to close. You just have time to try it on now.'

She was only a secretary and made half the money he did and did not have a name that resonated as his own did; his name was Lars Voss Andersen and although the Voss Andersen was not hyphenated – for the hyphenated version was protected by law, he presented himself on social occasions as 'Voss-Andersen.' It was the name of his father, a respected name in legal circles. Voss thought he could at least get that much out of his family background. Those who knew him called him just plain 'Voss,' those who didn't and tried to be familiar, upcomlings, made the mistake of using his first name, 'Lars,' which he used only to sign legal documents and bank draughts.

Still, despite his name and background, she had a more impressive dwelling than he, a Patrician five-room apartment on Crown Princess Street, overlooking the King's Garden, four-meter ceilings and exquisite molded plaster-work and high broad triptych windows. It had been her parents' home and rented for a song – the kind of apartment you had to know the devil's grandmother to get your nails into. He admired her taste, the way she arranged her furniture on the antique polished plank floors, the many pictures hung in artfully uneven groupings all the way up the high walls, the way her sofa and chairs were clustered in one part of the room beneath a low hanging ceiling lamp that had once graced a cathedral, so that they were united in a cozy light, the rest of the large room in shadow. On one window ledge, an enormous ceramic elephant planter spilled over with green ivy that she had started from a cutting filched from the yard behind a house where Hans Christian Andersen had lived for some years. She lit candles all around the room, giving it a sacred, passionate look.

With such taste anyone would think she was from an important old family, a contessa even. Denmark was full of contessas with small jobs. But breeding showed.

Voss's father had once taken him to visit a baroness who lived in a mansion on Kristiania Street. She was very old, and her home was filled with wonderful objects and had hosted members of the royal family. Voss's father had asked the baroness what it was like to be in company with royalty, what were they like?

The old baroness smiled at him. 'Oh, they're just like you or me. Only not quite as snobbish.'

Voss cherished that story, loved to tell it, to drop the baroness's name.

He and Michela sat on the sofa drinking Alsatian Cremant while Frank Sinatra sang from a CD about the summer wind. Barefoot on the cool floorplanks, he allowed his eyes to roam idly from the coffee-table fruit bowl, to a little stack of books, to her, legs tucked up beneath her on the sofa, breasts large and beautiful beneath her T-shirt, hanging slightly with their fullness and age, though the nipples were still uptilted.

He wanted to tell her about the baroness.

By most measures, he was her superior – education, position, family background – but he still felt ignorant, unknowing in comparison – her taste, her practical knowledge, her experience. Even the things she ate, the spices she used. He felt he grew just being with her, developed, learned. And her ease in the bedroom was something beyond anything he'd ever known. It was not the egoistic directness of the girls he had been with in school and university, knowing their rights and demanding their pleasure, but a quiet smiling complicity, an openness to their mutual opening.

On a hanger over the top edge of the door to the bedroom hung the red formal gown she'd bought at his urging, smoky and dim in the shadows, rich but not gaudy, sensuous but not vulgar, and he felt an intense sense of well-being, that she had bought what he wanted, that she would wear it even if she was slightly embarrassed how revealing it was, that all his colleagues in his company would see her in it; her beautiful shoulders and breasts, her mature ease with her body. Even if she was a bit plump – and no denying that. At more objective moments he had to bite his tongue from telling her to go on a diet – but what did it really matter? She could always lose weight later.

He sat across from her and set his flute of Cremant on the coffee table, reached for two of the grapefruits in the cut-glass bowl and balanced them on his palms. 'Almost as beautiful as yours,' he said.

She laughed. 'You're crazy.'

'About you.'

She raised her glass. 'Why do you sit so far away?'

'Want me closer?'

'Yes, please.'

He came round and sat. He kissed her, taking her glass to put it on the table, and laid the flat of one palm against her breast, breathing into her neck. 'Oh, God,' he whispered. 'I *want* you . . .'

75

15

Striptease

Afterwards, propped up in bed, she smoked a Prince Extra Ultra Light and watched him eat pink segments of the grapefruit. Chin on her palm, she blew smoke through pursed lips and wondered about the details of his life, things she didn't know. 'You've never told me anything about your mother,' she said, suddenly aware of this. 'Tell me about her.'

'My mother? Why my mother? You sound like a head-shrinker'

'Has yours been shrunk?'

'Not on your life!'

'I've told you about *my* mother. I'm curious. It's natural to want to know,' she said, although she could sense an almost troubling intensity in her own curiosity.

He popped a triangle of the pink fruit into his mouth and spoke with it on his tongue. 'No psychologisms.'

'Promise.'

His lips pursed as he sucked juice from the fruit. 'My mother was never able to admit what she wanted. As a result, she lived and died unfulfilled.'

'She died?'

'In a car accident. She wasn't driving.'

Her fingers leapt with comfort to his cheek. 'I'm so sorry.'

'She was in the car with a man who was not my father. She had no business being with him. Other than the obvious.'

Michela said nothing.

'So?' he said. 'Guess.'

'Guess?'

'What my mother wanted and was never able to admit.'

Michela shook her head and touched the sparse black hair at the center of his pale chest.

'Try and guess.'

She watched him, thinking. 'Did your mother ever . . . get closer to you than you wanted?'

'Closer than . . .' His face lit up as understanding reached him. 'No! *No no no no.* She wouldn't even have *dreamed* of that, you can be sure. She never touched me at all. Literally.'

'What about your father? Where was he?'

'Where my mother wanted to be.'

She shook her head.

'Free of me.' His smile, she thought, when he said that was like a child's, a smile of simple purity, pure simplicity, unaware of its own unknowingness.

'Your father left your mother?' Michela asked.

'No no, he was there, but he wasn't there, you know? He was free. Free to work, which was all he did. He was . . .' Voss flicked his fingers like quotation marks framing a phrase. '. . . a Very Important Person. The world needed him to solve all its many corporate legal problems. He was a recognized advocate in the high courts. I once found a list of all the corporations whose boards of directors he sits or sat on or chaired – there were something over 30 of them. He had his own bedroom and study at home, and my mother slept alone in a king-sized bed in a king-sized bedroom. A lonely queen. To be honest, I don't even think my father ever had a mistress. He might have, but I doubt it. The law was enough for him. She tried to leave him once, and he told her he would see to it that she did not get anything, not even custody of me. I understand those were his exact words – not *even* custody of me. He didn't want me, you see, but if she didn't do what he wanted, he'd take me from her anyway. The surprise was she agreed to it. She called it calling his bluff: *You want to have to take care of the kid by yourself?* But the bluff was all hers; she could risk the loss easily. So he had to tighten the screws, come up with a worse threat. He'd see to it she got nothing else either, beyond the basic support. Which amounts to about 700 crowns a month, not enough to keep her in king-sized beds and high-ceilinged rooms. She would even have to find a job. So she stayed. She seemed to think she stayed because of me. That was how she justified herself.'

'Are you sure you're not selling her short?'

'Don't get me wrong,' he said, 'I understand. It wouldn't be easy to go from a 12-room house in lovely Rungsted Kyst to a two-room apartment in Vesterbro or someplace worse. Even, God forbid, Albertslund.'

It occurred to her she should never have asked, should never have opened this door. She regretted having been witness to his telling her these things. It was not what he told her so much as the way he did so. She could abide a certain amount of immaturity – after all he was younger than she – but the self-pity he was exhibiting seemed suddenly to threaten everything. She could not have imagined that just a few words, a few related details could have had such a chilling impact on her.

'How do you know all this?' she asked. 'In so much detail.'

'I know.'

'Listen. She stayed. She did stay. Remember that. What would have happened to you if she hadn't?'

His eyes flicked at her, and his smile seemed to tell her that he knew something she did not, that he was about to reveal to her a fact that he was reluctant to let slip, but at the same time his expression belied an undeniable relish.

'*You* stayed,' he said. 'What happened to your daughter?'

Out of her stunned silence words rose. 'I will pretend you didn't make that unthinking comment,' she said. For an instant

79

she thought of asking him to leave, putting an end to this right now. She could hardly believe he had so blithely made things even worse. Hatred seethed in the pain of the wound he had so casually picked open and gloated over, and she wanted to smack him. She feared she might crumple into tears and that was the last thing she wanted him to see her do just now, for her trust was so suddenly, so fully, undermined. Viciously she stabbed her cigarette out in the ashtray on the bedside table, and it occurred to her that only a very immature person could be so callous. He was callow. For one intense moment she felt as though she had seen him truly, as she had never seen him in the year she had known him, as though in one instant he had ripped a mask from his face. But as the insight faded, another idea drifted into her consciousness which was more amenable to her, for she did not like to judge, to see a person in the worst light available. She could not bear to live that way, as some people she had known did, always thinking the worst of others, eager to do so, never looking for a way to understand.

What she thought now was that the game he played here with these statements was a striptease of sorts, but it was himself he teased. He wanted to be naked – for her to see him naked, in what he felt was his full shame. He wanted her to see him at his worst and still not turn away. The first she felt with this insight was embarrassment on his behalf, at his self-absorption, self-pity, self-seriousness, all the worst things that a Dane could exhibit. Grow up, she thought and almost said it, or something less direct, but colder, for in that way she would be able to dismiss all this, allow it to pass on into simple fleeting unpleasantness. Tomorrow or the next day it would be shrugged off, temporary foolishness. They would forget it. But then pity began to seep through, empathy, and her thoughts were eclipsed by the urgency of the emotion.

'How old were you when your mother died?'

'22.'

'It must have been terrible for you.'

He smirked. 'Terrible.'

'Why do you make that face when you say it?'

'Three guesses, the first two don't count.'

'Is your father still alive?'

'Who'd call that living?'

'Are you bitter?' she asked, hoping the question might be subtle enough to make him think and observe himself, subtler than a direct statement.

His pale-blue eyes gazing at her shimmered in the dim light of the bedroom so he seemed to be smiling and crying at the same time, and his lean cheekbones, broad flat bony pale chest with its tiny patch of dark hair touched her.

'I'm sorry,' he whispered then, and a light from outside the window caught in a tear sliding down his cheek. 'I'm sorry for what I said about your daughter.' The last words caught on his tongue like a sob. 'It was uncalled for.' And he swallowed, sniffled, cleared his throat loudly. 'I never want to hurt you,' he whispered.

'That must be my own responsibility,' she said. 'Not to get hurt.'

When he leaned forward to kiss her, she did not stop him.

16

Shall we dance?

In the enormous banquet hall, Voss and Michela were at the same table, though not side by side, and their being separated like that, near enough to see one another but not to exchange even a low, private word if they wished, raised a strange, giddy tension in Voss's chest. Michela was gorgeous in her red, low-cut gown, her bare shoulders exquisite, the top of her chest, the shadowed cleavage between her breasts – what Danes call the *cavalier passage*. Her light hair was piled and pinned on top of her head so when she turned to chat with the tuxedoed men on either side of her – Madsen, the bearded accountant, to her left; Vaever, who was Vice Chairman of the Board, on her right – Voss could see her almost Hebraic profile and the graceful line of her throat and shining interweave of blonde hair pinned at the nape of her neck which made him wish he could come round behind her to press his lips to the golden skin there. The lighting showed him something new about her, too: that her shoulders, the line of her nose, the whirling outline of her ears even, were downed with the finest, finest pale fuzz, as on a peach, though longer, sparser, and his heart lurched with excitement at this discovery.

It seemed a tribute of respect to Voss's position and promise that his companion had been seated beside the Vice Chairman of the Board, but it also meant that after the coffee, he would have the first dance with her, for she was the table lady on his right. This bothered Voss very much. He did not dance himself and would have to sit here and watch the older man moving and touching her body right out on the dance floor in full view of the entire company. He had not anticipated this when he picked out that gown for her. Madsen, to her left, was on Voss's own managerial level, so less threatening; they were also on good terms, although Voss felt intellectually superior to him. It amused him that the financial managers in the company always seemed to sport beards these days, just catching up with the style about 30 years too late.

Well, he thought, *That time, that sorrow.* The first course was being served now, and Voss consoled himself that there would be plenty of time and plenty of wine to prepare himself for the inevitable Michela-Vaever after-coffee dance, at the end of which he could whisk her away into his own company. They were staying in the hotel, on the executive floor, and he could barely wait to get her upstairs and undress her.

The first course was goose liver pâté, and Voss waited eagerly as a waitress in black livery poured Gewurztraminer round the table. There were four glasses before each plate he noted happily – white wine, red wine, desert wine, and water. Followed without doubt by a selection of strong digestifs.

To Voss's left, in a glittery blue dress, was a plump blond named Janne Splid who sat like a good little girl, hands folded on the very edge of the table before her. The man beside her, a young analyst named Bruno with a northwest Copenhagen accent, poked his pâté with a fork. 'Foie gras, bla bla,' he said. Then, under his breath, 'I hate this shit.'

'Get used to it,' said Voss quietly, pleased for the excuse to speak.

To his own right was Agnette Würm from personnel; he was trying not to remember how at the summer outing a year ago, in his cups, after repeatedly kissing her in the shadows behind the boat house, he had proposed that the two of them try to recruit her secretary into a menage à trois.

'You are sick,' she said and left him there.

Ever since, he had been avoiding her and was having trouble finding common topics of conversation now. Although he knew he should wait for Vaever, the senior person at the table, to initiate the first taste of the Gewurztraminer, he lifted his glass and quietly said '*Skål*' to Agnette, just to break the ice. At the sound of the word, all eight people at the table hastened to seize and lift their glasses, and Voss blushed, avoiding Vaever's gaze, hoping Michela had not noticed his blunder.

The wine was excellently fruity, and everyone held his glass aloft after tasting, *presenting* it to the company, glancing by turns into the eyes of each person at the table, before returning the glass to its place. Voss noted the level of wine in Vaever's glass after his first taste, for that would signal the rate at which he would be drinking that evening – the rate at which others at the table would be expected to drink. Voss was delighted to see he had taken half the glass in one snap.

He asked Agnette if she would be going away for summer holidays, and she seemed grateful for the question. He listened raptly as she told about the summer-house she and her mother had bought in North Zealand, practically on the fjord, as he took many small sips of his white wine, wondering why a grown young woman would vacation with her mother.

Between the first and second course was a speech by the Chairman of the Board, a short stocky man, who began by expressing special thanks to Lars Borg Sommer for honoring them with his presence this evening.

'Who's that?' Michela whispered to Vaever, loud enough for Voss – and everyone else at the table – to hear. He curled his toes as Vaever glanced at her. 'Lars Borg Sommer,' Vaever repeated discreetly, covering her gaff by pretending she had merely not heard the name. 'The Minister of Trade.' God, Voss thought. *Can't you just shut up and look good!*

The Chairman was saying that tonight they were all here to

dine, and converse, and dance, and enjoy one another's company, not to listen to speeches. But he then proceeded to give a speech all the same; it went on long enough for Voss to begin to get a cramp in his buttock while the waiters and waitresses stood to the side with their wine bottles poised like soldier's with rifles at port arms. Voss managed inconspicuously to catch the eye of his table's waitress to indicate his need to have wine in his glass for when the Chairman was finished speaking and toasted the whole assembly.

He was pleased to note she filled his glass almost to the lip, recognizing perhaps his greater dedication to content than bouquet. She only filled the glass of Janne Splid to his left halfway, and Voss whispered to her, 'You know what Jonathan Swift said to a waiter about that?'

The waitress shook her head.

'"Pray tell, sir, what is the function of the remainder of that glass?"'

Agnette chuckled behind her napkin, which cheered Voss, and he gazed across at Michela to see if she had witnessed his witty comment, but she was not looking his way. She was smiling raptly in the direction of the flannel-mouthed Chairman.

Phony! Voss thought. Ass kisser! And gulped down half his wine.

The Chairman finally finished, chairs were scraped back as the assembly rose, glasses were lifted, a chorus of *skål* rumbled across the room, and then they were seated again, and the lovely waitress refilled Voss's white-wine glass once more to the lip before she began clearing the starter plates away. This is a beautiful friendship, Voss thought. She was cute, too. He speculated a bit about the waitress as he chatted with Agnette, did a tad of cross-table verbal fencing with Madsen, tried in vain to prime a bit of chit-chat from Janne, who he concluded was a frump, noted with pleasure Michela's admiring smile fixed upon him in passing.

By the time, they were cutting into their pink strips of lamb in mint gelé and pleasuring their tongues with a '97 Mercurey *premièr cru*, it appeared that northwest Bruno had decided to affix himself to Voss with conversation about the vagaries of Danish football. Voss had nothing against having an ally, but cautioned himself not to appear dependent upon the attentions of a man with a marked northwest accent, so he began to pose the occasional question across to Vaever about a complicated item on the next agenda of the Board. Besides, he knew little about soccer, not having so much as even kicked a soccer ball since the required matches of primary school. He was pleased that Vaever seemed interested by his observation, and when Michela posed a question about it, Voss said – perhaps too quickly – 'That's very technical,' heard in his own ears the false sound of his tone, and turned back to Bruno while Vaever took upon himself to answer the question from Michela that Voss himself, he admitted to himself now, had been unable to manage.

Noting from her table card that Janne Splid's full name was, in fact, Janne Splid Hansen, while Agnette Würm's full name also included a Hansen, Voss began to tell her a story, partially fabricated, about a dinner he attended once at which everyone at his table was named Hansen or Jensen. 'There was a Hans Jensen and a Jens Hansen, too!' He began to chortle in anticipation of her laughter, but she ignored his story and said, 'Your companion is sweet,' with a curl to her lip that he didn't like. He wondered what she meant.

'Thanks,' he said, 'You're sweet yourself. Lovely dress,' he added, fingering the glittery chiffon gauze around her shoulders. *My maiden aunt has one just like it,* he wished he dared to add.

Janne Splid Hansen smiled, but he saw the glint of battle in her eye and cut across to Bruno, asking what he thought about Brian Nielsen's chances for that million-dollar heavyweight title fight with Hasim Rahman in China, boxing being one manly sport he did occasionally follow.

'Rahman's ascared a Super Bree-an,' said Bruno. 'He's gonna go for David Izon instead. Bree-an'd kill 'im, but Don King's pullin' all the strings anyhows.'

Voss didn't know who Izon or Don King were and didn't want to ask. Bruno rushed on to say, 'But the real question is when's

Bree-an get a shot at Tyson? That's the fight I want. Tyson and Shelly Finkel's in for a surprise.'

'You know what they call Bree-an in New Vork?' Madsen asked. 'A Danish. Like Kennedy in Berlin in 1960? *Ich bin ein Berliner.* I am a creampuff.' There was laughter, and Voss hastened to say, 'Bree-an better wear metal earguards if he doesn't want a love-bite on his ear,' and then, 'You know, I had a drink at Hvid's Wine Room last week and guess who served me? Old Hansen.'

'Who?' asked Bruno.

'Jørgen Gamle Hansen.'

'Who's 'at?'

'Former middleweight champion of Europe is who. He's serving at Hvid's now. I said, "How's it going, champ?" and he lit up like a birthday cake.' Voss thought he heard his own voice beginning to take on sympathetic echoes of northwest Copenhagen so he turned his attention to the label of the *premièr cru,* which the lovely waitress had left on the table within his reaching distance. He topped up the ladies' glasses to left and right before emptying the rest of the bottle into his own glass which he lifted to Agnette Würm Hansen on his right, who met his eyes with, he thought, a sparkle in her own. Which got Voss wondering if she might, in fact, have remembered his suggestion of a menage-à-trois last year and was reconsidering. Or at least reassessing the libido of a man with the passion to make such a proposal.

The grating sound of a motor distracted him. A curtain was being raised behind the dance floor, revealing all the musical instruments there. Voss noted that the thought of the dancing raised a nervous sweat in his armpits. He took another gulp of the Mercurey and popped a cherry tomato into his mouth. Then he said to Agnette, 'May I be so coarse,' as he slipped off his tuxedo jacket and draped it on back of his chair. Agnette laughed and snapped one of his white braces. Voss leaned intimately toward her, saying, 'I won't be responsible for my response if you do that again.'

She called his bluff and snapped it again, and he only laughed, though he noticed that he was seriously considering trying to snap the strap of her baby-blue breast-holder, which he had glimpsed provocatively peeking out of the hem of one of the puffed shoulders of her gown. He liked the look of her bare arms and the deep saltbox of her clavicle. She was, in fact, trimmer than Michela. He considered making reference to how much fun the company picnic had been last summer, considered asking if she were staying in the hotel also, but thought that might be misunderstood if overheard. He could wait until later when the others were up and dancing to ask her that, which he was certain she would find a more interesting question than, Shall we dance? In fact, who knew? She might well have thought again about what had happened last year, might be reconsidering, hoping for another chance.

He wondered if Michela would be so inclined. She was a racey woman, had nothing against spicing up their love-making with verbal pictures, fantasies, mostly of his own suggestion but also some of her own originals that she sketched into his ear with a breathy whisper.

'The father is word to the deed,' he said aloud but no one seemed to have heard. Then he was uncertain what he had said, though what he had meant to say was, The thought is father to the deed, or maybe, The word is father to the deed. Or was it, The thought is father to the word?

His mouth was very dry so he emptied his water glass in one draught and said, 'Ah! Water is life,' as the waitress filled his little dessert-wine glass.

'May I?' he asked and turned her pale slender wrist so he could pretend to read the label of the Sauterne bottle. The skin of her wrist was so soft, so warm, so alive with pulses, that he glanced at her eyes, and she smiled. How he would like to kiss her, massage her lovely poor over-worked body. I certainly hope your boyfriend massages your cute, tired feet for you when you get home, he wished he could say to her, but not while Vaever's and Michela's heads were leaned so intimately toward one another in conversation. About what? *Bitch!*

'Take care your companion doesn't begin to envy the

waitress,' said Janne Splid Hansen on his left, and Voss froze. The frump has some bitch in her, he wanted to say. Worst kind.

'Oh, no, don't worry,' Janne added. 'She only has eyes for Herr Vaever. She is completely *absorbed*.'

'Good thing you're here to keep an eye on it all,' said Voss, smiling, happy with his tongue. 'Who brought *you* by the way? I mean . . .' He smiled over his lazy amendment. 'Who is your escort? You're not alone, I hope?' And saw in the hurt of her grey eyes he'd cut too deep. *Well, sis,* he thought, *that's how it is when you play with the boys.*

'I am with my husband,' she said curtly and forked a wedge of fat-edged lamb into her plump face.

Good idea, he thought. *Have some more calories. Little more fat on your plump.* But the crack about Michela and Vaever still smarted. He sent his gaze across the table again, found himself studying Vaever's square-jawed face, the flattened bridge of his nose, must have taken a few shots in his time with that punched-in snothorn. He was older than Michela, Voss reckoned, by a good ten years, which would make him what? 50? At least. Probably's got a saggy ass, he thought, and at just that moment, Vaever looked across the table at him and smiled.

Voss beamed back at him as a plate of champagne sorbet and wild berries was placed before him by the lovely pale hand of his friend, the waitress. He raised his eyebrows at Vaever to indicate complicit appreciation of the dessert and the waitress, then hoped the older man had not thought he meant complicit appreciation of Michela for hell's sake!

Michela flashed a big happy smile at her plate of sorbet and said, 'Mmmmm . . .' which Voss found somewhat overstated and annoying and, in fact, poor manners, vulgar even, as he went for his Sauterne.

Then it was coffee and tiered dishes of dark pralines being passed, and Voss's favorite waitress stood behind him performing the miraculous feat of holding three *avec* bottles in one hand: Grand Marnier, Poire Guillaume, and an XO Hennessey. An XO! She smiled encouragingly.

'Do I dare?' he said.

'I think you owe it to yourself,' she said and twinkled as he touched the tip of his right index finger into the center of the O on the XO label, thinking, *You are the woman I was born to love, truly.* It occurred to him she seemed rather intelligent. Perhaps she was more than a waitress. Perhaps a university student earning some extra money on the side.

He could not believe the depth of the cognac she poured for him, could not believe this much XO cognac would be his at one time, glittering deep red-brown fluid in the bell of a snifter, cupped to warm in his palm, his nose at the edge of the glass inhaling the piquant bouquet, thinking how he would love to pour it into the salty pale palm of the waitress's hand and lap it out.

'All we lack now's a cigar,' he said, and Vaever reached into his inner breast pocket to extend across the table toward him an open three-tube leather humidor with three fat Cohiba robustos sticking out.

Some sexy gal, my date, hey VC? he thought, but said, 'Oh, Herr Vaever, it was only my joke.'

'Call me Jens,' the older man said, and 'Go on, take one!' Then he passed a little silver cutter. 'Keep me company, Voss. We're two of a vanishing breed. Cigar lovers.'

Noting that Vaever had offered a cigar to no one else, Voss did not look at Bruno, but enjoyed the thought of how the expression on the poor northwester's face no doubt looked, and said, 'Well *joyeuse fumée,*' leaning back in his chair and lighting up, filling his mouth with the rich Cuban smoke and letting the warm haze of XO well-being settle around him like a lovely elegant filmy garment.

Recalling something in the newspaper a while back about Clinton and Lewinsky and cigars, he ventured to say, "This cigar is perfect." I had one in the office the other day and it was bad. 'This cigar's bitter,' I said, and one of the secretaries looks at me. 'Well don't blame it on me, Voss!' she says.

The table roared with bawdy laughter, everyone, even Vaever, cigar between his smiling teeth, and Voss relished Michela's naughty smile.

He sighed lazily, marvelling again at, savoring, the fact that he was the only man at the table Vaever had offered a cigar.

Then he found himself considering why this might be the case. An acknowledgement of his ability, his promise, his future? A simple gesture of friendliness? Pity? A response to his idle comment about the lack of a cigar, interpreted as a put-down by Voss on the incompleteness of the dinner, of which, after all, Vaever as Vice Chairman, was among the hosts? Could it mean the opposite of what it seemed? A gesture of generosity that was in fact a put-down of himself? A set-up? Could it be, in fact, mockery? Here, have a cigar while I goose your lovely older girlfriend under the table? For if he were goosing her, surely Michela would be too discreet to object, or to let it show, for fear of compromising Voss's position. Or perhaps she was not objecting because she enjoyed it! Perhaps she had invited it! She knew how to send very subtle messages with her eyes, her lips, the stray, seeming spontaneous, touch of her fingers.

Voss's dress shirt was damp beneath the arms, down his spine, and at the small of his back. He blotted his forehead with his soiled napkin and hardly dared glance across the table. The musicians were taking their places by their instruments now, which meant people would soon be dancing. He and Agnette would be left alone at the table, and he didn't at all feel up to explaining to her that he just never danced. Of course I was sent to dance school as a boy – to Frøken Thomsen, in fact, in Hellerup. Just never got the knack. Count your blessings I won't be treading on your nice new pumps. No, what could he say? He wished he could just bolt. Maybe take a trip to the gents'?

Then he noticed the open bar had been set up at the back of the room, far from the dance floor, and he thought what he needed more than anything else just now was a good cold drink. He smacked his lips to advertize his thirst and set the Cohiba on the rim of the ashtray.

'Anyone for a nice cold drink?' he asked.

Michela leaned forward with a smile, and his blood jumped. He could see clear down the front of her dress. He could see her nipples!

'I would love a gin and tonic,' she said with a dazzling smile. Butter wouldn't melt in her mouth.

'Anyone else?' he asked, but all heads shook or ignored him, and he was gone just as the first notes of the first dance number began to crash across the floor.

Half-a-dozen others were quicker than he getting across the huge dining room to the bar, so he lined up, thinking he would order two G&Ts, one a double, for himself. No, make it a triple – they might be serving stingy two-centiliter measures. Michela wasn't accustomed to hard liquor, no sense doubling her up at all. In fact, he thought she had probably had quite enough by now, judging from all her cozy tête-a-têtes with Vaever. Call me Jens. Sure. The band was playing a slow number he didn't recognize, and he didn't dare look back. See his whole table on the floor, only Agnette left seated all by herself, abandoned by her table gentleman, and anyone who noticed would think badly of him for it. Dirty trick to pull on a woman. Really low. Better just ask her to the floor for one number when you get back. Shuffle around to a slow one. Manage that ok. Remember Frøken Thomsen's turkey-squawking voice when he was ten, ruthless pinching of his arm to try to get him to fall in with the rhythm. No wonder he hated to dance! But he could manage a single foxtrot. Then you've done your duty and you could get down to other matters with Agnette. Different people have different talents.

The slow number finished and melded into a zippier one, which he recognized as a jazzed up version of an old Beatles' song. He chanced a quick look over his shoulder, saw bearded Madsen dancing with two women at once – his own table lady and Agnette, too. Prick! Ass kisser! Better thank him for the courtesy.

Even northwest Bruno was dancing, though not with Janne Splid. He was rocking back and forth like a clump of wood in the arms of one of the legal secretaries, while Janne Splid danced gracefully with a tall handsome blond man. Her husband? Much better-looking than Voss would have expected her to have.

93

Threading his way back across the dimly lit dining room, a gin in each fist, single in his right for Michela, triple in his left for himself, he paused, spying Vaever and Michela out on the floor, dancing to 'Harlem Nocturne'. There was a good deal of space around them, and they moved slowly and elaborately to the vibrato sounds of the electric guitar and saxophone. She looked so beautiful and graceful as Vaever, in his tux, turned and twirled her, pulled her body up against his own so her breasts were pressed flat against the shiny lapels of his tux, and he smiled down into her smiling face, their eyes joined, crushing her breasts against his chest. Then he turned her away again, twirled and drew her back, while his Bali-clad little feet stepped deftly to the rhythm. His left hand clasped her right, their arms extended full so they were as far away from one another as they could be without breaking their grasp; arms extended, she curtsied slowly, gracefully before him so her sexy red dress bushed out around her, and her head bowed as though in homage. Then she lifted, and he spun her toward him so her dress twirled alluringly around and between her legs and the full front of her body met his.

Voss was frozen by the beauty of their movement. But in the midst of that radiant moment, a seething jealousy rose in him. He remembered her husband – Mads was his name – who she told him had beaten her sometimes out of a jealousy that was utterly unfounded and unjustified. Suddenly Voss, who had never even imagined striking a woman, or anybody, felt now he could understand beating her because gripping him as he watched her now was a furious wish to hurt her, to make her pay for curtsying to Vaever – *curtsying!* – and it appalled him to experience this passion.

He felt in this moment the turning point of the evening, knew that from here forward, it would be a fight for him to resist the urge to be evil and sarcastic toward her.

They returned to the table, flushed and smiling, just as he reached it. Vaever said something to her and went toward the bar, and Voss delivered her gin, told her he had a poisonous headache, that she should stay and enjoy herself and come up to him later, and before she could find her way through the amazement evident on her face to speak, he spun and walked quickly from her, relishing the confusion this surely had caused her.

Halfway expecting her to hurry after him, take his shoulder, hoping she would, hoping she wouldn't, he hurried toward the elevators, smiling and nodding at people he knew.

She did not follow him. In any event she did not catch him. And as the elevator doors bumped shut without her appearing, his rage rekindled. He banged the button for his floor, missed, tried to bang it again with the side of his fist but a sharp pain wracked the blade of his palm; his hand had hit the door-open button by mistake and a man and woman he did not know in tux and gown stepped into the elevator. He smiled crisply, nodded to their smiles, as they punched their floor and he his.

He felt he could kill her; pictured himself choking her, thumbs on her windpipe. He ground his teeth at the vision.

In his room, he filled the ice bucket, took a little bottle of Chivas from the minibar. He flung his tuxedo jacket across the room so it knocked a lamp from the bedtable. He slid his braces from his shoulders and sat, thought of the Cohiba still balanced on the lip of the ashtray on the table in the ballroom, cursed himself for not having taken it with him. Then he was glad he had left it for Vaever to see, the old fuck! That's what I think of your fake generosity!

In the little refrigerator were a bag of nuts, chips, a Mars bar. He took them all out and began munching them, one by one, chewing methodically, filling his mouth, chewing, swallowing, gulping whiskey. He poured another Chivas and peered at the green luminous numbers of the clock face shimmering in the base of the TV: 11:15.

Bitch! How long you plan to stay down there? I see you have no problem making contact with people you don't know. With my colleagues! My *boss!*

Again and again he pictured in his mind the movement of their bodies, parting, joining, their smiles, extended arms, Vaever's smile, her curtsy. Fucking *curtsy!* What a stupid fucking thing for her to do! To the vice chairman of the board! An embarrassment for him, a professional embarrassment!

He could not remember ever having witnessed anything in his life in such vivid detail. Except for what he could not see. The liberties of Vaever's hands down her back, her front, on her hip. His thumbs no doubt secretly moving to her nipples! And Voss knew very fucking well how responsive to touch they were! And who knew what *her* hands might have done? Did he have a hard-on when they danced? Did he rub it against her. Wedge his fucking agéd hip against her cunt? Was her cunt wet? Did he kiss her neck? Run his wrinkled 50-fucking-year-old finger down her cleavage?

Voss tore off his butterfly, snapped to his feet and glared into the mirror at himself. 'I hate you!' he snarled. 'I fucking hate you!'

Then his face grew cold, sly. 'Oh,' he said mildly. 'You decided to come back to our room after all, did you? How cozy. Did he kick you out of bed after he fucked you? You think he wants anything more than that from you? That's all he could possibly want from a low-life bitch like you!'

He stepped from the mirror, back again. 'God fucking damn it, you didn't even know who the Minister of Trade was, you ignorant fucking bitch!'

He grabbed the phone receiver and slammed it down into the cradle again, yelled, '*Shit!*' And '*Shit shit shit!*'

There were only two little bottles of Chivas in the minibar so he settled for the Ballantine 8-year-old, poured both 5-centiliter bottles into his rock glass and sat in the dark staring at the green numbers on the clock, felt himself nodding.

He woke to a scraping sound, realized she was sneaking in the door. He opened his eyes and saw her, black patent-leather slippers in one hand, holding her gown hitched up by the hem. It was after 2.00 by the green glowing numbers on the digital TV clock. She moved silently through the dark room without turning on the light. From her movement it was clear to him she'd had plenty more to drink after he left her, and she stopped short, startled, when she saw him sitting there. Her hand flew to her chest and she gasped.

He rose, felt the fury swelling in his fists, saw how fragile the dark taunting beauty of her face was, and he heard a sob choke in his throat as he lunged for her and buried his tongue into her mouth.

Then he was tearing at her gown, snarling, 'What did you do? Tell me!'

'I didn't do anything,' she whimpered. 'I was just dancing.'

He fucked her on top of the bedspread, and all the while he was in her, moving on her, rocking, sideways, forward, grabbing her up against him, he saw Vaever's hands on her, their bodies pressed together; saw Vaever's old freckled hand going up her dress beneath the table; saw him shove a Cohiba into her cunt and fuck her with it, smiling the way he had smiled at Voss when he held the pocket humidor out to him, the way he laughed at the Clinton joke. And he pictured her on her knees, Vaever's fat agéd cock in her mouth as her blue blue eyes looked up into Voss's, watching him as he watched her suck the Vice Chairman's dick and then raised her whorish mouth to Voss's, still wet with Vaever's cock, and buried her come-gobbling tongue into his mouth as his mind surrendered to the void. He shuddered, growled into her ear, arching up on the bed and came, crying out, 'O dear God, I *love* you! I fucking *love* you!'

17

Love in the morning

Voss opened his eyes and stared up at the shadowy ceiling over the hotel bed. Dusty egg white, it pressed down at him with the gloom of raw morning. A liquid pain moved in his skull, a blur of pressure from temple to temple, and his nose was dry and clogged. He wanted to pick it, but didn't know if she was awake, didn't know what to expect from her.

The events of the evening before were unclear to him. He remembered leaving her in the dining room and felt a fierce sense of justification for having done so, but could not quite recall why. Then he remembered it was because of her dancing with Vaever, the way Vaever had moved her, the way she curtsied without any concern for how it might have made him feel, without any concern about the fact that she was dancing with the second highest senior official in his organization.

He remembered the guilt all over her face when she came sneaking in – *sneaking!* – cocktail slippers in hand, tiptoeing, thinking she could get in without waking him, not aware he was awake and fully conscious of what was going on. *Guilt!* She owed him an apology all right. She had embarrassed him in front of his colleagues. Worse, his superiors. Curtsying! Right out on the dance floor like that where everyone could see.

But from the memory of that moment to when he was in the room was something of a blur. There were blank spots, and suddenly he was uncertain what he had done. He remembered being furious. Had they argued in the dining room? Had he shouted? Had others seen him, heard him? He remembered a couple getting onto the elevator. Who? Had he said something to them? Who were they?

He moaned, squinted his eyes against the pain behind them, trying to fill in the blanks. Then he remembered fucking her, how hot he had been, her guilty face, her whimper, 'I didn't do anything wrong. I was only dancing.' And he remembered more then, the excitement, the thought of Vaever feeling her up right out on the dance floor, rubbing his thigh between her legs and her thigh against his crotch.

He moaned again, remembering, as the memories grew in his mind. What had he told her? Was it only in his head? Did he tell her? His blood stirred at the thought, the images, the fear he might have told her something about how fucking excited it made him. A tiny whimper clicked out of his throat and he stirred his legs, reached down between them to calm himself and found himself, despite the pain, raging horny. His breath was heavy, and he smelt the hangover reek of his own body, and he wanted to wallow in it. He wanted to put his face between her legs, he didn't care about anything, but he was afraid even to look at her.

He feared the judgement he might see there on her face, feared what she might remember that he could not, how she might interpret what had happened. That whimper in his throat again, and he turned on his side toward her, knees drawing up to his chest, and started.

She was watching him, the side of her head propped on her palm, her eyes mild and sleepy.

'Good morning,' she said quietly.

He kept his voice neutral. 'Morning.' Hoped she couldn't read his face, couldn't remember more, or more clearly, than he could.

'Do you remember what you said to me last night?' she asked, reaching to riffle the close-clipped hair on the side of his head.

'Of course I do!' He heard the bang of a housemaid pushing her trolly in the corridor outside the room, wondered what time it was. 'What, uh, specifically do you mean?' he asked.

Her sneer was merry, gently chiding, and she leaned closer to his face. He could smell her breath which was not even sour, and that made him feel even more vulnerable. He didn't have it in him to stonewall, but he knew he must. Never let them get you when you're down the next morning. Human nature. Admit to a blackout, and they play with you like a cat. Show your throat and they go for it.

'Specifically,' she drawled with a little toss of her head, 'You said that you loved me.' She kissed his lips lightly. 'But of course it was probably just the heat of the moment. If so, I won't hold you to it.'

'Oh, Jesus, Michela,' he whispered, and he did love her at that moment, gave in to all resistance in gratitude, off the hook, to the beauty of her, to her sweet kindness in not recoiling at his stench. 'Oh, Jesus, Michela.' He kissed her neck, which was so delicious to his lips, murmured, 'Do you like to make love in the morning?'

'Do *you* like to make love in the morning?' she asked.

'Oh Christ, yes,' he murmured, 'I need you,' and she was naked under the sheets. He kissed her mouth, her throat, moving down, murmuring into her warm smooth skin. He wanted his face between her legs, to debase himself in the beauty of her cunt, to heal himself there.

She whimpered as his mouth found her, as he filled his senses with her, filled her beautiful cunt with his miserable face, felt tears in his eyes as her palms closed on the back of his skull, holding him there, so he said, 'Yes! Yes! Like that! Yes!' and she whispered, 'Darling, oh, darling,' and her smooth cool thighs closed around him.

18

A *little table music*

She hummed in the kitchen. He could smell the sweet, fried aroma of medister sausage on the pan, frying with onions, and the pungent reek of chopped red cabbage stewing in a pot, which with cold beer and iced snaps and hot mustard and dark rye bread, were the nearest things he knew to blissful salvation. A hangover was a high in itself. His senses had the keen edge of a razor, and he sat bare-foot, bare-chested in his jeans, no undershorts, reading a book of poetry by Pia Tafdrup, which he had taken from her shelf. A poem in which a woman held her lover's semen in her mouth, considering whether to swallow it or spit it out. In his condition, he identified happily with her as he listened to his own lover humming in the kitchen over the food she prepared for him.

'*Joyeuse fumée,*' he said aloud and wanted her in his arms again. He wanted to tell her things but did not know how much she might already know, could not differentiate between what he had only thought and what he might have said.

How much should a person tell? he asked himself and felt the answer in the knife edge of his senses. If this is a hangover, let me be hungover forever!

He reached for the bottle of Tuborg and tipped it up to his mouth, pulled a long rough draught down his throat, belched, and drank again.

Then the truth occurred to him in a clarity that dizzied him where he sat, his feet propped on the coffee table: I want her to know me as no one in the world has known me before. I want to share with her my innermost life. And for her to share hers with me.

He wondered if there were a difference between their shadows, or whether their shadows mingled already, whether they were together because they were two halves of a whole in every way. This confused him. Was she simply a canvas upon which it was for him to paint desire? Was it his place to act and hers to respond? Was a woman merely an answer to the question of a man's desire? Or was there as yet a half of the globe of their joining still unexplored? Was she merely reticent? Or was she truly passive? Was it for him to open this world for them to inhabit?

He took his feet from the table and placed them flat upon the cool polished planks of the floor, blew air through his pursed lips under the weight of his desire, his intention. Intention? He didn't know. Could he bear it? Did she know already? Did it need saying? What if he miscalculated, and he told her what had happened inside himself, what he had come to see, and saw aversion on her face, disgust? What if she said, You sick little fuck!

Then she would have seen him. She would know, and no going back, and who really knew how much he could trust another person? How well did he really know her at all? What if she just shut the door on him? What if she told other people? He thought about people they knew in common, people she might know well enough to tell about it, but there wasn't really anyone. Yet. She didn't really know anyone he worked with very well. Yet. Only Vaever and Madsen, but how well do you get to know anyone in a single evening of dinner conversation? (And dancing. How intimate do people actually get with each other on the dance floor?)

He remembered Agnette last year telling him, *You're sick*, but she didn't seem to hold anything against him last night. *Am I sick?* he wondered, but what was sick about explaining your own desires, your own *soul?* Sick is being closed off, locked inside yourself.

What am I thinking? Am I still drunk? Am I going mad? Am I opening to the world or closing into my own darkness? Is this me, or her? What is happening to me?

She came into the room in her tight faded jeans and a T-shirt, bearing a tray, and he could smell the sausage and cabbage and onions, and her voice was music saying, '*Værs go', skat.*' Be so good as to accept this dinner, darling. And the water ran in his mouth as he moved toward the table.

'Should I put on a shirt?' he asked.

'Why? You look good enough to eat, yourself.'

There was a fog over the King's Garden below her window, and it fit his mood perfectly. He stood by the CD player. 'A little table music?'

'Lovely.'

Hot spiced sausage on his tongue, mustard, and he lifted his aquavite glass to Miles Davis's trumpet blowing 'So What?' They snapped the iced liquor in one bite.

'You know,' he said, 'Snaps is a German word. It's from the German verb to bite. Best taken down in one bite, one mouthful.'

She laughed. 'You know so much,' she said, and he saw the look of love in her eye, like that old Bacharach song, *The look/Of love/Is in/Your eyes*, and he found himself asking, as he chewed medister sausage, wolfed red cabbage, 'Do you believe in people knowing each other? I mean, really knowing each other?'

'Tell me everything,' she said. 'Your dark secrets are safe with me, honey.'

He was remembering a girl he knew years ago, seven, maybe eight years since, who asked him once if he ever wanted to be beaten. She held a thick leather belt in her hands. 'Did you ever want to be beaten with something like this?' she asked him.

'I'd rather be the one doing the beating,' he said, which was a lie to cover the interest her question had stirred, and the look on

105

her face changed suddenly from provocation to submission. She'd lowered her eyes and looked up again. 'I'd let you,' she had said. 'You could if you wanted.'

He remembered that now with embarrassment because he had answered, 'No. That's sick,' and he was ashamed now for having so coldly closed the door she tried to open. It was just a game anyway. It reminded him of Agnette's response to him last summer. She was probably just as interested by his suggestion as he had been by Vivi's, the girl with the belt. Why was he so afraid? What was he really after? What did any of this mean? It was only a game. Or was he sick?

He refilled their snaps glasses and considered sharing that memory with Michela now. A memory from his youth, when he was only 23 or 24. More than half a dozen years ago. But she might misunderstand what he wanted, what he meant. It wasn't that.

What was it, then? What exactly?

He forked up the last bite of medister, dipped it in the mustard, chewed, watching her. 'How come you still have your shirt on?' he asked. She was wearing a corn-blue T-shirt of coarse silk, and he could see the outline of her nipples stretching against the blue silk. 'Your breasts are so beautiful,' he whispered.

She laid down her fork and pulled the shirt up over her head, crossing her arms to lift it off and smiled, watching him watch her, and he thought that her pleasure seemed to be in pleasing him, thought perhaps despite all the objection to women's being sex objects that a woman in love desired to be an object of desire for the man who loved her, that perhaps anatomy was an accurate reflection for the enactment of passion – a receptacle and a filler, passive and active – and watching her fulfill that role, he said, 'God, you are so beautiful.'

'Don't lie to me,' she said without changing her smile.

'I'm *not* lying.'

'It's ok,' she said. 'But you don't have to tell me lies.'

'I'm not,' he repeated. 'You *are* beautiful.'

'*Tak*,' she said, her voice meek and small and submissive and beautiful.

'*Og tak for mad*,' he said. Thanks for the meal.

'Did you get full?'

'I am full and happy and satisfied,' he said and saw through the triptych window the fog-blurred neon lights atop the buildings on the other side of the King's Garden, a blurred red bank sign, blurred green and amber and red traffic lights, blurred streetlamps. 'The fog,' he said quietly. 'I feel so . . . glad.'

'Do you want me to love you?' she asked.

He blinked, mouth open for breath because his nose was stuffed. 'You mean make love?'

'I mean love.'

'Do you?'

'I asked first.'

He tongued a scrap of sausage from between his teeth. 'I only know what I feel for you,' he said. 'I only know it feels so right. To be with you. Right here. I want to be right here with you. Nowhere else.'

In the silence, quiet piano notes and bass runs spoke and answered one another with Miles Davis's trumpet saying, asking, Soooo *what?* Soooo *what?* So simple and simply, until the horns of Cannonball Adderly and John Coltrane and Davis began to weave from that simplicity a more intricate pattern that lowered Voss's eyelids with the pleasure of the evening.

They sat together on the sofa with coffee and brandy, their bare shoulders touching, heads tilted together, and it seemed to him he might have forgotten what he started out thinking, what he had experienced the evening before when he waited for her in the hotel room, the force of that desire, that terror, that terrible passion. Had it been displaced with something else now? He was even less certain now than before. Had some change taken place? Was this something else? Was this the manipulation of his passion into the mould of what she wanted, what a woman wanted? Something less fierce, less wild, something more like 'love' and less like passion? He felt his desire clouding, but before he surrendered to that haze, he whispered to her, 'Could we make a promise to each other?'

She watched him. 'I don't know,' she said. 'Could we? What promise?'

'I mean a promise not to lie, never to lie.'

'I don't lie to you.'

'Are you certain?'

She shrugged, confused. 'What is it you think I lie about?'

'Everybody lies, but there are different kinds of lies. What I mean is if we could promise not to lie by silence. I don't care if you tell me you like my necktie if you hate it, but I mean for you to, for us to not hide in silence. People sometimes keep their mouth shut to hide what's in their heart. Things we would never guess at. So I don't tell you, you don't tell me, and little by little we become strangers, intimate strangers so close together but all wrapped around our secrets. Maybe we could go beyond that. Do you think we could?'

He did not know exactly what he meant. He felt a voice filling his mouth without connection to his consciousness, or perhaps greater than his consciousness, and he hoped she might know what he was moving toward and might help him know or preserve this thing that was visiting him that he could not quite grasp or be certain whether it had any real meaning at all.

Her smile gave him hope that there was meaning in it, and he wondered if he would feel differently later, if it would all blur away from him, or whether he could find some lasting truth in the rage of passion he had experienced the night before or if he was simply drunk, and whether in his drunkeness the night before and now was the truth. He knew that he wanted to tear open his heart to her without knowing whether he would regret it later, but what was this impulse really if not the truth of his heart stripped of restraint by drink.

If he let this moment pass, he feared it might never come again, and so he began.

And so he asked her if she knew, if she could imagine what he had felt the evening before when he watched her dance with Vaever, the beauty and the agony he had experienced, the pain it caused him to see her body touching his, to see her curtsy to him, to see her beautiful smile turned up to Vaever's face.

'It made me want to hurt you. Really. To hurt you.'

'I do not want to be hurt again,' she said.

'I wouldn't. I'm only telling you how I *felt*.'

'Do you want me not to dance with anyone else then?'

He peered into his brandy snifter, the amber liquid glittering in the light of the candles she had lit on the coffee table.

'No,' he whispered. 'That's not it at all. I *do* want you to. I want it very much. Because as much as it hurt me, it made me feel a love so deep I have never in all my life as long as I can remember felt before.'

She remained silent. Then her fingers touched the back of his head, moved through the stubble of his hair and squeezed the muscle of his shoulder.

'It was real,' he said and thought it must have been, could only have been something real that could explode with such force in him. And now the door was open and he felt her nails moving on the thick of his shoulder, on his neck, and he wanted her to know the rest, what he thought about when they made love, and he told her.

Her fingers stopped moving on him. 'Is it because you want to be free of me?' she asked.

'Oh God,' he said and knelt beside her knees. 'How could I think that? I'm crazy about you. It's because . . .' He lowered his face to her lap. 'I get so scared I'll lose you. But if I don't, if even then you come back to me, if all along you really love me, do it not to hurt me but *for* me, to please me, then it's beautiful. It's for me. For *us*.'

She put her arms around him, her face close to his ear. 'I could do that for you,' she whispered.

'You have to want to.'

'Yes. I do want to. But only because I love you,' she said, and he felt a happiness, a purity of happiness, he had never known before, not since he was a child.

In bed afterwards it seemed to him suddenly he didn't really know her at all. Her bedroom faced over the dark stubble of rooftops behind the street, picturesque in their loneliness, their abandonment. All those windows behind which people engaged in private lives about which no one knew. He stood naked at the windowsill, his desire spent, and it seemed to him he knew nothing about her really, knew only what she had said. In essence, she was willing to be a whore for him, and what did that mean really? Other than that she *was* a whore.

Am I drunk? he thought. Am I stupid? Am I crazy?

It was worse now than it had been the night before because then it had only been a dance. Perhaps Vaever had touched her, with his hands, his legs, his groin. Perhaps she had touched him. But then it was only a dance, and now suddenly it was much more, even if it was only words whispered between them, but now it was the very worst he imagined true, more than that. She would be a whore for him. And if she would be a whore for him, it meant she *was* a whore.

He thought maybe he was still drunk, but his mind was clear, his hands and legs steady, and the fury that gripped him felt right, righteous, and he turned back toward the bed and thought he would say something to her, question her, but he had not formulated it yet in his mind so by the time he reached her where she lay, leaning lazily back against the bunched up pillows behind her, smiling, he thought this was not love at all, this was madness, treachery.

The fingers of his left hand clutched into her hair, and he lifted her toward him. She cried out, and his right palm smacked her face, backhanded her. Her eyes went wide, her mouth opened raggedly, and he slapped her again.

'You are a fucking whore!' He had her arms in his grip and shook her. 'Fucking whore!'

'Don't you hit me!' she yelled, her voice stronger than he would ever have expected, and her shin lifted sharply and caught him full between his legs so he lost his grip, doubled forward, gasping, and dropped, sobbing for breath, to his knees.

'Oh, God,' she said, 'I'm sorry, did I hurt you? Are you all right?'

His face was in his palms, and he heard the strange keening sound that rose from his throat. He was not weeping, but moaning, and he realized how very drunk he really was, frightened to have thought he felt the clarity of sobriety when in fact he was as drunk as he had been the night before, drunker, so drunk he mistook drunknenness for sobriety, clarity.

He wrapped his arms around her hips and pulled her belly into his face and groaned. 'I'm sorry. I am so sorry. Please, God, forgive me, I didn't mean to hurt you, I just love you so much it is driving me crazy.'

19

Welcome to prison

Another chill wet day of June. Children screaming with joy on the lake bank – as if summer had actually come. This year summer came on a Tuesday as they say. Michela wore sunglasses against the glare of her headache.

Inside the entry of the home, wispy yellow flowers wept from the wisteria trees into the blue air. Michela rode the empty elevator to the sixth floor, a plastic shopping sack cradled in her arm.

Her father's rheumy eyes turned toward the door when she entered. His hand still clung to the trapeze. 'Welcome to prison,' he said.

'Prison?'

'Denmark's a prison. One of the worst.'

'As if you hadn't been a card-carrying social democrat all your life!'

'Yeah, I've always been an idiot.'

'Is it this home? Plenty of people would give the white out of their eyes for a place here.'

'Well good for them, and good for you. To me it is a prison.'

113

She noticed then that his thumb was holding his place in his book. 'Would you like me to bring some more cheerful reading for you, Dad?'

He laughed bitterly. 'Wouldn't help. I have bad dreams.'

Michela glanced at the window, smeared with dull light, thought of the sweet air beneath the trees around the lake. Regret that she had come began to cloud her mood. She pushed away from it. 'Dreams aren't real, Dad. Just remind yourself of that. If you wake from a bad dream, why don't you just turn on the lamp, sit up and have a cigarette. That's what I do.'

'I dream when I'm awake. I dream I'm wearing horns.'

'That again? Are you still worrying about hell?'

He was not looking at her. 'Not those horns.'

It occurred to her that he might be losing his mind, and that all this might be the result of hallucinations, misapprehensions. Then she wondered how life would look from his perspective. Maybe his simple straight everyday reality was worse than the worst nightmare she had ever had. She stepped closer into the smell, touched his hand. 'Dad, do you want to see a priest.'

'I do not.'

He still had not looked at her. Now he turned his good eye on her. 'What's with the sunglasses?' he asked. 'Someone give you a blue eye? Found yourself another charmer?'

Even this was better. She lifted the glasses, her smile ironic. 'Would you prefer to be alone?'

'What I prefer doesn't mean a Goddamn thing anymore.'

She set the plastic bag on his night table, still too close to the smell, and struggled not to gag as she emptied it, item by item: A tabloid, three bottles of strong beer, a greasy pastry in a little white baker's sack. 'Shall I open the paper to page nine for you? They're advertising Page-Nine Girl of the Month today.'

'What good'll that do me?'

'Don't tell me you've even lost your taste for naked women?'

He adjusted his grip on the trapeze, hoisted himself up a notch, his lips set sternly. 'Don't try to provoke me.'

She sighed. 'Maybe I should just go again.'

'I think you'll do what you damn please regardless, just as you always did.'

'Dad,' she said and dragged the visitor's chair as far from the bed as she could without being too obvious. 'Does it have to be like this?'

He said nothing. Only rumbled the phlegm in his throat and stared at the far wall.

'Want a beer? I brought strong ones.'

'Know what I want? I want you to stop wheeling your mother down here to insult me. I think I've earned the right to be spared that.'

'She doesn't know what she's saying.'

'She knows. Somewhere, she knows. Now she's got the power and she uses it.'

'So you had it for 50 years, and I don't remember you being squeamish about exercising it when you wanted.'

His watery eye shot toward her and for a moment she thought he would weep. 'Do you think she was kind to me?' he demanded, his voice faint with emotion. 'Do you really?'

'To be honest?' Michela said. 'Yes. She was. A lot kinder than you were to her. And I think you ought to try to think a little bit about how it is for *her* now, for her to have to be that way. At least your mind is intact.' *Or is it?* 'Don't you think it's about time for you to grow up and give *her* a thought for a change.'

'How *dare* you! I've treated her, the both of you, like a queen! And here's my thanks. *Kind?* Ha! You've heard her. You've heard her yourself! Tongue like a viper!'

'Well, who's kind to anyone in the long run?' she said, her eyes on the window, the dull light outside. 'Everyone's to blame.' Her words were routine, weary, marking time before she could leave, but she heard what she had said as though it had been spoken by someone else and wondered why. *Everyone's to blame.* Maybe that was true. But she had no time to think, for he tugged himself up higher in the bed and demanded, 'Did it ever occur to you, my dear *sweet* daughter, that your mother might be a *whore!*'

'I won't hear this.'

'No, you won't, will you?'

Now he had her, he thought he had her, she could hear it in his tone, so she gave him both barrels. 'It's your own guilt turning back on you. Do you think I don't know about all your little side-springs, Dad? Do you think mother doesn't?' She rose, emptied his heaped ashtray into the trash pail and slammed it back onto the bed table. 'Who are *you* to criticize? Your behavior was *despicable!*' Now he had her. A fight was what he always wanted. To keep from thinking about himself.

But he closed his mouth, met her glaring eyes with his one good one as silence lengthened between them, and she listened to the ugly echo of her own accusations. 'Dad,' she said, 'It doesn't have to be like this. If you wanted, we could make use of our time together. I could read to you. We could talk . . .'

'About what, for Christ's sake? What's left worth talking about?'

She thought of Torben at the elevator door, warning her not to expose herself to this, warning her about cancer. Then she got to thinking that Torben had visited her father, too. Possibly what the doctor had told her father was something other than what he had told her. 'What did Torben have to say to you when he was here?' she asked.

'Can't understand a word that man says. He doesn't speak standard Danish. Talks through his moustache, and he's got nothing to say anyway. Talks after your mouth. All he does is agree with whatever the Goddamn hell you say to him yourself. Then he asks me if I want morphine and . . .' He clamped his jaws, and she could see he was fighting pain, heard a groan with a sound from somewhere deep in his trunk. He squinted shut his eyes as his body stiffened.

'Oh, Dad,' she whispered and squeezed his shoulder. The stench was overpowering. 'Dad.'

'He'd like to kill me with drugs. Put me under the fog until I lose it all and disappear. That's what they want. Official policy. Free up a bed. Make room for the next zombie. Pay taxes all your life and then when it's time for you to use their precious services, they want to pull the plug. Well let me tell you this: If I decide to go out, it'll be *me* who decides!'

'Oh, Dad,' she whispered, and she wanted to ask him again if it wasn't time to let go of the trapeze, to lay back on his pillow and let it come to him, but the only words her mouth could find were, 'You poor man.'

Her date with Helle was not until two, but she took one look through the door of her mother's room, saw her sorting some imaginary items from an empty straw bowl on her lap, saying, 'This will do perfectly for Grandmother Edel,' and she couldn't find the will to enter the room, to pretend she could see whatever the old woman imagined to be in the basket, to ask her questions about the conversations she had with people who had been dead too many years for her to clearly remember their faces or their voices or their eyes for they were all ghosts now, faded into the fading shadows of memory. Then she noticed the old man sitting on the edge of her bed, watching her, his ruddy hands crossed on his lap, listening raptly as though he understood whatever in the world it was she was talking about.

Michela backed away from the room, saw the blond nurse watching her with a wan smile. 'She has her own little world,' the nurse said. 'They both do. I really don't think they're unhappy. I've never seen her sad, not for a minute, in all this time. Want a cup of coffee, honey?'

'Thanks,' said Michela. 'I have to meet someone.'

'Good. Don't forget to enjoy yourself. You've been better than most, let me tell you. Don't let them swallow you alive.'

And there it was again. Michela looked into the woman's kind, understanding eyes and wondered what lay behind them, what thoughts, what life of her own. Michela nodded. 'Thank you for being so good to her,' she said.

20

You've got mail

From his window Nardo watched the red-uniformed postman push his yellow bicycle along the pavement below. In a leather bag in front of the handlebars were stuffed rubber-banded bundles of large envelopes, periodicals and small packages; over the back fender leather saddlebags thick with business envelopes. He did not recognize the postman. He was tall, dark-haired. Usually it was a young blond woman, a smiling girl, who brought the mail; other times a burly, tough-faced Dane. This one today Nardo had not seen before. He did not look like a Dane. He did not look like a postman either, Nardo thought, his suspicion fleeting as a spider. Beneath the window he propped his yellow Post Danmark bicycle on its kickstand, took a bundle of envelopes from the saddlebags and let himself in the areaway gate with one of many keys on a chain hooked to his belt.

Quickly Nardo went to the door of his apartment and opened it a crack, listened. He heard the postman enter the ground-floor doorway, heard the quiet plop of an envelope on the little table there, the shuffling of paper. Then he heard more rustling, a scratching sound – the strike of a match? He left the door open as he edged toward the stairwell. The floor planking creaked beneath his weight.

He froze. Waited. Then he leaned forward at the waist, peered down over the railing. He smelled smoke. The dark-haired postman who did not look like a postman was slouched back against the wall, smoking a cigarette. Nardo studied him. He had a large smooth forehead. His skin was darkish. He did not look like a postman. He looked like someone you would see in an office, someone who would deal with vaguely specified matters. He did not look Danish.

On the light coloured wood of the little table there below were three letters in a neat row with a fourth set off to the side. From where he stood Nardo could not read the names on the envelopes. The postman licked his thumb and finger and pinched out his cigarette, returned it to the fliptop box in the breast pocket of his red shirt.

Nardo's brow was wet. He waited. Before letting himself out again, the postman reached to straighten the letter that lay by itself off to the side of the other three. It seemed a strange thing to do. Nardo waited until he heard the clatter of the bicycle moving off again before he descended the flight of wooden steps.

Hands held stiffly by his sides, his eyes swept across the faces of the letters. The three to the left were addressed to people who did not live in this building. Sweat sprang out on Nardo's back. The one was to a Dr T Kerrigan, another to Patrick Bluett, an American translator who lived one or two houses down – Nardo knew *of* him but did not know him personally, and the third to Samuel Finglas. Nardo's legs were trembling. The name Samuel Finglas he recognized as that of a man who had died last winter. There had been an ambulance and a lot of activity outside the building and Nardo had the idea some foul play had been involved. These people did not live here. He studied the addresses. Granted they were all on this street, granted the house numbers were scribbled carelessly . . .

He looked to the fourth envelope, the one off to the right, by itself. His name was typewritten on its face. The stamp was postmarked Copenhagen, the day before.

With trembling hand he lifted it from the table. There was no return address. Not on the front, not on the back. Sweat rolled down his back, beneath his arms.

21

I have told you nothing

'Can you explain, doctor,' Nardo asked. 'How an atheist can believe that his people are more beloved of God because they are wealthier? There is a sect in the United States I have heard of. Baptists, I think, in the southern states, southwestern. They believe that money is grace, given by God. This I can *almost* undervestand. But I do not see how it fits into the system of an atheist to be more beloved of a god that does not exist because you have more wealth?'

Rarely did he speak at such length to me, and the speech left him breathless. His voice quavered with the last words, and I sensed that he stopped not because he was finished, but because he feared exposing the anxiety that motivated him. We had made some progress last time. He had been exhausted afterwards, as exhausted as I, but clearly it had been painful for him, so I understood his reluctance to return to that place where the pain was hidden away.

I smiled ruefully. 'Tell me, Nardo, what are we really talking about here?'

He continued to stare past the side of my face, his mouth stiff.

His statement clearly was a challenge, but required the eye contact he would not give, so he has challenged me while staring at the wall with a false smile, at once grotesque and pathetic. Yet if I contemplated his words, I had to recognize the edge of truth to them, the perception of First World for Third, Europeans for Indians, northern intellectuals for southern 'primitives'. On some level we believe we are closer to the heavens while they dance with feet of clay. I smiled privately, suddenly remembering Jung in Africa with his rhinoceros whip, trapped amidst a tribe of dancing natives and realizing they were in the thrall of a primitivism that could have put him in mortal danger. He cracked his whip and laughed simultaneously, a pathetic bid for control. Jung the crackpot.

But a discussion of such matters was not the reason for our being together in my consultation room. 'Nardo,' I said. 'Let's not play games.'

'You no like games, doctor? Never trust a god who does not like play games.'

'Think about your arm, Nardo. How hard we worked to win back your control of that. We can do more.'

'You are perhaps thinking of some other limb that is not functioning.'

'Why not?'

If only he would look at me! I can see in his posture, in the sneer of his smile, that his little joke backfired on him, but he would not go further with it. 'We're getting nowhere with this, Nardo. I can understand your reluctance, but we have to go back. To where we were before. Last time. Last time you faced the pain, and it scared you. I can understand that. To get through what you experienced you had to build an armor so strong that no pain could penetrate. Now you have to take the armor off. You have to survive your own strength now before it crushes you.'

He looked at my chin, and his face was eerily mild and pleasant. 'Tell me,' he said, and I recognized that his manner would convey a secret cargo of poison. 'What do you know about what I have survived? Do you have information sources?'

'Only you, Nardo. You told me some things.'

'I have told you nothing, *doctor*.' The last word was sodden with contempt. 'I have told you not one millimeter of it.'

'Well I hope you will tell me more.'

'Why?' he asked, his voice mild and poisonous again. 'Do you enjoy hearing? Is it entertaining for you?'

And here we are again, I thought. Locked in. But abruptly he rose, moved across the room in a hunch, squatted down in the corner between the sofa and a bookshelf. His forehead glistened with perspiration. His eyes were wide, fixed on something I could not see.

'Where are you now, Nardo?' I asked.

He only stared at the wall.

'Nardo. What are you feeling, my friend?'

His mouth opened. He screamed. He lowered his face into his hands. He screamed again. The sound was high and startling. The shriek of rusted nails being prised from dead wood.

'What do you see, Nardo? What is happening?'

'I was not singing.' He spoke in a tight, gasping croak. 'I did not smile. I named no one. I did not. There were no names to give. I only waited here for my *turn*. It is cold. It is hot. I was not singing. I did not laugh. I never spoke any name. There are no names to give.'

'What name, Nardo? Who could blame you if you gave names. Nardo, you are only a man. You have done more than could be expected. You have shown great courage. Everyone gave names, it could not be helped. No one is *that* strong.'

His eyes focused, turned toward me. For one instant there was eye contact, but before I could engage him, they were gone from me again.

'What are you espeaking about, doctor?' he asked hoarsely. 'You are confuse.' He rose, supported himself on the shelf, on a chairback, on the edge of the desk, as he returned to the green chair. I could see where the sweat had soaked through his shirt in great circles beneath his arms, at his back, his chest, his stomach. 'You are a confuse man, doctor.'

'Nardo, how can I help you when you will not share your thoughts with me?'

He looked at my mouth. To my lips he said, 'Perhaps you already know all of it.' As he spoke, he reached into his jacket slung on back of the chair and withdrew an envelope, tossed it onto the desk before me. It was addressed to him, postmarked Copenhagen K, no return address. The flap was slit. I withdrew a sheet of paper, neatly creased. It crackled in my hands as I unfolded it. A blank sheet of bond paper with a single sentence typewritten on it: *They work hand in glove with the CIA.*

Who sends these things? I wondered. Disgruntled ex-clients taking revenge because they could not stick it out? Political enemies? Whose? His? Mine? The Center's? The Council's? Who *were* our enemies precisely? Xenophobes?

'Do you believe this, Nardo?'

'Perhaps I do. Perhaps I do not.'

Suddenly I was angry. I held the letter out to return it to him. He sat back in the chair, a tiny smile on his lips, looking at the sheet of paper extended in my hand.

'I think you know this is not true,' I told him. 'I think you know I am here to help you. This letter was sent by some impotent crank. It is meaningless. Why do you try to test me in this way? I think perhaps it is simply to avoid confronting your problems. As long as you can allow yourself to believe I am untrustworthy, you can avoid trusting me with your memories and avoid dealing with them.'

His eyes slowly opened wide, his mouth grew small, his face pale. 'I *know* what is real,' he whispered. His voice quavered. His head trembled. 'I saw them. Watched them. I studied their haircuts, the rings they wore, their wristwatches. I studied their hands, their knuckles, their fingernails, the hair on their fingers, their clothing, the buttons on their jackets and shirts. I never allowed myself to confuse what was real with what was not. When I was made to stand on my feet for three days wearing a hood and finally found myself on the floor reading from the Bible, I *knew* the Bible was not there. I knew the parrot-faced man who pecked at me in my sleep was not real. The enormous animals that chased me for hours while I slept, unconscious from a beating, were not real. The shower of stones that rained down onto my skull was not real. But the man in the yellow tweed suit was real. Frog-eyes was real. Flatnose was real. Moustache. And the three flies that lived in my cell for a time and visited me, touching me gently with their tiny feet, they were real. And the angels who came to me and their love was real!'

I waited, like a trout in the stream of his emotion. He leaned forward, whispered.

'And when they asked if I was hungry, would I like some meat, and the water ran in my mouth just at that word until Frog-eyes said, "Give our friend here some roast chicken, over easy," and they hung me upside down over the fire so I smelled the stink of my own hair burning, my own scalp. I *knew*, doctor, what was real and what was not. I am a witness, doctor. The only witness.'

22

No toys at the table

My wife tapped on the door of my study to call me to dinner. As she looked in, her eyes touched my notebook, and that one brief glance was all that was necessary for her to indicate many comments to me. How suspect it would sound if one of my patients should explain an action this way: Why did you shout at your wife? Because she looked at my notebook in a certain way.

But the glance articulated far better than words the years of quarrelling over an unresolved, unresolvable problem. My work. *It is unreasonable*, she had repeatedly told me, *for you, for me, for the children, that you should give so much of yourself to it. I realize you are dedicated, devoted, that the work is valuable, but you give it too much! And for what? What do you really get out of it? Is it even healthy?*

Here, as always, I stood fast, even if she rocked my certainty, I had to hold fast. So many times I tried to explain to her that I must do this, I must use myself in this way. I've told her, 'Humankind is a mystery; even if a man spends his entire life trying to solve that mystery and fails, he will not have wasted his time.' She turned her eyes, sighed. She was a wall. She wanted this energy for herself, but I had to apply it to my work, my prime passion, one of my two prime passions; she was the other one, she and the children. But I could not be who I was without my work, and she could not or would not understand, not any longer, not as she did in the beginning, before the children were born.

I wondered sometimes if she were more astute than I, if she perhaps could see something of me that I could not, the back of my head, so to speak. And what did she see there? That I was obsessed? Labored under an illusion? That I hid in this work? Used it to protect myself from my real life? These were questions I once could answer with professional ease, could see the layers of identity, natural to a dedicated professional, part charlatan, part shaman, part scientist, dedicated to the arts of medicine and healing, self-development and self-aggrandizement. Just as a surgeon was a knifesman in disguise, a civilized murderer. How easily I once could walk that line, bear those many masks, those many slivers of self. And where was I now? On the verge of burn-out? Was I there already? Could I do this at all anymore?

My wife said, 'It's on the table, getting cold.'

I closed my notebook, tried to close my thoughts about my wife, myself, Nardo. I sat at the table with my family and gave myself to them as best I could.

My son had a comic book folded over beside his plate. Forbidden. But neither my wife nor I said a word about it. I was trying to find my feelings about her, my real feelings, trying to remember all the aspects and phases of our life together, how it grew, had been seen to grow even during periods it felt hopelessly lost. We had to be able to deal with these things and continue to function. I had to set myself up as a clear and integrated person for Nardo despite any personal confusion I might feel. I recalled once reasoning with a patient, saying, 'You have got to try to work through these things and get your mind clear.'

'You mean to say,' he asked, 'that there are people in this world whose minds are clear?' Asked almost naively, but with a certain strength that caught me by surprise, exposed my own doubt. I blurted, 'Not, I confess, 100 per cent,' and I still could see his owlish smile.

My daughter had a small plastic toad on the table beside her spoon. She was hopping it along the edge of her plate, speaking to it, for it. 'Where is my pond, little toad, is it over here, around the knife? No, go find mommy daddy toad . . .'

I wanted to be here now at the table, to be with them, but I continued to wander inside myself even as I attempted to chat, as the conversation petered off, as my wife withdrew into herself, and the room filled slowly with silence. Only my little girl spoke, to her plastic toad, and my wife's eyes looked bruised with the tiredness of her day that I wanted to ask her about, to share if I could only remember what it felt like to care, if I could only remember some words and find some caring to fill them with, but I was too far away from myself. It would have been better if I had stayed in my study, carried my plate in to my desk and sat with one hand forking up my breaded fish as I leafed through my notebook with the other. *What are you feeling, Nardo? What did you feel just then?*

The echo of the question opened the floor of my confusion. Why did *they* not try to reach through to *me*? Couldn't they see my need? I was invisible to them. My wife's pale-blue eyes stared past me as her lips moved over the food in her mouth. I had never struck her. Only once. Never. She struck me first. 'Find your mommy daddy little toad . . .' The pages of my son's comic book rustled. He was reading a *Tin Tin* book. I felt myself drifting away from them, and they could not even see that I needed them to reach out and help me back.

Like a pinpoint in the distance of my consciousness I saw Nardo, almost equally distant a question: Why did that fate find him, why *him*? Did he invite it? They sought to change him from a man of will and conscience. Was I seeking to change him? A surgeon, I thought, is a knifesman in disguise. And who was I? What was I trying to do?

And someone else was there, too, whispering to me, reminding me of the one time I struck my wife, his voice both foreign and intimate as he moved closer to me, touching impulses beyond all reason, nudging me toward a dimension I have never seen, but which was there always nonetheless, where Nardo had been, perhaps still was, where Frog-eyes ruled, and were I there which side would I choose to be on? There, where you pay with freedom, comfort, safety, your life? Or where I would be safe, where my belly would be filled?

My eyes turned toward my daughter to find comfort in her sweet young face, but my mouth opened and I said, 'No toys at the table, Inge,' and heard the cold sharpness of my voice, felt an incongruous smile moving to form on my lips. Was I smiling?

'But Dad, it's just . . .'

'No *toys at the table!*' my voice rasped. I felt passion in my eyes. My wife laid down her knife and fork, her mouth opened to speak. My daughter's mouth drooped, my son looked up from his comic book in bewilderment, and he spoke first. 'Dad?' he said, and the tone in which he spoke that single word, a tone of astonished disbelief, gave me access to a view of myself at that instant: I had behaved in a way that was out of character, that had astonished my children. They did not berate me. They were not wounded. Not yet. They were startled. *This is not our father,* their eyes told me. *This is a mistake, a misunderstanding . . .* Which meant they believed in me – still.

You have worn this mask well, the voice whispered in my ear. *Even when you looked in the mirror! Who could know you?* Again he touched impulses he sought to connect with my children, pictures too ugly to forebear flashed in the darkness of my mind too quickly for identification as my little girl's troubled eyes sought solace from mine.

I had to turn away. Those pictures must not involve her face, her eyes, no, Christ save me.

My wife was watching me. Her eyes were not sympathetic. For one broken second, I wished to try to explain, to justify myself, and in that same second, I recognized the impossibility of that task, and the frustration hardened to anger, ran down my arm to my right hand which swelled with a fury to match the fury rising in my chest.

I scraped back my chair, rose, dropped my crumpled napkin on my plate. 'I will take my coffee in my study,' I snapped and left the room, feeling an odd sense of satisfaction with the bewildered gazes of my children at my back, simultaneously cursing that ugly satisfaction and wondering what I was doing as I slammed my study door behind me, sat in lamplight at my desk, face in my palms.

It was as if Frog-eyes was there, whispering, *Perhaps I will do you a favor, Nardo. Shall I? Wouldn't it be the kindest thing for all concerned? You are a sad escuse for a person. I tried to make you into a real human being but you are not a man. You are nothing.*

It was as if this voice explored for purchase in my throat, and his gaze was in my eyes, his hard hateful smile on my lips. I shuddered. 'No,' I said aloud. 'No.' Learn from this. This is a state of mind. Confusion. Use it. Learn from it. Let it happen as Nardo let his angels be. I relaxed my mind, and Frog-eyes was there in the room with me, in my study, breathing at my ear with foul breath and scummy lips. *So you see, doctor?* he whispered. *The man is not a person. He is a worthless invididual, you see? How else could we deal with such a one? You yourselv have invested weeks and weeks in him, for what doctor? He abuses your kindness. The man is not a person. He is a miserable trouble-maker. Do not waste your days on him. You understand me better than you wish to admit, doctor, no?*

Memories, images too ugly to bear, began to rise in me. I swept my arm across my desktop so paper, pens, clips were whisked to the floor, and I shouted, once, a single note, and stood staring at the mess on the floor, gritting my teeth.

My wife was at the door, watching me. I saw fear on her face. Of what? Me? My face? What did it show?

'Are you all right?' she whispered.

Acid filled my mouth. I would spit it at her, but then I saw she was my wife, aging, vulnerable, no longer the young girl who enchanted me years ago, yet dearer now in the vulnerability of her mortality, my mortality, the vulnerability of our children, and this insight, vision, stunned me, drained the poison from me.

131

Frog-eyes was gone, and my heart was open to her, this woman I had shared my life with for so many years.

I came out from behind the desk, crossed to her. My embrace startled her. She hesitated, then returned it, and I clung to her, felt with my palms the comfort of her back. Her arms calmed me, returned me to a world where Frog-eyes and Flatnose and the Yellow Tweed man and Moustache were nothing, distant rumors. I wanted to sink to my knees before her, to push my face against her belly, close my eyes, feel her hands on my head, releasing me from the fear of knowing things, of feeling them within me.

I did not kneel. Slowly, by degrees, I withdrew from our embrace, stepped back, looked into her pale-blue eyes. How like a familiar room they were; searching, welcoming, open to receive my gaze, to share the thoughts in my heart. She was my other passion, my precious friend. I recalled that Jung said we are no more responsible for the thoughts in our minds than for the animals in a forest. The cool-warm blue gaze of my wife's eyes soothed me.

'Come have coffee,' she said.

I followed her, into the living room.

23

That is not my father

Michela arrived at the French Café long before Helle. She ordered white wine and a glass of ice water to stretch the time before the next glass of wine. She watched a dark-skinned man on the bank of the lake feeding bread from a plastic bag to the swans and ducks and grebes. They paddled from across the lake toward him, congregating in a little patch of sunny green water near the lip of concrete where he stood. She saw then it was the man from the café and felt a lump in her throat at his kindness. Sitting up straight in her chair so he might see her if he turned, she kept her eyes on him, but he brushed crumbs from his palms and wandered off in the other direction, along the lake bank.

Someone had left a copy of *Ekstra Bladet* on the table, the same newspaper she had brought for her father. She lit a Prince Extra Ultra Light and leafed through the paper.

The front-page lead was titled *Murder for 24 Beers*, about one drunken Swede who had killed another in an argument over a case of Carlsberg. Both in their late 40s. Friends. They'd taken the ferry to Elsinore for a good time in liberal Denmark where you could drink to your heart's content. There was a photograph of one in handcuffs on his belly on the sidewalk a few feet away from the other man, crumpled in a doorway amidst broken bottles, a policeman and policewoman trying to resuscitate him.

The mention of Elsinore reminded Michela of her father, his obsession with *Hamlet*. She wondered what it was about the play that so captivated him. In gymnasium she had seen it at the Betty Nansen theatre, and she knew it was performed every summer in English in the castle at Elsinore, too. Perhaps she should see it again. All she could recall of it was someone holding a skull and saying 'To be or not to be?' Søren Pilmark it was, he had played Hamlet; she could still remember how good he looked in tights. Then she recalled her father's crack about her not reading good literature and Voss mentioning that she really ought to know the names of all the state ministers. Her face flushed with the memory, she looked back into the tabloid.

On page two was a picture of a bullfighter being gored in the groin by a bull, over a caption that said, *Lost his cajones*. She smirked, kept turning pages, got to the *Page-Nine Girl of the Month*, a pretty-faced 25-year-old named Aicha, kneeling on a white-sand beach, smiling sweetly, one forearm between her breasts.

Then she thought of her father not even bothering to look at this picture today when she visited, wondered if he took a peek anyway, after she'd left him. She thought how strong and passionate he had always seemed, how her mother had so often rebuffed him. But he had also been such a tyrant, impossible.

All his complaints about the lack of love in his life. He came to her old apartment in Nørrebro drunk one night, years before, to tell her he had just come from a prostitute – this when he was in his 70s:

'Do what you want,' she told him. 'Do what you have to do. But please don't come here and tell me about it.'

'Don't you tell me what to do, miss!'

'You can get out of my home if you can't act decently and speak decently. Go on, then. Get out. Go!'

'I'll sit right here and finish my beer and I'll go when I am Goddamned good and ready to go. If you want to throw me out, you can call the police.'

She stood up and tugged at his arm. 'Get out!' she yelled. 'I've had enough! This is my home. Get out!'

He glared at her. 'I will then,' he said. 'I'll get out. I'll go down to the lake and drown myself. That's what I'll do. And you, you're the killer.'

As he stumbled through the door, she saw how very drunk he was and tried to make him come back, but now he would not be stopped. He bundled down the staircase to the sidewalk, staggered off along the dark street, 74 or 75 years old, drunk as a sailor, acting like a baby, his fury fueled by self-righteous rage at having been kicked out by his own daughter.

She called after him again and again, her voice echoing down the empty road, but he wouldn't stop, wouldn't turn, trudged along swiftly, weaving, in the middle of the sidewalk. A taxi came roaring around the corner, and she thought he would hail it, but he let it pass, weaved up to the corner, turned, listing toward the curb, and was gone.

Then she had to phone the police, told them how drunk the old man had been, exaggerated, told them he was a danger to himself, threatening suicide, and they said they would try to find him. Sitting, waiting, she hated herself for not having gone after him, for having let him get away, and she hated herself for caring, for worrying. *He* was the parent. Why did *she* have to take care of *him*? He had always been a tyrant in the house, had ruined her chances for an education, blocked her from going to university, arguing that since he himself had made his way up to a high position without university why should she need it? He squandered all the money he earned, even had merchants coming from time to time to repossess furniture he hadn't kept up payments on, and now she had to sit and worry about him out drunk in the middle of the night, threatening like an adolescent to kill himself.

She wept and opened a bottle of wine and poured a glass, worrying that she might become an alcoholic, too, and chain-smoked and worried about that. Her husband Mads had been out drinking, too, and little Ria somewhere, probably also drinking . . . and Michela chewed her nails, remembering when she was a little girl, and her father had painted her nails with foul-tasting polish to cure her of the habit. He had held onto her hand; she could still see it pale and small in his thick, ruddy one as he painted the stuff onto her nails, saying, 'This'll cure you.'

'I'll learn to like the taste!' she shouted at him. And she did that, to spite him, and she felt panic rising in her heart at the thought of the old man she had turned out onto the long dark boulevard.

The doorbell rang and a policeman was there, a short man with a hard, scarred face and light eyes. 'I think we got your father,' he said.

'Is he ok?' She was terrified.

'Drunk as a priest in Hamburg, but he's breathing. We got him in the car. Come on down and see.'

Downstairs, a patrol car was parked outside her building, and she prayed no neighbors were at their windows. The squadcar motor idled, a plume of white exhaust rising into the autumn night, and a man in a torn suit jacket with a face filthy as the pavement sat hunched in the back seat. She peered into the window, and he stared back out at her, a bloody scab on his forehead, a face she had never seen in her life.

'That is not my father,' she said.

Next morning her mother called to complain that he'd come home with the smell of another woman on him and wouldn't get out of their bed, and now she'd had it, she wanted a divorce. 'Can I come stay with you and Mads, Michela, until I find my own place?'

'No, mother,' she had said. "Not this time. It's *your* marriage. Deal with it.' And slammed down the phone on her mother's whimpering voice.

Now, in the French Café, she stubbed out her cigarette and tried desperately to think of one happy family she had known in her whole life, one single truly happy harmonious family, as she turned the pages of the newspaper to an article about a member of a motorcycle gang who had been given a year in jail for forcing a young man to take out a loan for 20,000 crowns that the biker confiscated, telling the boy it was 'an asshole fine'. On the next page was a story about a gang of second generation immigrants who were routinely robbing and beating the old people who lived in the suburbs of Odense, followed by a two-page spread of advertisements for digital cameras and mobile telephones, a cartoon in which a man and woman lay facing away from each other in bed while a parrot in a cage alongside them said, 'I have a headache. I have a headache'.

Then there was an article about the coming wedding of the Crown Prince and his Australian fiancé. Every state employee in the country would be given the day off for the occasion, and the entrance to the Cathedral was being remodelled to accommodate the bride's 20-meter train. The day off would cost the tax-payers 100 million crowns in addition to the unpublicized amount that had been allocated for the event itself. Along the side of the page was a sampling of pedestrians' comment on the question of whether too much was being made of it. Three people had been asked. The first two thought it was appropriate, but the third complained that 100 million crowns would pay a year's salary for more than 500 ordinary people. 'Why should taxpayer's foot that bill?'

Michela thought about it. She felt a flutter in her stomach, a sense of helplessness, as her eyes scanned the page trying to find something that might clarify her own understanding of it. She studied the Crown Prince's handsome, smiling face; the Australian girl, Mary's face; the Queen's . . .

She turned to the horoscopes, looked first at her own, Virgo: 'You grasp something which logic can not clarify. Your intuition steers you through.' Then at Pisces, Voss's: 'You aren't afraid to talk about your feelings. You will get to know someone in a completely new and profound manner.'

She folded the paper, pitched it over to an empty table, hoping her father hadn't looked at it, hadn't read all the terrible news about what people were doing to each other in Denmark today.

A couple of tables over, two men sat drinking coffee, talking. 'You have a powerful mind,' the one, older man said to the younger. 'But I think you are a little too pessimistic, my friend.'

'Am I pessimistic if I look out the window and see it's raining and say it's raining today.'

'No, but you say, It's raining, we'll get soaked, we may drown.'

The boy chuckled. 'And if it's the deluge? 40 days and nights of rain?'

The older man laughed, too. 'Then look for the forty-first.'

They were both smiling, having fun. Michela liked them. She wished she knew them and watched as the waiter came to the men's table with two plates. 'Who has the frog's legs?' he asked and set them down before the older man.

'See that?' said the younger fellow. 'Would you tell those frogs to be optimistic, too?'

The older man looked down at his plate with a merry smile. 'Hello, my little friends,' he said. 'Thank you for being so delicious. I'm going to welcome you into my body, and you will give me strength and pleasure, and I will turn you into poetry.'

Michela smiled with appreciation, but they didn't notice her. She signalled the waitress for another glass of wine, and a thought she had been avoiding since the night before slipped unexpectedly into her consciousness, the fact that Voss had struck her, pulled her hair and smacked her face. Slapped and backhanded and slapped her. But Helle appeared, opening the glass door of the café, and Michela eagerly abandoned the memory.

Helle was a dozen years older than Michela, a secretary from another department in her office, and they had been seeing each other regularly enough for the past couple of years that a real friendship seemed to be developing. They always remembered each other's birthdays, ate lunch together once or twice a week met somewhere outside the office every month or so. But now that they both had boyfriends, they saw each other less frequently, and when they did, it was usually to compare notes, to share complaints or satisfactions, to try to interpret from the present what their futures might be.

'What's with the shades?' Helle asked, and remembering she still had them on, Michela removed the sunglasses and folded them on the table, wondering why she had worn them in the first place – the sun had hardly been blazing today. Was she playing abused woman?

'It's just such a dazzling day,' she said with an ironic smile.

'Isn't it awful?' Helle said. 'And they call this summer? Well it wasn't so bad for a while there earlier.' She sat, asked the waitress in what Michela thought was an unnecessarily condescending tone to bring another glass of wine.

Michela liked Helle's face, and her body. Her mouth was full and mysterious, somehow inward in its posture, as if her mouth sugggested private, sensual thoughts. And she dressed well, in clothes that didn't cling but still showed the graceful lines of her legs and hips. Occasionally they hugged and kissed on the mouth a little, and a year before, after two bottles of wine at Michela's, they had come close to doing more, but Michela cut it short by going out to pee and then changing chairs when she returned. Helle was a passionate woman. She liked to talk about what she did with men, and Michela enjoyed listening, although she never went into detail herself. Helle also rented a room in her apartment to a young woman from the university, a very cute, nervous young girl who, Helle had told her, had terrible problems with her mother who belonged to the *Indremissionsk* sect in Jutland – the sect members dressed in black, did not dance, drink, smoke; their only pastimes were drinking coffee and singing psalms, like the ones from the movie, *Babette's Feast*.

Michela had noticed how familiar Helle and the Jutland girl were with one another and wondered vaguely whether anything was going on between them, though she didn't like thinking that and tried not to.

'How's Bertold?' she asked now. Bertold was Helle's boyfriend, and Michela wondered if Helle had managed to get the commitment from him she had been working towards. Michela did not like Bertold, who was a loudmouth and a braggert, but Helle was terrified of being alone and put up with a lot from him. They did not live together – yet – and he was given to unexplained absences, vague business trips. Michela's intuition told her he had other girlfriends, or even boyfriends, but she wouldn't mention this unless Helle asked her opinion.

Helle had met him on a single's cruise. They still kept in touch with some of the others who had been on the cruise. Michela wondered if Helle never worried about AIDS, thought perhaps that had been her own reason for cutting it short that evening with Helle. She had never been with another woman, but saw no reason not to if she wanted. Except the worry about AIDS. She had called the public sex advice line to ask if a woman could get AIDS from another woman by oral contact and was disappointed and frightened to be told that you could, that it could be transmitted through a woman's secreta. She called again a few days later to ask the question again, and this time another counsellor told her it would be almost impossible because the bacteria of the mouth were such a powerful defense. She didn't know what to believe.

The waitress brought their wine, and Michela smiled and thanked her warmly, to try to make up for it if Helle had hurt her feelings. She could see that Helle was pale; she looked worried as she reached for Michela's pack of *Prince*. 'Can I smoke one of your cigarettes?' she asked.

'Of course.' Michela pushed the pack toward her, annoyed. Helle was not a smoker, except when it came to other people's cigarettes, especially Michela's.

She lit up and shook out the match, blew smoke through pursed lips. Her fingers were trembling.

'Is there something wrong?' Michela asked.

'I don't know what to do.'

'What is it?'

Helle told her that Bertold had taken one of his trips again and had given her the key to his apartment so she could water the plants and feed his cat.

'Would he do as much for you?'

'I don't care,' she said. 'I liked it. That he trusted me. And it was cozy. But after I took care of the cat and the palms, I dusted and vacuumed and straightened up. He'd left a bit of a mess. I washed the dishes and then I started dusting, and I saw his computer there. I just couldn't resist. I turned it on and went into his email.'

'You *didn't!*'

'I couldn't resist.'

'How did you know the code?'

'That wasn't hard to figure out. He actually told me once, in a way. I told him I was always forgetting my passwords, and he said, "Use one you can't forget. Sexsexsex." That turned out to be his.' She chuckled, but her fingers trembled as she lifted the cigarette to her lips. 'I couldn't help it. He doesn't tell me anything. And then giving me the key and there was the computer, right there. And in a way he *told* me the password. Just like that. I thought, maybe he wants me to look.'

'It's not right. You shouldn't have.'

She fell silent for a moment, staring at Michela with her half-lowered eyelids, that mysterious set to her lips. Michela remembered kissing them.

'Do you want to hear?' Helle asked.

Michela said nothing. She waited, listening.

'There was only one mail in his sent-post file. And one in his inbox. Otherwise there was nothing. It was all deleted. Only the one sent and the one received mail.' She sipped her wine and took several puffs of her cigarette as though she were in a hurry to finish it or perhaps eager for the narcotic effect of the tobacco.

Michela had to admit she was dying to know, but ashamed of herself for it, so did not ask, only waited.

'The mail was to his friend, Mario. Remember him? You met him at Krut's Karport, when we went to hear jazz one Sunday, a few months ago?'

Michela nodded.

'Mario is Bertold's best friend, and we go out together pretty often, Bertold and me and Mario and Signe, his wife, or whatever she is. She doesn't speak much. She's a doormat for him. But he's Bertold's friend, and he's nice enough to me . . .'

'He was nice enough to me, too,' Michela said dryly, remembering how he had come on to her at the bar when Signe went to the toilet, and Voss was at the bar.

Helle seemed not to catch the tone. 'You just never know how people think or talk when you're not there, behind your back.' She stubbed out the cigarette and took another without asking. 'I'm just smoking too much. This only happened a couple of hours ago.'

141

'What? What happened?'

'I read the mail he sent to Mario. And the one he got in response – which he hasn't seen yet himself. His mail seemed to be an answer to another one Mario had sent him. It was very short.' She snapped open her purse. 'Here, I ran a copy of it. It starts, "Yo Mario." What does that mean, anyway? "Yo." Do you know?'

'I think it's something American. Slang for hello.'

'So it says, "Yo Mario. Good to hear you have things set the way you want with Signe and the other cow."'

'Cow?'

'That's what it said.'

'Bastard.'

Helle chuckled. 'That's how they talk. It doesn't necessarily mean anything.'

'Doesn't mean anything? Cow? The prickhead.'

Helle laughed, but her fingers still trembled holding the cigarette between them. 'Then it says, "I think things with Helle are finally falling into place. She's going to clean my apartment when I'm gone, and I asked the bitch to cook up some food for me, dinners you know, wrap them and put them in my freezer for me." That's a lie, by the way. He never asked for that. So you see how it is. I did it for him once. Once. But he never asked that this time, and I never said I'd clean his place. Just feed the cat and the plants. The cleaning I did on my own, and see if I ever do it again.'

'Well he's a bastard,' Michela said. 'I can understand you're upset.'

'There's more,' Helle said and drew on the cigarette, inhaling deeply, held the smoke. 'What comes next, it says, "Always nice to have some meat in the deep freeze. Think I'll put Helle in there, too, while I have some strange stuff this weekend. Remember Karina? She invited me over when I'm in Århus, and I have definitely packed my bags in my bags."' She stubbed out the cigarette and took another.

'You can have another cigarette if you like,' Michela said, and Helle started. 'Oh, I'm sorry, wait, let me . . .' She reached toward the passing waitress. 'Do you have a 10-pack of Prince?'

'Only 20s,' the waitress said.

'Oh, never mind. I'll never smoke 20.'

'Go ahead,' Michela said. 'Take one of my mine.' This hardly seemed the time to make an issue of it.

'Here's what Mario answered,' Helle went on, exhaling smoke. '"Yo, Bertold!" That sounds so stupid. "Yo, Bertold, here is the gospel for today, straight from the mouth of the master seducer, Mr S K." Who's S K, do you know?'

Michela shook her head.

'It says, "When two people fall in love with each other and begin to suspect they were made for each other, it is time to have the courage to break it off. But it sounds like you have the best of both. Right on, bro!" – that part's written in English.'

She folded up the paper and put it back into her purse, snapped it shut and hung it on the corner of her chair.

'That's it?'

'Isn't that enough?'

'It's *too* much,' said Michela. 'Drop him fast.'

As though she hadn't heard, Helle said, 'Anyway one thing is positive – the last part. About packing his *bags*. At least he's being careful.'

'You can't mean that.'

'I don't know.'

'Drop him.'

'I should never have opened the computer. He never meant for me to see this. Maybe he was just, you know, bragging, the way men love to do. He looks up to Mario. Maybe he was just trying to sound like a big shot.'

'At your expense.'

'I don't know.'

'You're crazy, you know that?'

'I've invested so much in this relationship.'

'*Relationship!*' Michela opened her mouth to say more, but closed it again. The light from over the lake now fell obliquely across Helle's face, illuminating it in a way Michela thought she had never seen before. There was some quality to it, some indefinable movement of her lips, some desperate flicker of her eyes that left Michela breathless with an anxiety she could not identify. Not only for Helle, but for herself as well.

Helle's cigarette had burned to the filter. She dropped it in the ashtray and looked at Michela's cigarette pack, but what she said was, 'I don't know. I don't want to be alone.'

Michela watched Helle walk away in quick short strides along the lake bank, to the bridge, crossing the lake. The green of the chestnuts deepened as the afternoon deepened in shadow, and the bridge looked lonely with Helle walking so quickly away across it.

Her wine glass was empty. The two men who had talked about looking out a window at the rain were gone. She thought of the older one who had addressed the frogs legs. Perhaps he was a poet. She wished she knew him.

Absently she took out her cell phone with the thought of calling Voss, but remembered that he had slapped her, and it was as though she had not felt the sting of that blow until this moment, as though a spell of numbness suddenly lifted, and she felt the fingers of his one hand clawing at her hair and the red pain of his palm sharp against her cheek, the shock, the salt taste of blood on her tongue, and then tears in her eyes as she shouted at him. She could not remember what she said, why he had done it. They had been talking. They had made love. And he had been whispering about Jens Vaever, fantasies, exciting himself and her and then he was hitting her, and she struck back.

No man would ever beat her again. Not without a fight. That she had honored that determination gave some grim satisfaction, but still it could not overpower the question boiling beneath it all: Why do men hit me? Why is it happening again?

PART II

Mother is displeased with us, Chet

'Who then devised the torment? Love.
Love is the unfamiliar name
Behind the hands that wove
The intolerable shirt of flame
That human power cannot remove.'

T.S. ELIOT

24

I know a lawyer

The sky was a vast flat ceiling, the blank grey of an empty movie screen, and Michela was thinking, as she strolled toward her meeting with Voss, about the times that Mads had beaten her. It was much worse than what Voss had done two nights before. Voss had only slapped her, pulled her hair. Mads had struck her with his fists, torn hair from her scalp. The doctor, Torben, had seen Michela's blackened eye and swollen cheek, and without even asking who had done it told Michela, 'Leave him. Once they start hitting you they never stop. They weep and beg and apologize but once they start they never stop. It's like opening a door you can never shut again.'

But he hadn't been completely right. Mads had only beaten her a few times in their sixteen years together. It seemed to her there was some sort of logic to it: a number of conditions that had to exist at the same time for her to be in danger. He had to be under stress at work, there had to be trouble with Ria – her screaming fits –, Michela herself had to be in the grip of a bitchy mood which she recognized, in retrospect, as a kind of combined depression and discontent with the general lot of their life together; for all these reasons it was usually also a period when circumstances worked against Mads having time or opportunity to play his guitar, as well as a period where they were not having sex. And finally, it usually came about immediately following a situation in which they had been together with others – a party, a function, even a family gathering – where Mads had been drinking and another man had been paying a lot of attention to her. Sometimes, she knew, she had encouraged, even solicited the attention, innocent as it might be, and that too she saw as a factor of all the other circumstances – because everything else was so bad she looked for a fix of male attention to ease her troubled mind.

When all of these conditions converged, she had finally become able to recognize that she was in danger. It only happened perhaps six or seven times. Or maybe it was more, maybe a dozen times, twenty times, perhaps twice a year for sixteen years. She began to be able to see it coming after about the third time, but always too late, always when he already had that hot fixed stare in his eyes. Outwardly, to the others at the party, he hardly appeared drunk, but she knew the deliberate cunning and concentration with which he could disguise the intoxication. One sign was when he was into the hard liquor, neat whiskey or vodka or martinis, and as she spoke with the other man – it might be anyone, her brother-in-law, a complete stranger – she would suddenly see his glance focus on her too often for a second too long. Fear would open in her stomach, and she would try to catch his eye, to see if that look was there, but she already knew and it was too late to do anything about it.

That was the irony for her. She got to where she knew it was coming, but that knowledge was of little use other than to prolong the torment of expectation. For the remainder of the evening she would know that in a few hours she would be punched, kicked, smacked, pushed against the wall. He would hit her in the face and breasts, twist her arm until she thought it would break, cover her mouth with his sour palm and in a furious whisper threaten to kill her if her screams woke Ria or brought the neighbors or if she struggled.

148

Ultimately, she would surrender to it, having learned his rage spent itself more quickly without resistance so she would try to protect her face with her hands, her breasts with her forearms, her belly by drawing her legs together, her knees up, until he stopped, panting, over her. She would lay there, past tears, past pain even – until the morning – listening for the sound of him staggering on to the bedroom to tear the spread from the bed and retire to the couch, the throw pillows beneath his head. She would wait until his breathing grew quiet so she could safely crawl into the bedroom.

During the years they had Chet, the golden retriever Mads had named for Chet Atkins, he would lock the dog in the bathroom before he started on her. It fascinated her, that methodical detail. She watched him drag Chet by his collar toward the bathroom door, heard Chet's whimpering – even Chet knew what was about to happen, and he was as passive about it as she was. She would watch him, the current of fear mounting in her stomach, breath ragged in her lungs, trying desperately to think what she should do, but there was nothing, no door in the apartment she could lock herself behind. She could not run and leave Ria with him, and there was not enough time for her to get Ria and reach the door. Her hands were not quick or strong enough to fight back. Once, as he finished closing the dog into the bathroom and started toward her and she watched him coming from where she crouched in the corner of the darkened living room, her hand had slipped a heavy glass ashtray from an end table. She hid it behind her back and, just as he was reaching for her, swung it at his head.

He bellowed. Blood sprung from his scalp, and he dropped to one knee before her, groaning, his palm on his skull, blood oozing through his fingers. She gasped and reached for him, fearing she had really hurt him, damaged him, but then he was up again, his hands clenched at his sides, blood running down his face, rivuletting around his staring bright eyes, teeth bared, lips forming words: 'You bitch. You've had it.' And his pain, his wound, only increased the sum of her misery. Not even that the beating that time was any worse, maybe it was only the same as the other times, but her pain was worsened by the violence she herself had done, by the fact that now she too was actively involved, participating.

Afterwards, when he let the dog out, it would go to him, follow him, sit whimpering, rock uncertainly from side to side awaiting his orders, drag its belly across the carpet after him, lick his shoe. Sometimes, instead of sleeping right away, he would pour another drink and sit in the armchair and talk to the dog. She listened from behind the bedroom door once.

'Mother is very very displeased with us now, Chet,' he said, his voice slurring, the tight control that had bottled his rage all evening lost now, his head drooping. 'Now we've finally crossed over the line. We've gone and done it for good. Now mother will never want to love us again. It's just you and me now, Chet. Just the two of us.'

There was never sex involved. He never tried to rape her. This was not about sex. It was about his rage and hatred, about wounds so deep in him they were beyond reach, geysers of dormant pain that certain conditions could cause to erupt, like the geysers she had seen in Iceland once, that the tour guide primed to activity by putting soap flakes into the mouth of the dormant hole until the low rumbling began and then the jet, the explosion of a pillar of water jutting up into the light until it had spent itself.

She came to see it like that, a natural force, a phenomenon that existed because of the presence of invisible but unimpeachable circumstances, some of which were present in herself, and it seemed she could no more eliminate them than she could chop off her own hand.

Next morning she would be the first up. She limped into the bathroom to shower, to study her bruised face in the mirror over the sink, examine her body in the full length mirror on the door, assessing the damage. A cut, swollen lip, a blue eye, swollen cheekbones, welts and blue and yellow and violet patches on her arms and legs and hips and chest, a wobbly aching knee or ankle, strained wrist, elbow.

He lay face down on the sofa, perfectly still, pretending to sleep while she fed Ria in the kitchen, squeezed oranges, boiled eggs, brewed coffee, sat on the stepladder with a steaming mug and a cigarette. Then at last he stood in the kitchen door, fear in his eyes. 'Good morning,' he said, waited there in the doorway for a sign that he might enter the room.

'The dog needs to be walked.'

'I'll do it.' He cleared his throat. 'God I'm so thirsty.'

'There's juice.'

And he would go to the juice presser, 'Ah! Fresh squeezed!' and pour a pulpy sticky glass and guzzle it down, gasping, smacking his lips, as they moved into their day, back into their normal life, as it had been before the explosion.

He would be alert and tentative for several days. Sometimes he wept and cursed himself. She would give him credit for one thing: he never apologized. An apology would have been adding the worst insult to it all. His own pain showed in his posture, the way he moved about the apartment like a visitor, someone who was there by invitation, without full rights. Or in his brooding eyes as he sat hunched forward on his chair, elbows on his knees, one palm trying to cover the bruised knuckles of his right hand, and she took refuge in the knowledge that it was over for now, that for the next few months she was free of it.

Once she had to go to Torben to have him look at a finger she thought might have been broken. He examined all three joints carefully with the gentle tips of his own thumb and index finger. 'Just a sprain,' he said, 'a bad enough one,' then, without looking at her, asked, 'Do you enjoy it?'

She did not answer until he raised his eyes to hers, and she said, 'No.' Calmly. For she knew that only half-truths were expressed in indignation.

He nodded, clearly having decided to abandon his project of getting her to leave Mads. She wondered what his estimate of her staying might be, but was too proud to ask.

After Ria was gone, Mads never touched her again, neither in violence nor in affection. He didn't talk about what happened, would leave the room or the apartment when Michela had her crying fits. She wondered where he kept the emotion. Her own tears were like a necessary bleeding over a long period of months, but she never saw a thing on his face. He played his guitar and smoked cigarettes. He didn't drink. They both lost weight.

The nights were the worst. Her mind gave no peace from remembering. She didn't dare lay down in the dark without something to quiet her. At first she did it with wine, but then feared that was getting out of hand so she went to Torben for a prescription.

'You're only 36,' he said as he keyed the prescription into his computer and printed it out.

'I feel like 50.'

'You think you're old but you're still young. You think, my God! 36! 36 is young. And fertile. And you're a fine-looking woman.'

Her laugh was bitter, but Torben's pale blue eyes held her. 'I don't mean with him. You're a wonderful woman. You could have another man.' He snapped his fingers. 'Just like that.' His eyes were still on her face, and she received his gaze, his longing, like a warmth of light. 'You're sweet, Torben,' she said without addressing his unvoiced appeal.

She did consider it. Not Torben. He was sweet, but he was her doctor, and he was a friend, nothing more. But the possibility of another child. She considered if perhaps the loss of Ria might have changed Mads, created another wound so great, so substantial, it might nullify the effect of the other invisible suffering that had possessed him, had turned him against her in violence. Then she hesitated, remembering the time he struck Ria. Hardly anything, a slap at the back of the head and a shove, but the movement of his hand, the jerk of the child's head, the shock and hurt in her eyes, the fact that the blow had been enough to make her stumble, that his hand had chosen her head as a target, of all things, to strike a five-year-old child in the *head*, that he seemed to think he had the right to, was at liberty to raise a hand to her daughter was enough.

She dug her nails into his arm and backed him out of the room into the foyer with the strength of her fury, could feel the force of her own eyes searing into his. 'If you *ever*,' she whispered. '*Ever* raise a hand to my daughter again, you will lose her, me, and everything you own. I promise you. I know a lawyer. He *knows* about us. He has a record of it and photographs of me aferwards.'

The fear in his eyes was sweet to her, the trembling of his mouth before the power of her lie. She knew no lawyer, there were no photographs, but he never again touched Ria.

In the end, however, there was not enough time left for them to consider having another baby because then he was packing his suitcase and his guitar, and he was off to give his music a 'real' try. She saw him once again, only a few weeks later, from the window of a bus driving up Emdrup Way, a dull winding street of cheap, identical apartment buildings – a solid, flat-faced row of dirty yellow brick. He was entering the street door to one of the buildings with a woman. They each carried two plastic bags of groceries from Brugsens supermarket. She only caught a glimpse of the woman – very thin with a coarse face and too much make-up – and realized at once that Mads had known her for a long time. Who knew how long? She thought about his jealousy, his rages, and he himself, it now seemed certain to her, the one who was cheating, the wrong-doer punishing the wronged for his own misdeeds.

25

Death Extra Ultra Light

Voss wore sunglasses too, and his black leather three-quarter length coat. The sky of early evening had opened to let sunlight down on Coal Square, and he sat at one of the tables outside the White Lamb, a tall glass of beer before him, his coat lapels open. She saw him before he had noticed her, and she almost laughed at the thought of the two of them meeting here like spies, in sunglasses. The square was empty and quiet enough that she heard the whistle of a blackbird, looked and saw it perched on top of a larch tree, and she thought perhaps they would get some summer this year after all.

Voss's face was serious, inward, the face of a man awaiting news of a reprieve, or its denial. She had not let him off the hook yet. At least she had learned that much in her life. How like a little boy he looked sitting there, his milk-fed cheeks and lean narrow jaw and the black wrap-around sunglasses that he removed the moment he spotted her. She couldn't imagine ever being afraid of this boy. A smile brightened his face, and he half rose, scraping back a chair for her.

'*Hej!*' he said. 'What would you like to drink? Let me get it for you.' He leaned to kiss her. She gave her cheek and a measured smile and waited as he went to the bar for her wine. The fruit and flower vendors were closing up their stalls, packing their wares into open-sided vans, and the motor of the sausage man's wagon was puttering as he began to guide it along behind him on a rudder, across the square, leading it to wherever it was sausage wagons were berthed for the night. A woman about Michela's age stood with a little boy, watching. The boy was blonde, maybe three years old, standing sturdily on plump legs, his face lit with wonder at this spectacle of commerce. It occurred to her she was *still* fertile, at least for a little while yet.

Voss set the brimming wine glass before her. She opened her flip-top box of Prince Extra Ultra Light. Only one remained in the pack. 'Oh I need cigarettes,' she said, half rising.

'I'll get them for you! There's a 7-Eleven right there.'

'You don't have to.'

'I want to. Extra Ultra Lights, right?'

She remembered his crack then, *Death Extra Ultra Light*, and smiled, no longer annoyed, as she watched him stride away over the cobblestones, eager to please. She hoped he wouldn't try to buy her a flower from the vendor there. Let that be a test, she thought. If he buys me a flower, he's really full of crap.

When he returned he had only the cigarettes and a little paper bag of licorice sticks. She hadn't figured on candy. But he began to chew one himself, offered her a bite, and she took it to be civil. Strong salt licorice.

'How was your day?' he asked.

She thought for a moment, lit her cigarette. Then she said, 'This has to *never* happen again. Do you understand that?'

He nodded rapidly.

She looked squarely into his eyes and spoke quietly, firmly, 'Do you understand that?'

'Yes,' he whispered. 'I do.'

And she almost smiled at the sound of it, the suggestion, *I do.*

26

Burning a witch

Cutting grass was a privilege. The late June air had a touch of summer briskness on my face, and the aroma of the cuttings lifted to my nostrils, lifting me with it. A few pears had fallen from the tree by the house, shadow fruit suddenly exposed to the summer heat of the past few days, and begun to rot. Yellow wasps hovered over the brown mash, descended and lifted again, carrying a load to the hive. In the service of their queen.

The fallen pears had begun to smell like fruit brandy where they lay decomposing. My mower approached the square burnt-out patch where my wife stooped with a trowel and grass seed, hoping to get life back into it before the end of the season. Here was where we built our midsummer night fire the evening before. I placed a layer of bricks over the grass, then built a tripod of branches over a twig mass, and on top of the tripod my wife affixed a little rag witch she and the children had sewn together and wired to a splintered broom handle. The feet were a tiny pair of sneakers left over from when the kids were toddlers, and the hands were a pair of torn-up leather gloves. A black scarf was wrapped around the head, and my wife painted the beige cloth face with eye pencil and lipstick. The little creature was almost frighteningly real, an evil perverse little face on a body the size of a small animal.

The tradition was to stuff the witch with items related to people and events one wished to be delivered from, then set it ablaze. I had always smiled at my wife when she searched the house for things to burn, a letter from the tax authorities, a newspaper advertisement for a shop where she had been treated badly.

'Sometimes I really think you believe this nonsense,' I remember having told her last year. Her eyes smiled at me. 'Perhaps I do.'

This year, however, with black crayon, I drew a sketch of a man with bulging eyes and greasy black hair wearing a military hat, folded it into an envelope which, to make it seem official, I sealed with red candle drippings and shoved in through the split in the witch's breast.

After I touched a match to the twigs and balled-up newspaper inside the tripod, we stood with glasses of wine and watched the flames crawl up to the broomstick and lap up around the little white tennis shoes. I sipped my Beaujolais as smoke seeped then poured from her clothing. She tipped on her broom and black smoke billowed up from the flames into the sky as the fire engulfed her, but then the yellow sky darkened. There was a crack of thunder, lightning shot jaggedly down the sky and splashes of water began to fall. We gathered up our plates and glasses from the garden table and hurried beneath the glass overhang on our terrace. I ran back with a can of lighter fluid, stood back and squeezed the can, emptied it into the smouldering fire. The rain began to fall in earnest then and I sprinted back across the grass to the glass-roofed terrace.

The fire burned strangely against the pouring rain. Through slitted eyes I watched, imagining the frog-eyed face within the burning chamber of her breast, imagined his mouth contorted with rage, imagined the envelope and the slip of paper, the black lines which I had shaped to form his image, being chewed by flame. Now, however, the rain fell in a dense deep curtain, and we could see only the dim glimmer of fire from where we stood, dying beneath the flood.

The children were disconsolate for a while, until I got some charcoals glowing in the grill beneath the glass roof, and they speared globs of snow bread on pointed sticks and roasted them on the coal fire. My wife and I sat holding hands in the unnaturally dark evening. Although I knew it was pure rubbish, I could not help but play with superstitious fancies of cause and effect to explain the furious storm.

My wife watched me, a knowing smile rippling her sweet lips. She had no need to speak; I knew what she was thinking and she knew I knew. *So. Who believes the rubbish now, doctor?*

As a jagged spear of lightning staggered down the sky, followed by a massive grumble of thunder we could feel in the earth beneath our terrace, I wondered what Nardo might be up to this evening, what effect this unusual storm might have upon him. We had gone back to that place for a little time during our last meeting, but he was still not finished with it. It occurred to me that somewhere on the other side of the ocean, on the other side of the world, Frog-eyes might at this moment be at work. In the dark around the patio, around the glow of the grill reflected on the intent smiling faces of our little boy and little girl, somewhere in the miserable rain, I felt the presence of his spirit. I imagined him watching us from beneath the dripping magnolia tree, a cruel smile tilted across his mouth. *Safe and dry with your family, 'ey doctor? I am the one who makes the world safe for you, do you know that? Protect you from these, these ignorant peasants who seek to own what they have not earned. They would slit your throats in the night, you know that? They would do it for less than what you carry in your wallet right now. How much? 800 crowns? They would with pleasure put a knife into your back for those few bills. You are a naïve man, doctor. Without me, your so-called civilization would be a bog of nothingness, and you would be on the street begging. Yes. I know, Dr Goodie-goodie. I know.*

My wife leaned across to me and looked into my eyes. 'My

glass is empty,' she said, drawing me back with a start. I opened another bottle, listened with pleasure to the muffled pop of the wine cork beneath the drumming of rain on our glass roof.

An early sun this morning dried the grass before it disappeared again behind the clouds. I went to inspect the site of our little bonfire. It was a soggy mess. Bits of the witch were tangled in the wet remains, but the chest was gone and with it the envelope I had tucked in there. I cleared away the mess, lifted up the bricks I had laid on the grass as a platform. The grass beneath them was blackened, dead.

Now I steered the mower over the expanse of lawn while my wife reseeded that black patch. The gentle chattering sound of the mower filled my ears. A bird high in the beech tree whistled. I peered up through the branches but could not see it. Then I heard the quick rapping of a woodpecker and I paused, heard it again, blessing the pear-smelling air of this midsummer day, the first day of the long returning darkness.

Dirt washed from beneath my nails, I sat watching my hand that held two fingers of whiskey on ice in a rock glass. The hand was scratched from the rose branches I pruned away, and I was weary and gratified. Upstairs, my children slept, my wife awaited me, fresh from the shower, and I prolonged the moment, the whiskey cool in my mouth, my mind agreeably heavy. I leaned back in my easy chair listening to sixteenth-century music on the CD player and watching the wind slash about the branches of the tall birch tree at the edge of the lawn, the magnolia in the center. All I could see was branches moving against the grey-blue night sky, all I could hear was the violin and cello movements of music that had lasted centuries, and I felt a suspension of time, a suspension of its limitation, of the world's progress, of the ugliness that waited to be dealt with in my little room at the Center.

Do you enjoy hearing? Is it entertaining for you, doctor?

160

I once saw a photograph in a medical journal, looked at it for an instant, then shut the journal and dropped it in the trash. I would not look at it. I would banish the image from my mind, but of course it had already lodged itself there, lingering, a chink in my soul. The picture was of an African woman, one of the wives of a chief, punished for infidelity. A thick metal ring had been bolted into the bone of her forearm so that she could be hitched like a goat to a fence. I despised that photograph. I despised the photographer. I despised the editor of the medical journal who made the decision to publish it, for surely demons had negotiated with his will over whether to use the picture or not, over whether it could serve some good purpose, and who was to say who won? Who was to say whether some good purpose might have been served? I could only say I despised the fact that I had seen it, that it was communicated to my soul from the distant ugly place that spawned such ugliness, a thing I would never have imagined, invading my soul like blight.

27

Midsummer night madness

It was perhaps the way he was awakened that day, with the first light, not 4.00 in the morning, the sound of a car door smacking shut. Sweat sprang out across his back, his brow, pooled in the palms of his hands beneath the too-warm blanket. His lungs convulsed, pulling for air, useless sacks that could not fill.

He heard footsteps in the street and waited, peering from his bed through the tiny living room toward the apartment door. He had placed his bed so that he could see the outer door from there, and he knew in his mind, knew at this moment that no one was getting out of the car to enter his building, to climb the wooden stairway, to bang suddenly on his door, to wake the concierge for the key or just kick it open, to come in and rip the blanket from him, to take him by the hair and drag him naked to the floor. He knew, he *knew*, and yet they *were* here in Copenhagen, even here they were. It was not impossible. He had seen them. In the Center even. In the cafés. The ones from the wrong side of the door, the wrong side of the bars, ones who had left Santiago for reasons other than his own.

And why then? Why did they leave? To infiltrate? To find the ones like him who could go to the Hague, who could tell what they had seen, what they had experienced? To tell about the disappeared, give names to the faces, faces to the names? To tell about their filthy methods, their laughter, deceit. 'Go, Nardo. You can go. We are finished for the day. Go. Can you walk? Good.' And then, as he reached the door, dragging his legs, 'No, wait, come back, just another hour or two.' Or, 'You must have a powerful friend somewhere, Nardo. We have been ordered to release you. *Not!*'

The one with the bulging eyes, his smug smile: 'If you ever try to tell this, who would believe you? Can you even be sure it ever really happened? Oh, you have a few bruises, some more or less minor injuries, but these things can happen so many ways. You fell in the shower. You fell down the stairway up the mountainside in Valparaiso. Can you ever be sure of anything anymore, Greenebag? Can you!'

He had shaken his head no, but he was sure. He had only to close his eyes, and it happened again, it happened all over again.

You are a dangerous man. You are a danger to them. *(Man? You are not even a man. You will never be a man. I shall see to that, Greenebag. They will set you to guard the virgins because you will never be a danger to a woman.)*

He had seen faces in the center, seen the expressions, the eyes hiding knowledge when they looked at him. Eyes that said, *I know you. Just wait. I will get you again.* It was not impossible. It had happened before. Nothing was impossible. You have no rights. Rights? The right to fill your mouth with cake. Until it is decided they wish for you to eat something else.

Make no mistake. Only until they decide.

He was not certain how long he lay there waiting for the sound of footsteps that never came. Later, when they did come, they jolted him from his doze, continued past his door, up the next flight, into a door up above, the footsteps of a neighbor coming home from a nightshift or a late celebration of the Midsummer Night.

Midsummer Night. He remembered then the evening before,

in the Commons, the sprawling green park where Copenhageners gathered for the high day of summer . . . Now he remembered the details. Was that what had so unnerved him?

The Danes made so much of the midsummer night, the longest day of the year – and here it was long, nearly twenty hours. Everywhere in Denmark – in the countryside, on beaches, in harbors, in private gardens – people gathered to build heaping bonfires upon which they fashioned of rags and paper and wood the effigy of a witch on a broomstick, and as the last light of that longest day was fading, they torched it and huddled together to watch it burn. Some even stuffed objects into the witch's straw breast – names on a scrap of paper, in an envelope, photos to be devoured in the flames, freeing the supplicant of troubles associated with that name or image.

Nardo was fascinated by this glint of superstition from behind the Nordic façade of rationalism, so he decided to go over to the Commons on the northside where thousands of people gathered each year for the bonfire.

In the open restaurant there, he dined on sinewy beefsteak and listened to live music blare out on loudspeakers from the pavillion. A group of electric guitar players sang the anthem of the evening, Holger Drachmann's nineteenth-century hymn about Sankt Hans – St John: about the light of high summer, the dance of youth, the full-throated song of birds in the fields, the crowning of the patron saint with laurels, the witches and trolls of the countryside, and the love of country and rattling of sabers against all enemies of the Danish Kingdom. Meanwhile families and groups of young men and women grilled sausages and chickens out on the green expanse of grass. The as-yet unlit bonfire heap was huge, mounted with a life-sized witch with painted face, all ready for the torch.

Then suddenly the evening turned dark, a wind rose. The sky split open. Rain began to flood down on them and a quick soggy darkness fell with it. There was no place to go. The organizers of the festival rallied to throw up half a dozen open-walled canvas shelters, and as lightning cut jaggedly down the sky, cursing laughing shouting people gathered blankets and coolers and folding chairs from the grass and ran for cover while the thunder rumbled and cracked overhead, reverberated in the earth beneath their feet, and water was flung on the wind in thick sheets into their faces.

The hearty organizers brought out gasoline and managed to light the bonfire and the witch despite the rain, and it burned in eerie thick flames, darker and hotter than wood fire. Spires of dark light leapt and bent stiffly beneath wind and rain.

Nardo hurried from the one canvas shelter to the next, but they were stuffed to the outermost edges with wet, shivering people, hair plastered in faces, shirts stuck to bodies. Finally he saw a small place he could half wedge into. A young woman stood near the edge with a cooler beside her feet.

'Please excuse me,' he asked in Danish – and perhaps it was that, the words in Danish perhaps alerted the man in the shadows, perhaps they sounded exaggerated and sarcastic or just too foreign. '*Venligst undskyld,*' he said because there is no real word for *please* in Danish, 'Friendliest excuse me,' he asked, 'May I move your cooler a little bit so I have the possibility to stand in here where it is dry?'

The young woman smiled and moved the cooler herself, made room for him, but from the shadows inside, a man's voice said casually, 'There is of course also another possibility. You could go find somewhere else to stand.'

In a flicker of lightning, Nardo glimpsed a face, young and thick, close-cut yellow hair, a blunt nose. The faces of others standing nearby looked away.

'I meant no disrespect,' Nardo said in Danish.

'What language is that you're trying to speak?' the young man asked.

Nardo felt fear and anger crawling up his legs. 'I only wish to be in shelter,' he said.

'What you wish does not particularly interest me so why don't you do the smart thing and vanish, *Pedro?* What kind of Perker are you, anyway? I can't place the miscolor.'

Nardo's mouth opened, and he didn't know what he intended to say. 'I meant no disrespect. Is it too much to ask that I stand here where it is dry?'

'Is it too much for me to suggest you shut the asshole in your face? Or would you like us to shut it for you? We can do that for you if you like.'

Nardo remained silent. The calm of the young man's voice was somehow more ominous than if he snarled.

'What are you, Pedro, deaf? Or just so old you can't hear anymore? Or maybe you don't understand Danish at all. Is that it? Want us to explain it for you?'

The woman who had made room for Nardo looked back at the young man in the shadows and said, 'This gentleman was perfectly polite. Why are you talking like that to him?'

'I think I asked him very politely to close the asshole in his face. I even offered we could close it for him.'

'Why are you so interested in assholes?' the woman asked sharply. 'Is that what you like?'

'No,' Nardo said softly to her. 'It is all right. I will go.'

'Wise decision, Pedro,' said the young man, and Nardo stepped out into the rain, into the unnaturally dark summer night, past the huddled people beneath sagging canvas roofs, past the burning witch, the abandoned concert shell, and out to the deserted boulevard beneath the pounding rain.

He remembered now the wetness of his clothes, his puddled shoes, his soaked hair, his tweed jacket drenched through to his shirt, shirt drenched through to his skin, and chill rain running down his collar. At home, he stuffed newspaper into the shoes, hung his clothing on the cold radiators, from hangers in the bathroom, and sat naked at his window, shivering, a blanket around his shoulders, sipping brandy until finally the shaking of his body gave way to sleep.

Now again, he dozed, slept, dreamed of music. At first troubling, the strings of madness at the far edges of the mind, but then there was the gentle sound. The bandoneon. Step-step – step-step – close. The dance of sorrow. Music that reached into his heart. And he remembered today was the Tango Day advertised by Café Bopa. He considered it. There might be others from the south. *Porteños* who might be connected to his own country. And others. The Colonel's men. The generalissimo's.

Or would there?

Did it truly continue here? Or was it over with? Are you such a *cujon* that a stupid boy in the park unmans you with a threat? *Unmans*. How to unman what is no longer a man already?

He dozed again and woke with a start. He had an appointment at the Center that day with Thorkild Kristensen. But he heard at the open window a sluggish ugly rain, and even Thorkild Kristensen would not understand the deadly power of that rain, its sound, the dull vague images it stirred.

He threw back the blanket, moved on unsteady legs to his little kitchen and ate fruit standing by the dirty window, peering down at the rubbled backyards, sectioned off by shabby fences, saw unfamiliar tiny red flowers, called *tjern* in Danish, on a tall bush whose name he did not know in Spanish or English, elaborate berried flowers on another whose name he did not know in any language. Dirty walls, a heap of bricks, a yellow plastic watering can, the bent over back of a man in a green shirt performing some hidden task, a naked rubber doll in a soaked baby stroller.

And he remembered Thorkild Kristensen quoting some poem to him once. 'Sometimes the truth is found in a walk around the lake.' And he thought, *Sometimes the truth is found in my own heart when I talk to Thorkild Kristensen.*

He showered, dressed in clean clothes, for that was important, a pressed blue shirt, a brown necktie, polished shoes. His tweed jacket was dry on the hanger; he shook it out and brushed it. He removed the plastic bag of garbage from the cabinet beneath the sink and let himself out, pausing to listen if there were any sound on the wooden staircase. Nothing.

In the backyard below, there was a minor accident; when he lifted the lid of the large metal bin to throw in the trashbag, he missed, casting it against the rim so it spilled onto the gravel, and he had to stoop beneath the sluggish rain to retrieve soggy grapefruit shells, bannana skins, cigar ends, crumpled paper, coffee grounds.

Then, out on the street, it seemed as though people were purposefully walking in his way, cutting across his path, and he felt a destructive fury fluttering in his lungs. He wanted to push them roughly out of his way. He wanted to find the young man from the park, to look into his stupid eyes with challenge, to fight him, to twist his neck and bang his head into a brick wall. At a corner as he waited to cross, an automobile stopped right in the crossing, blocking him, and Nardo glared at the driver, a young Danish man who seemed to think of nothing but himself.

When he had walked all the way around the car, its radio pounding some electronic rhythm, and heard a distant voice in his mind planning an elaborate vengeful humiliation of the driver, he realized it would be best if he returned home, cancelled his therapy session and remained indoors today. He turned back and noted, spraypainted on a broken wall, the words *Blood and Honor*, and knew then that he had made the correct decision.

In his apartment again, he stood over his telephone thinking he must call to Thorkild Kristensen to say that he could not come, but he could not decide which language to use, for the doctor's Spanish was not very good, and his own Danish was insufficient to convey the politeness required of this situation – he had promised himself never again to use the word *venligst* – so he would have to speak to him in English, and he did not know the proper words to say in English. Should he say, *Something came up?* Or, *Sorry about that?* He hated those words, so casual and thoughtless, lacking human respect, but he could think of no others, so instead he turned away from the telephone and crawled, fully clothed, even wearing his shoes, beneath the blankets on his bed and lay there panting.

His head hurt with that dull, distant ache that seemed always to be with him everytime he remembered to look for it. His teeth were bothering him again. It felt as though there were a thread caught in along the root of the last remaining molar on one side, and he kept flicking at it with the tip of his tongue, but the thread would not come free.

He took the remote control from the floor beside the edge of the bed and clicked on the television, watched a few moments of a foolish American television drama in which two cheap-looking women said awkward, venomous things to one another, clicked past a show in which an American man with a round face and pale-framed spectacles interviewed several young black men who wore women's clothing, past an Italian channel he thought he might watch but it was some manner of studio contest in which people seemed to be trying to humiliate one another for the amusement of an invisible laughing audience, to a children's program in which a man in a long white clinical jacket said, 'Hello, kids, this is jolly gentle dental dad! Don't forget to brush your teeth everyday – today and tomorrow and tomorrow and tomorrow . . .'

He pressed the red button on the remote that extinguished the picture and lay there flicking at the string or whatever it was beneath his tooth. He would go mad if he could not eliminate that string and the gentle jolly dental dad seemed a deliberate provocation to enflame his mind, to make him desire to cause pain to someone, or to himself.

In the bathrom, he squeezed dental paste onto his toothbrush and he worked it along his molars, gently at first, for the few teeth he still had left were so sensitive from what had been done to them. Gingerly, he worked back toward the rear molar, trying to position the brush down along the edges where it might remove whatever the thing was that he felt there along his tongue. He poked the brush deeper down around the back, on the outer edge, probing, but whatever he tried, the thread-like thing was still there, so he plunged the brush backward and scrubbed furiously at the root until suddenly he felt something hard drop onto his tongue.

He spit into the sink and a large white-brown clump struck the porcelain with a dull click. A tooth. The size of the tip of his little finger. The root was still lodged in his gum. He ran his tongue into the jagged slick gap, watched his face in the mirror and saw there a man who was not a man, who had been reduced to a faulty crumbling fake. He held the chunk of molar between his fingertips and thought it might as well have been a kernel of his decayed and broken soul.

At the mouth of the bedroom, he stood staring at the crumple of blankets, but the sight of them, their gloomy beckon, seemed to reek of something worse than oblivion. Better to walk, to be out in the world, moving.

He brushed lint from his clothes, combed his hair, donned his tweed jacket for it was a chill wet day.

But outside on the street, the rain had stopped and a ragged patch of blue sky showed through the massive dark ceiling of sky. He felt sunlight on his face, the backs of his hands.

He walked the entire length of the lakes. Black Dam Lake, Pebblinge Lake, and when he reached the big white Lake Pavillion, turned in toward the Center, felt agreeably small walking the sidewalk of the great western boulevard to the Town Hall Square. Pausing there, he looked at the larger than life-size seated sculpture of Hans Christian Andersen wearing a tall hat, his gaze focused upward and across the street toward the Tivoli Gardens. Nardo followed Andersen's gaze and his own feet across toward the fairy tale domes and spires.

He paid his admission fee and strolled past the Chinese pantomime theater, the statue of a white-faced clown, a bronze fiddler on a pedestal surrounded by bronze naked children, a strange fountain of bubbling glasses that looked like enormous test tubes.

Bands of youngsters stalked the pleasures of the park, moving with swift determination toward the amusements, and he heard the screams of people who had paid to be rattled and cast about in various trains and compartments. Elegant elderly people sat over lunch behind the glass wall of a restaurant, and in a little booth on one path sat a man hand-rolling cigars. Nardo paused to watch his deft thick fingers, thought of the readers in Cuba hired to read poetry and stories and novels to the cigar rollers. He wondered if they were still in function.

The dark ceiling above the Gardens had closed again, and the air now was grey and chill, an unwelcoming air, yet still the people crowded round the amusements – rides and shooting galleries and gambling stations – queued up at the ice cream bars and candy-floss kiosks and beer taps. Still there was laughter and shouting, faces flushed with frenzied pleasure, couples arm in arm, fathers with infants on their shoulders, a little girl in short pants, her legs chilled pink, the drum and brass music of the uniformed Tivoli Guards Marching Band, boys and girls in red tunics and tall beaverskin hats playing a lively brass version of the stately Danish national anthem.

The miniature trolly rolled past, its bell constantly dinging, and he threaded through the gardens that bordered the path with their appealing scatter of flowers. No English or French gardens here, with flowers like rows of soldiers or forced into patterns; here they were planted in irregular sprays, which were delightful to Nardo's eye, calming.

Again the dark ceiling opened and sunlight brightened the drooping dessicated purple-white buds on a magnolia tree so Nardo recalled how the Danes were always saying, If you let the weather keep you indoors, you'll never go out.

Yet there seemed a frenzy in these gardens he did not understand; frenzy rather than awe or wonder or delight. Perhaps it was himself, his own tiredness, but he felt a need to be away from these enclosed walls of amusement, to be outside the walls someplace quiet, perhaps to read, or merely to gaze up at the sky and the trees. He had remembered to bring his Alberti with him today, in the side pocket of his jacket. Perhaps he would find a quiet place to sit and read. He thought of the Commons where people often went to sit and read, but rejected it immediately. Then he remembered the Café Bopa again, the Tango Day they had advertised.

28

The invention of the tango

Up past the triangular square, along East Bridge Street and across Jacob's Place his legs carried him. How unexpectedly strong they felt now, full of purpose, without pain or hesitation. His tongue flicked into the gap where his tooth had been but jumped away as he heard the music from Bopa Square, the wailing sorrowful strains of a bandoneon playing *La Viajera Perdida* and the violins and piano, too. There were tables on the concrete apron outside the café and the music played from a tape recorder amplified through a tall black speaker. A waiter, tall and dark-haired, heavy-faced, watched like a *compadrito* from the shabby doorway, framed by an electric strand of colored lights faint in competition with the sun. A woman in a black, split dress danced with a dark-suited moustached man, a wide-rimmed *fungi* tilted over one eye, their legs wound together as they moved across the concrete to the 2/4 rhythm: step-step – step-step – close. And then a long pause as he held her, one arm trapped behind her back in his grip, their faces turned in opposite directions like courting birds; then their eyes met, fixed, glaring, with a passion that she administered in her gaze, the power of his desire locked in the power of her eyes, as her arm was locked in his hand.

173

Nardo knew the history of this square, had been told it by Thorkild Kristensen. It had been here the Danish resistance operated during the German occupation in World War II. Bopa was an acronym for one of their main organisations, *BOrger PArtisaner* – Citizen Partisans. The Gestapo had dealt harshly with those they caught. They were tortured in the Gestapo headquarters in the old Shell Building, taken by car to the park now known as Memorial Place on the north of town, tied to stakes, blindfolded and shot, tens of them for every dead German. The Bopa leadership was held prisoner on the top floor of the Shell Building as a human shield against attack from the sky.

This seemed to Nardo somehow an appropriate place for the tango.

He took a table and signalled to the waiter, ordered red wine. The dancing couple, short and portly, were far from young, but they knew their dance, knew the rhythm of one another's body. Nardo felt a curious enthusiasm to see this exhibition of a dance from his continent, invented there by impoverished immigrants who sailed to Buenes Aires from Italy, France, Germany, England, Spain, Ireland, Turkey. Men who left their families behind with the plan of earning enough to send for them later, which they rarely managed to do. They fled poverty to find more poverty, found slave work in the meat-packing houses, lived themselves packed-in, half a dozen to a tiny barrio room, or worse, in sewer pipes. At night, to escape the heat and rotten stenches of the slum and butchered meat and their loneliness, they went to the taverns where they invented the tango, danced with prostitutes just to feel a woman's touch so they could close their eyes and dream of the women they had left at home, the hard postures of the dance echoing the relentlessness of passion deprived of love.

Now to see this dance performed in Europe touched in him memories of his student days when he and his friends danced in the cafés and taverns, playing, practising the sorrow that life would eventually teach him was reality. He closed his eyes and moved lightly in his chair to the rhythm, the emotion of the violins echoing in his blood. The waiter brought his wine, and

Nardo filled his mouth with it. It was not very good, but that was as it should be – like the cheap wine those immigrants had drunk in the *enramadas*.

For these moments he was home, the home of grief embraced, transformed into a cold, lonely passion. He looked around him at the other tables. Only a few blond heads sat over coffee and newspapers, sandwiches, amber glasses of beer giving off no light in the grey afternoon. But he no longer felt the chill. His blood was moving.

Strands of cloud drifted across the sun, touching it with a damp green chill, the threat that cold rain might at any instant wash away this moment's respite.

Then he saw at a table far across the patio to his right the woman and her young friend. The boy wore a black-leather coat that reached half down his thighs, and he sat huddled there, his hands thrust into the side pockets, chin tucked in, unsmiling, watching her as she watched the dancers, her smile broad and warm, chin lifted, eyes brilliant even from this distance, even in this flickering, dull, metal light of the north.

Nardo rose. His legs carried him across to their table before he had even thought. He addressed the young man respectfully, although he was really speaking to her.

'Will you permit me to invite this lovely lady to dance with me?'

The young man's shrug could only have been assent, and Nardo looked into the woman's blue eyes. She hesitated, half glanced to the boy but Nardo felt surer than he had about anything in a long time, and the uncertainty and concern vanished from her face in his gaze.

Then her hand was in his and the pebbly cement crackled beneath the soles of their shoes as they stepped across it to the *"Violines Gitanos."* Four steps across and a close, his thigh between hers as their eyes met and her lips parted to draw breath. He trapped her arm, but loosely, behind her as they did another *volta*, looking away from one another in one direction, in the other, and the woman in black clapped her hands once, crying out, *"Bravo, compadre!"*

175

They turned again, and his right hand at the small of her back, holding her wrist there, became more intimate, his left hand on her shoulder, but always holding her eyes which held him in their blue heat, and the music faded off.

'One more,' she said softly. As they waited for the music to begin again, she added, 'Such a passionate dance!'

'No,' he said. 'It is the dance of sorrow. The dance of those who are far away and alone.' He was embarrassed by what might have sounded like self-pitying melodrama in his own voice, but her gaze seemed intent to hear more.

The music began, *'Volver,'* and he said, 'Some say the word *tango* is from the Latin *tangere*, to touch,' and trapped her wrist more firmly now, her other hand at the nape of his neck, his other hand at her shoulder as he steered their progress across the concrete apron.

Another couple was up now, too, and in one turn Nardo saw the young man at his table, watching them, his face impassive, but Nardo thought it was a pose, a feigned indifference that might be dangerous, and he thought perhaps he should beware. The sky cleared again, opening for the warm sun, and her thigh was between his now, but the unexpected joy of his passion suddenly eluded him, replaced by the realization that this would have to be their last dance. 'Please,' he whispered. 'Just to tell me your name.'

'Michela,' she said quietly, a secret between them.

A few more steps and the music had ended, and they were no longer touching. He bowed and thanked her, and at his table again he drank the remainder of his wine in one pull to drench his parched tongue, signalled the waiter, thinking he would send a drink to them, but they were already up, leaving. She glanced back with a parting smile.

Michela!

And then their backs were moving away across the square, their bodies close, the young man's hand low and tight on her back.

The light shifted again. Blue clouds brought a premature end to the early evening. Nardo felt a few drops of rain touch his face and remembered the evening before. He carried his glass of wine into the café and sat by the yellow, half-timbered wall beneath the low ceiling. There was a cave-like dimness within, cloud-damped sunlight slanting through the three front windows, sectioned into triptyches and quintyches. The bandoneon music still played, although the tango couple was nowhere to be seen now, and Nardo felt himself at home in the dimness, sheltered. A strange electric light illuminated the many bottles shelved behind the elbowed bar, the row of taps offering varieties of Tuborg. At the end of the bar three tall fat candles burned at different heights. Here a man could hide and dream of home.

A long slender waitress, white apron tight around her hips, approached him. She smiled. Nardo looked into his empty glass. A flash of imagination spoke to him, predicting: *One blink of your eyes and you will be staggering out the door, lost forever in the bottom of a glass.*

With a smile, he shook his head no.

29

Grandmother's crystal

In the kitchen, she thawed chicken legs, boiled new potatoes, peeling them hot at the sink, prepared them with crème fraîche and chives and onion sauce. She saw herself there making his dinner while in truth she wished he would go back to his own apartment and leave her in peace. Her temple throbbed, and she was angry with herself for tippling the wine she had opened for their dinner. She thought of him inside, lying on the sofa, a pillow bunched behind his neck as he read one of her books. Not that she wanted him in the kitchen. She preferred to be alone here. With her guilt. The guilt angered her, too. Why should she feel guilty just for dancing? But guilt was a familiar emotion. She felt guilty about so many things. Guilty when she had sex and guilty when she denied herself, guilty when she drank to free her desire and guilty afterwards, in the memory, for having freed it, for having drunk too much, for drunken kisses, guilty when she partied too much and guilty when she avoided company.

But the guilt she felt now was specific; her dancing with that man had a meaning now she did not wish to think about. She had felt Voss's urgency as they walked away together from the café,

179

felt it in his hand on her, heard it in his breath and was not surprised when, at the top of the stairs to her apartment, just inside the door, he pushed her against the wall and pressed himself against her. She slipped away, chided him lightly when what she really wanted was to shove him off with all her might.

'Go in and relax while I make some food. I'm hungry,' she had said instead of, 'Go home, Voss. I've had enough of you for one day.'

It made her sick to think what he might be thinking. How dirty it made her feel, tainting the memory of that dance. She had never been good at the tango, but in that man's arms, led by his hands, his legs, his body, she had felt no doubt in her movement. She had forgotten herself, forgotten Voss there, watching, but she knew now what was on his mind.

Yet it was not only that. It was her mother; the personnel at the home, telling her they didn't have staff enough to change her mother's diapers. She thought it must feel degrading for her mother and, even worse, her father to have their own daughter change their diapers, to have to end life the way they began it. If a nurse changed them it would seem more clinical, but lately whenever she came to visit, the nurses gave her the diapers and made it clear they expected her to do the changing. At least her father had the catheter now, but her mother would be wearing diapers for a long time to come.

She realized she was also angry that her mother had never mustered the courage to leave her father. All the times she demanded Michela's energy to help her plan an escape, forcing her to hear again the whole list of grievances, enlisting her agreement, and then never going through with it after Michela had taken all the trouble to find an apartment for her, organized all the details, gas and electric and telephone and separation papers and lawyer, and it never came to anything.

'I can't leave him. What would become of him?' Which she knew really meant, *What would become of me?*

What was the use? It was too late now anyway.

She drank off the last of the wine in her glass, covered the casserole with alumiunium paper and slid it into the oven, set the timer. Then she poured another glass of wine and thought, *To hell with you anyway,* and was not quite certain if she were speaking to Voss or to her mother or her father or herself. She was also angry with her father because he had dominated both of them all his life with his schemes and his grandiose airs, his over-luxurious way of life, and all the times they'd lost an apartment and furniture and had to move in the middle of the night, and how it all left them both penniless and old, at the mercy of the state which was supposed to be bountiful with social provision for all – after all, they paid for it with their taxes – but when it was all you had, you learned otherwise. Life on welfare was no picnic.

The only thing she had got out of it all was this apartment, the last grand place her father had managed to finagle, and luckily she had had the sense to register her own address here long enough in advance before he'd lost it again, or would have, so she could move in. It was the only real asset she had to show for her 40 years, and now Voss sprawled out there on her sofa, reading her books, as if he owned the place.

The whole tangle hung like a stench in the gauze curtains drifting in the breeze through the tall kitchen window. They needed washing, too. She heard Voss moving around in the living room and felt another stab of guilt. Why? she asked herself. Why? Because I drink too much? Because I danced with someone? Because I smoke too much? Because I didn't go to university and he did? Because I'm not good enough for him? Because my life is a waste?

She knew she was spoiling for a fight as she banged the dirty utensils into the sink and just wished he would show his surly face and make one crack about her dancing in the café. Just one observation. One innuendo. One reference to the games he asked her to play and then grew furious over her agreeing to.

Her glass was already empty again, and the wine bottle more than half empty so she refilled her glass with the remainder and drank it down. She opened another bottle, easing the cork out so it wouldn't make a telltale pop, and that made her feel sneaky. More guilt. More anger. She looked into the mirror tacked over the sink and saw the corners of her mouth were stained red with wine, and she wet the corner of a dish towel with cold water from the tap and daubed at her mouth, went to get her lipstick from the bag on the kitchen table and started to cry.

She spun back to the sink and hunched over it, weeping silently into the dishtowel, but he was already there behind her, his large young hands on her shoulders.

'Hey,' he said. 'What's wrong, *skat*?'

And him calling her *skat*, treasure, which she didn't remember him ever having done before, made the tears even more bitter. He had used the "L" word enough in recent days, but always only in passion, in distress, in the weakness of his hangovers. Now the word on his boyish mouth seemed as fake to her as his passion.

He turned her body and looked into her face. 'What is it, honey? Tell me.'

She was about to say she didn't know and that's what was so stupid about it, but instead she heard herself say, 'That man at the café. He was so sad. So very . . . sad. His eyes.'

'Come on now,' he murmured, holding her to him, and the stove timer rang. 'It was beautiful to see you dance,' he whispered, and she stiffened. Were they doing this again? And why had she not considered what that tango might open again between them? Was she stupid? Why had she not declined when the grey-eyed man with his dark face held out his hand to her? It all seemed suddenly slipping out of control again. She didn't know what he was after, and she didn't know her own mind either.

They ate by candlelight at the butcherblock dining table in tattered rococo chairs that had been her grandmother's, and the sound of the wine chuckling into the old crystal glasses and his purring compliments about the food soothed her.

'It's nothing, she said. 'Simple. So ordinary.'

'Tastes wonderful to me, *skat*. You have a magic touch in the kitchen.'

There it was again. *Skat*. Treasure. What was he up to? He was smiling at her in a funny way, as if something was going on behind his big boyish forehead.

She reached across and tapped his head with her pointed red fingernail. 'What's going on up there?'

He shrugged, but the smile didn't leave his lips.

'What?' she said.

'When you danced,' he said. 'You know. With Vaever.'

'Vaever?' She thought for a moment that Vaever might be the name of the foreign man she had tangoed with, and it startled her unpleasantly to think Voss might know his name, might know him. She wished she had asked his name. When she told him hers. She remembered the moment he asked her and thought it was one of the most romantic moments she could remember in her life. *Please, just to tell me your name.*

'Yeah, you know, Vaever.' He had a strange look on his face, impatience, incredulity, as though she had forgotten something very essential. 'Mr Vaever. At the company dinner. Jens Vaever.'

'Jens?'

'Yeah. Jens Vaever. You danced with him at the dinner, remember?'

'I didn't know who you meant. He only told me his name was Jens.'

'Well he's the Vice Chairman of the Board. You danced with him when I went to get us drinks. You asked me for a G&T, and I went to get it and when I came back the two of you were dancing. You were dancing to a song called "Harlem Nocturne".'

'Are we going to go through this whole thing all over again?' She smiled as she said it, but could feel the coldness of her eyes, and Voss blushed. 'You looked so . . . beautiful. Dancing with him. So beautiful. I just can't forget it.'

And still they hadn't talked about the tango, and she couldn't think. What was he up to? Talking about this all over again as though they hadn't whispered about it all in the dark already. Suddenly she was in doubt about what she remembered, what had happened between them, whether she had clearly understood the things he had said to her.

He was silent for the time being, gazing at the dark windowpane where she could see the reflection of the candles burning in her grandmother's Holmegaard-crystal candlesticks.

183

Down below her window, in the King's Garden, she could faintly see the green illuminated head of the sculpture of Hans Christian Andersen jutting up over a hedge, and further away the illuminated towers of Rosenborg Castle where the crown jewels were stored in a basement vault. She remembered once a few months ago, Voss had asked her to sit naked on the armchair wearing only jewels, her amber and ivory pearls around her neck, the big amber pendant between her breasts, silver and turquoise around her wrists, a silver chain around her belly and around her ankles, hanging down behind her, rings of silver and gold on her fingers and toes. She had been touched, excited by his desire, that he had pictured her in this way, desired her naked and adorned. He knelt before her, naked himself, and kissed her knees, one at a time, slowly, tenderly, and said in English, 'You are a queen. My queen.' The word was so much like the Danish word for woman, *kvinde*.

Now he turned his face from the window and said, 'I still think about that.'

She refilled their wine glasses. 'About what, *skat?*'

'That's nice,' he said. 'When you call me *skat*.' And she was struck again, as she had been the first time she saw him, by the handsomeness of his face, his strong chin, his light clear eyes.

Suddenly shy, she said, 'The same. You never said it to me either before tonight."

'*Skat*,' he said, gazing at her with his young eyes which she could not help but feel seemed shallow, caught up in their own . . . What? Impression of himself? Her impatience with him made her feel disappointment with herself. Why was she so hard on him? He was younger. Was there really such a difference in the nine years between them? Was he only a boy? What was this all about? A game they almost played that went sour before it even started?

She sipped her wine, reached for her cigarettes.

'Death Extra Ultra Light,' he said, smiling, and she could have smacked his smirking mouth.

'It is my business that I smoke,' she said curtly.

'Hey, *skat*, I was only teasing.'

184

'You are going to wear that word out,' she said. 'And don't tease me. I don't like it anymore than you would.'

The conversation had derailed, but she couldn't figure where. 'Do you want coffee?' she asked.

'Sounds great.' His eagerness to be served.

'Good,' she said. 'Make me some, too, will you? Milk but no sugar in case you never noticed.'

But he was not to hook or stick in. He served the coffee and sat beside her on the sofa with her bare foot in his palms, a Stan Getz record playing. Brazilian music.

'I do think about it still,' he said, massaging her foot.

She only looked at him.

'About you and Vaever. Dancing.'

She said nothing, reached for her cigarettes.

'I think about it when we make love.'

Well *joyeuse fumée*, she thought, and there was a long silence while Joao Gilberto sang Portuguese lyrics that had been the theme music of her early years with Mads, before Ria, before all of it, when she was 20, her parents just past 60. How unreal those years seemed now. What children they had been, and had she ever really grown up? Ever? She thought of Ria, how she had looked in her bed, so pale, eyes shut, mouth open, her chest unmoving. My baby is dead. And why should I think of that? What is any of this really at the end of the day? What will any of it mean? *Dødens Triumf.* The triumph of death.

Cut to the chase, she thought. What is he after now? And she thought of the man whose name she did not know, his grey eyes staring into hers, his body moving her body, and she asked, 'What is this all about, Voss? What is it really about? That you got jealous when I danced but liked the way it made you feel, too? I haven't forgotten all the things you told me the other night.'

She saw excitement in his eyes and quickly added, 'And I haven't forgotten what happened afterwards either. What you called me. You called me a whore. And what you did to me. You hit me. And I haven't forgotten your promise either.'

He lowered his face. 'Do I have to pay for that again?'

185

'I hope not,' she said, looking into the tiny monkish bald spot on the crown of his blond head.

'Hey, why are you getting so tough with me? Remember me? I'm the guy who loves you.'

'You use that word so easily now.'

'I mean it.'

She liked the feel of his fingers on her foot. She liked where they were – or did she? What did he want? What was he thinking? Did he even know himself?

'Would you like for me to be with another man?'

His thumb, massaging deeply into the sole of her foot, stopped moving. 'Do you want to?'

'Wasn't that what we talked about? It was your idea. You asked me if I would. And then when I agreed to do it for you, for us, you blew up, you called me a whore.'

'I got confused,' he said, his voice husky. 'It excited me. I was jealous, but somehow, it doesn't make sense, it made me feel so close to you. I didn't tell you this but today at the café, when you danced with that man, it was exciting. Were you excited?'

She reached for her wine. 'I don't know. I was only dancing. I want us to have it good together, we're free to do what we please, but I don't want you to go through that again, to go through that like the other night.'

'No, no, it's not like that. With him, it would be different. Were you excited?'

She thought about it for a long moment, listening to the music, staring at a painting on her wall, a still life of two fish on a cutting board. By a Danish Academy painter, a painting she had from her grandmother. His eyes were on her, waiting for her to make the decision. It frightened her that he seemed to want this so much, and it was simple, she knew what he wanted. He wanted her to be with another man. It was the thing he wanted, maybe the thing he needed, maybe it was the only way he could love her, and she wanted to love him, she wanted them to be able to love each other and have the pleasure of each other.

30

The child screams and looks at me

Progress followed by setbacks. Nardo had skipped his last appointment without letting me know. A delicate situation. It was difficult for me to know whether his behavior was irresponsible, some manner of adolescent-style challenge, or whether he had in fact been immobilized by his demons, unable to attend, unable to contact me. Now, due to problems in the center, I had to change our scheduled time for this appointment. There have been internal problems, conflicts, policy and scheduling disagreements, and one bright soul suggested that we put all that aside and hold a staff party to try to ease the strain cropping up amongst us. Unable to reach Nardo by telephone, I sent him a card in the mail informing him of the schedule change. A tricky situation within a delicate balance. I told myself the greater good demanded it, which was true, but could not ignore my ambivalence about Nardo's prognosis. I had no way of knowing whether he would come today, whether he had already abandoned treatment, whether he was holed up in his apartment in terror of opening the door or answering the telephone. And there was, had to be, a limit to my own commitment. I would go a long way, had gone a

187

long way, but there was a limit. I had other patients, too – though none, at the moment, quite as demanding as Nardo. Or, as threatening to my own balance.

I waited at my desk, half-heartedly studying a file, glancing up from time to time to peer through the slats of the venetian blinds at sunlight on the brick wall across the way. My ritual was to close the blinds when Nardo appeared. I did not want a glimpse of the State Hospital across the way to upset him, obstruct the sense of openness it was my aim to foster here. Yet today I could sense a reluctance even to do that. Perhaps we had reached an impasse. Perhaps I was as weary of this as he was, as steeped in hopelessness. Perhaps another therapist would do better with him than I had done.

Still I could not forget our last meeting, the unexpected glimpse of breakthrough, near breakthrough. He had been back there, but I lost him before we could do anything with it. If he came today there might be another chance. It came like a change of the Danish weather, sudden and unannounced. The appearance of light, the disappearance of light. One moment he was here, in the moment, resisting me, quibbling, posing behind ideological arguments; then suddenly something happened inside him, suddenly he was back there again, terror rose like floodwater into his eyes, the horror . . . I had to remind myself constantly that the quibbling sometimes masked the stirring of old demons inside him.

But if he did not come today . . .

At just that moment he appeared in my doorway. His face was clear. He seemed relaxed. I motioned to the green chair, rose and closed the blinds, returned to my own chair, facing him at a slant at an opposite edge of the blue oval carpet.

'I apologize for the change in schedule,' I said.

His lips tightened slightly. 'It was no convenient,' he said.

'Yes, I am sorry. It was not convenient for me either that you missed the appointment before this. Please remember that it is necessary to let me know if you are going to miss an appointment. Another client could have been fitted in.'

I saw resistance mount suddenly in him. He blurted, 'There was . . .'

I waited, but he said no more. Then, 'There were many reasons.'

'You might have phoned.'

'I could not. I tried. I could not.'

I nodded, deciding not to push the matter.

Then he said, 'A good thing happened to me this week. I danced with a woman. I feel I am in the world of light again.'

'Good. You *are* in the world of light. This is a good development, Nardo. But we're not finished with the other place yet. You need to go back again and finish with it. There is more to be done there.'

After a silence, he asked, 'In what way do you know this?'

'I feel sure of it.'

'You *feel!*' he snarled and seemed startled by his own emotion. Perhaps he could see it confirmed what I had said, but he retreated nonetheless, fell silent again. He reached to the edge of my desk for a little block of paper, small yellow slips with light adhesive on one edge. He fiddled with it, turned the pad in his fingers, first this way, then that, aligning the edges to his fingertips. Many moments passed with no words between us. I questioned him. He ignored my questions. I prodded gently, waited, prodded, provoked, waited. Nothing.

It occurred to me that we had reached the end of possibility. I was tired of this expense of time with so little result. So many months had passed. The cost was too great. His arm was healed. That was good, a substantial result. But so much remained still, and we were getting nowhere. I plumbed my heart for emotion, but there was nothing. No anger, no real interest left, nothing. I seemed to have taken a final step beyond caring. Caring, I realized, was not an act of will, but a resource, a thing, which existed in a man in a finite quantity. Perhaps a man could squander his caring. Perhaps this was a wrong choice to make, to turn too much attention to a thing that required too much of a limited precious resource.

Yet the prospect of turning him away was frightening, too. What cost might that have? For him? For myself?

Half an hour of our time remained, and I thought to myself

that I was being paid, the money was already home, my salary was secure. If I did more or less was not subject to scrutiny. I could have pronounced him a burnt-out case, simple as that, file a report to the evaluation board recommending alternative treatment, attention by a less expensive professional. Perhaps someone else might have wanted to try with him, but who? We all had a heavy caseload. I could place a question mark beside the very considerable resources being devoted by the State to the care and economic support extended to him. He was subsidizing his own expenses with his translation; perhaps he could work more, earn more, become independent. There were ugly aspects to my own power that glimmered in the dark of my mind, yet at times unpleasant decisions needed making. Even if I continued to slog through this to another small breakthrough, once again we would have to begin. How many times would we have to go back to that place where he had been broken down, only to retreat from it, try to deny it. And who could blame him? Why should anyone voluntarily return to the horror of such memories? Perhaps he had been sufficiently repaired to go on in his life here, to pass through his days half-functioning, half-broken. How many people in fact were already walking the streets in that condition, not only refugees, but Danes as well? Who was to decide on their fate? Who was I to decide on the fate of anyone?

Nardo did not even have a family. There were others here, other clients who had families to think of. The wife with her own set of problems, the children who lived with the shame of a father who had been so humiliated and abused, a mother terrorized by their father when finally he returned to them as a ticking bomb of shame and pain. Such an enormous task.

I could simply report that this man is beyond further progress, beyond my powers of further progress. I could recommend pharmaceutical treatment, perhaps voluntary warding, brush him off to another sector, let someone else deal with it. There were so many others waiting for treatment, so many broken people in this world. The streets were full of them. Young men who sat at the mouth of the underground trains, a sign propped up against a hat: *I am homeless and hungry.*

There had to be a limit to caring.

The silence of the room was the color of the day, a pale leaden color smeared around the edges of the venetian blinds. No air. The air in this room had already been breathed. It did not matter whether we spoke or not. My mind was blank, like the weatherless sky. I rose and went to the window, reached behind the blind to let in air, and Nardo's eyes did not even follow my movement. I sat again, watched his brown fingers turn the little yellow pad, black hair on brown knuckles and yellow paper, and realized that I scarcely perceived him. I scarcely perceived myself. How could my mind become so blank, drained? I tried to imagine my children, my daughter at the daycare, my son in third grade, but even they seemed far away from my consciousness. My wife was doing some administrative task at the university psychology department – what task? Chatting perhaps with a colleague – about what? My imagination was empty, my consciousness drained.

Who controlled this moment? Why did no thoughts, no pictures, no words come to me? The silence in the room was palpable. The room was still but for the constant lethargic movement of Nardo's fingers, a little clattering flutter of the blinds on the stream of air from outside. A puff of clean air entered my nostrils. Eagerly I breathed it in, felt it fill my throat, and a memory flickered into mind, a man from Uruguay who sat in this room with crimped, shrivelled fingertips, what they had done to him. Antonio was his name, a grey-haired man with a fine-featured face and grey-green eyes much like Nardo's, whose expression was so quiet, so distant. Yet he embraced me like a comrade the day he left to return to his homeland, to help establish a rehabilitation center for torture victims in his own land.

He did that. He went back into it again. I thought about the courage required to do that, the clarity of mind. And he said to me the last time, 'So many broken people. But like everything else, they must to be repaired each one at a time. This you have taught me, my friend.'

191

Here in this room, Nardo turned the little yellow pad in his fingers, and we said nothing.

My wife beneath me, palms on my back, barely touching – barely a touch – and our breath mingled heavily between us as I entered her. Scummy lips whispered at my ear, *Do you enjoy hearing, doctor? Does it entertain you? You miss those little entertainments, don't you, doctor? Your plaything of a patient. Oh, by the way doctor, when you saw the picture, the sketch of the naked woman having picana torture right in her bushy cunt, what did you feel, doctor? You felt a little bit electricity in your own pic, no? You try to ignore this, but I see. Yes. Oh, and tell me, where are your children right now, doctor? Where are your children at just this moment? Someplace safe? Perhaps we could to work with them?*

Do not put words of my children into your disgusting mouth! The protruding eyes watched me, watched the eyes of my wife who did not understand what was happening inside me, who could as well be a naked stranger beneath me, who could not see the ugly face that had thrust itself between us, watching me, watching her, leering.

I touched her hair and did not know what I was feeling. If I cried, if I could cry, she might understand that perhaps, but I could neither cry nor shout nor plead for help.

I went slack, rolled off her, and we lay side by side in the stillness of the dark bedroom, the night air sucking the curtain against the open window as against a mouth, the mouth of night that Nardo must now lie facing with open eyes, midnight after midnight in his little apartment over the lake. Perhaps he could not sleep. Perhaps he rose and stood at the window, looked across the lake to the walls of windows on the other side behind which other people slept or made love or lay awake in anguish over their own scarred and broken lives.

The faint shush of traffic from the avenue at the end of the street lapped against the silence of my bedroom in which two naked people lay side by side on a bed, their attempt to join broken beneath the ugly gaze of a frog-eyed face that ruled my world, sent me patients, broke people and sent them to me to be repaired again as best I could, which was not very good, laughing at how much better he was at his job than I was at mine.

It occurred to me that I would not like my children to meet Nardo. Was that thought irrational, racist? Why shouldn't they meet him? Should the occasion arise. He was my job, my salary. It did not matter if we spoke. He sat there in his chair. I sat here in mine. Not a sound in the room. And my family stayed alive, while his disappeared. My mortgage payments were made. We ate, enjoyed priviliges, burned a stuffed witch in our garden on the midsummer night, dragged an amputated tree into our living room at Christmas, mounted it in a pot of water to keep it alive while we adorned it with burning candles and glass balls, colored objects, paper hearts; we joined hands and circled round it singing songs of the child born in Bethlehem whose meaning long since had become perfunctory, worn thin from mindless handling. On warm afternoons, we loaded charcoals in the grill out on the lawn or under the glass-roofed terrace, doused it with flammable fluid and struck a match, shovelled on steaks or sausage, a spit of meat and vegetables. We drank wine in the summer evenings, entertained guests like ourselves, the murmur of our conversation in the dusk a gentle reassurance, small bursts of laughter, merriment, while on the other side of town Nardo battled his demons, sat at home facing the night like a black mouth before him, knowing that he would not sleep, that if he did sleep he would dream of stones raining down on his body, of huge animals chasing him all through the night so that even if he slept a few hours, he would awake more exhausted than before he slept to face a day filled with the foreign faces of a country which was not his, where Nordic eyes looked down on him, Nordic hands reached down to help.

And when I asked him, 'What was in your mind as you lay awake, Nardo?' he neither looked at me nor indicated with any movement that he had heard, and he said nothing, only turned the little yellow pad in his fingers.

It would have been a favor to the world if I had ended his pathetic life, Frog-eyes whispered. *He is not a man. I could have done him a favor, just like that!* Unconsciously I snapped my fingers lightly. Nardo's face turned in my direction for a moment, then back to the activity of his fingertips and yellow pad.

Then his head angled obliquely toward me. His eyes watching the side of my nose, he said very quietly, lips barely moving, 'You are having a party?'

'I beg your pardon.'

'You are having a party. The personnel here at the institute are gathering this afternoon for a party. That is why I had to change my appointment time again. To accommodate this party for all the personnel of this institute.'

'Yes,' I said then, remembering. 'We are having a get-together.' It was necessary to do this occasionally. Something was needed to bring us together under relaxed circumstances. Sometimes so many months passed with no contact but the meetings where we discussed our failures and maneuvered for organizational advantage. So we threw a party where we would stand in knots in the library, sip bad wine from plastic cups, nibble peanuts, try to speak to one another as if we were connected in some way beyond our failures and ambitions. No, I thought, this is self-defeating. Life was not so simple. We sought contact, despite it all, we had a purpose and we sought contact with one another, to acknowledge what was important in our work. This must be remembered.

'Do you know there are clients here who still have their family in custody? Do you know what that means? What they are experiencing just now, at this very moment? What is being done to them? And they are the lucky ones. The ones who have not disappeared forever.'

'It is a terrible thought,' I said, wondering how to explain to him why we are coming together, wishing to unburden myself on him. But how could I tell him, *We are having a party so that we can forget for a few moments what an agonizing, maddening burden you are to us!*

'Terrible?' he said. 'What do you know of terrible, doctor? What do you care? You of the God-beloved north who do not believe in God, only believe that you are chosen by Him? What do you really care? Go to your party, doctor. Enjoy.'

'Nardo, sometimes the troubles of the world have to take care of themselves for a while. Sometimes we have to relax and stop worrying for a time.'

'You are not serious, doctor. This is not a serious place.'

'Well,' I said. 'Perhaps this is a decision you will have to consider.' I heard the chill edge of my own voice, wondered at it. Was I baiting him? No, this was not a bluff. I felt in myself that I was ready finally to draw this to a halt. I saw that he registered this as well. His face was pale, his eyes showed fear, but he said, 'I have no use for a place that is so unserious its personnel hold a frivolous party while people in custody suffer horrors you could not even imagine.'

'It is terrible to think of, I know.'

'*Know?* What do you know, doctor? You know nothing of human nature. You have never even had a blow on the ear. Try a flying lesson one time, or a ride in the submarine. Perhaps it should be part of your training, to try for yourself. Then tell me what is terrible.'

I felt the blood drain from my face. I despised those words so, that such evil should be ensconced in such innocent-seeming phrases. I saw from the look of Nardo's face that he could see on my face what I felt. It stopped him for a moment.

'What you know,' he whispered, 'what you think you know, is nothing. *Nothing.*' He was rising from his chair as he spoke, and something, I realized, was happening. I felt something opening in him, flowing from him. I did not dare move for fear of destroying this moment. I merely watched, perhaps I nodded slightly. My eyes were on his face, open to his if he sought to engage me, but he still had not met my eyes.

He was on his feet now, pacing. He tugged a grey

handkerchief from his pocket and blew his nose. 'What you know is less than nothing, doctor.' His face was warped with scorn. He slashed at the air with one arm. *Nothing!* I could see water in his dark eyes as he squatted in the corner of the room, his elbows tucked between his knees.

'I told nothing,' he whispered. 'I never told a thing. I could tell you of a man I know who would not break when they beat him. No matter what they did to his body he would not break because he knew himself, he knew his emotions, which would trick him, put him in just that frame of mind they were looking for. He was innocent. He had done nothing, and he remembered that he had done nothing . . .' His face lifted, eyes fixed in fury. 'He had a right to *think!* He had a right to speak his thoughts! This is no crime! And he would not break. They could break his body, but they could not break his will, they could not break his mind because he focused. He watched. He reminded himself of what was real and what was not real. They tried. They told him he was laughing when he was not, that he was singing the republican anthem when he was praying the *Pater Noster*. But he knew what he did and what he did not do. He remembered to notice what was real and what was not. He always questioned himself. What is real? What is not real? And they could not break him. Only one way they found that they could get to him.'

He stopped speaking abruptly, his lips pressed tight together, and lifted stiffly to his feet to limp across the room to his chair. His face turned to mine but his eyes were closed, and I felt as though he could see me through his eyelids, as though two black eyes burnt through the flesh and saw me as he whispered, 'What you know is nothing.'

Outside in the street a car door slammed, and Nardo's eyes fluttered open. He stared directly into my eyes. Then his face jerked to the side, his eyes moved rapidly back and forth. He shivered, crossed the room, touched his forehead.

'What did they do, Nardo?' I whispered, alert, watchful. 'How did they break you?'

He crouched in the corner again. Sweat rolled down his face, his shirt was drenched with it. His arms between his knees trembled violently, and his eyes, his face, reflected a horror I knew I had to witness.

'I am in the room,' he said, and his voice was different, he was not speaking to me, he was merely speaking. 'They bring in a little girl. She is five, six perhaps. She is naken. Then they bring in the mother. She is pregnant. She is naken. The little girl tries to run to her, but the yellow tweed suit holds her back. He caresses her black hair. Moustache is holding a piece of cable. He says to the woman, *If you cry out, we whip your daughter, too. Simple. You decide.* Frog-eyes steps across and takes the little girl by the hand. He watches me. *This is your show, Greenebag,* he says. *Here we have the piece of paper for you to sign. The paper says merely that you wish us to stop doing this. Sign and we stop at once.* The cable lifts and cuts the woman's chest. It cuts deep into the skin over her ribs. She holds her mouth shut tight. Water runs from the corners of her eyes. The little girl's mouth is open wide and no sound comes from it. Moustache raises the cable again and it whips down across the woman's belly. The woman's grunt is muffled in her locked mouth. The child screams and looks at me. I begin to beg to Frog-eyes. *Please!* I say. *Please do not, please please, I beg you.* I shout, scream, *I will do it, I will do anything, whatever you say, please stop please!'*

Nardo was crawling now, on hands and knees to the table, gripping the edges with both hands. 'They kicked my stomach until I vomited blood again and again so in my mouth I always tasted blood. They made me lick it up, but they could not make me sign to what I did not do, nothing could make me, but the little girl, the mother . . .' His sobbing was high-pitched, pure and uncontrolled; there was a beauty to it, a beauty that demarcates the place where a human being is irrevocably human. I was on my knees too, and Nardo crawled into my arms. I heard the sound of my own voice trying to bring him back from that place, trying to bring us both back. I talked about the weather, a soccer match this weekend in the new stadium, about the kind of flowers I have on my lawn. I told him about the pears that smelt like brandy, the aroma of the grass. I told him about the Pablo Neruda poems I had read recently, the ones he had recommended to me, wonderful love poems . . .

Slowly Nardo rose from the floor, stood teetering on his feet, and I handed him the Kleenex box. He took it in both hands, mopped his face, blew his nose. He lowered himself to the chair, his eyelids closed again, his mouth soft, at rest.

Then he opened his eyes and looked into mine, and we sat that way for many moments.

PART III

Concerning the Angels

'Then I confirmed that walls are broken with sighs
And that some doors to the sea are opened with words.'

– Rafael Alberti
translated from the Spanish by
Christopher Sawyer-Laucanno

31

Greene's Summer

In the Café Noir, Nardo sat with his Alberti, and he expected nothing. The tall Kashmiri was behind the bar speaking to a man Nardo recognized as a Uruguayan who had published a chronicle in *Politiken* about the so-called torture school he asserted the Americans had established in Central America, about how they had employed the research of the Spanish fascists into the use of modern art to torment, the use of an image from Luis Bunuel's *Un Chien Andalou* – the image of an eyeball being cut by a razor blade, the variation of colors to influence the prisoners' moods, irregularity of the surface of the floor to induce uncertainty. The bartender stood his full height behind the taps, smirking. 'It was a stupid, ignorant article, pandering to a people who know nothing,' he said.

'You doubt my facts?' the Uruguayan asked. He was a free-lance journalist, a stringer for a number of Latin-American periodicals who sometimes worked as a translator for the rehabilitation center. 'Can you refute them?'

'I would not waste my breath,' the barman said. 'This is a country where if you open your mouth to complain, they stuff a

201

piece of cake into it. Here they have never known the conditions of other countries where other methods are required. You should pay a visit to my homeland in Kashmir. There you will see imagination at work. Do you think the allied forces in the second war were concerned about such niceties? And do you think those who were liberated worried either? The world is not black and white, my friend.'

Nardo's heart beat unevenly. He knew this argument, and he feared it to the point that he feared his own capacity to commit violence. He fondled the Alberti volume in his hands, peering into it, though his eyes saw only blurred dark lines on the pages. There was no escape from this, yet he marvelled at the Uruguayan, a vain grey-haired man wearing a jacket and tie that matched the color of his hair.

'Refute me,' the man said. 'Refute my facts.'

'I would not bother,' said the barman.

'And you did not see in the newspaper today, *today!* that 100 neo-nazis marched in Hilleroed in honor of Hess? It was called a "peaceful" event.'

'I laugh at this,' said the barman. 'You speak from two sides of your mouth. The left and the right. With two different messages. You would muzzle the neo-nazis, but you support the autonomes who attack them violently.'

'They are both stupid.'

'And you, my friend, are not very clever either. Have a drink on me.'

Outside, the lake was deep silver and two birds careened across its stippled surface beneath a sky that was lighter than the earth beneath it. These were men who did not fear their ideas for they had never been put to the test of their bodies. If Nardo could only find his breath he would tell them a joke, about the man who had gone to court with a complaint he had been tortured:

'Did you tell them what they wanted to know?' the judge asked.

'I did not, your honor,' the man said, and the judge banged his gavel.

'Case dismissed. This man has not been tortured. Tortured men always talk.'

Nardo raised his glass and sniffed into his wine. He would not speak with these men. He would read Alberti and let them speak of things they did not understand:

Angel muerto. Awaken!
Donde estas?
Paraiso perdido.
I look for a green gate
in the black depth.

'*Hej!*'

His gaze lifted from the page to her face, the blue fire of her eyes, and he was mute. *Michela.*

'What are you reading?' she asked and without waiting for a reply she reached for the book – 'May I?' – and turned back the cover. '*Concerning the Angels*'. She smiled, and he wondered if those words were adequate for her. What he read was *Sobre los Angelos*. It was in both languages, which helped him. Perhaps he would try to translate it into Danish. Perhaps Michela would help him.

Because he could think of nothing else to say, he said, 'Lorca read this book in 1929 when he was sailing to New York from Paris,' and could see in her face she had no idea what he was talking about. 'Seven years before the fascists assassinated him,' he added, lowering his voice, and still she looked confused. Nardo thought about the executioner who was reported to have said, 'I shot him twice in the ass because he was queer.' He decided not to tell her that.

She asked, 'May I sit down?'

And then they were across from one another, each with a glass of wine, his red, hers white, and in his mind was a picture of Araucanians drunk in the taverns of Temuco. She ordered something to eat as well, a piece of dark bread with a beige spread on it and chives.

'What do you eat?' he asked.

'*Rygeost.* It is delicious. Here, taste.' She cut a sliver of the bread and held it out to him on her fork. He received it between his teeth, not to soil the tines of her fork with his lips. His heart lifted while he chewed. The taste was indescribable – at once bitter and rich, wet and dry, sour and sharp. Perhaps it was simply because she had given it to him on her own fork, but he thought it was the most delicious thing he had tasted in this country.

She smiled. 'You like it? It is very Danish. Smoked cheese.'

'How you say it? *Ru-a os?*'

She laughed and pursed her lips as if for a kiss and pronounced a rolling 'r' and slanted vowels he could not duplicate. He gave her a scrap of paper, his pen. 'Will you write it for me, this *ro oost?*'

Chuckling as she wrote the word down, she said, 'It is difficult. You will learn. You already have so many languages.'

There was silence then as she ate her cheese. She offered another taste, but he shook his head.

Then she asked, 'Do you believe in them? Angels?'

'Your name,' he said. 'Michela. It is the name of an angel. I believe in you.'

'My father's name is Michael. He is more devil than angel. He wanted a son, so I am Michela.'

'I am glad he had you instead,' Nardo said, and then, afraid he had been too intimate, quickly added, 'I am Bernardo Greene. Nardo.'

She lifted her glass. '*Skål*, then – Nardo?' She said it as a question, an unfamiliar name in her northern mouth. 'If this was 25 years ago we could drink *dus*,' and they clinked their glasses.

'We still have that difference in Spanish,' he said, 'between *usted* and *tu*,' and the silence that followed terrified him as it lengthened and tilted the easiness of her smile. Finally she asked another question. 'Where are you from?'

He told her. One word. Two syllables. And what would those sounds tell her?

'Do you miss it?' she asked, a Danish woman taking the lead

from the man. He answered with subdued pride. 'Sometimes I miss the pounding of the sea. The *Pacífico* the Spanish conquistadores called it, what you in Denmark call the "Still Sea", but it is anything but peaceful or still. It roars. It booms.'

'You should visit west Jutland,' she said. 'The West Sea, *Vesterhavet* in Jutland. See the North Sea breakers on the coast. They are wild, too,'

Perhaps we could do it together, he thought, but spoke with unexpected anger hidden in the stillness of his voice. 'There are no rivers here, no mountains. The sea lies all around us but makes no sound. I miss *empanadas*. I miss bargaining with the Indians for a hen, a lamb, chicken, eggs, a bolt of cloth. I miss the sudden appearance of drunken Araucanians emerging from taverns to ride their horses into the hills.' How foolish he sounded in his own ears, a complainer, an ingrate, an ungrateful guest in this country which had tried so hard to heal and shelter him, the country of Thorkild Kristensen. He wanted to tell her about the doctor, of the hard work they had done together and how far they had come. He wanted to tell her of the things he admired here, but she had already lowered her eyes to the table, and his heart went cold with the fear she would quickly find a way to slip away from him.

'Michela,' he said and smiled, hoping she would know what beauty he was thinking about her name, but she said only, 'My father's name.'

'It is a lovely name. It suits you perfectly.'

Her thank you was dismissive, and his fingers touched the red cover of his book as his thoughts took refuge in another language, *Merci quand même, madame*, thanks anyway, *non rien*, no, nothing. Remembering once how the welcoming smile of a girl had borne the fragrance of honeysuckle, he said, 'The honeysuckle here has no fragrance,' and the pity in her smile sent his eyes out toward the lake, the sky now dark blue, the chestnut tree outside and the lamp pole silhouettes against the darker blue of the lake and the weeping yellow and blue flowers of wisteria.

'In my country,' he said, 'There are beetles larger than your hand. Snake-mother beetles, black and shiny and with a shell so strong a large child can stand on it with both feet without cracking it. They need no bite or sting, their shells are so strong.'

She shuddered and smiled at the thought, and still he felt they had failed to meet. His wine glass was nearly empty, hers more than half-full. The Uruguayan had left, and the tall Kashmiri was reading a newspaper opened flat before him on the bar.

'How did you happen to come here?' she asked, and he realized she wanted them to speak, to meet, for whatever reason, and he ran his fingers across the cover of the Alberti book and heard himself say, 'I could tell a story of my own about the angels. Let us say that I once met a man back home who had been mistreated, tortured.'

She shivered and watched him.

'He was taken from his family, his wife, his little boy, who were themselves imprisoned in a place they did not survive. They joined the *desaparecido*, the ones who disappeared. He told me a story, and I believe it completely. I know it is true. He was held in a dark windowless cell and visited daily by his keepers. They came at varying times, unpredictable. No moment was safe from their intrusion. At any time the door might burst open and their boots surround him where he lay on the concrete floor.'

'What did they want?' she whispered. 'Did he have some kind of information?'

'They were not seeking information or secrets or a confession from him. Their objective was to break his spirit only because he had been a man the people of his community respected, a teacher, they looked up to him, trusted him, a man not without dignity or the courage to examine his thoughts, his experience, and to tell of what he believed to be so. Not a hero, but a man nonetheless, still a man. Then. He believed what the philosopher Socrates said, that an unexamined life is not worth living. To break the spirit of such a man is to break the spirit of those who looked to him for their identity, for a way to think of themselves as human beings.'

'What happened to him?'

Nardo shrugged. He sipped his wine.

'They held him for months in the airless filthy cell, employing upon him the skills they had been taught by their neighbors to the north, and they were succeeding. Isolate a man, keep him from his family, ignorant of their welfare, tell him one day they are dead, the next day still living, that his wife had been . . . *used* by a dozen soldiers, that his boy had lost an eye, two eyes, has been . . . used. Deprive him of sleep, of books, of light, of human company, bind his hands behind his back and plunge his head into a tank of water afloat with excrement and bludgeon his kidneys until he opens his mouth to scream with the pain. Hang him upside down above an open fire. Bind him to a swinging trapeze by his wrists or his ankles and beat him. Tell him daily, nightly, at all hours wake him, to tell him he is nothing, less, not even a man, not a human being, tell him that even if his wife survives, which she will not, he will never be a man for her again, will never be a father for his little *maricon* son who is being used now for the pleasure of other *maricons*. Tell him that you would do him a favor to kill him, but that you will not do him that favor, you will do worse, you will make him live, you will condemn him to survive his family, knowing he does not even have the *cajones* to end his own miserable living nothingness. Do these things and you will kill his spirit.

That is what this man was experiencing, the loss of his spirit. He told me these things, how he felt it seeping out with a chill sting through his clenched bloody teeth, out into the dark stink of his cell, a thin vapor that hovered on the black puddled floor. He felt it bleeding from his heart with the sound of every other voice screaming from elsewhere in the prison.

He lay on the floor of his cell, open-eyed, slack-mouthed, finished. He lost count of the days and of the months. He was arrested in winter and at first he counted days, promising himself he would be free by summer, that he would not allow them to steal from him one precious summer of his life. But he lost all time finally. He never saw the daylight. He did not know the month. He waited only for the mercy of death.' Nardo paused, coughed, took a minute sip of his wine.

Softly she asked, 'Did he die?'

'Just when he thought he would be released from ever again caring, from ever again feeling anything, released into a death of one sort or another, at just that moment, he felt a warmth on his face. It came as the breath of a dog he once had and loved very much. As of sunlight, and he turned by reflex toward it to see two angels standing over him. Yes, angels. Real angels, this man insisted to me. With feathered wings, with glories, long-haired, in radiant array.

They spoke to him respectfully, with quiet formality. They apologized for his condition, for what had been done to him, for their inability to protect him from it. They told him that the summer had come and that they were there to take him out of the filthy room in which he had been locked for months so that for just a few moments he could feel the warm sunlight on his skin, smell the freshness of the grass, see the blue sky and white clouds. And then he was *there*, outside. He swore that he was truly there. They took him there, these two angels. He felt the sun soothing the skin of his face, his arms, easing his many sores. He inhaled the aroma of grass and weed and flowers. The blue sky sheltered him; an infinite radiant umbrella, and he felt calm, peace.

The angels apologized to him that they had to take him back again, but explained they had been allowed to show him this, to bring him out, as a promise, assurance that after a time he would again be free, that these things of beauty still existed, that he would again experience them, that he must remember this, to keep his strength.

And he did remember. Those few moments in the light were all the summer he had that year, but it was enough. It and the promise that the angels made to him. Another year passed, but he was freed, he was treated, then finally he came to this land and he again experienced the sun, the grass, the sky, the inestimable glory of freely drawing breath into his lungs, of walking the earth, seeing the sky, feeling the rain upon his hair.

He then said to me, because he knew my family, "I know your English head. You think this I tell you is mere superstition, hallucination, religious hysteria, some psychological device of survival. You see this as some primitive reaction," he told me. "I know you will not believe this, but I tell you this story is true," he told me. And I believe his story. I believe it as it were my own story.'

She was touching the sides of her wine glass with the tips of her fingers. Her eyes were fixed upon his face and she was silent for a long while.

Finally, she asked, 'Where is he now?'

Nardo did not answer at once. When he spoke, his voice cracked. 'Who knows? Perhaps he went back.'

Her blue eyes looked into his. 'To your country?'

He nodded. 'Perhaps he grew weary of being safe. Perhaps he went back to help the others.'

'Oh, my God,' she whispered. 'Wouldn't they kill him?'

Nardo's head turned slowly from side to side. He regretted having told this story to her, especially to her, here, now, in the way he had told it, and he only turned his head from side to side and said no more. Could she not guess who that man was? He could tell it no other way than as the story of another man. And now he heard from his own mouth the suggestion of his own future: *Wouldn't they kill him? If he went back to help the others?*

He wanted to run from her, from this place, just to run, but he remembered Thorkild Kristensen's eyes looking into his, what they had been through together last time, and his breathing stilled.

Now the café door opened and the young man was there, her friend, smiling as he entered. Standing beside the table, he told Nardo his name and held out his hand.

'May I give a glass?' he asked, sitting at the table with them. Nardo tried to find his voice by wetting it with wine. The glass trembled in his fingers, and to his amazement, the woman, Michela, abruptly stood and said, 'Thank you for telling me that story,' and walked quickly to the door.

The young man, Voss, watched her back with a confused smile that Nardo found repugnant. Then to Nardo, he said, 'I admired your tango. You are *really* good.'

Nardo said nothing.

They both glanced out the door that swung shut behind Michela.

32

This is not fair

Halfway across the bridge, Michela heard footsteps behind her. She didn't have to turn to know who it was and to know she had no wish to see him, so as crazy as it seemed, even to her, she began to run. When he called out to her, she ran faster. It had been so long since she ran, she couldn't believe how light she felt, her legs stretching easily out before her, balls of her feet striking the concrete bridgeway, the bounce and leap of her body, swing of her elbows.

His call fell further behind and stopped as she bounded across the lake road, down through the row houses of Weber Street and over Silver Square, down the long avenue siding the National Art Museum, over Brandes Place and along the side of the King's Garden.

When she stopped at her street door, she had to bend forward, leaning on her thighs to catch her breath. Sweat rolled down her face, and there was a stitch in her shoulder. Panting, she stared at the heavy door, overlaid with grafitti tags, symbols of some creeps who came by at night and spraypainted their stupid symbols on this elegant old carved wood. From where she stood she saw someone that might have been Voss crossing Brandes Place, moving at an ordinary pace, just as he would, so confident he knew what was right and reasonable behavior, except he didn't. She recalled the expression on his face as he stood over the table at Café Noir, the trembling smile on his foolish young mouth, the hunger in his eyes, completely unaware of what she had just heard. Perhaps he would have been indifferent even if he knew, perhaps he would not even have heard if he had been present, a youngster who could not find his way past the wall of his own desire.

You are weak, she thought. But weak was not the word. She did not know the word, and she did not know if she was being unfair. She knew only one thing. She could not bear to see him tonight, to talk to him, to have him try to touch her.

She keyed in her code on the door lock and slowly climbed the two flights to her apartment. In her living room, she sprawled back on the armchair. He had the outside door code, but thank God she had never given him a key to the apartment. When he rang the bell and knocked, she didn't move from her chair.

'Michela,' he called, a hushed shout. 'Open the door!'

She lit a cigarette. How good it felt to draw the smoke into her lungs, to blow it out in a long stream into the blue air behind the gauze curtains of her tall windows without Voss criticizing her for smoking. Was that unfair of her? He was concerned for her health after all.

'*Michela!*'

She went and stood close behind the door, laid her hand flat on the panel, pleased, liberated by this concrete slab of painted wood between them, this barrier.

'Michela!'

'Go away,' she said quietly. 'I want to be alone this evening.'

'*Why!*' He rattled the doorknob. '*Why!* This is not fair. What did I do wrong? Let me in so we can talk.'

'No.'

'You're being completely unfair. I opened myself to you. We both agreed. You're–'

'Go home,' she said and went into the bathroom, bent down to stuff the black rubber cork into the tub drain and opened the hot-water tap full. She could not hear him now if he was still there, if he was still speaking her name into the flat locked barrier of painted wood. What might the neighbors think? Who cared? She draped her clothes over the washing machine cabinet and climbed into the tub, lowering herself gingerly into the steaming water, sighing as her body adjusted to the heat. She hugged her knees to her breasts and pictured Nardo's grey eyes, remembered his words.

She closed her own, conjured up the angels that had come to take him out of that dark, windowless cell; imagined his moment of feeling the sun on his skin, the smell of grass and clean cool air.

33

The child is laughing

Instead of just picking something out from the kiosk in the home, today she had stopped at the bakery and the cheese shop for a seed roll and sixteen-week-old cheese, things he had always loved. But he turned his good eye on the cheese and said, 'Grand. Maybe they'll let me put my bridge in to eat them. The seeds are like shark paper under it. Feels good. Reminds me I'm alive.'

'Well you know what they say: What does it mean if you wake up without a headache, stomachache, or toothache, not a pain or care? That you're dead.'

'Funny!' he barked. 'Where did you learn your humor?'

'You're in fine form today, aren't you?' she said, aware of her desire to provoke him and doing her best to stifle it as, with a plastic knife, she scraped the seeds off the roll into the waste basket and halved and buttered the bread from a tiny tub of *Lurpak*.

Voss had been phoning everyday, many times, five, six, more. Sometimes he spoke, sometimes not. And three nights ago he let himself into the lobby door and slept on her doormat, which led to a visit from the superintendent whom she did not much care

215

for in the first place, a little peacock of a fellow with short kinky blond hair, delighted to be in charge of something for once in his life.

'We can't have this,' he said.

'Then do something about it.'

'That's what I am doing. We can't have it.'

'So throw him out.'

'He's your friend.'

'Are you afraid of him? He is big, isn't he?'

The little man slapped his chest. 'I'm not afraid of nothin'.'

'Good. Then get rid of him. I don't want him there anymore than you do.'

There was a letter under her door and more phone calls that progressed from professions of love to appeals for mercy to veiled threats to silence to accusations that she was a whore.

Her legs trembled as she left for work in the morning and when she returned in the evening, as she left again to visit her parents. It startled her to realize you could be with someone for nearly a year and be so surprised – not only by him but by herself.

The slap had startled her, the backhand shocked her from her trance to defend herself, but worst of all was the fact that she had not thrown him out at once, had acted as though they could continue even when he started with his plans again. She was surprised at herself for agreeing, not so much the first time, but the second.

How could she have failed to see his weakness? Or did she see it and pretend not to? Was she so desperate? How could she have fallen for a man who was so weak?

On the phone, he said, 'You can't do this. You have to give me a chance to talk to you.' And every plea, every demand made him more despicable to her.

'Voss, I have nothing left to say to you. Let's cut our losses and quit before we really hurt ourselves.'

'*You* could get hurt,' he said.

'I'll pretend you didn't say that this time. I was with a man who hurt me once, and that is not going to happen again.'

'I would never hurt you.'

'You just threatened to. And you did it once.'

His voice rose two octaves, she could picture his face, red and puffy like a baby's. 'I was confused! I *love* you!'

'You think you do.'

'I do!'

'I'm sorry to say it,' she said, 'but I don't love you.'

'You're not sorry to say it! You love saying it! You're a cruel bitch!'

It was so childish she could hardly keep from laughing.

'Listen,' he went on. 'I know you. You agreed and now you try to put it on me. Do you think I don't know you wanted to suck his spic cock? Is that what this is about? You want me out of the picture so you can have him to yourself and suck his spic cock! Why don't I tell him what we had in mind? Why don't I do that?'

You sick little worm, she thought, but said, 'Voss, I'm sorry but you should get help, really. Please consider it.' And she hung up, remembering the time she went to Mads about Ria, when the girl had been brought home for the third time almost unconscious with drink. 'We need to get help for her, Mads. She needs to see a psychologist.'

He had been sitting in his favorite chair, his guitar across his lap, a whiskey balanced on the arm of the chair, one she herself had served him: *Three fingers and three ice cubes and stir it with your little finger.* The third drink of the evening so she thought he would be primed to discuss this, to listen, but his mouth grew small and officious, and he said, 'Psychology. It's sad that Denmark has begun to psychologize everything. What we need are stronger minds, stronger wills. And anyway.' He lifted his chin to look at her. 'It was not I who shied from disciplining her.'

Now, in the home, she buttered the two halves of the de-seeded roll, applying butter the way her father liked it, spread with a uniform thickness from edge to edge so it left the imprint of your teeth when you bit into it – 'tooth butter', they called it. She laid a slice of the pungent cheese on each half of the roll and cut it into small segments with the serated edge of the plastic knife. She handed it to him on a paper plate. 'Do you want juice with it? Water? Would you like a bitter snaps?'

His hand on the trapeze above his head adjusted its grasp, and he asked, 'Are you still sleeping around?'

'Dad.'

'Well why not? Like mother, like daughter.'

'Don't you start on Mom again!'

'No. Let her have her fun with Kragh. Pair of idiotic smiling cheaters, the pair of them. You're just like her.'

'I don't have to listen to this. I won't listen to this.'

'I only hope if you are sleeping around again that it's not with one of my friends this time at least.'

'Dad. He was *not* your friend.'

'Damn right he wasn't.'

'He was twenty years younger than you and . . .'

'And fifteen years older than you.'

'How . . .'

'But I fixed him. I did. He never wrote a line for *Politiken* again. Not a line.'

Her wish to strike back, stopped in her throat. It occurred to her she was old enough now to let him have his delusions. He never had enough influence on any newspaper to blacklist anybody. The 'friend' he was so upset about was a free-lance journalist Michela had been with for a few weeks after her divorce, a man whose own marriage had just gone under and who she met at Bernikow's Wine Room when her father invited her in for a drink to show her off. She stopped herself from trying to explain to him how little it had meant, how it had had nothing to do with him, how they had treated one another well for a few weeks and then parted company. Instead, aiming to bolster his ego, she said, 'I hope you weren't too hard on him.'

'Just hard enough,' he said. 'He got what he asked for.' And turned his attention to the paper plate, apparently satisfied enough now to enjoy his breakfast. He popped one of the little squares of bread and cheese into his mouth and chewed gingerly with his corner teeth, the only functional ones remaining.

'What will you have to drink with it, Dad?' she asked, but he spit carefully out onto the paper plate and reached it back to his bed table.

'What's the use?' he said. 'I can't even gum my food anymore.'

'Would you like smaller pieces?'

He bowed his head and squinted his eyes, and she saw a tear roll down his mottled cheek, and she put her arms around his shoulders, slowing her breath not to inhale the smell. She kissed his temple.

'Dad,' she whispered. 'Do you know that I love you?'

Slowly he lifted his head and looked into her face, his wet eyes blurry, the scrawny bird-like red folds of his neck stretched up. Fearing her affection might trigger his self-pity she tried another tact. 'I see you're reading *Hamlet* again. Does it still end the same?'

He turned away. 'Yes. It's always the same. But still a mystery. Same as my own life.'

How did Hamlet end again? She wondered. A lot of dead people on the stage. She tried to find a joke to make of it, but he cut her off. 'What is a man if all he does is sleep and eat,' he said, staring with that one yellow eye. It was not a question, but she tried to find an answer anyway. Not fast enough. He plunged on.

'I did not do what I might have done when I had cause and will and means and strength to do it.'

'Dad,' she said, 'You've had a good long life. You've lived. Look at all you wrote and published. You've had a great life.' And thought but did not add, *You just have to realize that it's over* – a fact that seemed to her ghastly and unreasonable for any human being to have to accept.

'No.' He shook his head. 'To be great is not to stir without great cause. I did think my cause was great. I really thought it was. The Danish social democracy. Do you know how hard I worked for it?'

'Of course you did,' she said, though she could not particularly remember his being involved in social democratic politics. 'And what you did mattered.'

219

'Ha. I fattened pigs to fatten myself and fattened myself for maggots.'

'Oh, Dad, you are so unhappy. It breaks my heart. What can I do for you?'

'You want to do something for me?' he asked, and the faintness of his voice frightened her. 'Will you do something for me?'

She touched the forearm that clung to the trapeze. 'If I can.'

'Will you laugh?'

'Laugh?'

'Yeah. Laugh.'

'Laugh? At what?'

'At whatever. At anything. Laugh at me. Just laugh.'

'Laugh at you?'

'Do I have to explain everything!'

She bowed her face toward his crumpled stained sheets, saw his bare scrawny thigh where the covers had lifted from it. She could see the tube running from his catheter to a half full plastic bag suspended on the bedframe and felt a burst of air snicker through her nostrils, a flat mean tone in her throat.

His voice was barely audible. 'No no *no*, not sarcastic. Merry. I want to hear your merry laughter. Your voice is so beautiful in laughter. My only daughter.'

She had to close her eyes, lift her shoulders, searching for something she could not fake, an emotion this smell, this bed, this room could not call forth, and yet that scrawny yellow chicken bone of thigh, that plastic tube running from the fork between his legs, it had so pained her to see, to wash, when she had changed his diaper, that rumpled sheet and wizened chest that she remembered on the beach when she was a girl, full and matted with red curls, it all reached into her own breast, her throat, she remembered the one time in a whole childhood he had spanked her, shouting, 'That's it, I've tried everything and there's nothing left, you have to get across my knee,' and his hopeless attempt to smack her bottom had produced not tears but laughter, as he yelled in rage, 'She's *laughing!* The child is *laughing!*' and her mother intervened indignantly, 'The poor girl is hysterical!' But even as a child she knew she had not been laughing out of hysteria or fear. She laughed because it was so foolishly funny, so absurd, the whole spectacle, and now she threw back her head and laughter rolled from her throat.

'No,' he whispered. 'You have to smile. You have to smile when you laugh. Show me your beautiful smile. Laugh! Smile, my little darling!'

And she sat there on the grey plastic-cushioned chair, amidst four white walls, grey Copenhagen light slanting in across his scrawny leg, his taut tendoned arm gripping the trapeze, his withered chest, and she felt the laughter grow from its first few false notes to a chuckle that blazed out through her open smiling mouth. And she saw his terrified eyes and grinning toothless face, the wolflike peaks of the four corner-teeth jutting up from his gums, 'Yes yes, laugh, like that, like when you were a little girl, *my* little girl, laugh, my girl, laugh!'

In the hall by the elevator bank, she leaned against the wall, her face in her palm and felt the silent tears against her fingers, thinking, *How fucked, how fucked it is, how fucked it all is.*

The elevator doors bumped open, and she stepped in, wiping the corners of her eyes with the heel of her palm. She stared at the button for her mother's floor, sighed, pressed it and rode up, blowing her nose into a scrap of paper napkin she found in the pocket of her jacket.

34

Rain-haunted days

Nardo laid his pen down on the desk and rubbed his eyes, looked at the yellow pad, its pale blue lines filled with the coils of black inked words, the opened red-bound dictionaries, the pile of business documents to one side. He earned far more money here translating than he could ever have hoped to earn teaching at home. It amazed him that companies would pay him so well to translate such meaningless words. Management babble. Personnel newsletters. Who would read these words? Who would find anything of value in them?

He drew his chair away from the desk and opened the door to his little balcony, turned the chair around and folded his arms across the back. The lake watched him with its multitude of glittering eyes. The swans floating past looked up at him. People out for a stroll watched him with the backs of their heads just as when he sat in the café to read he was watched by the Kashmiri, the dessert counter, the many colored rows of bottles, the strangers at tables drinking their coffee and waters.

The sadness of these past rain-haunted days swelled in his heart, and still he had not seen her again. Perhaps it was fortunate, for he could not bear the unhappiness of his desire, the story he had shared with her, the taste of smoked cheese from her fork, the memory of their dance. He remembered now the taverns of Valparaiso when he was a boy, doors along a dark street behind which women danced, into which passers-by were drawn, sailors, lonely men. To dance the tango, they thought in those days, was the best use of a whore, the closest thing to sharing with a woman you had to pay, even if the sharing was of sorrow. Nardo could not imagine using a woman in that way now, could not imagine paying for a touch, a false smile, could not imagine such a charade of affection, passion. To dance with a stranger as he had done as a boy. Even his wife he saw now had been a stranger, though her memory was still a wound – no, a scar where a wound had been. Where wife and child had been was now but an unfeeling scar.

He remembered the steep stairways of the city where they had met, how a man could perch there on the face of a cliff and hear the grumbling voice of the earth that could swallow houses, people, cars, buildings. Somewhere there now his wife and son were swallowed, *desparecido*, though not by natural forces. Or was it natural? All things human. What would this Michela know of that? What could it possibly mean to her, a woman from this flat low land of blond hair and blue eyes and Danish smiles? What could there ever be between them?

You are not even a man. You will never again be a man to a woman.

But he remembered the morsel of cheese from her fork, the taste of it, and 'No,' he said aloud and closed his eyes, listened instead for Thorkild Kristensen's voice, felt the Dane's strong hand gripping his as he wept on the floor of his office and saw that Thorkild's eyes were wet, too. When he saw that, he knew what had happened held meaning, that it was true.

'I don't want to go back there again now, doctor.'

'I think maybe you don't have to, Nardo. I think maybe you're finished there. Now I think it is time for you to find and follow your desires. You are a free man.' He lifted his hands upward

224

and smiled. 'The sky is the limit,' he said in English. 'Whatever you want.'

And what was it he wanted? What was it even to desire? Had he learned anything in his years?

A blackbird whistled in the damp, light evening, *una canción despesperada.*

And what held him back now, what kept him indoors with a nearly empty kitchen, a ghost at his own window? The unthinking behavior of a foolish young man. His own foolish response. Last time he was out walking on North Free-Harbor Street, Nardo saw a little basement cheese shop and thought of Michela, the delicious morsel of smoked cheese she had fed him on the tip of her own fork. He had the name of the cheese written on a scrap of paper folded into his wallet, written by her own hand.

In the shop he had stood in line at the counter, the paper in his palm, and when it was his turn, he said, '*Rooka os?*'

A young Danish man beside him, wearing the white overalls of a workman, laughed loudly. 'Listen here now, comrade,' he said to Nardo. '*Rygeost*. Try it again now, *rygeost*, come on.'

Nardo began to tremble. *Leave me alone*, he thought, and without warning anger rose more quickly than he could stop it, fury.

'Come on,' the young man said, putting on a show for the amusement of the other customers, moving his hands as though he were conducting a choir. 'Give it a try. *Ryg-e ost.*'

'Give this a try,' Nardo said in Spanish. 'Stick it in your ass!' And saw, in the instant before he fled, barged out without his cheese, in the surprise on the young man's face that he had not meant any harm.

A stupid, inappropriate response. Yet it haunted him. Does every word I say in this language put me on exhibit as a fool? To be condescended to by every village idiot! But it was nothing, he knew it; thoughtless. The young man no doubt thought that because he found it humorous, Nardo surely must as well. Have I lost all control? And in his mind he heard the voice of Thorkild Kristensen: 'Learn from it, Nardo. Try again. Otherwise you'll never get to taste that cheese again!'

He closed the balcony door, washed his face, knotted a necktie at his throat, donned his beret and with his jacket over his shoulder, he went down to cross the lake. And the tremor of fear he felt with the bridge beneath his feet was not disagreeable.

35

Blithe vacancy

From the hallway outside her mother's room, Michela could hear the humming. *'Grand Amour'* mixed with strains of *'La Mer'*: Somewhere/Beyond the sea/My love/Waits there for me . . . She could see from where she stood her mother's vacant eyes staring into the mirror at her own reflection, a vague smile on her face, that incessant melody. What great love did the old woman remember? Could that year she spent in Paris as a seventeen-year old have been a year of great love left behind? It was so difficult to believe. Did she come home to meet her father with a lost and secret love in her heart, hidden from the man she would marry a year later, hidden for the remainder of her life, a great love briefly tasted that never could be?

Or was she singing now about the great love she never even glimpsed, only yearned for, never tasted, never saw the hope of, so she settled for a man she never really loved? Or was what she felt for her father, the life they knew together precisely what was meant by the word love, precisely the reality of a lifetime's love. Is that where it all led? From meeting to desire to passion to acquaintance to estrangement again, a worse estrangement?

Michela considered the fact that her mother had stopped her from having a year in Paris when she herself was a girl, would not allow, would not support it. Why? To protect her from some pain of love her mother had experienced there?

Love, she thought. Had she herself ever loved? Truly? Ever felt a great love? A love beyond all else, beyond all others, all calculations, perceptions, all balancing of pros and cons? Or was it all just a coupling with phantoms? Had she ever loved? Was there truly such a thing? Or was it just romantic drivel? Myth? At best, a lifelong complex of emotion shared with an intimate stranger you were bound to by a mix of contempt and need and familiarity. She remembered once seeing an interview with some American writer on television; the interviewer said to him, 'You must love writing more than anything in your life.'

'Oh, no,' he said. 'A writer has got to *hate* writing, the way a man hates his wife.'

Somehow it was her mother she found most difficult to visit now. This blithe vacancy, this ceaseless humming about the great love that never was – or had been and was never revealed and was now lost in the vanishing mind of the fading light which once was a woman in love, or almost a woman in love, or a woman who had imagined a love never known? And who did not even now have a mind capable of recalling it.

Why go in? she thought. The woman was happier alone, floating on the ceaseless melody that filled what was left of her brain. Or in the company of Kragh. Her father's rival. Michela smiled at the thought, but ruefully, fleetingly, understanding her father's pain and anger even as she smiled at it.

It had been five days since Michela had been here, five days since she had been to work, five days since her break with Voss. Five days she had stayed indoors, stomach cramped against a pillow, curtains drawn.

She tried to read but could not, tried phoning Helle to talk but hung up as soon as she heard her friend's voice, switched on the TV and almost immediately switched it off again.

Whatever it was she had felt for Voss was finished, vanished.

What had she felt? The wish for love? Is that all it was? All it could be? That and physical desire, and what exactly was physical desire? What started in her body and sparked an urgency in her mind, a blindness of some sort that eclipsed thought.

How could she wish to love such a foolish young man who had such confidence in the value of his name, of his education, of his title as a jurist, and who was so weak?

Perhaps she was unfair to him. He was a boy still, and she was old enough, had seen enough of life that she should be a woman now, adult. She had no right to try to reach back into another person's youth as though she could recreate lost years of her own life in the years of his, in his foolish boyish confidence and, yes, his illusion of love for her, his game of desire. It was not love, it was hardly even desire. She did not know what it was, but it certainly was not what she had hoped for, had always hoped for, settling first for Mads, then, almost, for Voss.

If there was not something greater than that, she wanted nothing, would rather be alone.

She thought about the story the man Nardo had told her, about the angels. How it had chastened her, put her foolishness to shame with its power, its dignity. There are things in the world that matter, she thought. Things that do matter. Things that are serious.

It reminded her of a poem she had read once, by Halfdan Rasmussen, and she rummaged through her books until she found it:

> My fear is not of torture
> Or the body's natural fall,
> Not the bore of foreign rifle
> Not the hatred on the wall,
> Nor the night that from the skies
> Pain's last explosion falls –
> But the blindness of indifference
> That is deaf to mercy's call.

Hugging the pillow to her stomach each morning after stopping the alarm clock, she heard children in the courtyard, a young family leaving for work, the bustle of last minutes after breakfast, cozy bickering at the curb by the car before its doors smacked shut and they drove off to their day.

Perhaps that was love, perhaps that's all it was.

She dozed, woke to the sound of the old couple from upstairs with whom she sometimes chatted in the hall and whose children never visited them. The old couple always asked about her parents, praised her devotion to her mother and father.

'Every parent should be so fortunate to have such a daughter. So sweet. So pretty and kind. You make us believe in goodness.'

They left flowers at her door sometimes, came with small gifts, a cake, fruit, and occasionally she invited them in for a glass of wine, such lovely noble old people.

'What a beautiful marriage you have,' she said once, and they were silent for a moment.

'We have been fortunate in that way,' the old woman said.
'If not in others,' said the old man and chuckled and did not mention the disappointment of the children who had moved away and all but forgotten them.

Why? Did their love and concern for one another exclude the children somehow? Or was this too a sham – their love for one another, just a facade, as they perceived her devotion to her own parents as love, while she felt it as little more than duty, little more than an instinct that had her do what seemed had to be done?

On the fifth day she decided it was time to visit her parents again. For whatever reason. Something within moved her to go to them. Is it because I've never grown up myself? Will always be a daughter, never a woman? Is that why I lost Mads? Why Ria could not survive? Why I hoped to hide myself in the illusory devotion and desire of Voss's immaturity?

Michela looked into the doorway of her mother's room. The man in the striped bathrobe, Herr Kragh, was standing behind her, reaching down on either side of her head to run his long fingers up through the white hair. Michela could see her mother's face in the mirror, eyes closed placidly, a smile on her thin lips, humming that tune. She could see Herr Kragh's face, too, beaming with delight, mouth and teeth parted in a large open smile.

She turned from the doorway; saw the blond nurse watching her.

The nurse nodded encouragement at Michela's retreat.

PART IV

Forgiveness

'*Act well your part, there the honor lies.*'

EDGAR LEE MASTERS

36

Almost like a bird that knows

When she saw him there she almost fled, back into the rain, but he had already seen her and his eyes were so full of welcome she could not find it in her to turn from him. She smiled, gave a little wave, shook water from her jacket and hung it on back of a chair two tables from his and ordered a glass of wine and an ice water from the Kashmiri barman.

The man, Nardo, sat with a book open on the table in front of him, the same book with the red cover, but he was not looking into it. He was looking at her with glistening eyes that embarrassed her.

Break this silence. 'What is the significance of your grey beret?'

'The significance?' He smiled. 'To keep my head dry.'

'But it is not raining in here.'

With a sweep of his hand he removed the beret from his head, and she hoped he hadn't thought her critical. 'Still with your angels?' she asked, nodding toward his book and thought she saw hurt on his face, remembering the intensity of the story he had told her, knowing suddenly with a certainty what she had already half-suspected: that the story he had told was his own. The recognition startled her. She did not know what to say.

Then he asked, 'How is your friend? The young man.'

So, she thought. Even he sees it. The *young* man! 'I don't know,' she said. 'I haven't seen him.'

Nardo registered the information with his gaze. 'You were close?'

She shrugged as the Kashmiri served her wine. 'You are well?' the barman asked her, apparently wanting to get into the act himself. Suddenly she felt like a woman on the loose, a subject of attention.

'No complaints,' she said and remembered she would have to return to work in the morning. 'Other than work.'

The Kashmiri's pouchy eyes took her in. 'Work,' he said with a thick smile, 'is a blessing.'

'Oh,' she said. 'I forgot.'

'Are you another spoiled young European?'

'I used to be young, but I don't think I've ever been spoiled. So far anyway.'

He laughed, and she still felt the other man's eyes on her, Nardo. She wanted to ask about his story, about the real story, but didn't dare. She wished he would join her, but he remained where he was.

'May I see?' she asked, reaching across the empty table between them toward his book, receiving it where his finger held it open. Her eye swept down the page:

> *She was walking with the casual air of a pensive lilly,*
> *almost like a bird that knows it's about to be born . . .*
> *Yes, yes! My life was to be, was already a loosened*
> > *shore . . .*
> *But you, awakening, drowned me in your eyes . . .*
> *Then I confirmed that walls are broken with sighs*
> *and that some doors to the sea are opened with words.*

She drew in breath, an inhalated affirmation, but she could

not speak; her throat was too thick. Her eyes filled with foolish tears that embarrassed her, and she closed the book, passed it back across the empty table. She swallowed twice, sipped her wine; then she lit a cigarette and offered one across to him. He took it, held it, unlit, between his fingers.

'Thank you,' he said, and the sound of his voice, soft and deep in his throat, made her feel something she did not want to feel. It was too impossibly soon after the foolishness with Voss.

'From the face of a certain woman shines hope,' said Nardo.

Now she would defend herself. 'You have a way with words it seems,' she said. 'Are you a poet yourself?'

His eyes went dull. 'No.'

'Have I offended you?'

'No. No. I am not a poet. I was a teacher. Now I am a translator. All I can do here.'

'Do you translate poetry?'

'Hardly. Who would pay me for this? I translate the business documents. The pay is infinitely better.'

Outside, dusk gathered in the wet green leaves beside the lake. The dull milky blue of the sky was one with the color of the lake, and she could not bear not to ask the question pressing up within her.

'Why did they do those things to you?'

So. She had understood. He shrugged, his uppper lip protruding wetly, and said nothing.

'But there must be a reason.'

'You mean what did I do to draw their attention? To anger them?'

She nodded, shrugged her shoulders in quiet insistence, waiting.

He cleared his throat, reached for her box of matches and lit the cigarette she had given him. He smoked it without inhaling.

'You don't actually smoke, do you?' she said when he had not spoken for some time.

'This cigarette,' he said and drew smoke into his mouth again, puffed it out. 'This cigarette was a gift from you. I am enjoying it.'

237

Now she wanted to retreat again. It was too intense. She looked to the door, trying to prepare a graceful exit and saw Voss at the window in his black leather coat, staring in at her, his hair slick with rain. Her breath caught. She turned away. Hopeless. What is wrong with me? What am I doing? From wrong to wrong. Only two swallows remained in her wine glass. She had not paid yet. She would ask the waiter to order a taxi so she didn't have to confront Voss out there. She glanced to the window again. He was gone. Out of sight at least. Or had she only imagined him there? Her fingers were trembling and she was about to ask for the bill when Nardo said, 'I told some children about a poet.'

'Excuse me?'

'I told some children about a poet who sang dangerous songs.'

'Songs? Dangerous?'

'Songs dangerous enough to get me noticed. To earn a place on the *lista negra*. Songs that called the eyes of the world to human misery. Families who had nothing to eat and were thrown in jail on behalf of men whose families had enough to eat for ten people, garments for a dozen, servants to ease their unused muscles and soft aching feet.' He trimmed the cigarette against the rim of the ashtray. 'Our police hunted for the songs of these poets who sang of such impoverishment. The poets were captured but not their songs. For a song, once it is let loose in the air, can only be captured by one person at a time and cannot be stopped for there are not ever enough policemen, will never be enough policemen or enough soldiers to stop a song. Even all the money of all the rich cannot stop a song from reaching the ears of those who will hear it. If only one person hears it and learns it, others will, too, and others again. And they will teach the songs to others. But they stopped the teachers, too. Yes. In some cases very efficiently. The teeth of a panther are not so cruel as human beings. Nothing is that cruel.'

'You were teaching these songs to the children?'

'I was a teacher. My job was to teach them.'

'Did you know? That teaching those poems would . . . get you into trouble?'

He smiled ruefully. 'I did not think anything would happen just for teaching a poem. I didn't think. Now I think. So they won.'

'How did they find out?'

'The usual ways. A pupil who is moved by the poem says something at home. A parent complains. The principal called me in one day. He asked if I had told the pupils that the poet Domingo Gómez Rojas had been tortured by the police and went mad and died in a dungeon. I told him yes, I had, and he asked me why. I said because it was so. He asked me what good such informations did for the pupils.' Nardo twisted out the last fire of his cigarette. 'What good it did? I do not know. Do you know? I don't think you have such songs here. Not anymore. Perhaps once. I don't know. Perhaps there are no dangerous songs in this part of the world anymore. And perhaps that is a good thing. Perhaps there is no need of them. Or perhaps the dangerous songs now are ones you do not recognize because they offend you, because they sound *wrong*. Who am I to say? Your country has given me shelter. In some countries today, you know, the big developed countries, you lose your job if you teach that the world was not made by God in seven days. I have even heard that in America, in the universities, a professor can be fired for looking with pleasure at the body of a woman student.' He laughed, and the sound was shrill in his own ears. 'Is crazy.'

'Would you recite me one of his poems?' she asked.

'Whose?'

'The poet you mentioned. What was his name? Dominigo something?'

'Domingo Gómez Rojas. There is no meaning here for that. I would rather recite Matthew Arnold.'

'Arnold?'

'Do you not know the poem "Dover Beach"?'

'Perhaps. I don't remember.'

He studied her. 'May I say to you something? Do not be ashamed to say you do not know something. For a person to e-say *I do not know* require wisdom.'

'Still it can be embarrassing.'

'No embarrasing. Now I recite "Dover Beach" for you. My mother teach me to remember it in English, and I say it to myself many times when I am in the prison. This poem is written so long time ago. Is written almost same time as the building where I now live was built, 1880, only few years before. I like to think this poem when I look at the water on the lake. You want me to say it for you?'

'Yes, please.'

' "The Sea is calm tonight.
   The tide is full, the moon lies fair
   Upon the straits; on the French coast the light
   Gleams and is gone; the cliffs of England stand
   Glimmering and vast, out in the tranquil bay.
   Come to the window, sweet is the night-air!
   Only, from the long line of spray
   Where the sea meets the moon-blanched land,
   Listen! You hear the grating roar
   Of pebbles which the waves draw back, and fling,
   At their return, up the high strand,
   Begin, and cease, and then again begin,
   With tremulous cadence slow, and bring
   The eternal note of sadness in.

   Sophocles long ago
   Heard it on the Aegean, and it brought
   Into his mind the turbid ebb and flow
   Of human misery; we
   Find also in the sound a thought,
   Hearing it by this distant northern sea.

   The Sea of Faith
   Was once, too, at the full, and round earth's shore
   Lay like the folds of a bright girdle furled.
   But now I only hear

Its melancholy, long, withdrawing roar,
Retreating to the breath
Of the night-wind, down the vast edges drear
And naked shingles of the world.

Ah, love, let us be true
to one another! for the world which seems
to lie before us like a land of dreams,
So various, so beautiful, so new
Hath really neither joy, nor love, nor light,
Nor certitude, nor peace, nor help for pain;
And we are here as on a darkling plain
Swept with confused alarms of struggle and flight,
Where ignorant armies clash by night . . ." '

She looked at him, admired the clarity of pronounciation; watched him exhale.

'You like this poem?' he asked. 'It has meaning for you?'

'I do like it. I don't know so much about understanding. But yes, it has meaning for me. I can feel it.'

'This poem says to me about the loss of all faith except for one. That two people can be true in their love. I remember this poem and I remember once I hear a professor here in the university say this poem is, how you say, "elitist". That it have no interest more for the popular people. I say that is giving up. Every person can know this poem. This poem has save my mind.'

37

Green shadows on a damp evening in summer

It was late. Past midnight. He sat alone at his table watching the water and the sky, observing the faint tremors in the hollow of his body, of his limbs.

He removed the paper from his shirt pocket – a small sheet torn from her diary – and unfolded it on the pale wooden surface of the table. She had doubled it and doubled it again, and now he undid the work that he had watched with fascination her fingers do, and he read what she had written there in her careful hand: eight digits and a name. He smoothed it out on the table-top, read the name, the numbers.

'May I call you?' he had asked when she requested the Kashmiri barman to phone for a taxi, was gathering her things to leave. The question, he could hear, was blurted, slightly breathless, and she looked at him for a moment, then opened her purse, removed a small book with a pattern on the cover of multi-colored butterflies – green, red, purple, blue, with eyes in their wings. She tore out a page and wrote her name, her number, carefully: Michela Ibsen and eight digits. Folded the ragged-edged sheet carefully, twice, and handed it to him.

'That would be nice,' she said.

Now he lifted the unfolded paper from the table and watched it tremble between his fingers. He reached for a pen and copied the name and number inside the back of his Alberti so that he would have it written in two places.

A duck laughed somewhere beneath the trees along the lake. Such dark green. *Green shadows on a damp evening in summer.* He thought of Baudelaire, saw floating past in shadow the neck of a great white swan that questioned him. Lonely swan, alone on the water at night: where is your mate?

He whispered aloud in French, 'The supreme and unique pleasure of love lies in the certainty that one is doing evil,' closed his fist and bowed his face against it, smelling the flesh of his fingers, and heard the ragged shallow sound of breath in his lungs.

38

Melancholy, long, withdrawing roar

She knew she should not sit up tonight. She had to go to work in the morning. It was time to return to the world, and she should be rested. But she had no wish to sleep. She felt a febrile energy driving at her to *do* something. She had opened a bottle of wine, smoked many cigarettes, paced the room pulling books from her shelves, searching for the poems she used to love and had neglected for so long, like forgotten friends who might no longer open their hearts to her. Michael Strunge and Pia Tafdrup, Jørgen Sonne, Jørgen Gustava Brandt, Henrik Nordbrandt, Dan Turrell. She had half a dozen volumes open on the table and could not stay with any one poem or poet long enough to read it through, she wanted to read them all at once, as though she had been starving and admitted to a feast, but could not settle to anything, only to taste this and that and something else, unable to digest.

And the question that always nagged at her reappeared: What were these things for really? Of what use were they? *Love let us be true to one another* . . . That anyway was something she had understood. Or was it only the sound of his voice speaking that she understood, like the sound of a voice praying? She thought of him in that prison, hearing that poem repeated again and again in his brain. And she thought of the thing he had told her: Not to fear saying I do not know.

But God! she thought. There is so much I do not know.

Then she came upon her old gymnasium anthology of British verse and located the poem he had recited by Matthew Arnold and that calmed her. She read it through, slowly, contemplating the lines that she could, reading the footnotes of others, trying to open to the meaning, the sound. *The sea of faith was once too at the full . . . Love, let us be true to one another . . .* She read it aloud for herself and felt in its melancholy, long, withdrawing roar a stillness at the center of her heart.

She sat back on the sofa, smoking, and wished she had asked for his telephone number, too, then was glad she had not for she was not certain she could have resisted phoning him now if she had the number, and it was much too soon for her to pitch herself into such a thing. You cannot just continue going on from one thing to another like this. She had been foolish, wreckless, with Voss. And how could she have hitched her own wrecklessness to his, following him in something so truly foreign to her. White fever, Pia Tafdrup called it. White fever and the dark language. But not *her* language, not *her* fever –Voss's, his ungrown heart, his stunted soul.

She had to find her own way now. It was too soon to love again. If she had ever loved at all. That word again. Was it anything at all beyond a word? A wish? Retreat? A shadow to hide in?

Am I anyone at all? Am I nothing but a response to a man's desire for me? Am I nothing in and of myself?

She sighed, closed the book and set it down on the coffee table with a hollow thump.

The telephone rang. The sound elated and terrified her. How could he know she would so badly want him to call already? And how dare he call at this hour? What intentions could he have to do so? To think she would allow it? Did he think she was desperate? A whore? Yet she *did* want to speak to him, *did* want him to want to contact her immediately. So why resist? She *was* awake. Why put on airs? Why pretend?

She caught it on the fourth ring, gauged her voice. 'Hello?' she said very quietly.

'Is it to torture me?' Voss.

She hung up.

It rang again.

'You're with *him*, aren't you?'

'Can't you see what a fool you are making of yourself, Voss?'

'Then I'll be a fool. A fool for love. I'd be a worse fool to lose you out of fear of looking foolish.'

'Voss. Grow up. I'm hanging up now. And if the phone rings again I'll just unplug it. So give up.'

It did not ring again that night.

39

Angels and visitations

Trees silhouetted against the yellow sky. She stood with him on the bridge in the cool evening. The water of the lake ran in the breeze like a river, a gleaming metallic blue. They had walked round the lake together at his suggestion. He had phoned her.

'I have to be home no later than 10.30,' she said so that he would know not to expect more than a stroll, an hour or two of talk. Whether or not, in time, there would be more she did not know, did not want to know. Whatever meaning this might have, or not have, depended upon the construction of borders behind which she could for once in her life wait and make up her mind in peace.

So far so good. It was as though the truth consisted in their walk around the lake. They moved at an easy pace, told each other a little bit about themselves. He asked a few questions, and she found herself candid about her marriage, her daughter, her parents.

'Your daughter is how old?' he asked, and she realized she had not been clear. In any event he had not understood. 'She died when she was just seventeen.' After a moment she added, 'She took her life.' She heard the statement in her own ears, a simple

249

formality. The words achieved a distance that seemed to her to lift to a level that might begin to release her, as though these facts might now begin to join the flow of the past and move away, downstream, in time.

From the corner of her eye she saw his hand lift. It touched her arm, once, and drew back. His palm warm on the bare skin of her forearm. Only for an instant.

They walked a while in silence beneath the trees. The swans and ducks had retired for the night. There were only the dark green trees, gleaming water, sky, the occasional hushed gabble of a bird. They had nearly completed the circuit of the lake when his fingers took her elbow, squeezed gently. His gaze was fixed toward the shadowy pathway ahead, and he stopped walking.

'Look!' he whispered. She whispered, too. 'What is it? You're frightening me.'

'No, how you say? A fowx.'

Then she saw it there. Grey in the moonlight, shiny, then red beneath the light of a path lamp, slipping away up the slope. 'A fox. Haven't you seen any before? There are lots of them in Copenhagen.'

'Is the first time for me to see this here,' he said, smiling, and his boyish excitement touched her.

The Café Noir was just ahead, and he asked, 'Shall we have a coffee before we say goodnight?' his voice so unassuming.

'I'll never sleep if I have coffee now.'

'Tea perhaps? Or chocolate?'

'Well all right,' she said, and they moved toward the café only to find it was already closed.

He gestured across to the row houses at the end of the bridge. 'I live just there. We could have tea at my window.'

'Oh! In the Potato Row houses?'

'Potato houses?'

'You must know they are called the "Potato Row" houses – they were built for the workers in the late nineteenth-century, built like potatoes are planted, in rows. They're very sought after. You're fortunate to live there.'

'Come see how I am living then. For a tea.'

She waited before replying. 'That would be nice,' she said. 'Just a cup. But it is important that you do not misunderstand."

'Please,' he said and laid his palm on his chest. 'I am no misunderstand. I am no danger. It is only for the cup of tea. It would be pleasant for me to have a visitor. The first.'

Upstairs, she was startled by the number of windows, the view of the lake. You could not see the road unless you stood by a window and looked directly down. It was as though they were suspended over the lake.

'This must have been expensive,' she said.

'No espensive. A friend help me find it.' One more kind thought of Thorkild Kristensen.

'And you've never seen a fox from all these windows?'

'Never,' he said. 'I never see. Now I look.'

'They're considered a nuisance.'

'A beautiful nuisance,' he said with a smile that for an instant made her wish he would kiss her. Instead she touched his hand and turned away. Beneath the path lamps she saw a large unleashed dog trotting along, hump-backed, snouting through the grass, its master 30 meters behind. 'That's what I don't like,' she said.

'You no like dogs?'

'I like dogs, I mean I like dogs, but I don't like people who let them run unleashed. My daughter was bitten once, when she was very little. And when I was a child one of my girlfriends was attacked, horribly.'

He nodded, eyes distant. 'My dog, our dog was shot.' He cleared his throat. 'When the police come for me the second time, my little dog bark at the police. Very angry. The policeman laugh. Then he take out his pistol and . . .' He looked at her. 'I shall make tea.'

He boiled water, and they sat in the light of a dim yellow lamp by the white wainscotting, and the tranquil beauty of the moving, gleaming lake surface calmed her. She did not want to think about the little glimpse he had given her of the life he had left behind. She noticed, too, that his Danish wavered, sometimes it

251

was close to fluent, then suddenly grew heavy and awkward. She wondered if he was nervous. She peeled open the envelope of a teabag. It was from Bewley's. 'Have you been to Dublin?' she asked.

'Yes. I have to see the place where James Joyce would no longer live in, but spend his whole life to construc in word.' His face was side-lit in the lamplight, shadowed on one side, so his eyes seemed deep, and she hoped he could not see on her face that she had no idea what he was talking about. The name he mentioned was only vaguely famliar to her. I do not know, she thought.

'And the country of my mother,' he added. 'Even if she never see it for 50 years. Beautiful country . . .'

'Your mother is Irish?'

'But we speak Spanish together. She read to me in Spanish the great poets.'

'Except that one you recited in English. Matthew Arnold.'

He beamed. 'Yes!'

Michela said nothing for a time, and the silence grew uneasy in her. 'You should have candles to light with such a view,' she said then.

'I shall buy some. For next time. If you will come again.'

She lifted the bag from the steaming water on her teaspoon, wrapped the string around it to squeeze the last flavor from the bag, stirred in sugar. 'Do you mind if I smoke?'

'Please.'

In the shadows by the far wall she saw shelves of books, wondered what they were, but did not want to ask in case she knew none of them and appeared ignorant. *I do not know.* She felt stupid and wanted to leave as soon as possible not to be exposed. But the fear made her angry. She knew things, too. About Danish poetry.

'You have been to Dublin, too?' he asked.

'No. I only recognized the tea. I had an aunt who drank it.' It occurred to her then, it had been her Aunt Ida – who had also taken her own life. What would he think of that?

'You have read something of Joyce?'

'A little perhaps, no. I'm not certain. In school. I . . . don't know. Would you put on some music?'

He rose and she watched him go to the stereo and select a CD, hoping she would recognize what he put on, but she didn't. It was slow, ponderous music, unlike anything she had ever heard, almost like the music of some strange film, grinding deeply, escalating so it filled the room, then suddenly dropping, replaced by the light ringing of a triangle, then again the deep ponderous grinding. And although it was foreign to her, it seemed the perfect music for this view, this light, for the hour.

'Is this music from your country?' she asked.

'No, from Finland. Rautavaara. It is called "Angels and Visitations".'

'Angels again,' she said, and the teasing lightness of her voice seemed inappropriate in her own ears. 'It's beautiful.'

'You like?'

'Very much.' And she did, and felt less stupid. 'Would you write his name down for me?'

'I will copy it for you on a tape. This symphony was inspired by the writings of the Austrian poet, Rainer Maria Rilke, who spoke of the power of angels, of the fear of engaging them, which reminded Rautavaara of a dream he have many time when he was a child, where some force visit him, try to visit him when he lay in bed at night to sleep. And he resisted. He was terrified. In the symphony you hear that terror, and in a little while it become more intenser, and finally you hear a man scream. It is the scream of a surrender. He give up to the angel. I think it is a moment of transformation that is brought about by a meeting between human consciousness and some alien reality. Perhas the divine reality."

As he spoke she noticed his language became finer again. She looked at the paintings on the wall above his sofa, floating bodiless figures, dark eyes that stared out, and she chuckled self-consciously. 'I think you are frightening me.'

His eyes started, then calmed. 'Why? There is nothing here to be frightened. The fear is without grounds. These powers are enormous and beautiful in their enormity. There is nothing so small and so frightening as human beings in the smallness of their evil. In divinity there is no evil. Even the divine destruction is a creation. Not like the destruction of resentment and envy, the hatred for intelligence, spiritual leprosy. That is Unamuno who say these thing. Like the destruction of a man who bragged he fired two bullets in the ass of Lorca because he was a queer."

'Who?'

'Lorca. The Spanish poet. Very beautiful.'

The music lifted now to a crescendo of horns, warped plucked strings, frantic violins, a rhythmic cacaphony, kettle drums, climaxing in a human scream, the scream Nardo had predicted, the scream of a man surrendering to a power that has overtaken him. She felt her eyes open wide at that moment and she shivered.

In the quiet that followed she lit another cigarette and watched Nardo. His eyes were lowered to the raw wood table, his lips joined, protruding. His face might have been a mask in its stillness, its cryptic repose. She wished now that she had left earlier, that she had not come, that she had not exposed herself to the possibility of this moment turning ugly. She did not know how to leave.

Finally she asked, 'Do you have family? Brothers? Sisters?'

'I have one brother who die before he has a name. My sister disappeared. I have cousins, several. They left Chile when Allende was elected. And returned when Pinochet took over. They thought him a great man.'

He spoke so neutrally she could barely read his meaning, though she knew enough about Pinochet to catch the drift. She knew that terrible things had happened there, but hadn't it been long ago? When she was only a child. Or was it more recent? She wondered now how old Nardo might be. 50 perhaps? Not so old. Or maybe he was younger, aged by what he had gone through.

'Do you have a wife and children there?'

'A wife and son. They are gone, like my sister. People disappeared.'

It was too much to offer comfort for. She wanted to be away.

She did not want to ask more, did not want to know more. She glanced again at the paintings on the wall, the large dark staring eyes without a face, and waited for a moment that would allow her to say that it was late, that she must be going.

'I am sorry,' he said then.

'For what?'

'You are a woman. I have not acted like a man. I have been alone for very long.'

'You have nothing to apologize for. I came here for a cup of tea and nothing more. In Denmark a woman can visit a man like this. I hope there was no misunderstanding.'

'Of course no,' he said.

'It is late now. I must go.'

'Of course,' he said, and she could not see if the short taut line of his mouth was set in pain or anger. At the door she said, 'Your Danish is really very good. And you speak such a beautiful English, too.'

His brow lifted. 'You think this?'

'I do.'

'Sometimes I cannot to say the simplest of things in any language spoken in this land. I do not to know the word or the arrangement they must have. Thank you for making me not to espeak only Danis. That I may shift. We meet on the neutral ground.'

'But you must learn more Danish,' she said and smiled. 'You will be more comfortable when you have the language. And even if we speak like throat disease, we have poetry too. We have poets.'

'But I would,' he said eagerly. 'I wish to. Then I can speak only Danis with you. Will you not tell to me some names of the Danis poets to read? We read some Danis poet in my language school. I would to know more of them. We can to learn each other.'

40

From A to B

In the cup of her palm she held the glittering little treasure he had given her at the door, had placed into her hand with a self-ironic smile. A thing to win a child with really, but somehow it had moved her, in the same way he had touched her with his words about the cigarette she gave him. *Because you gave to me this cigarette, I am enjoying it.*

The summer dusk had finally settled on the city, a faintly glowing yellow darkness in the sky above the dark row houses of Webersgade, itself illuminated by strange, other-worldly yellow-copper light of the street lamps suspended on cables high above. There was little traffic but she waited at Silver Square for the light to turn green, as Danes will do, traffic or not. And beneath the streetlamp she peered into her palm at the sweet he had pressed into it. A hard sweet wrapped in transparent blue cellophane with a darker blue border and the word *Hartmint* printed over a red heart. The wrapper crinkled in her fingers as she unfolded it and slipped the mint between her lips, pressed it between her tongue and palate to sweeten her saliva. She smoothed the crinkling glittering paper in her fingers and the sound made her recall as a

257

child how attractive such a wrapper seemed, how amazing and valuable such a simple, insignificant thing had seemed, how marvellous the sound it made in her fingers.

The light changed and she crossed East Farimags Street, passed the corner of dark Stockholms Street, walking more quickly on the long empty sidewalk of the boulevard alongside the now darkened National Museum of Art toward Brandes Place. The cellophane between her fingers, the sweetness melting on her tongue was a charm against fear, against the shadows of the long broad road that opened at the dark mouth of the King's Garden.

Yet she worked to hold her natural enthusiasm in check, the excitement, which struggled to replace her caution, her determination now to be herself alone for a time, to resist the desire to find life in a man rather than in herself. But the memory of Nardo's angels bringing him to summer, the humility of his request to bring him to Danish poetry – as if *she* were a teacher – touched her. But what did *she* know really? Something. She knew something. She was not stupid. She had lived, she had read some things, and even if she did not know so much, she believed that poetry was in the heart, and there was nothing wrong with her heart. Yet all the emotion and hope roused by the time she had spent with him seemed now split into two: her desire for a man, for *him*, standing against the need to find herself alone first. And somewhere at the heart of it her fearful question: Why do men hit me? And with that question the memory of Voss in his black jacket peering into the café window at her and then disappearing. Or did she imagine it? And with that the memory of a story a girl at the office had told the other day at lunch time, about one of her best friends the weekend before who had been napping on the big bed with her children and woke as her husband came in and pulled her off the bed by her ankles, dragged her across the floor and down the stairs while her two small sons watched, eyes and mouths wide with terror. Next day, when the husband was at work she marshalled her friends to help empty the house; each of the kids carried out a caged hamster, the youngest saying, *We have to get them away or Daddy will beat them and they didn't do anything.* As if *she* had done something that could merit what he had done to her! Yet there was more to the story. The girl put her things in storage and moved in with the two boys to her parents' tiny apartment until she could find a place of their own; but next day she went forward with her appointment for an operation to have her breasts enlarged from an A to a B cup with the 30 thousand crowns she had saved up – even if she didn't have money for the beds they needed for the new apartment.

Nothing is simple to understand, Michela thought, and the thought was troubling because it complicated her own question: Why do men hit me? She tried to simplify it by considering the fact that only two had hit her, Mads and Voss. No other man had ever hit her. She'd had other boyfriends. None had ever hit her. Was that why she lost interest in them? No, she refused to believe that. Not even her father had hit her, except for that one spanking which had been a joke really, a laughing matter. And Voss had only hit her the one time, and she had given better than she got.

But was it over? He kept phoning, sometimes on his belly, sometimes on his hind legs. And he did something strange. It must have been he, who else could it have been? He mailed an envelope to her, a sealed envelope. There was no return address and nothing inside the envelope, and foolish and meaningless as it seemed, it had frightened her. What did it mean? She could not prove *he* had sent it, but who else could it be? And even if she could prove it, who could she complain to? She would sound mad. *He sent me an empty envelope and I am frightened.* She was sure she recognized his hand in the printed address. What could it mean? Had he forgotten to put the letter in the envelope? Or was it someone else? No, it must have been Voss. And on the table where she sat when she had torn back the flap and shoved her fingers into the empty envelope, she found, a few minutes later, a small dark hair. Had it come out of the envelope? Was it a hair from his body? A pubic hair? Or had it already been there on the table?

She waited for the light outside the front of the museum before crossing Brandes Place as she cracked what remained of the hard sweet between her teeth and chewed it, tried smoothening out the wrapper again, but it was so wrinkled now it no longer glittered in the street light. Her legs and arms felt hollow with the thought of the envelope, of Voss peering into the café window, and a current started in her stomach as three men came out the gate of the King's Garden diagonally across. Her breath caught. She averted her eyes, praying they would not see her. They crossed the other way, against the light, and she decided not to wait for the green signal, walked swiftly across to Crown Princess Street. Her knees were trembling now, and she cursed her fear, dug into her purse with quivering fingers for her apartment keys, touched the code on the front door lock and was in the lobby.

She shouldered the door shut to hear the reassuring catch of the lock and stood there for a moment in the dark lobby, breathing deeply until her lungs settled. Then she pressed the timer light for the stairwell and began the climb to the third floor.

At each landing, before she turned to the next flight, she braced herself to come face to face with someone waiting just there, by the bannister, or on the shadowed landing above, hating the fear which strangely heightened with each confirmation that there was no one.

Of course there is no one, she thought and despised herself for her fear, for the quivering of her fingers as they worked to fit the key into the lock of the apartment door, at each false click of the key against the brass cylinder.

'Pull yourself together,' she said aloud.

'Yeah, pull yourself together,' a voice from behind said in mocking mimicry, and she heard the scrape of a shoe. She whimpered and the keys dropped from her hand as she turned to see Voss standing in his leather jacket on the landing above, peering down at her. The timer light cicked off, and she fumbled for the switch on her doorjamb to reactivate it, looked towards the stairway down as light flooded it, and her eyes scanned the tiled floor for her keys.

Voss still watched from above, made no move toward her. 'Where were you?' he asked quietly.

'None of your business.' The quavering of her voice angered her. 'Now get out of here or I'll call the police.' She wanted to kneel to find the keys, but something told her to stay upright.

'They won't come.' He began slowly down the stairs toward her.

'Stay away or I'll scream. The superintendent knows all about you.'

'I'm shaking in my trousers,' he said, but stopped. 'What is it you're so afraid of? Feeling guilty? You know, I know you have a great big liberal bleeding heart and all, but I advise you to stay away from that spic. He's poison.'

'So now you're a racist. Why don't you go sign up with Pia Kjærsgaard and the National Democrats.'

'I'm no racist, but he *is* a spic. The word has a meaning, you know. I've looked into his background, and he's no innocent survivor, believe me. He's a bad guy. He wasn't tortured – he was a torturer himself, a lot of them slipped in when Pinochet stepped down. I'm worried about you. I know some people in Amsterdam who'd like to get their hands on him.'

Abruptly, then, she saw how pathetic he was, this overgrown boy with his bravado and his lies, and her fear lifted. She could only smile and the easiness of it lightened her heart. 'Go home, Voss,' she said and stooped for her keys.

He said, 'You know I sit there at night by the window with my brandy and look out into the darkness and all I see is you, *skat*.'

'Maybe you should cut back on the brandy then,' she said, looking for the key she wanted in the ring, as he took another step down. 'It's your femininity. You bring out the best and the worst in men. It's not your fault. He'll bring you nothing but misery, believe me. Where he comes from women are dirt.'

Despite herself a question rose in her mind: What if Nardo hit me? The thought was unbearable, but she said, 'Go home. There's nothing left here for you. Use your head.'

He was coming closer, slowly, as she lifted the key to the lock, willing herself to move slowly, naturally, and he was speaking, reciting, 'Love knows no virtue, no profit. It loves and forgives and suffers everything because it must. It is not our judgement that leads us when we love, not the advantages or the faults we discover that make us abandon ourselves or that turn us away. It is the sweet compelling force that drives us onward. We no longer think, feel, will. We give ourselves to it wholly so that it may carry us off, and we do not ask where.'

The key was in the cylinder now, turning the deadbolt out of its slot, and he was an arm's length from her. She cautioned herself not to hurry, not to invite attack by sudden retreat. 'Who wrote that?' she asked, feigning an amused tone of voice. The door was open. She could see from the edge of smugness to his smile that he had not seen through her guile.

'An . . . Austrian writer,' he said. 'Guess.'

She leaped inside and slammed the door, twisted the deadbolt and gulped for breath.

The door trembled as he slammed at it from outside with the flat of his hands. 'You deceitful treacherous bitch! You're a whore who'd fuck anybody for a kind word!'

She spoke quietly through the door. 'Keep it up. Now I've got witnesses. Shall I call the police or do you want to go now?'

He lowered his voice. 'Michela, please, let me in. I'm going crazy, honey, we've got to talk.'

'We have nothing to talk about. *Go!*'

He slammed at the door with his shoulder so it rattled on its hinges. Then she heard the super's voice. 'We can't have this here, mac.'

'Disappear,' Voss hissed and banged the door again. 'Michela, honey, let me in, I lost my key.'

'You never had a key and you don't live here and you're not welcome,' she said loudly. 'Now leave me alone!' Through the peephole she saw the little super step closer. He stood a head shorter than Voss. 'That's it,' he said, putting his body between Voss and the door so the stairwell was behind the taller man. 'Let's go home now.'

'Oh, did *you* fuck her, too?' Voss said. 'How was she? She's got the clap you know.'

The super kept moving closer, but Voss wouldn't yield. He shoved out with the heels of his hands, and 'Oh?' the super said quietly. 'You put your hands on me?' And lunged. At once Voss's arm was twisted up behind his back and the super was marching him, whimpering and cursing, down the stairway.

Michela returned to the kitchen and filled a glass of water from the tap, which she gulped down. Then she refilled the glass with wine, hearing with mean satisfaction the echo of Voss's whimper in her mind, yet loathing it, loathing the scene she had witnessed, the ugliness of the words and her attraction to his humiliation. The wine bottle had been opened the day before and left uncorked and it tasted sour and weak. She poured a bitter snaps instead, but the doorbell rang in one sharp tone, and her hand shook; the dark liquor sloshed over the edge of the snaps glass onto the kitchen counter.

'Who is it?' Her voice was a hushed rasp.

'Peder.' The super. But she had never called him Peder.

She opened the door just wide enough to look out. 'Thank you, 'she whispered, braced for a lecture, but the little super was smiling. She noticed suddenly how deep his chest was, how thick his forearms beneath the turned up cuffs of his workshirt. 'You won't have no more trouble with superboy there no more. Just give me a call if you need help.'

'Thank you,' she said. 'Thank you and I'm sorry for this.' Then she saw the look in his eye, and how he stood his ground at the door, peering conspiratorially in over her shoulder.

'Goodnight,' she said coldly and shut the door, twisting the deadbolt, latching the chainlock, which she had never used before.

41

The Word

The initial, minuscule, informational particle of each bolt of pain
was indistinguishable from the start of ecstasy, but only for that
tiny dot of time. Immediately then it transformed to a blade of
white heat, molten ore up the arse, through the gut, and all he
had to hold his nose above the sea of brackwater that would
drown him was the trapeze his right hand clung to. The hand that
all his life had held the pen. He swallowed it. Whether he was
alone or whether someone was in the room, he swallowed the
groan, considered it a point of pride to lock it deep in his throat,
inside his chest.

Easiest was when someone was there, for then he had
someone to hide it from. Easiest of all with strangers. The little
push-face one who came with his food, if you could call it food,
but he could barely eat it anyway so what did it matter? Even the
big blond who came and greased the catheter and emptied the
bag and gave him a wash in his head and his arse. As long as he
had words left he could charm them and as long as he could
charm them he knew he was still alive.

How are we today, Mikhail? First name liberties they took. Do

I *know* you, sweetheart? But he let them. *How are YOU today, little treasure? I see I won the lottery again if you're on duty today, darling. Your big eyes give me reason to go on, dearest.*

Who was he, then? The gravedigger who could fence verbally with a prince? Not even with a prince anymore. With a bloody hospital orderly! But he had words still. As long as he had an eye to see, ears to hear, even if he sank into the dim broth of senselessness but was still awake, the words came. To express the sense of the light that slanted in from the big sky over the lake, through the slats of the blinds. The texture of the air through the open window. Words rose up in him from wherever it was words rose up from to describe these things, to describe everything, the currents of his soul. If he had a soul anymore, if he'd ever had a soul. Too late to worry about unanswered questions he'd never bothered to engage, but sometimes, increasingly, it seemed to him that existence after all might really be as simple as pictures for children – God and Satan, heaven and hell, good and evil and the thing in between he learned about in Catholic school, purgatory, where you drag your chains through the torment and fire of regret for all you thought you did right but now saw was wrong, for all you didn't or wouldn't see you needed to do and so didn't, for the theft of pleasures at the cost of others' pain or neglect, for the use you made of your talent, for its misuse, the misuse of the words. Until you were clean again, the way Isiah cleaned his lips with a burning coal. Clean? Had he ever been clean? Yes. In the beginning.

In the beginning was the word, and the word was with God and the word was God. Or was it? Truly, in the true beginning, was something wordless, and he was the vehicle, the instrument that saw it and forged words of it – the flat blue grey of light cast from the big sky, say, and he saw it, and simultaneous with the register of his eyes, his one good remaining eye, something moved somewhere at his center, his core, and lifted upward to someplace where the words took form on it like snowflakes caught on a pillar of wind, defining its shape as it lifted from your lungs to your throat, the words already there perhaps but needing your mouth to cut their shape and release them on your breath to the world. But even your own ears were involved then, listening to test the words your mouth released, to hear if they were true or false, if they succeeded in conveying the impulse started in your body or in the spirit it carried – spirit? soul? what? – by the light cast down over the lake from the sky.

Even if that most excellent canopy of air, the overhanging sky, the majestic roof fretted with golden fire began to seem nothing but foul vapors, even then, if he lost all delight in fellow men, in fellow women even, there were still words.

This was one thing about which he had no doubt, that this is what he had been made for, the thing that he could do, and he did it as he could, where he could, to fulfill ends he needed to fulfill for one reason or another, for himself, for his family, for whatever. Words were the leaves and fruit that grew from his tree to define his relationship with the world in which he lived, the water which geysered from his fountain. No, he had some will in the process, the power could be directed for various purposes, and that was why he found it easier now to deal with the strangers peopling these days – these, face it, last days of his life. Women mostly, whom he could charm with words, he knew he could, always had been able to, saw it on them, women were mad for words, with words he could undress them and lay them on the cool white sheets and spread their gorgeous limbs and fill their gorgeous hole. He saw it on them. Young, old, beautiful, homely, ugly-toothed, full-breasted. Sometimes it was so easy, too easy, sometimes he let it pass, let them slip away, and that was his morality. Let her go, Mikhail, let the lady keep her sweet for someone who will honor it truly.

He knew he stank now, sometimes even his own nose was offended by the stench. And he looked like hell, but even so, he could light their eyes, he saw it, and even that much told him he was still in force, even if only a shattered fragment of what he had been.

The strangers were the easiest. Give him a parade of nurses and sweet nurses' aides through here, and before they could gag at the stench of him, he could charm them, because one look at them and the army of his words fell to his service.

The strangers were no problem. It was the family he found it harder and harder to abide. Lise, denying his existence so she could carry on like a ridiculous tramp with that decerebrated cretin lech Kragh. Pernicious woman! Refusing to admit she recognized him as a ruse to insult him in revenge for what she no doubt saw as all the wrongs he had done her in the course of doing what he had been designed to do as the person responsible for their material circumstances. Oh he had things to account for, he knew that – taking too many barebacked chances in bed with her, thinking, 'I'll get off at Roskilde,' but he never could hold back, and there she was again, knocked up, so he had to make some dirty deal with some broken-down doctor, engineering favors to get them to make the cut that started her bleeding so she lost the thing. Of course, it hurt her! How could you have managed not to think about how it hurt her! A woman cutting a life out of her belly!

And he hid his shame, he knew it, he knew, he hid his shame in rage. The gravy plate smashed against the wall, the warmed-up dinner dumped into her bed. But she was no angel, even if the whole world thought so. Poor Lise. Poor dear Lise. Poor dear Lise could crack a man's nuts in ways no one heard or saw or dreamed.

And Michela with all her plain-dealing truths now she had the tables turned on him. He always had the power over her and now she had him down, she wasn't letting him forget. As if he hadn't deified the two of them all his life. Treated them like Goddesses, and now the tables were turned, they had him down, foot on the windpipe and press, *How's that dear? How do you like that, Mikhail, darling, dear husband, dear father?*

That's what women waited for all their life, to get the upper hand. They didn't *want* it; it didn't make them happy; they only respected a man who could keep *them* down. But they find out your weakness; they can run you by opening and shutting the honeypot. Then they find out control is not enough, they want

268

absolute power over you, and they work at it, chip chip chip. And as soon as they get you down they go for it, close the windpipe and let him beg for air, shut your gob for you with their incessant nagging and their *judgement*, and that's it. End game. The judgement in their eyes, their mouths, their lips, their probing questions questions questions, and sorry, honey, no honey tonight. Freeze you in your tracks if you were mobile at all, but now they got you on your back. Check and mate, my dear sweet *skat.*

And that's not the half of it. Bad enough with them, but then you got the system on you, too. System is all loused up. The great system he believed was the great cause of which he was a part. The great social Democracy he and all the good hearts of his generation had put their blood and sweat into building, and that was the joke. He employed his wits as a journalist to help get the tax system into place for them until finally these Goddamned nazis in disguise took over, keep the taxes, drop the services, devil take the hindmost.

We were building a great society, a truly enlightened one where everybody got a full education, the health care they needed, libraries, good roads, well-paved streets, bridges without tolls, the needy fed and sheltered, bigotry a crime, trains and buses that ran on time, taxi drivers who came at your call and leapt out to open the door for you, happy to take you where you wanted to go because they had a piece of the whole good system, too.

Illusion. Lie. Dared greatness for a bloody eggshell. Words flew up, thoughts remained below.

With his left hand he reached to the bed table for his cigarettes and lighter. He lit a Cecil, inhaled wrong and coughed, and his catheter popped out. *Goddammit!*

He got hold of the buzzer pinned to the sheet beside his pillow and pressed. See what nurse would come and play with his pencil today. He waited, dragging deeply on the Cecil, waited. The coughing fit had tired him, but he didn't dare sleep. To sleep perchance to piss. Then they'd be fussing all around him, changing sheets and dressing gown and the Goddamned shame of it. Concentrate to keep that sphincter shut!

Finally Edel came in, one of his favorites with her plump young face.

'Ah! Edel! You know you look like you're about 17 years old, darling?'

'Come on now, Mikahil.'

'True! Y'do!'

'And you smoke too much.'

'Right. Smoking kills. Well, then I'm giving the system a break.'

'How about giving me a break? You rang, *monsieur?*'

'Eh, yeah, sorry, but the thing, you know, it slipped out of my, eh, you know . . .'

'Well, we'll just get it back in place again then.'

As she turned back the sheet and clipped off a strip of white adhesive tape and went to work, he spoke to her to keep from thinking about what her hands were up to.

'You know what Holmes said, *skat?*'

'Sherlock Holmes?'

Mikhail laughed merrily. 'Could use him to solve some Danish mysteries. I'm talking about Oliver Wendell Holmes. American. He said, "With taxes you build civilization." Took an American to give it those words and that was ironic all right, a country where they live in gated communities with armed guards. You know that, Edel? They do! To protect their private fortunes. Madman at the lead, madder son of a madman bombing the whole arse-fucked world to his will, to protect the private massive fortunes of the few. And who supports him *now?* Denmark by God. Anders in the fog and George in the bush!'

'Now now, Mikhail. Be careful. You don't know who I might have voted for.'

'Do not tell me you juice-sizzle-me let that coalition of boobs dupe you?'

'Ask no questions, I'll tell no lies.'

'*Why?*' he pleaded. 'For *what?*'

She patted his cheek and smiled. 'Just to make your piss cook, sweetie.'

'So you're teasing me, right? *Right?*'

She winked. 'Sometimes I think you're best off when you're mad.' She wiggled her fingers. 'Bye bye, treasure.'

'*You!*' he called after her. 'Come back here and argue!' He could hear her laughing in the hallway. 'She really knows how to take the piss off me,' he muttered. Still he wondered, was she one of them? Tearing down what he had spent his life trying to build up.

It was a vision, a Danish vision, and where did it go wrong, then? When had it been taken over by cynical bastards, rightwing and leftwing alike?

Or did it go wrong? Or was it only himself, Mikhail Viggo Ibsen who'd gone wrong? Blind in one eye like Odin, seeing only half the light?

The war was part of it. The Germans. It did something. Brought us together and smashed us into millions of individual pieces, too. The stupid greedy Teutonic fools. March in and take a country, occupy a neighbor's house, imprison and kill the jews, the gypsies, the communists.

Right outside this window, over the lakes here, he had seen with his own eyes their planes flying in, and B52s, too, and later the British coming in formations of Mosquito fighters to take out the Gestapo headquarters in the Shell Building, and they did it, too, but they also bombed the Catholic school where his sister's little girl Birthe was in kindergarten, and they were buried in the rubble, boiled to death in the water from the firehoses and the pipes that burst so the water level rose to fill the basement of the burning school where they took shelter. 89 of them. Kids and teachers. They found Birthe in the arms of a headless nun beneath a table in the basement. Say what you will about the Catholic Church but those nuns were brave girls. 89 of them dead, nothing alongside the tragedies of today, but why the fuck can't they learn? Why is Denmark supporting powers that go in and bomb one country after another to Goddamn ass-fucked splinters. Don't they know what bombs do to people?

271

Years later, long after the occupation was history, in a serving house on Gammel Strand, a young German tourist took a chair at the table where Mikhail sat writing – where he often sat and worked toward a deadline. But the young German wanted to talk. He wanted to apologize to a Dane for the sins of his fathers. The year was perhaps 1974, and this young Bavarian-lipped breast-beater was, he told Mikhail, 26 years old, born in 1948, after the war. *Apres la guerre.* He said it in French for some damn reason.

'You see, I haf had no part for it and it shames me, the actions of my country then. Even mein own fadder who was an officer and died in battle I can haf no pride of. I feel shame of it.'

Mikhail had been moved. This young man was now a few years older than he himself had been during the occupation, and he could think of actions by himself and by others he knew, of which he was not particularly proud. Five years of biting back and swallowing fear, anger, hatred and shame does something to a man, to a people. Some even start to learn to like the taste, it becomes a natural thing. Well he had done his best not to eat it. He went where they were not, the grey-coats, and if they showed up, he left quickly and when another of his nieces, Helle, was almost killed in an anti-sabotage action, he found her in the rubble, her blue eyes shining from the soot that covered her – still alive, thank God, thank God, still alive. And only then, finally, the next to last year of the five, did he join the resistance himself, printed coded messages in his articles – obituaries and society pieces that sent news of weapon movements, sabotage targets. Yet he had already swallowed enough shame and humiliation, manipulating as best he could for some butter, for a little bit of real coffee, a bottle of cognac at Christmas time . . . So he understood shame himself, thought perhaps his long wait to have children, the many abortions, might have come from that shame, and he was moved by this young German thumping his breast for his father's misdeeds.

He might have been Mikhail's own son in years, the son Mikhail regretted never having, though he would not trade his beautiful daughter, born when Mikhail was well into his forties, for a dozen sons even if, truth be told and to his shame, he was at first disappointed. Lise must have seen the disappointment on his face. 'We'll call her Michela,' she said. 'After her father.' Nice gesture. Poor Lise. It was not always the way it is now.

And he would not trade his daughter for a dozen sons.

'You could have been *my* son in years,' he said to the young German and ordered a beer for him, an Easter brew, for it was April – a little irony there for that had been the month of the occupation, nearly 35 years before, and the month of resurrection, too – resurrection of the earth, the cycle of the egg. Strong beer to heal a wound. They filled their glasses, and Mikhail did what he would not have believed he would ever do. He lifted his glass of Easter brew to a German, in April no less, and spoke the words his heart dictated to his throat, his mouth: 'Here's to friendship, then, young friend, and to healing. *Skål.*'

They presented their glasses, nodded formally, drank deeply, presented the glasses again, and so help him God the little kraut said, 'Ah, the Danish beer. Is goot. But the Cherman beer is the *best* in der *worlt!*'

Mikhail laughed, then as now a furious laughter, which stoked another bolt of white hot pain that started at his bumhole so he gripped the trapeze and felt the bulging of his eyes, of the veins in his head, of the inarticulate groan strangling in his throat. His good eye looked in desperation to his nightstand for the ketogan he tried always not to take so he could add to the stockpile he was saving for his own final solution should that moment come, so *he* could choose the moment, so *he* could decide. But while the prick of death fucked him up the arse, he could only stare helplessly from his one bulging good eye at the pills in their plastic bubble and try to measure the duration of the attack, but even that he could not manage.

He only knew at some point that he no longer felt anything, and he remembered Michela's joke about death as the absence of pain, and with that memory realized that the pain finally had blotted out all consciousness for however long it had lasted. He could see no change in the light over the lake, but the days were so long now he might have been gone for minutes or tens of minutes or longer.

Now, however, there was peace for whatever time it chose to remain with him, until the arse fucking started up again, and he reached with his almost useless left arm for the two ketogan and fisted them into the metal box inside the nightstand where he kept the hoard of his private final solution, his own to take if and when he chose. For he was determined the last decision would be his and not a decision nudged across the table at him by some hospital administrator like a luger to an SS officer.

The State had stripped him of everything, but would be denied the right to strip him of his life. Free up a bed, save resources from being squandered on a dead end. I am 86 years old, cancer eat my eyes. I have survived all the indignity you delivered, and *I* will decide when I shit my last!

If he still had the power to write, he would write it all. One last chronicle about the final lying indignity heaped upon a man who had devoted a major portion of his power to building this system.

It had always been his plan to work until he dropped, and that plan was reinforced by the time he was 65 and realized that the pittance offered by the State in retirement would never support Lise and himself in anything but a notch above poverty. It was a lie. There was no security. The money was spent. Collected and spent.

Finally, when he was 74, he had been ready to take a real retirement, had built up a private fund to make it possible to live a life of reasonable comfort for his last years – and nothing grand mind you, just reasonable comfort, he didn't even have a house, they lived in a rented flat, or a summer house either, or even a Goddamned colony bungalow, or even a car. He had some cash, and he invested the cash in secure bonds, and it was finally possible. But they smelled it and gobbled it up.

He had a letter from the tax authorities, signed by one Felix Kissmyer and one Birthe Sternlieb, 'proposing' that they come to have a look at the private office whose expenses he had been deducting from his income and to 'review' the receipts and records of his expenditures and income for the preceding six years.

The comedy team of Felix and Birthe appeared at ten in the morning on a Monday, equipped with blurry photocopies of paragraphs of relevant legislation and decisions taken by high instances about deduction claims and regulations. They came with a tape measure and measured his 'office' and each room of his dwelling to determine what percentage of the whole his 'office' constituted. When they pronounced the word 'office', he could hear the inverted commas in which it was couched. They called Mikhail by his given name. He called them nothing. He did, by reflex, against his wish not to, help Birthe Sternleib off with her Persian lamb wintercoat and showed her to his books and his files, and he showed Felix Kissmyer – a long-jawed, emaciated, living example of the proverbial anal triad (detail, regulations, economy) – to an easy chair to which he delicately lowered his protruding butt and said, 'I am a realist, Mikhail. I believe that no matter what form our documentation might take, it all comes from the realistic impulse. I am from Århus and have a well-nourished skepticism for the anti-realistic documentation I have sadly witnessed flourishing amongst inner Copenhageners.' He paused, looked around the walls of the apartment. 'Such a wealth of art you have on your walls!' he exclaimed.

'Hm,' said Mikhail.

'I note,' said Felix Kissmyer, adjusting his bottom on the cushion, 'that you have said nothing about the art.' And duly made a note in a spiral notepad that he extracted from behind the pen-holster in the breast pocket of his striped shirt. 'I note further that you and your wife Lise are not the sole tenants here.'

'My daughter is also on the lease.'

'She doesn't actually live here, does she, Mikhail?' said Felix Kissmyer.

Mikhail allowed silence to be his reply.

'Smart,' said Felix Kissmyer, by which clearly he meant a combination of 'sneaky' and 'stupidly obvious'. 'So even though she does not live here, even though her actual public registry address is elsewhere, she will – if there are no regulations prohibiting it – have someplace nice to live one day, a lovely old Patrician rent-controlled dwelling of . . ." He consulted his note pad. ". . .190 square meters floorspace. When you folks, so to speak, *fall away* – as, of course, everyone does do one day. You know, Mikhail, not everyone has the good fortune to live in such a beautiful and very reasonably-priced dwelling. The tax department is in fact currently looking into possible legislative regulations that might take this into consideration. A very low rent on a large abode is, in a very real sense, as much like income as, say, a company car or company telephone. Eminently tax-worthy, I would think.'

Mikhail's heartbeat began slowly to accelerate. Caught in a bureaucratic clamp. Impaled on a technicality. If Kafka doesn't come to the Castle, let the Castle come to Kafka.

And contrary to his resolve to utter no word that was not absolutely necessary, said, 'I have worked for over 50 years and paid taxes for over 50 years . . .'

'Everyone pays taxes.'

'I have never taken welfare. I have paid unemployment insurance and never was unemployed for a day.'

'What you pay for is the insurance, the peace of mind of being insured.'

'I have paid into the system and have taken out nothing in these 50 years.'

'Of course you took out. You took out public subsidies on transport, health care, education for your daughter . . . But you were fortunate as well that the system employed you all your life. Not everyone is that fortunate.'

Then he told Felix Kissmyer a story about a woman he knew who had with her husband owned and operated a small dry-cleaning establishment. Her husband was called in for an audit one day and informed that his income for the past six years had been re-assessed and that he owed 150 thousand crowns in back taxes.

'That's only 25 thousand a year,' said Felix Kissmyer, 'a hairline over two thousand a month. It sounds to me as though he wasn't even fined. He might have been, you know.'

'No, but he dropped dead on the spot,' said Mikhail, locking eyes with the taxman. 'Right on the tax-office desk.'

'That's sad,' said Felix Kissmyer. 'For all concerned I'm certain it was a trauma. Certainly for the investigator as well.'

'Could be,' Mikhail said with evil glee, warming to his tale, 'but the investigator visited the man's widow next day and presented *her* with the bill. Next day.'

They sat for what seemed a long time without speaking, during which Mikhail meditated the facts that he had been incredibly stupid to tell that story about the dry-cleaner couple and that Birthe Sternleib – who wore, in contrast to his own Lise's blue woolen overcoat, Persian lamb against the cold – was now stripping and raping his books and his files, and that he would keep his resolution to offer these oppressors no refreshment, which was in blatant opposition to his hospitable nature: not a beer, not a cup of coffee, not a cheese sandwich, not a glass of juice-sizzle-me luke-warm tap water!

Two hours later, bearing between them a sealed cardboard carton containing his books and files for the past six years for which he had been requested to sign a receipt, a carbon copy of which was provided to him, they told him that he would be receiving a letter and said, '*Tak for idag.*' Thanks for today.

'Hm,' said Mikhail and shut the door behind them, resisting the urge to smack it for, as some poet once said, the door is rarely to blame in such cases.

The letter arrived two weeks later. Virtually nothing was allowed, although he had the right of appeal. If he appealed, of course, Michela would most likely lose her right to take over this rent-controlled apartment when he and Lise had shuffled off, and the contract on his elegant, rent-controlled apartment was all he had of a life-time's effort to bequeath her – that and his modest 'fortune' (as it was called in taxman language), but given the extent of the decision to disallow, his 'fortune' would become an even more ludicrous candidate to be categorized as such. Furthermore, the fate of those who appealed was well known. If an appeal was won, firstly, contrary to all other juridical actions, all court costs were born by the appealer; secondly, though this was not written into the law, it was common practice, the tax authorities would take a special, detailed interest in the triumphant appealer's income tax returns in future for all the years of his or her life.

They took slightly more than half of the 900 thousand crowns he had stashed away to supplement the base-line state pension he was entitled to – no supplementary retirement payments would be forthcoming due to the fact that he still was in possession of a 'fortune'.

The other half of the 'fortune' came to the attention of his bank advisor, who sat in an office overlooking the Western Gate train terminal.

'Ibsen,' the portly advisor, slightly more than half of Mikhail's age, said – unlike the emaciated taxman Felix Kissmyer, the bankman accorded him the courtesy of addressing him by his surname rather than his given name. 'Ibsen,' he said. 'It makes no sense having all that money sitting in short-term bonds.'

'*All that money?*' repeated Mikhail incredulously, ironically. 'I don't even have a lousy half million crowns to show for my whole juice-sizzle-me life!'

'No, but you could have a tax deduction that would considerably enhance what you do have.'

'I am not allowed to deduct anything.'

'What I am about to propose, you would be allowed to deduct. Believe me. I guarantee it. You can deduct ten per cent of the capital per year, each and every year, for ten years without even touching the capital. Figure it out. That means you get your money tax-free before you even touch it.'

'It's already tax-free. That is net money.'

'Earning nothing.'

'It's in bonds.'

'Virtually nothing. When you calculate inflation. Look here . . .'

He produced a chart, followed lines from one column to another with the retracted tip of his ballpoint pen. 'A ten year retrospective of that money in short-term bonds shows it would have earned two per cent. That hardly matches inflation. What you have is a virtual *negative* investment. Project it ten years in the future under the plan I am proposing and you will see a profit of . . .' The retracted pen point traversed the page of columns. '. . . eight per cent. That's a profit difference of 400 per cent!'

'Ten years from now? I'm 74 years old.'

'And strong as a Jutland farmer. You have a choice. Eat your capital now or let the tax department finance a fat dividend for you and *then:* collect your capital, too. You don't even have to wait ten years. Ten is optimal, but you can take it in five. If you start eating your capital now it will be gone in five years.' He patted his portly tummy. 'Men of appetite need fuel. Furthermore, under the plan I am proposing, in the event that you should *fall away* – and let's face it, we are all going to fall away someday – the money will be there for your daughter, who will inherit everything remaining in the account, minus of course 40 per cent for the state.'

The portly bankman also had a female advisor, one Gretchen Deepdale, who had sparkling blue eyes and a pale blond moustache and sideburns. 'You know the proverb that says, You can't exhale with a mouthful of flour? Well with this investment, you can do both.' Her eyes glittered at him above the firm set of her palely bearded lips.

'Ibsen,' said the portly bankman. 'You can have your cake and eat it, too.'

'Well, I am, was, always have been, always will be, to the end of my days, an asshole,' said Mikhail aloud now as he clutched his trapeze and gazed through his single eye out upon the waters of the lake which was the same color as the cloudless sky. As above, so below, he thought.

He signed the bank papers which locked up his cash – from everybody that is, except the taxman. The plan worked as the portly bankman and the palely bearded lips of Gretchen

Deepdale had promised – except that they had not factored in that within three years it would be discovered that his intestines were an intricate roadmap of cancerous cells, simultaneous with the increasing exhibition of his sweet little Lise's now undeniable and increasingly progressive decerebration. Call it Alzheimer's, call it dementia, call it senile or presenile dementia, call it her second childhood, whatever, her consciousness was in rapid decay.

With the pulling of the last few strings Mikhail had available to him, the authorities provided him and Lise with these relatively comfortable but tiny two rooms in the same sheltered old-age dwelling – in return for which they confiscated his remaining 'fortune' which no one would have known anything about had his portly bankman and Gretchen Deepdale not proposed their strategic investment. Apparently it was locked away from everyone but the taxman whose long slender fingers could fit supplely through the eye of any lock known to the Great Social Democratic Kingdom of Denmark.

And that is when he realized they were all after him all along – the social democrats, the socialists, the national democrats, the conservatives, the left party (which was right), the whole rainbow fan of hungry political parties stuffing their hands in. All of them, his employers, his wife, his child, the newspapers he wrote for, the Queen, the Prince Consort, the Crown Prince and his girlfriend, Copenhagen electric and water authorities, the women he had occasionally danced a side-swing with, the telephone company, all had a single aim manifested via a variety of techniques – to drain him, to keep him from his job as a man of finding pleasure in existence, the pleasure of work, of women, of drink, of fat, smoked eels on dark rye bread with scrambled egg and chives and well-aged cheese that reeked of the sour beauty of life itself accompanied by cold pilsner and a Swedish portion of iced snaps followed by a lungful of good, hot, tasty smoke from a green Cecil and the supreme joy of a blank sheet of paper and fine-nibbed pen of black ink upon which and with which to describe in words these wonderful phenomena.

It was all a sham. You were a man of pleasure and not of thought even if your pleasure was coopted by words. So you had no real part at all in the play. All he had left of dignity was to stand up and face it, toe to toe, nose to nose, and never give in, *never*, to hold tight to this trapeze and keep the spirit of the breath that served what was left of his rotting body going.

Still going strong, thank you.

And he would write one more thing, one final document, a chronicle that would record all that he had learned of this treachery. All his life he had written about everything he knew and learned and experienced. He wrote about the dead and about the living, the dying and the boring and the useless and the used. He wrote to the best of his ability, such as that might be. He wrote honestly, and if he had been deceived all his life by a vision that became a lie or proved to be an illusion or was all along nothing but self-deceit, still he had written from the source of honesty as best he could see it. He had honored his talent. He was a fountain of words and if his pieces were little read, little noted, mere fillers amidst the jungle of columns and features and editorials of whatever papers would publish them, he wrote them from what best he understood to be the truth as he saw it at the time. He wrote for whoever would take what he wrote, and he wrote whatever anyone would ask him to write about for whatever they would pay, whether it was a bottle or two of wine or a thousand or more crowns or a contact he could cash in later (for the rooms he and his wife now lived in, for example – a realization that tickled a hard bark of laughter from his phlegmy throat). And his wife and his daughter and the women he sometimes slept with didn't see he was doing what he could until finally he got just a little bit ahead, and he was already too old for anyone to care about except the taxman and the portly banker who never lost interest as long as there was still a little scrawny meat to pick from the bones with their greedy pointed beaks and their long skinny legal fingers.

Now he was a member of the skeleton club and blind in one eye and near dead in one arm and his arsehole didn't even work anymore else he could shit out his words, scrawl them in crap on the bedclothes, but it was over, gone, dead, all except his chin that was still up above the surface he was sinking down into and his writing hand that clung to the trapeze and kept him up above the shitpool of his life into which, unless the water came to him, he would not sink one second before he – HE – decided to.

Down below where Satan waited to laugh in his face with an evil grin and get him down by the neck.

And that was the catch. Does the light just go out? Or is there more? And if so, what?

In the drawer of his nightstand, along with the cache of ketogan he could not decide whether to use, were a legal pad and six finely sharpened number-three yellow pencils with which he could yet write his final chronicle, telling it all, *I will tell all,* all that he had finally learned, right to now and the moment of his death.

And there was the catch.

To write it he would have to let go of the trapeze.

42

La Doloroso

Brazilian jazz on the CD player – a CD they purchased from a man they'd listened to earlier in the day at Krut's Karport. Lars Albertsen was his name, and he told them the mouthpiece of his tenor sax had once belonged to Ben Webster. Visible above the top of his shirt pocket was the blue edge of a city bus pass – no pampered rich boy here – as he played a dreamy melody, the valves of the sax squeaking faintly with his improvisations. He smoked while he played, resting his cigarette in the curve of his sax – 'That's what the guard on the C note is really for,' he said and proceeded to blow a stream of notes that danced Michela's soul in its unexpected changes, lifting, spinning, dropping her.

During one number she had watched a yellow bus drive past on Øster Farimagsgade, could hear its motor and the sound of its airbrakes against the background of his tenor sax and the rhythm of bass and drums and the combination seemed blessed to her, sitting there with Nardo at a corner table, sipping red wine, watching his face, eyes closed, serene. What demons of memory resting behind the gentle curve of his lids, this man who had been in the company of angels? Then he opened his eyes, and she said, 'I was watching you.'

'I know this,' Nardo said. 'And I was essunning my face in the warm of your eyes.'

Lars Albertsen's tenor sax played a melody whose words were about love and dreaming, dreaming and love, and she was no longer even trying to resist any of it. She sipped her wine, sad to hear the musicians finish, but happy. 'We'll be right here again tomorrow,' Lars Albertsen said. 'Hope you will, too. When Stan gets in your eyes!'

'Now comes *La Doloroso*,' said Nardo.

'That sounds sad.'

'Thee bill,' he said with a smile.

Now she watched the leaves on the chestnut trees down below his window, trembling in time to the melodic stream of notes from the CD and the rippling glint of light on the lake surface while Nardo sat barefoot in shirt and slacks in the wooden chair by the window, across the coffee table from her. His face was bowed into his palms, as though he were praying, though she feared he was fighting shame at the failure of his body their first time together.

He had not wanted her to see him naked, drew the curtains over the bedroom window and undressed himself, and as her hands explored his body in the dim light she understood why, as the tips of her fingers found the lumps and hollows and bands and swirls of scar tissue. He winced with each discovery, and she whispered, 'Are they still painful?'

'Painful? No. Only shameful. It is almost more worse.' And he lay staring at the ceiling. 'I think I should to like one of your cigarettes now,' he said and what the words told her was, *Stop trying please. You are wasting your time. Do not kiss me or try to excite me.*

She lit two cigarettes and put one of them between his lips, remembering having seen this done in some old American film, remembering how erotic it had seemed to her – such a contrast to this reality. She could not see his eyes in the dim light, saw only shadowed hollows, but she tried to imagine them. It was important to know if they glittered with pain or smoldered or were flat and still. She considered things to say to him, ways to challenge him from this mood that had immobilized him, but she didn't dare to speak for the words of challenge that suggested themselves seemed so brazen against the horror of what he had known.

For some reason, watching Nardo on his back, blue smoke drifting from his mouth, the echo of the knobs of scars still throbbing against her fingertips, she found herself thinking of a neighbor of the country house her parents had rented a couple of summers and Easters. His name was Flemming and he was hunch-backed, with only one leg, and he seemed an old old man to her at ten, though probably he was only in his 20s. She could see from his eyes and his mouth when he looked at her and from the kindness of his manner that he loved her so. He lived next door in a year-round house with his mother, and one Easter when they came for the long weekend, he showed her how he planted tomato seeds in a window box and told her that when she came back in a few months for the summer, they would have grown to vines with small tomatoes on them. And she remembered; when she came back, she went right to his door, and he knew immediately what she was there to see and led her right to them. Perfect tiny tomatoes on the vines. They stood close together admiring them. Michela could feel the warmth of his body, could smell the unusual sweetness of him as his palm shyly touched the crown of her hair – only once – never again, though she wished he had done it once more, more firmly.

He died young, poor man, so young. Next time they came back, he was gone, just gone. Flemming dead and the mother moved away, the house empty, closed, its windows like empty eyes as she stood on the dirt path outside and looked at it.

Sorrow hung heavy in her stomach now remembering, and there seemed some lesson in the memory, though what that might be she did not know – other, perhaps, than to believe in goodness, to nourish it as one can, to hold it gently.

She excused herself and went to the little water closet alongside Nardo's kitchen. As she was about to sit, she saw trickles of blood down the curve of the porcelain. He had been in here before they made their way to the bedroom. She peered closely at it. It was blood for sure, and the water, too, was tinted red. *What have they done to you, Bernardo?* She wanted to go back to him and wrap her arms and legs around his body so he could feel her breasts and her breath and the warmth of her sex against him, so he could know she cared for him no matter what.

But he was already up, dressed, sitting in the wood armchair by the living-room window where she could not sit beside him. She went to him anyway, began to lower herself to her knees, but he waved her off with a turn of his wrist.

'Please, do not kneel to me,' he whispered.

The CD was on repeat. Lars Albertsen was playing 'Desafinado' again.

'Esslightly out of tune,' said Nardo.

'Excuse me?'

'Esslightly out of, how you say, tune? *Desafinado*. It is to mean esslightly out of tune. In Portuguese.' His smile was tart.

'Are you . . . injured?' she asked. 'Are you bleeding? Inside you?'

His response was the smallest of laughs, a tiny chuckle of breath out a rounded mouth, almost no sound at all.

'What did they do to you, Nardo? Why are you bleeding inside?'

'Just a little thumping. A keedney massage they say it calls.' His mouth tightened instantly, became small. She noticed that his language was worse again, both his Danish and his English – it seemed that some confusion took hold of his mind at certain moments and disrupted his grasp of words. She leaned toward him from the other side of the pine coffee table and whispered, 'Don't close. You mustn't close to me. Please.' She was grateful they were speaking mostly English so she had that word. *Please. Por favor.* There was not really a word for it in Danish, only syntactical and tonal expressions, which hardly really carried plea. Danes did not like to beg.

He lowered his face.

She waited, and she did not know if she waited in vain, if he had already relocked a door that would never open again. Why? Because his prick had misbehaved? Such nonsense. Men are so vain! Her impatience almost found words until she remembered who he was, what he had been through, what they might have done to him physically that was far worse than suggested by the mildness of his words.

'It doesn't matter, you know,' she said. 'To me. Whatever it is, whatever is wrong. I care for you.'

He did not answer, did not move for so long that her gaze wandered to the window, the walls, his pictures hanging there in the reddening light of summer evening. Strange figures that seemed to suggest disembodied souls. It occurred to her that the man who had painted those images must have seen them in his mind, in his dreams perhaps, in pictures; animations, that lifted from within the dark beneath consciousness to become visible, to request existence in the light of day, to deliver themselves to the artist's brush – all beyond words, beyond language. She thought of the word 'insight' and it seemed to have a marvellous new level of meaning. The sight within.

Then it occurred to her that Nardo had taken the trouble to acquire and hang these pictures. That he lived here surrounded by them. Perhaps they were a way to find him. She looked from the one to the other, settled on a picture of a huge golden fish swimming in yellow light filtering through a green jungle, as though it were flying through the air, or swimming through the light. Its beauty filled her eyes, warming her. 'I like your fish,' she said. 'Who painted it?'

'A poor fool.'

'But it's fantastic.'

'Precizely. Fantastic. Fish only swim with the current. Only fish swim with the current.'

'Not that one.'

He lifted his face but looked straight ahead. 'Precizely. This is why this fish is doomed. My father always tell me, only fish swim with the current. Has he been a fish he might still live.'

'You live.'

Slight rapid nods of his head, and his gaze blank, he said, 'Lived. To know he was true.'

Confused, she waited. Then, 'Your father?'

Now he turned his face to her, and his eyes seemed to have forgotten and only now remembered she was there, too. 'No. The one with the flat-creased nose, and ugly teeth, and the eyes of a frog. He was true when he tell me I would never be a man again.'

'You *are* a man.'

'Not in this way: *You will never be a man again for a woman.*'

'You are a man for me. You are strong. *So* strong.'

Blindly again his eyes focused on her, and she was afraid of his gaze. She was afraid suddenly of the violence smoldering there, dormant beneath the rubble of memory that buried him. But he looked away, and she was desperate to know what she should say that might save this moment, but asked herself then, Why? What did she expect to find here? What of value did she have to give him? Or would he just draw her into the pain of his own unhealing wounds? She wondered if she should go, take this small pain now to avoid a much worse one later, get away while there was time. But there seemed some unpaid debt here. Something she owed him, now that she had tugged at this door, had perhaps opened it a crack. Where could it lead? But she knew already, thought she knew, thought she saw the place it led: *Why do men hit me?* Voss: They treat women like dirt. Was this just another variation of the man she somehow had been programmed to seek? A variety of masks to allow her the sufficient self-deception until she was deeply enough entangled for them to drop the mask and let the violence show?

'We are the produce, the product of our lifes,' he said then. 'Of our esperiencies. If you had meet me twenty years ago, who would you have meet? Who would I have meet in you? Could I then have been a man enough for you? Could we have some kind of passion together? Some kind of love? You have me speaking now for you have touch me but you have see in me the man who is not there. You have open up the door upon my closet and see

288

that it is emptiness. No, perhaps more bad than that even. And I have been a fool again for I believe I have see in you a life I could live upon with.'

Abruptly he rose and began to pace the bare plank floor, moving rapidly, and she was frightened.

'But no,' he said. No, this is no possible, you see? You see this floor? You see this floor beneath my feet? You see my feet upon this floor? These these, what you call them? I do not even know what word you call them. These *plonks* . . . these planks of wood from the tree. They are 140 years old, cut from forest pine in Norway, shipped on the boats into the old western harbor of Copenhagen, Hafnia – hear? Latin name! To the timber factory that uséd to exis on Reventlows Street, a small walk from here. And they were hammered into their place in this floor before I was born, before you was born, before my father or your father was born, at the time when Matthew Arnold write his poem on Dover Beach, and the nails . . . you see these nails, these nails are make of casted metal by the men who lived then. I know this because when I cannot work and cannot sleep and cannot find the peace in my head . . .' He rapped at his skull with the knuckles of both hands so she could hear the sharpness of the sound, and she felt her own eyes open wide with fear, but with his pain, too, for like it or not, she was part of this now, of whatever he might prove to be beneath the mask of calm and indifference that was falling from his face.

'And I walk on my broken feet with concentrations so I do not limp like a cripple man to the bibliotheque to read of the history of the house in which I live to try to find a time that is older than the time which has done its work upon me. But is no good for you cannot to return to other time. Is not possible. You see they did their works so well upon me. They turn me into a chicken like that chicken that light up in naon – how you say, neon – upon the wall across the lake advertising the eggs of Irma.' He cranked his elbows like the wings of a hen and squawked – an eerie tinny sound from his throat. 'But I have got no egg, you see? I am not a man, I am a chicken, you see, but I have got no egg, you see, they turn me to a sterile chicken. No man, no woman, no nothing.' His eyes were astonished wide beneath his sweated brow, and somehow she had moved beyond fear.

'No,' she said. 'You are not a chicken, you are a man. You are a strong man. Strong. Stronger than any man I know.'

'No no no no. I was never man of violence. And I am less than this. I could no lift a fingers to defend my own self or my . . . or others. I am, and this is why I am of no use to a woman in a bed. Behind the door inside my heart there is nothing left. No violence, no passion. There is nothing. Only the little heart of a chicken."

'You are so wrong,' she said, and now she stood, too, to be taller in his eyes, to face him and make him see her and hear her, and she knew what she would say now to him because it made sense to her suddenly, Mads and Voss and the violence they let loose on her. It was not *her* weakness, it was *theirs*! It wasn't her fault, it wasn't Nardo's fault, it was the fear men had in their hearts, fear of themselves, of other men, of women who could see their fear if they did not stop them seeing with their fists.

'Do you really think a man needs to be violent?' she asked. 'Do you really believe that is what a man is? Or that it helps? There will always be someone more violent. You don't have to be violent. To add violence to the violence. You only need to be strong. You *are* strong.'

43

He won't hurt you

The sky over the lake was a miracle, a Danish miracle. The July sun was nearly down when she left him. She stood alone on the corner of East Lake Street and watched the last of its red light draining beneath the horizon of buildings to the west, above its pastel levels of pale yellow, orange, green, blue.

A great sky above our little Copenhagen, she thought, and felt pride and pleasure in her city, her land, that those who came before had not built a city which hid the sky from them as she thought had been done in some cities – New York and other places maybe. On the lake bank she could see that eerie luminesence of the light nights of northern summer. Instead of turning her back to it and going home, she crossed the road and sat on a bench along the deserted lakefront. In one direction she could see across the whole expanse of water to the dark boulevard, in the other to the still light sky, the exotic green lushness of the summer trees, the lake water ranging from a shimmering onyx on one end to a pale yellow mirror on the other and the here-again gone-again reflection of the neon signs on the faces of the buildings along the opposite embankment – a red bank sign in neon script, a yellow glass of Tuborg filling, the neon chicken, neon eggs, in their endless cycle.

Directly across was the silhouette of a solitary man walking a dog. Otherwise, nothing stirred. Even the joggers had gone home to their families, their gardens, whatever it is joggers go home to – bottles of sparkling water with tofu and TV; cool showers and 3 per cent cheese; mentolatum on tired muscles.

She felt as though she herself had run for miles, could feel in her muscles the struggle she had been through to drag herself out of her fear, to reach the other side, resisting the frightening deluge of his anger, allowing it to build up before her eyes until there was nothing left for him but to break. And she feared that, too, but knew somehow she mustn't run from it. She stood where she was, facing him across the coffee table, and when the fury reached its peak, when the anger of his voice dropped into a spiteful rage, he crouched forward across the table, hissing, 'Go away, you *puta*, you whore! I don't have anything for you!'

'No,' she said. 'I won't. Not like this.'

His crouch seemed for a moment predatory – like a panther that lowers itself to spring, and she thought she might scream, words, a plea, *Don't hit me! Please don't hit me!* She thought she had misjudged, had once again placed herself in the path of a man's violence, but instead of retreating she leaned into it, open now to whatever this moment would be, and of course then she saw the inevitable, the only place it could lead up above the broken rubbish of their lives.

His face became another mask, an ancient mask. It seemed ugly for a moment, theatrical even, but the judgement of her eyes was deceived by the raw power of its grief, at the great pain of human betrayal he had known. His mouth and eyes turned downwards, became a caricature, a Greek mask of tragedy, and the sound from his chest was awesome in its agony, in its expression of what they had done to him, the cruelty and injustice and irreversible harm they had done. The pain was not his alone, it was theirs together, a place that had waited to be discovered by what she saw now as an indefatigable wish to love.

They ended kneeling on the floor together, blubbering – that was the word some part of her consciousness had used to identify the sound. Beyond restraint or shame. To cry as a baby cries, but as an adult – perhaps as an adult can cry only once in a lifetime, with the grief a lifetime's effort is invested to deny.

Afterwards, spent, they sat together on the sofa, holding hands. No music now. Only silence and the night. The hollow sound of footsteps from the apartment above, the hum of a motor on the road below.

And still she felt that reverent silence as she sat here on the bench by the lake watching a man on the opposite bank walk his dog. She noticed the dog was rather far from the man, padding erratically from side to side along the broad dirt embankment, sniffing, peering, moving quickly ahead. It turned and headed across the transverse to where she sat, and the snout of fear began to nudge against the surface of her calm. Her instinct was to retreat before the animal got too close, to climb up the easy angle of the grass slope behind her and retreat towards home, but she did not move, only watched as the dog padded closer, the distance between it and the man increasing as its distance from her shortened.

The light on the dog's fur seemed dreamlike. It was a large animal, at least part German Shepherd, and she could see from here that instead of a collar, a bandana was knotted around its muscular neck – something she had seen on the large dogs kept by rough unemployed men because the authorities allowed a supplementary payment to those on welfare who had a large dog to feed.

It rounded the transverse now, 100 meters from her, its owner twice as far or more behind, a hulking shadowy figure walking slowly, perhaps truculently. Now it seemed too late for her to retreat, and the fear she had known all those years since the German Shepherd up in the country had attacked her friend Nette pushed up more urgently against her calm. She remembered the snarling, the flattened ears and twitching thin lips as teeth bared, the slow approach and finally the pounce and Nette's screaming, the strips of flesh torn open on her arms as she tried to use them to protect her throat. And then again, like a repetition of the nightmare, the one who bit her own little girl, Ria, the sudden flurry of attack and the blood on her child's arm as Michela kicked and kicked at it.

This dog saw her now. Its head snapped up with the recognition of her presence, and she pictured herself through its eyes, remembering in some nature program on TV having seen a representation of the imperfect images a dog's eyes perceive, greyish and unclear, more shape than detail.

Why am I just sitting here? she thought, recalling advice on handling dogs – show your height, be firm, avoid eye contact, pick up something large that the dog can see . . .

Then, when it was perhaps two or three meters from her, it lay on the ground, its deep chest flat to the dust, foreleg extended, massive head aloft, amber eyes watching her. The light of the parklamp illuminated the eyes as they watched her. Thinking what? Waiting for what? A false move? Its jaws were shut. She saw no sign of breathing. It might have been a statue, but she was all too aware of the life beating within its powerful chest. What thoughts, what images, what impulses, what reflexes lay coiled within that small skull, more snout than cranium? Want to play? Want to bite? Should she speak gently to it? Firmly?

She watched it obliquely, the two of them, two alien species, perfectly still, watching each other, perhaps equally ignorant of one another's intentions. Then suddenly the animal twitched, turned its head with a snap, twisting its flank, and began to chew at a flea beneath its ribs, and the spell of her nerves broke.

The owner approached now, a burly, bearded man, slouching along the edge of the lake.

'Evening!' he called.

'Evening.'

'He won't hurt you.'

'I know,' Michela said.

Only later, when she was crossing Brandes Place, almost home, did it occur to her that the animal might have felt some sense of what she had been through that evening with Nardo.

44

The rules of the game

The sky was yellow as the surface of the lake with a strand of red over the grey buildings to the west, and he realized he had just opened his eyes again. Sleep sometimes came as a thief, snatching his consciousness before he ever knew.

Someone stood in the doorway of his room, and he turned his good eye toward the figure. It looked like Michela, though he was not certain. Perhaps it was a nurse. He took a chance.

'So,' he growled. 'It's you, is it?' And saw then for sure by the way her head moved that it was Michela. 'Think of that. A daughter finding time for her father.'

'Is that how we have it today? Shall I leave again?'

He saw she had a plastic bag from the shop downstairs and glanced at the large illuminated green letters of the clock on his nightstand. It was well past noon, which confused him. Without thinking about it he had felt it was Sunday – somehow the light seemed to suggest it, the quality of the silence – but that shop closed at noon on Sunday. 'Isn't it Sunday?' he growled and heard in the sound of his own voice a plaintive note of fear, confusion, and saw the sound register on Michela's face which had drawn within range of his vision now, in a softening of her mouth which she immediately buried in an ironic smile. Just at the rim of consciousness he recognized in this little series of adjustments the contract they had entered into somewhere in the past, a never spoken agreement that had developed between them to conceal their love in irony, to mock sentiment for fear it might soften the crusty façade that protected them from having to share unwieldy emotion. The recognition saddened him, for there was so little time remaining between them now, yet they had not found their way around their self-imposed rules, his own rules perhaps, foisted upon her. She could touch him, but he could not touch her – thus it was up to her to touch. He could not request understanding or care as need, but must demand it, circuitously, as an ironic complaint.

'It's Saturday, Dad,' she said. 'You'll have to wait another day to go to church if that's what you were thinking about.'

'Ha! Church!' And remembered his breach some days before when he had asked right out if she thought he might go to hell. What had he been thinking of? It seemed to him at just this moment to have been *her* fault that he asked. Just as it seemed her fault that he confused the days, her and her false mother's, throwing him off balance, and he didn't like it. Didn't like her enjoyment of their turned tables. She and Lise coming down to insult him under the guise of a visit. Michela rouges her face and brings her down like some painted circus clown to insult him behind the mask of her dementia, but she knew full well, they both knew. And that flathead pervert decerebrate Kragh knew, too. Trying to seduce his own wife and coming down to brag. Danish dog! Pernicious woman! Treat me like a fool, a cuckold and a fool. Well, good luck with her, Kragh – she's cold as a bloody cod.

He cleared his throat raucously and felt the shaft of pain probing tentatively at his anus, his rectum, and opened his mouth to speak not knowing what he would say – perhaps he was responding to her denial of a request he had not even made because he was so certain she would refuse, deny him. He wanted to ask her to pack him up in a wheelchair and take him out to his favorite pub, just *once*, just once more, over to the Toga Wine Room for a strong beer and a bitter, to see the faces of the men he knew there, if any of them he knew were left, to show himself capable of sitting up and swapping stories. He wanted to ask her to let him dictate his chronicle to her, 'Last Words,' he would call it, no, 'Last Words on the State of Denmark' is what he would call it. He would use an epigraph from *Hamlet*. Marcellus? 'There is something rotten in the State of Denmark.' Too blatant. Maybe Hamlet himself on the Danish smile – 'That one can smile and be a villain.' Too portentous. Maybe just a shortening of the Marcellus – 'Rotten in Denmark'. Make a good title, that.

And in the chronicle itself, which he would compose for *Politiken*, he would refer to Buster Larsen and his TV comedy sketch from when? '80s? '70s? '60s? The bitter old man calling Denmark '*Lorteland*'. The Shit Land. Shit State. Though he wondered now if the irony would be lost, if he would seem himself to be nothing but a sour, word-spitting, ruined old dying bag of bones that stank of physical corruption. And because he could not even ask these questions according to the rules of their game – *his* rules of *his* game – and because she was unpacking from the plastic bag the things she had been so thoughtful as to bring for him – a three-pack of little bottles of Gammel Dansk, his staple bitter, two packs of green Cecils God bless her, *Ekstra Bladet* with the naked girl on page nine that never failed to please his eye and which he had never made a secret of enjoying, a delicate sugary pastry snail; a cellophane bag of salt fish licorice – because of her kindness and because he could still hear the echo of her beautiful laughter from last time – when? – and stupid old Polonius's words – no, Hamlet's mocking Polonius, 'One fair daughter and no more, the which he loved passing well.' – in embrace of all these things, he opened his mouth to open his heart, but the words he heard slurred across his toothless gums were, 'It is embarrassing how self-absorbed and selfish young people are – all the way up into their 40s. Embarrassing and astonishing.'

She had just placed the last of the items from the bag on his table and she paused, still holding the empty plastic sack, sideways to him. Her motionlessness seemed to his one-eyed regard suspended in time, outside of time. The crackled surface of his field of vision made it seem an oil painting, and he could no sooner call back his words, to try to undo them or fob them off as a joke, than he could weep or beg for her help, her kindness, her forgiveness, her affection – the affection she readily gave and he allowed himself the luxury of receiving without comment or with irony, as though it were suspect, as though it reeked of self-interest instead of being given as it was, like milk from a breast.

He thought, *Now she will leave.* She would sigh and look at him with pity and surrender and shake her head and leave. The thought tasted of the same kind of bitterness he had learned to savor as a young man during the war, the occupation, swallowing back all his anger and fear and helplessness and shame at being under the boots of the sausage-eating krauts.

But the set of her shoulders relaxed and the oil painting dissolved in movement. 'Dad,' she said. 'Don't you know that I can see right through you. I know what a bluff you are. You talk in such big letters because you feel so little and you're so afraid that someone will see it. Well *I* see it. I do see it.'

He laughed once, a bark really, meant to convey supreme irony, but in his own ear he heard it fill the room like a pitiful old man's breaking cry. He tried at once to correct the sound, conceal it with another, a sound of force, but the second time no sound at all came from his throat, only a spurt of air and in his own nostrils he could smell its foul stench – air from the pits of his cancered self. He set his gums, his jaw, and lifted his chin, face, pointed away from her, though he felt her gaze on him and did not know what it might convey. To turn his face to see seemed impossible. Her face might be a mirror of his own, of his whole existence, reflecting the pitiful helpless futility of his entire life, its sum total equalling this: a decrepit dying father helpless before his own daughter.

He heard air leave his throat again, a ragged expulsion,

wordless yet eloquent for it was an admission to himself of who he was, who he had been, who he had become, of a life of words building to inarticulation, ending in wordless air, leading to toothless silence.

He felt water spill from his good eye and dribble down his cheek. And then he heard the sound of words that had been composed somewhere beyond the reach or control of his conscious mind.

'I've done terrible things in my life,' he said and heard the soft whispering growl of his voice as if he had spoken aloud, in privacy, to himself.

'I know you have,' Michela said. 'You've hurt me, and you've hurt mother, too. Very much.'

'She's gone from me, Michela. She's *gone!* And I can't even tell her I don't know what happened. What went wrong? I can't even tell her I'm sorry. She's *gone!*'

Of all the emotions she had seen in her father's face, smug arrogance, impotence, rage, Michela could not bear to see this broken grief.

'You've been selfish, Dad,' she said. 'But you've also done good things. You've also taken care of us. And you've given us a lot of happiness, too. We've had happy times. I don't know what happened to you to make it so hard for you to show your love, but I always knew there was love there, too. Inside you! And I love you for that and for the good things you did. And the happy times we had. There were a lot of happy times, too.'

'There were!' he said eagerly. 'There were, weren't there?'

'And I forgive you,' she said, 'for the bad things you did to us.'

Now his voice was small. He turned his face to her and saw in her eyes a kindness that astounded him. For he did not understand how a daughter of his could possess such a power of kindness. He said only one word. *'Tak.'* He said it again. *'Tak.'* And, *'Tak, min pige.'* Thank you, my girl.

PART V

Grand Amour

'The wind will take me away
And I won't know my own name
And I won't be there when I wake.
Then I will sing in the silence.'

PABLO NERUDA

translation by Ilan Stavans

45

Perhaps if I killed her?

He had made mistakes. He could see that now. For one thing he had underestimated her, misgauged her natural intelligence, which he could see now was more refined than he had first supposed.

At a table in Krut's Karport, he sat sipping sugared Absinthe, jotting occasional notes on a pocket-sized pad she had once given him for no reason other than to be kind, an elegant block of unusual dimensions which fit perfectly into the side pocket of his leather jacket; there was an interesting primitive sketch of a salamander on the cover and the pages were of fine vellum.

It was just this sort of thing that caused him rue now, the memory of her small kindnesses and of his own doltish behavior. For example, when he insisted on walking out of that last Kubrick film. Granted he had not insisted she leave with him, but of course he knew her nature was such that she would be more loyal to her companion than to her own pleasure of the film.

'I thought there were some interesting things about it,' she said outside.

And instead of enquiring deeper into her view – as he realized

305

now he ought to have done (*a lesson learned*, he scribbled on the pad – *won't happen again*), he had lectured her forcefully on his own view which he assumed to be more considered, informed and, well, correct; that the film was portentously slow, laboredly symbol-mongering, and obvious.

'But we'll never know how it might have . . .'

'It had *already* failed,' he snapped. 'After 30 minutes it failed. Kubrick clearly lost his touch. The film was out of control. A waste of 30 minutes on a failure is sufficient.' And with the force of his gaze and his tone, he silenced her – though, fortunately, without, he thought now, having had to resort to the next weapon he had marshalled and ready from his armory: *Oh, did they teach you film criticism in your high school?* Or, *Oh, does a high school diploma qualify you as a film critic?*

He could feel the heat of his blush now, considering that he had nearly said that. Yet he was sure he was right about the film. She was so gullible, her taste, so . . . well, ill-informed, lower middle class. Why should he be sorry about walking out on that junk, for having the correct response. She might have learned from his action.

The jazz trio, which had been playing at Krut's and took a break at the little bar looked ready now for another set – tenor sax (or was it alto?), bass and drum. Brazilian supermarket music. Advanced elevator muzak. He might have walked out on this, too, for fear of being thought to endorse it if anyone whose opinion he cared about spotted him here – and wasn't this just the kind of junk she would find so appealing? – but he didn't care to be alone on the street just now, and he was enjoying the absinthe – Krut's own brand – which was 136 proof. It sometimes had a vaguely psychedelic effect on him, which he thought might be useful if he decided to pay Michela a visit later. He could tell her that it was under the influence of absinthe that Van Gogh cut off his ear. He pictured himself telling her that, peering into her eyes until she looked away. The reverie, however, led him to a memory of his humiliation at the hands of the midget superintendent who'd ignominiously hammer-locked him down three flights and ejected him into the street the other night.

Bitch!

He assumed it was her fault. She must have called the dwarf. Or complained to him previously. She no doubt watched his humiliation through her little fish-eye spy hole. Unexpectedly the thought gave him an erection of outrage and confusion, but an erection nonetheless, which pressed distractingly against the heavy flies of his hand-tailored leather jeans.

Oh I'll get that bitch, he thought, but the eruption of venomous emotion did not redeem him from his misery, from the pain of the love whose depths he had surveyed too late. On a fresh sheet of the pad, he wrote, *It could have been. It still might be.* And, *Make her see that I was blind but now can see.* He studied the last sentence for a time until what seemed its initial brilliance faded, revealing its utter banality. He ran his pen harshly through the words.

Just as the saxman fitted his cigarette between two valves up near the curve of the neck of the instrument and began to blow some vaguely familiar melody Voss was certain he'd heard recently on a telephone hold-line, the glass door of the café swung open and a group of people somewhere near his own age spilled in. Strange-looking people, three or four of them, including a young woman wearing a brown leather vest and leather pants with laces up the legs and a laced leather Australian bush hat. Beneath her vest she appeared to be wearing nothing. With her was a man with bushy scraggly rusty red hair and matching beard who surveyed the front tables with haughty beady black eyes as he danced past the saxman, hands up waving in the air, hips swaying. His eyes locked on Voss's and narrowed. Voss looked away, nodded amicably to the leather-vested woman who returned his nod blandly. They sat a few tables away, ordered strong beer. The third was an Asian woman, Thai perhaps, though coarse-faced, thick-bodied, and the fourth a lean muscular black man with close-cropped blond curls and fine western features that gave him a sympathetic, reasonable look. They were a striking group, unsettling in some way. Voss took advantage of the proximity of the waitress to order another double absinthe.

'No, make it a triple,' he said. It occurred to him he might befriend them and make use of them somehow. They looked like they might be into kinky sex. Perhaps he could use them to frighten Michela. Then he became aware of that thought and studied it for a time, wondering about its source. Maybe it was the absinthe. The pretty waitress measured three two-centiliter drams through the sugar spoon on top of his glass and smiled at him. He tipped her a five-crown coin. She was sweet-looking, short, maybe 35. Her hands were older than her face. Sometimes he saw her without that smile on her face, and she looked like an utterly different person, cold and harsh instead of warm and sweet. He wondered if her smile were conscious. A tool. Cynical. It was a cynical world. He wondered if he could enlist her, then wondered what he meant by the thought.

The rusty-bearded young man was doing his strange dance again to the Brazilian music, and Voss studied the man's body in movement. It was supple and lean, perhaps muscular, perhaps menacing. There was something unsettling about him, something maybe perverted which both repulsed and attracted him, and he found himself thinking once again how he might employ them to frighten Michela. Perhaps he could devise a plan to save her from them and win her back, but he was instantly startled to catch himself thinking that, at what such a thought might say about his maturity, the solidity of his emotional balance which he had always before prided himself on, his cool.

She had the shovel under him all right, did old Michela. She really had the shovel under him.

Wondering if the absinthe was thinking for him, he turned his gaze to the plate glass window to study his vision of the world. It was fifteen hours into one of the longest days of the year, the sun at a sharp angle to the earth, but the light was grey and drizzly, jacket weather, and matched his mood. It made him feel again the pain of his separation from Michela, a pain he had dwelled on so long now that he could hardly separate it from his wish to have her back. It all seemed part and parcel of itself, that he had fucked up with her, that he lost her, that he wanted her back, needed her back, that he had been humiliated by her midget superintendent right in front of her door, that she had humiliated him with Jens Vaever on the dance floor in front of all his colleagues. He thought again about how surprised he was when the little superintendant proved to be so much stronger and quicker than he was. He had planned to push the little man against the wall, bunch up his shirt at the collar and ram him against the wall, tell him, *If you don't want a bloody mouth, get lost.* He had wanted Michela to see him doing that. But suddenly his arm was twisted up in a hammer-lock or whatever you call it, and it *hurt!* And he had whimpered, all while she could have been watching through her spy hole, surely was. He wondered if it made her wet to see him hurt. The sensation this aroused was interesting. He pictured her laughing at him, pictured himself naked outside her door – what if she had thrown him out naked and watched while the super twisted his arm and laughed, opened the door, said, *Let little Voss in again, we'll give him another chance.*

He didn't want to think these things. Not about her. Not about that stupid-looking ignorant midget. One thing was the fantasies they played with, but this, this . . . Maybe she did get wet and saw it as part of the game they had started playing, which she had agreed to engage in and had then so abruptly betrayed. It was a bad business to do that to someone who opened his heart; he opened the door and she slammed it on his dick. Nothing short of betrayal when he was at his most open, most vulnerable, to turn away, abandon him. *Tell me your secrets, darling, so I can use them against you.* In truth, the whole game was her fault. That dance she did with Vaever. Did she think he was a fool? It was her sweetness combined with the fact she could have done that to him, as if she didn't realize how it would humiliate him. She was playing with him, that sweet smile combined with that dark part of her behind it.

There was a whole literature about this kind of thing. Right back to the Bible: Judith, *The Almighty Lord hath struck him and hath delivered him into the hands of a woman.* He had recorded it in the little note book along with something else he found in a Victorian novel he'd been reading, never mind which: *There is a painful joy in the unfaithfulness of the woman you love. The highest ecstasy.* And in some of the Romantics – Goethe, in Keats, *Joy's grape burst against her palate fine, gaze gaze into her peerless eyes . . .*

Suddenly he realized he had been watching a woman at the table between him and the window, a very much older woman whose raw red hands were rolling a cigarette. Her features were coarsened with age, her skin pocked by years. He thought she might be 70 or more. She reminded him of a woman from the accounting department of his company who had been employed there for 37 years and never missed a day, who smoked cigars and still addressed everyone by the formal *De* and insisted upon the same respect. Voss had taken to smoking Prince Extra Ultra Lights to honor his lingering love for Michela – it made him feel closer to her – and he tapped one out of the pack now and offered it to the woman, assuming she was rolling her own to save money, thinking it would be a treat for her.

But her raw red fingers continued their work. 'Those are like kissing your sister,' she said.

Voss laughed. He wondered if she would let him kiss her, what it would be like, having her ancient tongue in his mouth. 'May I give a drink?' he said.

'Ask again when I'm finished this one.' She nodded at the half-empty pint of classic before her. It looked flat.

'I see you're not afraid of lung cancer,' he said.

'It's all genetic, honey. I'm 78 years old, smoke 20 a day and haven't even coughed since 1980.'

'You're not 78.'

'No. I lied. I'm 79. Next month.'

'You look a lot younger than that. How old's your husband.'

'Ain't you sweet. You know what? He was ok, Verner, but he's been dead these 20 years, and it's been the time of my life.'

Michela would love this woman. Michela loved to talk to salty old people in bars, and he remembered ruefully how impatient he'd been with her when she did so.

'You on your own then, are you?' he asked.

'Why? You lookin' for a girlfriend.' She cackled and stuck her tongue between her drifted teeth.

'Stranger things have happened.'

'Hope I never get *that* strange,' she said, and they both laughed, and he saw in her blue bloodshot eyes that he could make this happen if he wanted. He pictured her in his bed. No, better himself in hers, better strategy if a quick post-coital escape was called for. He wondered about her legs, but she was wearing slacks. His gaze dropped to her sandalled feet – no, no, no! Even if her toenails were painted red, the ankles were swollen and mottled, speckled with blue-cheese veins, no!

'Do I pass inspection?' she asked, and he laughed in a manner he hoped would confirm it had all been a mere flirt and turned his attention back to the pad sweet Michela had given him. The absinthe had completely melted through the sugar cube. He added water and sipped, tilted back the glass and held the green anis liquor on his tongue, savoring the 138-proof jolt as he leafed back to the start of the pad where he had copied some notes he planned to share in some way with Michela.

Bestow your gifts on us and shed on our faces the light of your impartial cruelty, your wanton hatred, unfold above our eyes your arms laden with flowers and murders.

How beautiful it seemed to him sometimes, alone in his bed, the windowpane suffused with blue summer night, to picture her in the room, naked, her light hair, her light eyes, a great bouquet of flowers on one arm, pressed against her naked breasts, the blade of a knife gleaming in her right hand as she approached his bed smiling tenderly. The Goddess of Camus' Caligula. He pictured her saying, *I am going to hurt you a little. And I am going to give you pleasure . . .* He brought himself off with the vision, always approaching, never reaching him, his brain crazy with a deep sniff from a vial of red poppers, his own left palm smothering his face as a substitute for her blond cunt.

Which was gone from him. Gone forever.

Evigt ejes kun det tabte. Eternal possession is possible only of that which has been lost.

Perhaps if *he* killed *her.* He contemplated this for a moment. How? No blood, not one sweet drop of it. No, his thumbs at her throat, her slender throat. In theory. Theory only. Perhaps if he should tell her, write, no, no, phone, and say, 'In death our love would be eternal.' He lowered his eyelids considering how this might frighten her, but found himself more frightened by the possibility that he might lose sight of the game he was playing with himself and actually *do* it and wind up in prison at the mercy of that society of sadistic sociopaths, stories you hear about what they do to the weak prisoners. He shuddered.

No, he only wanted to frighten her a little, to see fear in her eyes instead of that maddening confidence in her voice, her manner, her eyes, when she told him it was over.

Sometimes when your dark beauty becomes too much for me, my right hand begins to swell. But he hit the wall of the thought. For her beauty was not dark. Or was it?

No, not dark, sweet, a sweetness which nurtured. As the sweet decay of fruit in the earth nurtures fertility. Nurtured rage. False bitch! You empty bitch.

You are an empty envelope. You are not worth one hair from my balls.

Sometimes, he thought, you like to talk more than I care to listen. To your vapid chatter.

Talk to me, Michela.

Sex is sacred, she said to me once, and I snapped back, No it's not, it's carnal, it's meat, you and your weepy woman novels. *The Thorn Birds.* Saw it on your shelf. Hopeless love for a priest. Give me a break. All those weepy people falling into each other's arms.

You think you're so sweet, so nice. Well you're not. You know nothing about yourself, so little. About your own dark shadow. *To keep a man it is essential to be unfaithful to him. All women have the instinct, the profound desire to take advantage of a man's love and admiration. The woman must cultivate the capacity to give herself without love, without desire, without pleasure, for in cold blood lies the possibility for the greatest advantage.*

'What's her name?'

Voss looked from the pages of the notebook. The old woman was staring at him. 'The girl who's made you so unhappy?'

Only a tiny measure of the absinthe remained in his glass. Was it his second or third triple? Or fourth? He thought for a moment he might have spoken aloud, but she said, 'I been around the block more than once. It's written all over your cutie-pie face.'

There is a painful joy in the unfaithfulness of the woman you love. The highest ecstasy.

Voss said, 'The moral of the story is this. Whoever allows himself to be whipped deserves to be whipped.'

'Oops.' She drained the few drops remaining in her beer glass. 'I think this is my stop.'

Voss worked to maintain a posture of dignity, of indifference, as he watched her thick ankles carry her swiftly through the door, watched her walk past the front plate window without glancing in at him. All the rats desert the loser, he thought. He raised a forefinger to the waitress who stood idly behind the bar, unsmiling now, but his signal lit her face again like a pushed button and salvaged a scrap of his pride. He held up three horizontal fingers and her smile brightened with comprehension and acknowledgement. Apparently his foolish flirtation with the old lady had not been noticed or judged.

As the smiling waitress measured absinthe over the sugar in the perforated spoon on the glass, his gaze wandered among the faces of the others seated around the café tables. A short thin man with choppy henna hair who he'd heard was a reporter for *Information*, a heavy smooth-faced woman hunched over her glass, elbows on the table, a very thin blond woman, hair cut tight against her skull, reading a book. His eyes lingered on her, her face so very thin he could see the bones beneath the tight radiance of her skin. His prick was hard. Then his eyes moved to the table where the strange group sat and he saw the woman in laced brown leather jeans was watching him, a small enigmatic smile on her lips. Ineffable; but was she eff-able? Her eyes were green, her lips at once slender and ripe. They parted so he saw her

313

white even teeth, and he wondered what the opening of her mouth was meant to tell him. Her eyes still watched. He lifted his glass and presented it toward her. She responded with her own glass, and he noticed her knees were parted so he could see the alluring pouch of brown leather between them. The red-bearded man turned his smirk toward Voss. Even that seemed an invitation. He lifted his finger again to the waitress and, when he had caught her eye and smile, he swept the finger across the width of their table, raised four fingers vertically. Redbeard nodded, his feet propped on the stool alongside. The girl in brown leather lowered her face slightly to look up through her lashes at him. The trio was playing its romantic pap, the saxophone doing reedy 'improvisations' no doubt memorized from somebody else's recording, labored copies of someone else's spontaneous inventions, and Voss felt confident as he stood, carried his absinthe with him, moving toward them.

Redbeard lifted his feet from the empty stool, turning it with the toe of his boot toward Voss.

46

Almost sacred

This was what Nardo had forgotten. Or perhaps he had never really experienced it before. Perhaps what he had known before was not really love but only a preliminary to love. Perhaps he had needed to live through all that came before in order to reach a place where this experience of love was possible. Or did he deceive himself? Was he drunk on the honeysuckle fragrance of requited love?

She slept beside him, snoring quietly as a cat. He did not want to disturb her sleep, but felt a need to touch her. His palm on her hip, barely touching, reaffirmed, for as long as it was there, the fact of her, body and person, the warmth from her silken skin. *That you exist is proof.*

In the dark vault of the night she is here with me, has been here with me, believed in me, opened herself to that belief, and in that opening made it possible for me to believe in myself and thus also in her. He could not deny this reality. It seemed a miracle to him that she still wanted to be with him after that last night, after he had shown her the broken face behind the mask, that she would give him another chance to be a man for her.

He felt an almost religious experience lying next to her body in the summer night. Almost sacred.

And now the meaning of the words of his tormenor took depth they could never have had before: *You will never be a man again, you will never be a man for a woman again.* Now they turned back upon themselves and made of this moment something worthier. For it is precisely what they had been in one another's arms – he had been a man for her and she a woman for him, and that was so now and could not be undone by the past and was perhaps even more so because of the past, his and hers. All mistakes, pain, stupidity, injustice, preparing them to become something new together, something more certain and genuine.

After they made love the first time, he had gone to the kitchen to get something for them to drink, and when he returned he saw Michela from behind, naked on the padded bench by her vanity table, pinning up her hair. He saw in the dim evening light, in the flicker of a single candle she had lighted on the vanity, both her back and her face and breasts reflected in the oval mirror before her, saw the graceful gutter of her spine, the curve of her hips on the stool, the start of the split between her buttocks, the delicate swirl of hair at the nape of her neck as her fingers arranged it. His breath caught, and he remembered the promise of the angels who had visited him. At that moment, in that moment, he knew once more, perhaps more fully than ever before since his childhood, the possibility of life.

In bed again the sheets had an other-worldly glow, and they lay on their sides facing each other, propped on elbows and pillows and spoke quietly, sharing a cigarette and a glass of chilled wine. There was a sadness in the moment, too, but it seemed to him a reverent sadness, stirring at the heart of the night. The true and sweet sadness of two human beings coming this close. We are alone in the envelope of our bodies – he remembered having read that sentence somewhere, but there are things that diminish our solitude, that make it possible for us to speak across the chasm between us, to reach across and touch if only for an instant, for instants at a time.

This is what he had never seen before, but could see now, and in seeing it, he thought perhaps the angels had known that this moment, too, lay before him.

There was something he had been wishing for these years in this new land. He wanted an apology. He wanted certain persons to tell him they regretted what they had done to him. He wanted to see in their eyes that they regretted and that they carried regret as the burden true regret must be. That wish now seemed less central. He remembered discussing it with Thorkild Kristensen, after they had worked through so much together, all they had done to him, the use of dogs, the mock executions, all of it, after finally he and Thorkild Kristensen had returned together to that worst of all days with the little girl and her pregnant mother – *It is up to you, Greenebag. You decide. You sign, we stop, and the little girl and her mother go free.* He signed the paper and there was even someone there, in that filthy room, to notarize it with a little round stamp and stamp pad and a signature in purple ink, and the confession was the evidence by which they continued to extend his detention.

'What do you want now?' Thorkild Kristensen asked him.

'I want an apology from them. Something I will never get.'

'Instead of thinking of them,' the doctor said, 'Think of someone you admire. Is there no one great in your world?'

'My champions are dead,' Nardo told him.

'In time maybe you will find new champions. Maybe you will see that you yourself are a champion, Nardo. You have already shown how strong you are. Stronger than most. There are few who could survive what you have survived, my friend. I do not think that I could.'

Nardo realized now that he had not one, but two champions in his world. He had Thorkild Christensen who had chosen the work of undoing the effects of that ugliness, who entered the burning rooms of their souls to drag them out into safety. And now he had her, too, Michela, who touched his broken face with love.

The second time he tried, faltering, before he could succumb to fear, she whispered, 'Just touch me. Let me touch you. We are here together. That itself is to make love.'

So he made love to her with his hands and his mouth and

317

released her passion, felt her body tense and buck as she cried out beneath him, cried out his name, and they floated down from that height, light as leaves falling. She fell asleep beside him, this beautiful woman, this kind person.

He dozed. His dreams were quiet, his sleep agreeably light. The breath of the summer night stirred the gauze curtains at her tall bedroom windows. He watched through half-closed eyes. From the street below there was laughter, loud talk, the shattering of glass. Then footsteps in the stairwell outside her door, the sound of many feet. His eyes shot open and fixed upon the white ceiling high above the bed. Perspiration wet his forehead, his lip. The footsteps stopped at her door, voices. The doorbell rang.

Nardo was in a crouch by the side of the bed, saw Michela sitting up, her face pale in the light, blond hair askew. The bell sounded again, a long buzz. Then there was a banging on the door and a voice shouting, 'Come on! Come to the door! Open up!'

'It's him, Voss,' she whispered. 'He's *drunk*. I can hear it.' She moved quickly from the bedroom, down the narrow hall to the front door. Nardo hung back, clinging to the frame of the bedroom doorway and saw her peer through the peephole. 'He has a lot of people with him,' she whispered, looking back at Nardo, and her face seemed to him a mirror reflecting a broken, useless man who crouched in the door while his woman advanced toward the danger, while she faced the intruders.

'I am confuse,' he said. Their eyes held a moment. Then she turned from him and yelled through the door, 'Go away, Voss! *Now!* Or I call the police!'

Nardo gulped in air, looked at his trembling hand.

More pounding.

'Open the door, you bitch!'

And Nardo darted back to the bedroom, heard the jangling of his belt buckle, as he stumbled getting his feet into his pantlegs, heard Michela yelling as he pinched on his shoes.

'I'm calling the police, Voss!'

'I got someone here who wants to meet you, Michela!'

'The police are coming!'

Now Nardo was back in the hall, drawing deep slow breaths. 'I shall espeak with him,' he said quietly. Michela blocked his path.

'No, don't,' she pleaded. 'It's better if you don't. He's out of control. There are people with him I don't know. We mustn't open the door. There are too many of them. It would be foolish.' Her resistance was strong. He would have to use force to get around her. He was trusting himself to know what to say, but his eyes leaped about him for something to use as a weapon. Then they heard another voice. 'Come on, man. This is bullshit.' And then the trample of footsteps as they receeded down the staircase. Michela was trembling in Nardo's arms. The struggle now was transformed to an embrace, but he stepped out of it because he could feel the quivering begin in his own knees. His mouth was dry with shame.

'I'll make tea,' she said then which frightened him. Could she feel even his thirst? She went to the kitchen, and Nardo stood at the tall window of the living room. He could hear their voices in the street below, moving away, but they were on this side of the street, and he could not see them.

His lungs were still heaving, though more slowly, when she returned, bearing a tray with a teapot, covered by a patchwork cozy, and two mugs. She lit a lamp, and they sat in silence in the yellow lamplight at the sofa table as the tea steeped. He knew better than to speak. He still could hear the weakness of what he had said before. *I am confuse.* If he spoke now it would be to try to explain himself, to justify his fear, his uselessness.

Finally she removed the cozy from the pot, lifted out the strainer of leaves and tapped it, twice, against the rim of the pot before lidding it again. He watched her hands lay the strainer on the tray, watched water seep onto its lacquered surface, watched as her one hand lifted the pot, the other holding the lid in place, as she poured, first for him, then herself. 'There is sugar and milk there,' she told him.

'Thank you.'

'I need my cigarettes,' she said, and he thought at first she meant she needed to go down to buy cigarettes, and the thought of going to the street stoked terror again, but she was only going to the bedroom for the open pack she had left there, and the fear left him again, trailing bitterness and shame behind it. He sat there massaging one clenched, white-knuckled, useless fist with the palm of the other hand.

'Thank you,' she said when she returned.

'For what?' His voice was flat, and he did not look up from his useless hands.

'For wanting to send them away.'

'I did nothing.'

'What good would it have done? There were five or six of them, they did not look friendly. If Voss found out you were here . . .'

'Shall I to hide myself from him? This boy?' *You will never be a man again.*

'Of course not. But he was stinking drunk. It would have done no good at all. But I really appreciate that you were willing. That you wanted to help me.'

Nardo's hand trembled as he tried to lift the tea mug so he put it down again, wondering if she had noticed, and stirred in two lumps of sugar, tried lifting it once more and managed this time to get it to his lips without spilling. His eyes looked sidewise at her to see if she was watching him, but she was looking toward the window.

They sat for some time without speaking, the only sound the slow tick of an antique clock atop her bookshelves, and the occasional sound of talk, of laughter in the street, the whisper of a car motor, lifting in the summer night through her window. The clock struck 11.00, a tinny reedy sound.

A moment later the telephone rang.

Michela started. '*Shit!*' she whispered. Then she sighed deeply.

'Shall I not to take it?' Nardo said, but she shook her head and rose from the chair, crossing toward the burbling maroon instrument that seemed to Nardo an embodiment of evil.

47

Salt fish

It seemed to Voss this happened again and again, that he tricked himself into it every time. His clothes were dirty, mud-spattered and soiled, and there was blood on his shirt. He stripped them off, down to his underpants and socks, thinking it perfectly acceptable to nip down to the laundry room in his underpants and put these soiled garments in the washing machine while everybody slept. It was late. He would have the washroom to himself, and in any event, he had nothing to hide, nothing to be ashamed of, it was perfectly natural.

He rode the little elevator down four flights to the basement. The dusty walls and concrete floor were strange. He could see darkness at the end of the corridor to his left, to his right, but there was a light in the washroom. He ran from the elevator to the lighted doorway and filled the machine with his dirty clothes. There was still plenty of room for more, so he slipped his briefs down over his hips, pulled off his socks, and stuffed them in, too, smacked the machine door and twisted the switch to the wash program.

It felt good to be naked. He was free.

Only then, when it was too late to open the machine again – it locked until the entire cycle was done – only then did he understand that he was completely naked in the basement, and if anyone saw him here or in the elevator, who knew what they might think of him? That it was perfectly natural was one thing, but they might not see it that way, and the force of his belief might not equal the strength of their judgement.

The only thing to do was go outside, get out of the building. It was summer. He didn't need his clothes, and he had nothing to hide. He was confident in his nakedness.

Then he was on the street. The sun was up already. That was better. To be naked in the dark might be misinterpreted, but in the sunlight at least he couldn't be accused of trying to hide it. The streets were empty. It was good to feel his bare feet on the cool morning pavement, the summer air washing across his bare skin. There was nothing to fear. He kept walking, further from his building. He could see the park up ahead, the King's Garden, and he could sleep in the grass there as the warm sun dried the dew.

But a group of people emerged from the gateway. They were moving in his direction, and then he realized he'd tricked himself. They would *see* him. It was too late to get back to his building. His keys were in the washer. He could hear them rattling. The people were moving toward him like a dark cloud. He had to move his bowels. There was a park bench. He could defecate through the slats, and no one would be able to see his ass or his front either. He could hunch over. They wouldn't know. He had to do it quickly before they got to him. He sat and let his bowels open, but he had misjudged. The excrement didn't go neatly through the space between the bench slats. It squeezed out raggedly in a sticky clump, hung from his anus and oozed in under his buttocks, clung to the edges of the slats. There was nowhere to escape as the dark cloud of people drifted closer, he was not only naked, but had shit all over his ass and the backs of his legs and his hands, he had tricked himself again, and if he

322

leapt up to run they would see everything, the shit on his ass, on the backs of his thighs!

He woke with a start, the sheet, his body soaked with sweat. It took some moments for the terror to lift, before he saw it was a dream, that none of it had happened. He was here in his bed, not naked in the street, shitting on a bench, about to be discovered. He hugged his damp pillow, rocked himself against it, grateful in his misery.

Then it occurred to him he might have soiled the bed in his sleep. He whipped the sheet off to examine the bedclothes beneath him, but they were clean, wrinkled and sweated but not soiled. His relief was profound.

He limped to the watercloset to relieve himself, stood blearily over the bowl, listening to the splash of his water. His face hurt, but he thought there was something to be happy about. His ribs hurt, too, and the muscles of one leg and his shoulder, all on the same side. But he remembered kissing a woman. He remembered her mouth, her tongue, and his hands inside her vest, on her ass. He smiled dreamily with the memory, eyes sagging, as the last of his water trickled off.

Then the pain spread, rising to his head, his brain, and he reeled to the little handwash sink and leaned his palms on its rim, hunching over it until the pain and giddiness settled.

He remembered then, as a single dark image in a dark blur, the leather girl's mouth. He had been kissing her mouth somewhere, not in Krut's, on a street somewhere, outside the King's Garden. She was pressed up against the stucco wall at the entrance, alongside the bust of Brandes, her tongue in his mouth as he felt her up, leather thighs and the warm fork between them while someone questioned him.

'Where is it? Where's the place? Where's the big party you promised us?'

'He's drunk as snot, man!'

She was feeling his ass, too, clutching it, and he tried to shove the other person, the questioner, away with one arm.

'Where's the place, man?'

He looked up into the mirror now and saw his lip was fat, there was blood between his teeth, and yellow bruises on his leg, his ribs.

'Where's this ass-fucked party, you asshole!'

He closed his eyes, and in the dark blur of memory saw the redbearded man with his beady eyes, his glowering face.

More memories then opened in the blur. Inviting the four of them to Michela's for a party, thinking he could make her let them in, telling the redbeard – what was his name? Ole – telling Ole that Michela would fuck him and the other guy. He remembered amidst the blur his fumbling at the outer door lock, trying to code it in, and then in the stairs hoping the little dwarf superintendent would come out now there were so many of them. He remembered shouting at Michela's door.

Then it was blank again until they were outside the King's Garden. Or was that before? Kissing the leather girl, Janine was her name, kissing her and her hands inside his pants, saying, 'He's got a big dick, Maimai,' to the Asian girl. Voss wanted to kiss her, too, but her laughter was mocking. Ole tugged him away from Janine, jerked him from her arms and offered his hand to shake. Voss extended his own, but Ole lifted his away again and thumbed his nose with an ugly grin.

'That was not very nice,' Voss said, and abruptly Ole's forehead shot forward to butt him in the teeth. A smear of red pain, and Voss fell back against the wall, banged his head, fell.

Voss hawked into the sink and saw his spit was pink. He remembered the cool rough pavement against his cheek. His head ached, and the girl Janine, saying, 'I got his wallet.'

'Just take what he owes us.'

'How much does he owe us?'

'Whatever he's got there.'

Laughter.

324

Where were the others? Someone kicked him in the ribs. And a girl's voice – Maimai, laughing, said, 'Kick him in his ass! Kick it!'

There were more kicks. He could remember being surprised it didn't hurt very much, only his mouth and the back of his head hurt, and someone was putting his wallet back into his pocket, the wrong pocket actually, but he thought it was pretty nice of them and heard himself say through a mouthful of bloody spit and its metal taste, 'Fank you. Nice of you.'

'He says, "Fank you,"' one of the girls said. The shriek of laughter. Then he was alone.

He didn't remember more, couldn't be certain what he remembered was real. It might have been the absinthe, a mix of real and not real, what happened, what he dreamed, what was fantasy. But he knew for sure he had taken them to Michela's, had pounded on her door, he could still feel it in the sting of his palms.

He cupped his hand under the cold-water tap and rinsed his mouth, fumbled in the cabinet for aspirin and swallowed four tablets. In the kitchen, he drank juice from the waxed carton, then stood looking at the knives in a woodblock beside the toaster. He focused especially on one of them, blackhandled with a long slender blade, thinking how it might feel to stick it into the hollow of his throat, slide the blade slowly downward. Or up into the soft hollow under the left side of his ribcage.

In a crumple on the kitchen counter was a cellophane bag of salt fish, torn raggedly open, a few left in the bag. He must have bought them in the all-night kiosk on the corner – they would have seen his drink-smudged face! He would have to avoid them now, they would think of it everytime they saw him, he would think of it, remembering what he could not even remember.

He stuffed a handful of the black strong salmiak salted fish into his mouth and chewed gingerly where his teeth were sore from Ole's fat head butting him. The strong sweet salt of the licorice mixed with his spit, stung the tear inside his upper lip and he ran the tip of his tongue along the cut, exploring it. He ate the rest of the licorice in the bag, one black fish after the other, until his tongue felt dried and cracked and he found a cold bottle of Faxe Fad in the refrigerator which he tipped back, swallowing until he thought he might faint, put the half-empty bottle back into the refrigerator door rack.

Then he limped back to bed, pulled the eiderdown up over his head and masturbated, listening to the echo of the laughing girl's words, *Kick him in his ass! Kick it!* over and over, like a tiny scrap of film run again and again and again on the blurry screen of his memory until with a powerful groan he came into his hand and lay slumped there, drying his fingers on the sheets, wishing he could weep, waiting for the sweet death of sleep to bury him.

48

City of foxes

It was not seeing the fox in itself that seemed strange; it was the manner and the place of the sighting that startled her.

Mid-July: A glorious morning and she woke at five, alone in her bed, on the left hand side of it, no longer sleeping dead center of the mattress. She ran her palm over the cool, unmussed sheet of the opposite side. He had gone home to himself, respecting her need to be alone with this; he would join her in the cemetery. She missed the smell and the warmth of his body.

It was a good day for the cemetery.

Soon the aroma of brewing coffee filled the kitchen, and the edge of her sorrow was softened by the happy sleepiness of a summer morning after a night of peaceful slumber. That poem by Baggesen:

> Sweet brief oft-repeated sleep!
> Foreword of that place which kindly smiles
> From the dust where sweet my father lies.

She was at Garnison by 7.00. The city was not yet in full

327

swing; traffic on Dag Hammarskjolds Boulevard and Kristiania Street was light, its sounds muffled from amidst the trees within the churchyard. She collected rake and watering can from the shed alongside the administration building, filled the can at the open faucet and took a long, circuitous walk to the site, crisscrossing through the little tree-sheltered dirt paths flanked with stones and monuments, fenced plots with little benches for visiting friends and families. Birdsong tinkled in the quiet gentle air, the green scent of summer morning filtering to her nostrils, lush and bitter, the smell of new-turned earth.

There was little to do at the gravesite. The hole was fresh, neatly rimmed with mounds of clay. She raked patterns in the dust around it, obliterating the footprints of the diggers, and watered the shrubbery. 'No *buskbane* for me,' he said once. 'Smells like piss! I want to *know* if someone pisses on my grave.' She ran her palm across the waxy leaves of the four small cypress that defined the boundaries of the place. The stone for her paternal grandparents – Alfred the barber who, when his wife grew too much for him, would take to the fields with his canvas and brushes, and Maud who devoted herself to smothering Mikhail with care – warm garments, nutritious food, and prohibitions meant to protect him from the fate of his two older brothers and sister who proceeded their parents into the earth, dead from the Spanish flu, their ashes here in three urns buried at the feet of their parents' caskets.

Here, now, in a few hours, Mikhail would join them, one place remaining alongside for Lise when and if she chose to join him in the earth. If Michela wanted to be buried here she would have to be burnt, for she had given her own place – the last space big enough for a coffin – to Ria; she could not bear to have her burnt or to bury her in the common grave as Mads had wanted. She looked at the little shrine on her daughter's plot. It carried both her and Mads's last names, hyphenated: Ria Ibsen-Paludan. Such a fine-sounding name. It hardly seemed the name of a girl who took her own life at seventeen. Willingly or by accident Michela would never know. A mix of drink and pills. No note.

My little girl. *We did not manage to give you the hope and joy necessary to survival.*

To either side of the low wrought-iron fence surrounding the plot was a meter-long iron bench. Michela sat and breathed deep of the summer morning amidst her dead.

A quiet movement through the yew hedges across the path drew her eyes. She expected a cat or a jay hopping through the leaves, but there, not 20 feet away, was a fox, red-brown and full-tailed, lean as appetite itself, though it must already have eaten for it paused there, gazing across at her where she sat, its fur the color the hair on Mikhail's chest and arms and legs once had been. She remembered him on the beach, as naked as she had ever seen him then, when he was young and beautiful, dashing for the water to dive in, slicing the surface in a knife of sleek muscle, surfacing again with water rolling from his head, teeth flashing in the sun, his laughter ringing out. 'Michela, Lise! Come on in! It's fresh as life!' Those years when Michela's childhood filled their days with all the irrational hope of expectation a child gives its parents.

I love you, Dad. Your memory is safe with me. As long as I live.

The fox lowered its head, then glanced back warily over its shoulder, looked once more and disappeared with a sleek red flash into the yews.

She was old enough to recall when telephones actually did ring. Why it was still called ringing was beyond her; the sound that night had been an electronic burble, less insistent than invasive. She had risen from the coffee table, the tea, her bare-chested lover, his grey eyes alert with terrors far greater than any Voss could pose, the terrors of a past that might never give him peace. Voss was a mere nuisance. She would deal with him.

She lifted the receiver and said, in a voice more resigned than welcoming, 'Yes?' She heard not Voss but a woman's voice she did not recognize. She listened to the news it brought, cushioned in the protection of clichés that said everything short of the one word at its core: death.

She placed the receiver back on its cradle and sat in the rickety wood chair beside the telephone table.

'What is happen?' asked Nardo.

'My father,' she had said. 'He just died.'

It was a comfort that Nardo's insistence on joining her outlasted her insistence that it was unnecessary. They reached the home just past midnight, by taxi. They might have walked – there was no rush – but the last thing she wanted now was to encounter Voss again, perhaps still roaming the streets with his bar friends, drunk and belligerent, bolstered by the force of their number behind him and the liquor in his blood.

The lake at midnight was a deep blue-black, rippling with sharp sparkles of unnatural light. They had to ring for the watch, a white-clad orderly with tattooed wrists who came out on the second ring to unlock the front gate for them.

On the sixth floor she went straight to his room and was startled to see the bed had already been stripped to the bare, plastic-sheathed mattress, the surface of his night table cleared. The metal flower vase on the window ledge – which she had filled with yellow carnations two days before, his favorite flower – was empty. Nothing that had been his remained, not that he had ever bothered to decorate the room. She had pasted up some of his by-lined news stories over the months but they were gone too. She opened the drawer of the nightstand – no Cecil packs or lighter, no pad or pens or envelopes, the tin box with his 'secret' stash of ketogan gone. His books and the little photograph album and his scrapbook of news clippings were gone, too – no doubt all assembled in a cardboard box in the nurses station.

A nurse Michela had not seen before looked in, black-haired and pretty with a cool white complexion. 'Mrs Ibsen?'

'You don't waste time, do you?' Michela said and regretted her words when she saw the cool face soften with sympathy and embarrassment.

'I suppose you need the room. Plenty waiting I suppose.'

His body, already washed and prepared for viewing, lay under a thin blanket in a back hall by the elevators. Nardo stood close behind her as she lifted the sheet. Someone at least had bothered to comb his sparse white hair, and his face looked clean and scrubbed. He appeared younger in death than he had for the past year or more, and she realized fully then how much pain must have driven him, clouding his humor, tensing his muscles, creasing the skin of his face. His jaws seemed smoother now, relaxed finally, his eyelids calm. The only line of movement in the pale face was the hook of his nose. Illusion. It might as well have been stuffed with cotton. But a *vatpik*, a cotton prick, she thought, is one thing he had never been.

'Would you like to have a private moment with him,' the nurse asked softly. Michela nodded, not trusting herself to speak. Nardo stepped away as well.

Alone, it occurred to her that she should kiss his lips; for a moment it seemed to her that if she kissed his lips he might wake, might sit up on the table, strong again, turn a clear brown gaze upon her and grumble affectionately. Instead she laid her palm on his brow but drew it back quickly, stung by its lifelessness. It was good, she thought, that she had touched him. For now there was no doubt.

'How did he go?' Michela asked the nurse in her little, lighted station.

'In his sleep. There was no warning. He spent all day yesterday writing . . .'

'Writing?'

'Yes. He asked for a lap desk.'

'He let go?'

The white face tilted quizzically.

'Of the trapeze?'

'I'm new on this ward,' she said. 'I didn't really know him yet. He went in his sleep. He had been in a lot of pain, but he accepted a double dose of ketogan, and he, well, he slept and never woke

331

again. There was no crisis. We found a box of pills he had been saving in the night board. Apparently he hadn't been taking the pain killers.'

'Has my mother been told? She's up on eight.'

'I know, no, we thought she would only be confused if we woke her. Perhaps you would like to come tomorrow? And bring her down to view the body?'

And Michela did that, though she might as well have not.

'Father is dead, mother.'

'*Who?*'

'Dad. He died last night. Peacefully.´'

'Well of course. He died years and years ago when your brother was just a child.' Michela didn't bother to remind her she had no brother.

Down in the basement, in the morgue, the old lady's face was skeptical. 'Who is *that?*'

'Your husband, mother. My father. Mikhail Viggo Ibsen.'

'I doubt it. He's upstairs hiding. From his responsibilities. As he has always done.'

Michela signalled the orderly who had taken the body from its drawer, and as the young man adjusted the wheels and placed his hands on the end of the table to roll it away, the old lady said quickly, 'No, don't, you'll wake him! Let him sleep. It's so much more peaceful when they're sleeping.' And a tear rolled from the corner of each eye as she peered into the face of the dead man.

Upstairs again, Herr Kragh was lingering at the door of her mother's room in his striped bathrobe. 'Alexandria!' he exclaimed happily, as though he had chanced upon a long lost love, his arms flung open in embrace. 'You are a *queen!*'

The old lady giggled. 'Oh, Mikhail, you old charmer, you!' She glanced at Michela, pride in her smile. 'He *insists* my name is Alexandria. I think he's a little touched.'

The eighth-floor nurse hurried after Michela and stopped the elevator from closing with her shoulder. 'The watch on six asked me to give you this. She forgot last night.' And she handed an envelope into the elevator car. 'He left it under his pillow. You *are* Michela, aren't you?'

It was sealed, and written in a spidery, shaky script on its blank white face was a single word: *Michela.*

49

Do not burn me

Many more came than Michela would ever have expected. They crowded into the little chapel and stood in line along the path to either side, past the American Embassy on the one side, the Russian Embassy on the other. It seemed somehow incongruous to her, so many people crowding to a burial on such a lovely morning, so many people who, so far as she knew, had never visited him in the home. And there were flowers, wreathed and scattered, mounted on wire stands, mounded and trailed around the front of the chapel and up the aisle to the brace where the polished white casket lay.

Up front in the chapel sat Michela's mother in a wheelchair, face powdered and rouged for the occasion, white hair curled and tinted the palest auburn, fingernails painted red as her lips, and – at her insistence – every major piece of jewelry she owned adorning fingers, wrists, throat and breast. In her lap she held an antique cut-glass *bonbonière* in which lay an unopened packet of M&M chocolate-covered peanuts. Four brooches were arranged as though they were diplomatic orders over her left breast – fitting, she told Michela, for the funeral of a foreign dignitary.

335

She was convinced they were burying the Deputy Chief of Mission of the French Embassy, whom she claimed to have known as Marcel. 'We are *very* old friends,' she explained with a smile that intimated much, Michela thought, about the shadows of the old lady's long past time as an *au pair* in Paris. Or about her fantasy life. She was also convinced that Nardo was the diplomat's son, and when Michela explained that he was her friend – 'My *best* friend,' she added and squeezed Nardo's hand – her mother tipped her head coquettishly and said, 'Runs in the family.' Then she gazed at Nardo from beneath her lashes and asked, 'Well where have you been hiding *him*, dear?'

'Nardo is from Chile, mother,' she said.

'I doubt it.'

There were a few journalists and editors whose names and faces were vaguely familiar to her. Some whose pictures she thought she had seen in the newspapers, another whose face she might have seen on television, and cultured voices who spoke as through a microphone as they *condolerede* with formal bows, handclasps, shoulder squeezes.

Michela, who as far as she knew was to be the only speaker, grew nervous about having to address this unexpectedly distinguished gathering. The editor-in-chief of one of the regional newspapers – *him* she knew, a well-known lecher and corrupt drunkard who stocked his wine cellar, her father had told her, by publishing strategic news features – bowed curtly over his enormous belly and broke wind. 'Excuse me,' he said with no evident embarrassment, and then, 'It is the end of an era.'

She wanted to enquire what era that might be – the era of drunken would-be patriarchs at their favorite wine room or journalists fueling themselves up for the ratwatch at Bernkikow's or the Bobi Bar? But she recognized her own skepticism for what it was – a protection against the realization that her father had been a respected professional, something she had never granted him. She was afraid she might begin to sob, knew that sorrow lingered somewhere close beneath her surface calm.

Folded thrice and doubled in her black clutch bag was the

letter he had left her and, similarly folded, its enclosure which he had 'instructed' her to read out for whoever might come, 'if there are any left who would bother to come.' *Oh, dad, if only you could see. Maybe you can,* she thought.

'*My dearest sweet daughter,*' *he had written.* '*Here are my instructions:*

Bury me out of the chapel and in the plot at Garnison's Churchyard. Do not burn me. I do not want to tempt the flames below. When the time comes, I hope Lise might choose to lie with me in the earth. As Paulus said, "It is better to marry than to burn", the only sensible words of his that I know.

I want no priest unless they come privately, out of respect. I will not risk the spectacle that the Bishop of Århus visited upon us when my father shuffled off – a 20-minute exegesis on some dubious proclamation by Paulus that "We will not surrunder the courage." "The courage," he called it. Well I say surrender courage for we are all headed to the same blind capital city, Das Grab, and the undiscovered country from whose bourne no traveler returns. The Bishop also uttered ghastly sentiments about the beloved psalm book clasped in the deceased's "now cold hand."

No books in my hand, please, and do not refer to me as "the deceased". Mikhail will do. Or Viggo to those who knew me under that by-line. Or just plain Ibsen. No church, then, just the chapel, and no priest, and announce the service simply in Politiken, I wrote most for them. Let come who wants to come, if any are left who remember me – they're all dead anyway, the ones I knew, the most of them. And those who want to bring flowers; let them. I won't give instructions about charity. I've always loved flowers and will be happy to receive any that anyone might care to remember me with – if there is any capacity left in my dead bones to be happy at all.

I want you to read the attached text. Let speak who might wish. But: no readings from scripture, no words of bogus solace from Paulus and others of his ilk. And I appeal to you, no politicians, regardless of their party colors. They're all a sham, an embarrassment and a lot of self-interested bottom-holes.

Michela, my precious daughter, thank you for your beautiful heart, for the beautiful words you gave me last time we spoke. Now I have let slip the trapeze as you wisely counselled and made it possible for me to do. If any power at all is left to me, I will be the summer breeze that caresses your sweet face some evening when you think you are most alone. Kiss your mother's face for me and tell her that her husband loved her. And give Kragh a swift kick in his boney backside.

With most loving greetings from your Father.'

Michela stood at the head of the white casket and unfolded not the letter but the enclosure. Those outside the chapel were pressing in now and the little, windowless, vaulted room was hot and airless. She felt perspiration trickle from beneath her arms down the side of the black nylon blouse she had purchased from Jaeger up the street for this occasion. She swallowed, cleared her throat and thanked everyone for coming to say goodbye to her father, her mother's husband. She said that he had asked her to read this text and looked down to the sheet quietly rattling in her trembling fingers:

'Last Words from a Dying Writer:

My beginning was the word
That stirred the water of my blood.
I don't know if it was God,
Don't know if it was good,
But served it as I could.

No words remain to still my soul,
But still my soul will be.
Crossed my arms on blood-free heart,
Crossed my hands now cold to touch,
Lightless eyes no longer see,
A brain no longer nagging me
To set it free.

338

These last words were born in rage
But anger too now leaves my song.
The struggle of my days is gone
Right and wrong, wrong to wrong,
All withers in its yellow age.

Regret at pages never born
No longer daunts my flickering end.
The easy time is what I mourn,
The loss of hours milling words
I might have spent with friends.

One word alone remains, goodbye
To all of it, goodbye, goodbye.
Dear wife, forgive my love that failed.
Dear child, my thanks for your kind care.
Goodbye the light, the air, the sky, the earth.
Goodbye.

The rest is silence.'

There were perhaps two seconds of silence after the last word, the last goodbye – enough for a single cough, the single clearing of a throat – before Michela's mother exclaimed in a piping cry from her wheelchair, 'Oh! That was funny! Hoorah! Three short and a long: Rah! Rah! Rah! And so the long: Rrrraaaah! Now who brought the cake?'

Michela tried not to hear the smothered chuckles as she and Nardo wheeled the old lady out of the chapel along the path to the gravesite, labored not to chuckle herself for fear even a single snigger might unleash an unstoppable cascade of laughter, sobbing, both, a collapse into hyseteria.

They followed the trolly that bore the casket as the witnesses and mourners fell to behind them in a broad row. Then gears and ropes were purring silkily as the box lowered slowly into its carefully measured and cut rectangular hole in the earth. Michela stepped forward to cast the first ritual dirt on top of the casket. But a chill anger stopped her as she saw Voss, standing a few meters from the other end of the hole, in an open-throated shirt, his leather jacket unbuttoned, hands clasped at his leather flies.

The air that filled her lungs was rage, mounting to a scream of fury that never reached her throat. Nardo's quiet voice was at her ear. 'I will espeak to him,' he said and stepped around the grave, took Voss by the elbow, steering him away.

Michela knelt and dug her fingers into the loose earth at the rim of the grave and tossed it so it spattered across the lid of the white box. Then a spade sliced into the mound of earth and clay, twigs and stone, and emptied onto the coffin. She looked up. Voss and Nardo sat on a bench by the roundabout, 50 meters away. Then they stood. Voss had a dirty crumpled handkerchief at his face, mopped his nose with it. He shook Nardo's hand and without looking back at Michela walked swiftly on his heel-worn boots toward the exit to Dag Hammarskjolds Allé.

Nardo returned to Michela's side. She had not prepared refreshments, and the gathering began to break up. Last well-wishers extended hands for a last squeeze of her shoulder, a last word of solace.

'What did you say to him?' Michela asked Nardo.

'I tell him a story.'

'A story? What story?'

'I tell him of the angels.'

50

In the beginning

Voss could still see her. Flush to the gateway on Dag Hammarskjold's Allé, he peered around the edge of pale brick, watched her there by the grave. In black. So simple, beautiful, a black summer dress, shoulderless, close over her hips, a black lacey shawl around her shoulders, blond hair piled up on her head with a black velvet bow at the back where the wispy hair knotted together in a chignon. So pretty, the exposed ears, the nape of her neck, painful for him to see, stirring memories of before, when he was welcome to touch his lips there, the pale honey skin, wisps of light hair, ears a bit large for her face, almost comical, touchingly so, and she would turn her smiling face to him, her gaze tender and humble as though she felt unworthy to receive his affection. Then. Before.

His eyes still watered. He daubed them with the handkerchief balled in his fist, blew his nose, and the honking sound made him feel like a clown.

I have lost everything, he thought as he watched the Chilean lift the slipping shawl up onto her bare shoulder. She bowed to the wheelchair, whispered something in the ear of the wild-haired

341

old woman who looked up at her with a vacant smile. The Chilean squeezed her shoulder and spoke to her.

Voss was confused at how easily the man had taken charge of him. Why did I just . . . *give in* to him, allow him to steer me away, why did I sit and listen? But there had been so many people, he had expected only Michela, one or two others. That, and the quiet power of the man's voice had taken him by surprise.

This is very esad time for Michela. She ask me to say you her thanks because you come to her father's grave. But she cannot see you now. She hope you understand.

Voss had no power against the words, against the sound of them, the deep quiet sound of the man's voice, the sympathy and understanding it extended to him. And as he waited for some words of his own to rise inside of him in response, the man began to tell him a story, a strange story about a prison, about a moment's escape into sunlight from a dark filthy cell in the company of angels who promised him that one day he would be free.

'They give to me their word,' he said. 'And they keep it. They are keep it.'

The story was so strange that Voss could find no response to it. At one moment he nearly interrupted – *Hey, Pedro, spare me your religious bullshit, please.* But he hesitated, his mouth would not give form to those words. The man's eyes held him, glanced away, but returned again. Grey eyes that absorbed Voss's pain. The man squeezed his forearm. 'You shall be free of this pain, too, my friend,' he said and despite himself, Voss's eyes filled. He wanted to hide it but already could feel a tear spilling from the edge of one eye, rolling to the corner of his mouth.

Only now, watching them from the gate, did he find the words he would have said: *Her beauty is my pain. I'll never be free of that.* He wanted to throw a challenge into the calm of those grey eyes. *You stole that beauty from me.* But he knew it was untrue. No one had stolen anything from him. He had driven her away himself. What he felt for her might have been love, but somehow turned to stupidity, to ugliness as it rose to expression. He could see that now. If only he could tell her that; if only she would let him try to explain, it might still be possible . . .

The men and women in their dark clothes were drifting away now from the graveside along the paths of the cemetery, and Michela walked toward the place where Voss stood, rolling her mother's chair before her, the Chilean at her side. Voss's breath was heavy as she neared him. When she was a dozen steps away, he showed himself, came out from behind the brick gateway and waited.

You have to understand, Michela, he thought. *You have to listen, to let me . . .*

She stopped and looked at him. The Chilean's eyes were on him, too. Voss's hands doubled into fists at his sides. The Chilean lowered his eyelids, shook his head almost imperceptibly. Michela's gaze; her face was cold. She was a stranger to him now, less, worse than a stranger.

'Don't you understand?' he said, his voice tight, strangling in his throat. 'It might as well have been *me* you buried there today. I have lost everything.'

The old woman smiled vacantly at him from her chair. Michela murmured something to the Chilean, and they turned onto the path that led behind the embassy to the far exit. Voss saw himself there so clearly then; he had to swallow hard to keep from throwing up. Their receding backs might have been mirrors reflecting his own pathetic hatefulness.

She wouldn't even say hello to me, wouldn't even look at me, you didn't even give me that much common courtesy, Michela. Christ! How he wanted to hurt her, to capture her attention, back her into a corner, smile meanly: *You know, now I begin to understand why your husband beat you, you cold-hearted bitch! Why your own kid killed herself! To be free of you!* But even as the words echoed in his head, he recognized them as hollow, hateful lies, his own pathetic, impotent wish to make her hurt. He couldn't hurt her. He could only hurt himself. It was over.

He walked. Turned his own back and crossed the boulevard to

Stockholm Street, walked quickly, fists tight in the side pockets of his leather jacket, eyes fixed on the sunlit pavement in front of his feet, concrete slabs divided by a strip of cobblestone. He passed unseeing beneath the trees that flanked the edge of the east side park, across Silver Square and Webersgade to the street lakes. He stood for a moment at the foot of Peace Bridge, uncertain which direction to take.

A young woman glanced at him as she passed, tight low-slung jeans and a middie blouse, pierced navel winking in the sunlight. He watched her go, but the jump of his blood was not toward her rolling hips. The images in his brain, stirring in his groin were of ruin. He imagined Michela and the Chilean discussing him, pity, laughter. *Laughter!* Michela laughing. At *him!*

Move!

He turned left along the lakes. Black Dam Lake to Queen Louise Bridge, past the sculptures of Neptune and Tiberus, across the bridge and past the sculpture of a young man and young woman who sat gazing at one another, down into the pedestrian tunnel with its graffitied walls, and up along the bank of Pebblinge Lake toward the Lake Pavillion, sprawling white fairy-tale of a house, toward St John's Lake, the ancient leper colony, and he *wanted* her to laugh, *wanted* her to relish his destruction, he lusted for her ridicule. *Why? Why!*

Sweat plastered his shirt to his back, trickled from beneath his armpits, rolled from his forehead, guttered to the corners of his eyes. He peeled off his leather jacket and flung it over his shoulder.

Laugh! He *wanted* her to laugh. At him, at his pain. He *wanted* it. And she wouldn't even give him that. She wouldn't even kill him. She turned her back. She wanted nothing of him. He did not even exist for her now.

Sick. You are a sick little fuck, Voss!

And across Danas Way, across Kampmann Street, on the bank of St John's Lake, it all caught up with him.

He stopped, crouched, shouted, '*Fuck!*'

Two passing women jerked their heads toward him, veered away.

'*Fuck!*' he yelled again. '*Fuck!*' His jacket fell to the grass. He stooped, picked it up, swung it by the collar above his head in a whipping circle, once, twice, and let it fly. It shot out arcing up a few feet from the bank, then opened like a parachute and floated down to the water. He watched the leather glisten as it sank slowly beneath the slimey green surface.

'*Good,*' he muttered. '*Good.* Sink.'

He sat in the grass, face in his hands, smelling the sweaty meat of his palms. Out on the roadway, the air brakes of a bus wheezed. A truck rumbled past, cars beeped and revved. The tympani of a passing car radio reverbrated in the earth. His breathing stilled. He sighed, looked out at the lake again where his jacket had been. He could see its vague shadow beneath the surface, still sinking slowly.

'That was fucking smart,' he muttered. 'A 5,000-crown jacket. Cell phone in the pocket, too. *Smart.*'

Diagonally across from him was a sculpture he had vaguely noticed before – a sculpture carved, he knew, in the wood of a dead elm tree. Some years before, the elms of Copenhagen had been stricken with a blight and instead of cutting them down, the city had commissioned a number of artists to turn their remains into sculptures, rooted to the earth. Voss remembered reading about it. The sculptures were temporary, their survival at the weather's mercy. In the course of time, they would be worn away by wind, rain, frost, the rot of moss.

This one Voss had seen perhaps a hundred times in passing but never actually looked at it before. The remains of the tree trunk formed a thick 'Y' – a thick trunk perhaps two meters in diameter, three meters high, with two uneven bulky arms protruding out from it diagonally up to either side. In the crotch of the 'Y' stood a naked woman, her legs rooted from the knees down into a rough nub of wood, her arms pulled tightly behind her back, as if bound there, but her posture seemed at once that of captive and judge in her relentless gaze peering down at the world beneath her, at *him*. The woman's body was fertile – large-breasted, thick-hipped, long hair hanging down her back – but

345

her face showed hurt, anger, her mouth small and eyes deep in shadow.

Voss studied her, wondered who she was, what it meant for her to be there, rooted to that dead tree, born of it, rising from it, standing up amidst a scratchwork of dead branches, twigs, looming against the blue sky. He thought about the artist who had cut her into wood, the skill and dedication, the years it must have taken to learn and master that skill so that he could use it to cut beauty from death, from disease.

Then he noticed beneath her feet, to the right, a smaller figure, an infant, on all fours, seen from its left side, face turned outward, that same hurt, angry face, accusation beaming darkly from the shadow of its eyes. And lower still, cut into a hollow pulpit in the trunk itself, a rough-hewn man standing behind a lectern, face bowed over a tablet held in one thick wooden hand. The dark gaze of the man was fixed downward, upon the tablet.

Voss rose from the grass, moved closer, read the brass plaque at the base of the tree: *Ole Barslund Nielsen: 'In the beginning was the word.'*

A quote, though he could not recall from where. The Bible perhaps. Yes. *In the beginning was the word and the word was . . .* something, something. He would have to look it up when he got back to his apartment.

Then he thought of the story the Chilean had told him in the graveyard, of the angels who had shown him freedom and given their word. That one day he would be free.

51

A well-earned holiday

I locked my office door and pocketed the keys, peeked into the reception area and waved to the bright-faced smiling girl there. 'See you in a month!'

'Don't make me envious!' she said with a laugh. Then, 'You've really earned it, Kristensen!'

I smiled, continued out to the street, past the looming structure of the State Hospital toward the east side. I could have taken the bus from there, but decided to walk all the way to Østerport Station for the train. The walk would do me good. Perhaps I would stop at the Irma supermarket there and pick up some nice thick steaks for the barbecue and a bottle of the Spanish red my wife was so fond of. Couple corncobs.

'*You've really earned it!*' that nice girl at the reception said. I really ought to have known her name. Nice of her to say. Smile and a kind word means a lot. But it was my wife who deserved it, my kids. A whole long month with them, and I would learn to let my thoughts go free, would keep the door of my office at home shut from the outside, close down the computer. No writing, no email, no more preoccupation and speculation for a

347

whole long month. Just my wife, my kids, our garden. Load up the car for the beach once in a while. Picnic in the woods, in Frederiksberg Gardens. And no sad stories, no broken, suffering minds in the way.

I turned right on Østerbrogade and walked in the sunlight up to Dag Hammarskjolds Allé. Across the Allé something caught my eye, some people leaving the back exit of the cemetery. Three people: A man and woman pushing a wheelchair with an old white-haired woman in it. Then I saw the man was Nardo. The woman was attractive, and I saw Nardo's hand on her shoulder and peace in his face.

I smiled to myself. I did not wave. Just continued toward the station.

52

A kiss from the dead

As usual, Herr Kragh waited at the door of Michela's mother's room. Michela saw him as soon as the elevator doors bumped open, saw the anxiety evaporate from his eyes. His shiny red face opened with delight. 'Alex*and*ria!' he exclaimed.

Her mother sniffed. 'I am not certain I want visitors just now,' she said.

'But Alexandria! I have been waiting for hours!'

'This was a great loss,' she said. 'I am very sad.' She looked up around her from the old man to Nardo to Michela to the blond nurse. Her eyes were intensely blue. 'He was the love of my life,' she said softly.

'Oh, Mom.'

'And I only knew him for two months.' The intensity of her gaze stilled, and she added with formal resolution, 'But two months in Paris can be a lifetime.'

Michela leaned forward and tenderly kissed her mother's forehead and her cheek, looked into her eyes. 'That kiss was from my father, Mom. From your husband.'

The old woman's eyes opened wide. 'It *was?*' she said.

349

Nardo waited by the window, thinking how patient and gentle Michela was with the old woman. He glanced down to the lake bank and saw a young mother pushing a pram. She stopped to lean in and adjust the bedding, speaking smiling words that Nardo could not hear to the child bundled in there. Sunlight glittered on the lake behind her. What a wonder it seemed to him, what a perfect, complete moment: A mother, an infant there; a daughter, a mother here. He reached for Michela's hand and squeezed. She glanced at him with a questioning smile.

'You are smiling,' she said.

'With admiration.'

Herr Kragh, tall and hunched in his striped bathrobe, watched with hopeful, eager expectation, his bony blue hands clenched in the air before him as Michela wheeled her mother back into her room, and an almost inaudible melody rose on the old woman's breath, a song of three words, repeated again and again, '*O Grand Amour . . .*'

PRAISE FOR THOMAS E. KENNEDY'S WRITING

Greene's Summer

"What a gorgeous novel this is! With generous and elegant prose, Kennedy takes us from the darkest, most violent regions of our collective behavior to our most exalted: our enduring hope for something higher, our need to forgive and be forgiven, our human hunger to love and be loved. *Greene's Summer* is a deeply stirring novel suffused with intelligence, grace, and that rarest of qualities – written or otherwise – wisdom."

– Andre Dubus III, author of *House of Sand and Fog*

"A terrible, wonderful, horrible, truthful, heartbreaking and heart-mending book. The word masterpiece should never be used lightly, but *Greene's Summer* is exactly that, a masterpiece written by a master. How can anyone know so much about the human heart?"

– Duff Brenna, author of
Too Cool, The Book of Mamie, The Altar of the Body

"*Greene's Summer* is a most ambitious and complex undertaking, a triumphant achievement!"

– Gordon Weaver, author of
Cadence, Last Stands, Men Who Would be Good.

Kerrigan's Copenhagen

"Here is Copenhagen . . . conscious and sensual . . . a Cathedral of the night with fantastic chapels of cafés and restaurants . . . and women . . . a loving hymn to Copenhagen . . . everything is more beautiful written in English ink from an Irish-American fountain pen."

– Boa Tao Michaëlis, *Politiken*

". . . a can-opener to Danish cultural life . . . the more Kerrigan learns about Copenhagen the happier he gets . . ."

– Danish Television DR 2 'Bestseller'

"This must be the first time that The King's Copenhagen to this extent has been both scene and stuff for such a comprehensive novel . . ."

– Niels Barfoed, *Politiken*

"Kennedy has placed Copenhagen on a level with Joyce's Dublin."

– David Applefield, *Frank* (Paris)

"... an exciting journey for the reader, a wonderful, delightful read . . .
a remarkable achievement . . . an excellent companion for a visit to
Copenhagen."   – *Books Ireland*

"... a wildly inventive novel, simultaneously tender, raunchy,
intelligent and uproariously funny . . ."

– *Cape Cod Voice* ("Our Favorite Fiction 2002")

"... sumptuous and rich, sensuous and intelligent, witty and joyous,
like Copenhagen itself, the living heart of this wonderful novel . . ."

– Linda Lappin, *The Literary Review*

Bluett's Blue Hours

"... like blues from a saxophone, yes, in jazz style and blue tone,
comparable with Dan Turrell's Copenhagen crime books with
murder in the dark and much more . . ."

– Bo Tao Michaëlis, *Politiken*

"... Kennedy's second part of a planned noir quartet about
Copenhagen is a moody and charming acquaintance . . ."

– Tonny Vorm, *Information*

"... all the accouterments you'd expect from this inventive author –
unflinching characterizations, a wildly inventive plot, and the taste
of jazz and booze on every page. Kennedy is a writer's writer and a
reader's fortunate discovery."

– Michael Lee, *Cape Cod Voice*
("Our Favorite Books, 2003")

"... a great novel!" – *Irish Voice*

"... A beautifully sculpted novel, *Bluett's Blue Hours* showcases
Kennedy's peculiar genius for physical and emotional description."

– *Irish Edition*

"No one writes about the loves and lives of men better than
Kennedy, including their relationships with their own children. . ."

– John Mark Eberhart, *Kansas City Star*

**Readers interested in the story behind the writing of the Copenhagen
Quartet can learn more from the DVD, Thomas E. Kennedy: The
Copenhagen Quartet (www. deworde.com)**